KT-381-868

The author of twenty-five books, Erica Spindler is best known for her spine-tingling thrillers. Her novels have been published all over the world, selling over six million copies, and critics have dubbed her stories "thrill-packed, page-turners, white-knuckle rides and edge-of-your-seat whodunits."

Erica is a *New York Times* and *USA TODAY* bestselling author. In 2002, her novel *Bone Cold* won the prestigious Daphne du Maurier Award for excellence.

Also by *Erica Spindler*

ERICA SPINDLER
LAST KNOWN VICTIM

MIRA

All the characters in this book have no existence outside the
imagination of the author, and have no relation whatsoever to anyone
bearing the same name or names. They are not even distantly inspired
by any individual known or unknown to the author, and all the
incidents are pure invention.

First published in Great Britain 2007.
MIRA Books, Eton House, 18-24 Paradise Road,
Richmond, Surrey, TW9 1SR

© Erica Spindler 2007

ISBN: 978 0 7783 0162 2

58-0907

Printed and bound in Spain
by Litografia Rosés S.A., Barcelona

I dedicate this book to the city of New Orleans: To her beauty and grace. Her history, diversity and colour. To the strength and joie de vivre of her people. *Laissez les bons temps rouler!*

Author's Note

When hurricane Katrina hit New Orleans and the Mississippi Gulf Coast, my novel *Killer Takes All* had just recently been released in hard cover in North America. Set in present-day New Orleans, the book suddenly felt dated to me. Wrong. This piece of the world had dramatically changed, never to be the same.

A psychologist friend told me he and his colleagues "were the wounded attempting to treat the wounded." We of the Gulf Coast region have all been profoundly changed by Katrina, even those with no or minimal damage to our personal property.

I simply had to continue the story of Detectives Stacy Killian, Spencer Malone and the entire Malone family (first introduced in *Bone Cold*.) I felt compelled to pick up their lives post-K and show how they had been affected by the disaster.

I loved writing this story. Perhaps, I was attempting to heal myself through storytelling—using my gift to come to grips with this new, changed world, to set my little piece of the universe right. Life does, indeed, go on.

In creating *Last Known Victim* I had to make some educated guesses about two years in the future. How far along would the rebuilding process be? Surely the NOPD would be back in their Perdido Street headquarters, the wheels of justice turning smoothly?

Some of my guesses were wrong. As of the writing of this note, the police force is still scattered between many locations, ISD is defunct and nothing is running smoothly—with the exception of our beloved Saints. (Go Saints!)

I'd like to thank all those who helped bring *Last Known Victim* to life: my agent Evan Marshall, assistant Beth Jackson, editor Dianne Moggy and the entire MIRA® Books crew. Donald Martin at the LSU Fire & Emergency Training Institute for information on fire forensics and Bob Becker, CEO City Park, New Orleans. Thanks also to Scott Greenbaum at GlockFAQ.com, Barrett Brockhage at LockPicks.com and Russ at Lockpicksonline.com.

I can't end this without expressing my gratitude to my family—I hear a writer isn't always the easiest person to live with—and my God, for His many blessings.

PART

1

1

New Orleans, Louisiana
Sunday, August 28, 2005
4:00 p.m.

The gods were watching over New Orleans. Or so it seemed. How else could this historic city built below sea level, this beautiful jewel set in a swamp, have survived?

Survival. Of the species. The fittest. The self. An instinctual response to fight for life. To fight back.

Would she?

Walk to the door. Open it.

There she was. Lying on the bed. Asleep. Bitch! Cheap, faithless whore!

She deserves it. She betrayed you. Broke your heart.

She stirred. Moaned. Her eyelids fluttered.

Quickly! Cross to the bed. Put your hands around her throat and squeeze.

Her eyes snapped open. Pools of blue terror. She bucked and clawed.

Tighter. Tighter. Her fault. Hers. Bitch! Betrayer!

Her creamy skin mottled, then purpled. Her eyes bulged, popping out like those of some freakish cartoon character.

No pity. No second thoughts. She brought this on herself. She deserves it.

Her hands dropped. Her body shuddered, then stilled.

Halfway there. Breathe deeply. Calm yourself. Finish what she forced you to do.

A scream shattered the silence. A loud crack, like a gunshot, shook the house.

Only the wind. Katrina's fury. Move, quickly! Good. Now check your equipment. Make certain you have everything you need.

Industrial-strength trash bags. Rubber gloves and boots. Foul-weather gear. Shiny new bone saw. Pretty, pretty saw.

Zip-closure plastic bag.

No one to hear. No one to come. All gone.

An empty city.

2

New Orleans, Louisiana
Wednesday, August 31, 2005
3:00 p.m.

A ghost town, Captain Patti O'Shay thought. Or a scene from some post-apocalyptic horror flick. No cars or buses. No people on the sidewalks or lounging on porches. Eerily quiet.

She crept along Tchoupitoulas Street, heading uptown, maneuvering past downed power lines, branches and trees, sometimes having to go off road. Struggling to keep her attention on the task of driving. And to keep exhaustion and despair at bay.

Katrina had hit and all the "Doomsday" predictions had come true: the levees had begun to break and the bowl that was the Big Easy had begun to fill with water.

Ninety percent of the metro area—including police head-quarters—had flooded. Only the high ground had escaped: the French Quarter, parts of the Central Business District, pockets of the Garden District and Uptown. And this street, which ran along the ridge of the Mississippi River.

The city was without power. Without running water. Without access to supplies. Twenty-five percent of the NOPD's vehicles had flooded.

Citizens who hadn't evacuated were now trapped. On rooftops and in attics. On the interstates and bridges. Dying in the brutal heat, without food, water or medical care.

Now the looters, junkies and thugs had taken to the streets.

The NOPD had established Harrah's Casino, located high and dry at the foot of Canal Street, as their staging area. The Royal Sonesta, one of the French Quarter's swankiest hotels, now served as the temporary police headquarters.

She tightened her fingers on the steering wheel. All communications were down. The police department had been reduced to using a handful of walkie-talkies and one ad hoc, mutual-aid radio channel. A channel they were sharing with all other parish agencies and the state police.

Because of a "talk around" feature, communication between parties more than five miles apart was impossible, rendering unit commanders without a chain of command. To make matters worse, the various agencies kept cutting over one another, creating the cacophony she was listening to now—a stream of disjointed alerts, updates, conversations and requests for assistance.

It was something, at least. Fellow survivors, agencies struggling to restore normalcy. Audible proof that the world had not come to an end.

Though she feared hers had.

Her husband, Captain Sammy O'Shay, was missing.

She had neither seen nor heard from him since the Sunday before the storm. All officers had been required to remain on duty during the hurricane. She and Sammy had attended early mass at St. Louis Cathedral, then prepared to go out separately on patrol.

She remembered stepping outside of the church and being struck by an overwhelming sense of loss. Of dread. It gripped her so tightly, she caught her breath.

Sammy looked at her. "What is it, love?"

She shook her head. "Nothing."

But he had known better and curled his fingers around hers. Always her rock, her shelter in a storm.

"It's going to be fine, Patti. Business as usual by Wednesday."

They had hugged and parted. Then all hell had broken loose.

Today was Wednesday, Patti realized, thoughts returning to the present. And nothing was business as usual.

Where was he?

Patti suddenly felt chilled, despite the oppressively hot, humid air streaming through the cruiser's open windows. She shook her head, against the fear, the sense of dread.

Sammy was fine. He'd gone home to check on the house or look for her and been trapped by floodwaters. Or he had gotten trapped trying to help citizens escape. That's the kind of man Sammy was.

He was resourceful. If he had been injured, he knew to take refuge and await help.

So many were missing. So many were dead.

The walkie-talkie crackled and squawked. A number of buildings burned out of control in the metro area. There were reports of hundreds of displaced citizens converging on the convention center, of gunshots fired at the Superdome, of private militia teams arriving by choppers.

Hearsay and rumor. With no way of being substantiated because of the breakdown in communication.

Where was Sammy?

Suddenly the conversations stopped, overridden by an extended squeal. The sound affected her like a blow. Pressing and holding the radio's emergency button was one way to clear the channel for an emergency alert on this primitive form of communication. The protocol signaled users to stay off the channel until the alert was issued.

"Officer down. Repeat, officer down. Audubon Place."

Patti unclipped her walkie-talkie and brought it to her mouth. "Captain Patti O'Shay here. I'm on Tchoupitoulas, approaching Jackson Avenue. Can I get to Audubon Place from here? Advise."

She was immediately inundated with advice on which streets were passable: one lane on both Jackson and Louisiana Avenues had been cleared. Once she hit St. Charles Avenue, she would have to drive the streetcar tracks on the neutral ground, which had been cleared by Bobcats.

Audubon Place was the most palatial street in New Orleans, perhaps the entire South. A gated community of twenty-eight mansions, it was home to wealthy old-line, New Orleans families, captains of industry and the president of Tulane University.

Located uptown on St. Charles Avenue, across from Audubon Park and bounded by the university campus, it'd been left mostly unscathed by the storm.

A juicy—and vulnerable—sitting duck for looters.

Patti made her way there, thoughts whirling. The report could turn out to be false—many had in the past couple of days. If it wasn't, who was the officer? How extensive were his injuries—and how the hell would she get him medical treatment?

Patti reached her destination. She saw another cruiser had made the scene before her. And that reports of private militia had not been exaggerated.

Four heavily armed men in camouflage stood at the neighborhood's graceful, gated archway. Around them, private Hummers and a bulldozer.

She climbed out. The other cruiser's driver's-side door opened. One of her guys. Detective Tony Sciame. A thirty-year veteran of the force, Tony had now, truly, seen it all.

He started toward her. He looked like he'd aged ten years since she'd seen him last.

She didn't mention the fact, knowing she looked it, too.

"What's the status?" she asked.

"Not certain. I arrived a couple minutes before you. They wouldn't let me in."

"Excuse me?"

"Said they were in control of the area. Private security, hired by the residents to protect their property."

Money might not be able to buy love, but everything else was for sale at a price.

They approached the guards. As they did, Patti saw a third cruiser inside the gate, several houses down. Her heart sank.

"Who's in charge?" she asked the men.

"I am. Major Stephens. Blackwater USA."

"Captain Patti O'Shay, NOPD." She held out her credentials. "We got word of an officer down."

He inspected her ID, then waved them inside. "Follow me."

He led them through the gates and toward the third cruiser. She heard the hum of the generators powering the mansions. It was the way of the world, catastrophe affected the poor so much more profoundly than the rich.

And apparently, proved little more than an inconvenience to the superrich.

The victim lay several yards in front of the vehicle. Facedown in the muck.

"No badge," the man said. "Weapon's gone."

As they closed in on the victim, the smell of death strengthened. Despite the heat, Patti's hands were cold as ice.

"It appears the back of his head was bashed in by a heavy object," the major continued. "Then he was shot. Twice. In the back."

They reached the corpse. Patti gazed down at the victim, light-headed, the blood pounding crazily in her head.

"Decomposition's too far along for it to have happened after the storm," Tony said.

She opened her mouth to respond but found she couldn't

speak. She recognized this officer. From a lifetime together, sharing their trials, hopes and dreams. From nearly thirty years of marriage.

It couldn't be true. But it was.

Her husband was dead.

3

Thursday, October 20, 2005
11:00 a.m.

Patti stared at the computer screen, at the almost two-month-old NOLA.com news story.

Decorated NOPD Captain Shot by Looters
9/01/05 8:10 a.m.

Captain Sammy O'Shay, thirty-year veteran of the police force, was found shot to death at Audubon Place. His body was discovered by fellow officers Wednesday. Police Chief Eddie Compass believes his murder to have been the work of looters targeting the affluent neighbor-hood. An investigation is under way.

What a joke. There had been no investigation "under way" then; there wasn't one now. The city and all its agencies, in-cluding the NOPD, were in turmoil, their focus on survival. How did one investigate without evidence, equipment or manpower? Without facilities to house them all? Hell, parts of the city still didn't have safe drinking water.

Patti frowned. She wanted answers. Absolutes. She didn't even know for certain if Sammy had been shot before the storm hit, or after.

The chief had decided that Sammy had interrupted looters and been killed. It made sense, considering the neighborhood and timing. But if that was the case, why hadn't she heard from her husband in the hours between their parting at the cathe-dral and the time when all forms of communication had been cut off?

Any number of reasons. More unknowns. Frustrating.

She massaged her temple, the knot of tension there, as she reviewed what she knew of Sammy's death. He'd suffered a blunt-force trauma to the back of his head, suggesting that the killer had attacked from behind, catching him by surprise. He'd disarmed him, then used Sammy's own gun against him, shooting him twice in the back.

His cruiser had been unlocked, the keys in it. The vehicle's interior had been clean. When they found him, both Sammy's badge and gun had been missing. The scene hadn't been processed; any evidence that might have been useful was long gone now.

"Captain? You okay?"

Patti blinked and dragged her gaze from the computer monitor. Detective Spencer Malone stood at the door to what served as her makeshift office. Not only a detective under her command, he was her nephew and godson. He was frowning.

"I'm fine. What's up?"

He ignored her question. "You were rubbing your temple."

"Was I?" She dropped her hands to her lap, irritated. It'd been almost two months since Sammy had been killed, and being hovered over had gotten damn old. She hurt enough without being constantly reminded of her loss by people treating her as if she might shatter at any moment.

She was part of an NOPD family dynasty that included her father and grandfather, her brother-in-law, three nephews and a niece. But working with so many of her family members meant she had no way to escape the microscope.

"Just a little headache, that's all."

"You're certain? Before your heart attack—"

"I was tired all the time? Rubbing my temples?"

"Yes."

She had suffered a minor heart attack the spring before Katrina, but this was completely different. "I'm fine. You needed something?"

"We have a situation," Spencer said. "At one of the refrigerator graveyards."

New Orleanians had evacuated for Hurricane Katrina,

leaving behind fully stocked refrigerators and freezers. Now they were returning to those same appliances, which had been without power all these weeks. Most people just strapped the reeking units closed and wheeled them out to the curb. There they were collected and hauled to various dump sites to be cleaned by the Environmental Protection Agency. These sites had earned the nickname "Refrigerator Graveyards."

"A situation?" she repeated.

"A big one. EPA made an interesting discovery in one of the units. A half-dozen human hands."

Patti decided she wanted to go on this call with Spencer. The EPA supervisor, a man named Jim Douglas, met them at the car.

"Damnedest thing I've ever seen," Douglas said. "At first I thought Paul, he's the one who was cleaning the unit, was pullin' my leg. When you spend your day doing this—" he motioned around them "—a good gag's a welcome thing. You know what I mean?"

"Absolutely," Spencer murmured. "I'd say this detail gives new meaning to having a job that stinks."

"You know it. Don't worry, you get used to the smell."

Patti didn't bother telling him that one of the first, and most important, lessons a cop learned was to smear some Vicks under the nose before arriving at a scene where there was a "stinker."

She had to admit, this place smelled about as bad as anything she'd ever encountered—and that was saying something. Her eyes watered even though she still stood at the periphery of the site.

The man led them to a trailer. "Got a couple HazMat suits and masks for you. You'll want 'em."

He motioned them inside, then handed them each a white Tyvek jumpsuit, complete with hood and booties, and respirator masks.

When they had suited up, they started for the unit in question. Patti found the scene surreal: row after row of discarded refrigerators and freezers, food tombs in this great, stinking graveyard.

And like tombs and tombstones, the refrigerators bore messages. New Orleanians had begun to use their discarded appliances as a sounding board, spray-painting messages on them, some of frustration or anger, some of hopelessness. One proclaimed in orange spray paint across its front, "Heck of a job, Brownie," referring to what President Bush had said to his incompetent FEMA head days after the storm. One in black, "So long, Sir-Stinks-a-Lot," and another, "Here lies Uncle Fester. Thanks a lot, Katrina."

Interestingly, many of the units were still adorned with calendars, children's drawings and photos. Each a kind of snapshot of lives upended, time stopped.

"These units are classified as containing hazardous waste," Douglas explained as they walked down a row lined with the ruined appliances. "That's why the EPA's here. First we clean out the contents, which, by the way, is when the hands showed up. After the unit's been pressure-washed, we drain and dispose of freon from the coils and oil from the compressor."

"How many units are here?" Spencer asked. By his tone, Patti suspected he was having the same reaction to this bizarre scene as she. Of course, since August 29, not much about life in New Orleans *hadn't* been bizarre.

"Ten thousand," Douglas answered. "And we're just getting started. We expect a quarter of a million before it's all over."

Spencer whistled. "That's a whole lot of funky Frigidaires."

The man snickered, even though "funky" didn't cover it. "The good news is, they're being recycled. When we're done with 'em, they're compacted, then sent to a facility where they go through a shredder, then separators. Pretty cool, if you'll pardon the pun.

"Here we are," Douglas said unnecessarily, as neither Patti nor Spencer could have missed the unit in question; the first officer had encircled it and the immediate area with crime-scene tape. Two men, similarly outfitted in HazMat suits, stood just beyond the tape.

Then she saw the hands. Or what was left of them, anyway. Mostly skeletal, laid out on a plastic sheet on the ground. By each sat a plastic zip-type bag. She wondered if they would be able to extract any usable DNA from what remained, either from the hands or what looked like the "gumbo" inside the bags.

DNA soup. Lovely.

Patti shifted her gaze to the refrigerator itself. A typical freezer-on-top variety, white and low tech, no ice or water dispenser in the door. It didn't come from the Taj Mahal, that was for certain.

The larger of the two men stepped forward. "Officer Connelly, Captain. I answered the call."

"You set up the perimeter?"

"Yes. Verified the find and called it in."

"Good. Contact the department, see if they were able to round us up a crime-scene crew." She turned to the other man. "Paul, I'm Captain O'Shay and this is Detective Malone. I understand you're the one who found the hands."

He bobbed his head in agreement. "I suppose I should've gotten Jim right away, but I kinda couldn't believe what I was seeing. Surprised the hell out of me, that's for sure."

"It would anyone, Paul. Why don't you tell us exactly what happened."

"See, we have a procedure we follow. First, we empty the units. Dump what we can in the bins. By hand or with the help of a grapple machine. When that's done we pressure-wash 'em.

"Most of what's in these things is sludge. I mean, these babies have been without power for a long time. It's damn disgusting, I'll tell you that."

Patti wouldn't disagree. "How'd you find the hands?"

"They were there—"he pointed "—in the freezer. Wouldn't have found 'em if one of the bags hadn't broken. Slipped out of my hands and busted open. Act of God, it was."

The act she had interest in was one of pure evil.

"But you didn't go get Mr. Douglas?"

"I was kinda blown away, you know? Thought maybe this wasn't the real thing. That one of the other guys planted it as a joke."

His voice shook slightly, though Patti was uncertain whether from anxiety or excitement.

"So I laid that one out to take a real good look at it, and you know it didn't look like plastic. That's when I found another one." He glanced at Douglas. "And went and got Jim."

"And together you removed four more?"

He bobbed his head once more. "After we realized what we had, we were real careful."

"We appreciate that." She glanced at Douglas. "Do we know where this refrigerator came from?"

"The Metro New Orleans area."

"You don't have a street, a neighborhood or—"

"Just the Parish. Orleans."

Although frustrated, she wasn't surprised. The cleanup effort was immense. She'd heard the debris from this storm alone was going to equal thirty-four years' worth of regular New Orleans debris. Something like one hundred million cubic yards, enough to fill the Superdome twenty-two times over.

She turned back to Paul. "Notice anything else different about this unit?"

He thought a moment. "Nope. Sorry."

"If you think of anything, let us know." She held a hand out to Jim Douglas. "We'll take it from here. When our crime-scene crew arrives, you'll send them our way?"

He said he would, and as he and Paul walked away, she turned back to Spencer. He had crossed to the hands and was squatted down beside them.

"They're all right hands," he said. "That's six different victims."

She frowned. "Why right hands?"

"Why hands at all?" he countered.

"They're trophies. Obviously."

"Katrina comes into town and our sick bastard here loses his collection." He fitted on a pair of latex gloves, then held his own hand to the skeletal remains. "Women's hands. Too small to be a man's."

She slipped on a pair of gloves and joined him. When she compared, she saw that the hands were a similar size to hers. "Still, they could have belonged to a young male, maybe a teen?"

"Maybe." Spencer cocked his head. "Look at this. These four were very neatly severed."

"But these two," Patti murmured, "real hack jobs."

"As time passed, he got better at what he did."

"Practice makes perfect."

"Grim thought."

"Well, here's another." She stood. "They were all frozen. They all began the decomposition process at the same time— when the power went out."

Spencer took over. "So we're not going to be able to say when the mutilation occurred. Could have been right before the storm—"

"Or years ago."

"Exactly."

"Grim fact number two. No telling how many people have handled this refrigerator or how long it's been outside, exposed to the elements."

"Finding any trace will be a miracle."

He referred to trace evidence, she knew. Things like hair and fiber. "As will usable prints. We've got no way to pinpoint where this refrigerator came from, so no frame of reference to hang our investigation on."

"Grim fact number three," Spencer offered.

"Exactly. And DNA, if we can get an uncontaminated sample, won't do us jack without something to compare it with."

"Grim fact number four," Spencer murmured, trying for levity. "Thanks, I needed that."

The crime-scene crew, consisting of one tech, arrived. She recognized him from his gear. Obviously this lone tech would be doing it all, from photography to fingerprint-and-evidence collection.

Where they'd scraped him up, Patti could only imagine. Without housing, there was nowhere for people to live, even those who still had jobs. Currently hundreds of NOPD officers were living on the Carnival cruise ship *Ecstasy,* docked downtown on the Mississippi River.

"Yo," the tech said, setting down the gear. "What do we have?"

Spencer pointed. "Somebody's collection."

The guy made a face and shook his head. "This is so screwed-up. The tipping point for me was them spotting a shark swimming down Veterans Boulevard. I mean, how do you come back from that?"

He loaded the camera. "Mom lives in St. Tammany, I evacuated to her place. Lost forty trees on her property, but not one hit her house. Can you believe it?"

He didn't expect an answer and got to work. His story wasn't new. Patti heard a version of it from everybody she ran into. Nobody connected in this "post-Katrina world" without sharing their storm story.

She turned to the other officer. "Connelly, help him out here. Make certain the evidence is collected. Check in with me when it's done."

She and Spencer started back to their vehicle. They didn't speak until they had removed their HazMat gear and climbed into Spencer's vintage Camaro.

She turned to him. "We look for a victim. See if the computer turns up a vic that was missing a hand. Have Tony give you a——"

She had been about to say "a hand." He realized it, too, and glanced her way, eyebrow cocked.

A grim smile touched her mouth. "Detective Sciame assists. Keep me posted."

He agreed and they fell silent again. As Spencer drove, Patti gazed out at the ravaged landscape, one thought playing through her head: it wasn't enough the city had Katrina's devastation and rebuilding process to face, now they had a serial killer to catch as well.

PART

4

City Park was a sprawling thirteen-hundred-acre park in the heart of New Orleans. Before Katrina, it had boasted three eighteen-hole golf courses, a tennis center, and lagoons complete with a gondola and paddle boats, Storybook Land and Carousel Gardens, and the New Orleans Museum of Art. Limping back to its previous glory or not, it was still one of the oldest urban parks in the United States.

Today it was the location of a gruesome discovery: human remains.

Spencer parked his 1977 Camaro in front of the Bayou Oaks golf center's two-story practice range and climbed out. The dispatcher had described the remains as "skeletal." Certainly not the first of his career. Louisiana's sub-tropic climate, with its abundance of rain, long hot summers and acidic soil, accelerated the decomposition process. Here, a body could be reduced to nothing but bones and a few tendons in two weeks.

Detective Tony Sciame roared into the gravel lot. Spencer crossed to his partner's seen-better-days Ford Taurus just as the driver's-side door flew open and Tony heaved himself out.

The smell of French fries followed him. The call had obviously interrupted his lunch.

"Pasta Man," Spencer greeted him. "Betty know you're eating that garbage?"

Betty, Tony's wife of thirty-four years, monitored her husband's food consumption like a hawk—something Tony had no intention of doing for himself—and it had become a sort of battle of wills between them.

"Of course she does, Slick. My Betty's a very bright woman."

Spencer chuckled and glanced up at the sky. "Good day for a round of golf."

Tony hooted in amusement. "Slick, the closest you've ever come to swinging a golf club is the time you broke up a fight between those two guys in plaid knickers."

"Doesn't mean it couldn't happen." They fell into step together, and he sent his partner an amused glance. "And if I were you I wouldn't say anything about other guys' fashion choices."

"What?" Tony looked down at himself. "I look good."

He wore trousers in a shade too green to be called khaki and too brown to really be green. Puke or vomit would describe it nicely. Tony had paired the pants with a wild print shirt whose predominant color was orange.

"Sure, you do. For a color blind old fart."

Tony snorted. "You're just jealous I have the self-confidence to wear bright colors."

"Whatever you need to tell yourself, my friend," Spencer teased. Spencer had nicknamed the older man for his "pasta" gut, while Tony's nickname for Spencer aimed at his youth and inexperience. Though they swapped insults much of the day, they liked, respected and, most importantly, trusted each other to watch their backs.

In the NOPD, detectives weren't assigned partners, per se. They worked rotation. When a case came in, whoever was next in line got it and chose someone to assist. It was in the "choosing" that most of the detectives paired up.

Spencer and Tony's was an admittedly odd pairing. Spencer was thirty-three and single; Tony had been married longer than Spencer had been alive and had four children. Spencer was a relative rookie to Investigative Support Division, ISD for short, and homicide; Tony had been working homicide for twenty-seven years. Spencer had a reputation for being a brash hothead; Tony, one as a cautious plodder.

The tortoise and the hare. Not very sexy but, in their case, effective.

"Yo, Mikey," Spencer greeted the first officer, a guy who'd been in his brother Percy's graduating class at the academy. The two had been pals and bottle buddies before Mike had gotten married. "What do we have?"

The officer grinned. "Hey, Spencer, Detective Sciame. First tee, west course. Skeletal remains. Mostly intact."

"Man or woman?"

"Dunno. Not my area."

"Who'd the coroner's office send?"

"The bone lady. Elizabeth Walker."

"ID?"

"Nope. And no personal effects, though there might be something more in the grave. We didn't move the body. Called DIU, district three. They sent Landry."

Nearly ten years ago, the NOPD brass had decided the best place to fight crime was where it happened. They had decentralized the department, relocating the various detective units, taking them out of headquarters and moving them into the eight district stations, bundling them into what they named the Detective Investigative Unit. The detectives in DIU didn't specialize; they handled everything except rape, child abuse and high-profile murders. For those crimes, ISD took over.

"Glad to hear that, Mikey. You might make a decent cop, after all."

"Bite me, Malone."

"Nah, you'd like it too much."

"Can we save your personal issues for later?" Tony asked dryly. "The rest of the friggin' department's already here. I'd like to make an appearance before the vic's bagged and tagged."

Unfazed, the junior officer went on. "The engineer and

landscape artist who're planning the course's restoration found the grave. Stumbled over it, actually."

Spencer frowned. "What does that mean, stumbled over it?"

"Just what it sounds like. Really freaked the engineer out. Landed right on top of it, poor bastard. If he hadn't, they might've missed the grave altogether."

"You have names and numbers for these guys?"

He said he did and added, "I told them both to expect a visit from the NOPD this afternoon." The officer motioned toward the row of golf carts. "Choose your wheels. Keys are in 'em. Follow the signs."

They crossed to a cart and climbed in, Tony behind the wheel.

Spencer looked at his partner. "Ironic, finding a body here now."

Until a few months ago, when they'd moved back into their Broad Street headquarters, the entire detective division had been operating out of trailers here at the park.

"No joke."

While Tony drove, Spencer took in the surroundings. City Park had been decimated by Hurricane Katrina. The day after the storm, ninety percent of the park had been under anywhere from one to ten feet of water. Adding insult to injury, the water had been from the Gulf of Mexico, and its salt content had killed all the grass in the park, as well as a tremendous number of delicate plant species.

And like the city itself, in the two years since Katrina, the park had hobbled back to life—though to nowhere near its pre-Katrina glory.

They reached the site. With crime-scene tape, Mikey and his partner had created a wide swathe around the first tee. Tony parked the cart just beyond the tape; they climbed out and crossed to the officer. Spencer didn't recognize him and decided he must be a post-Katrina hire.

That's the way everything was in the Big Easy these days: pre- or post-Katrina. It served as New Orleanians' frame of reference to mark time and personal history.

It certainly served as Spencer's.

Before "The Thing," as local columnist Chris Rose had nicknamed it, Spencer had been confident he had finally conquered his demons. He'd felt secure in his own skin, his place in the universe, tiny as it was.

Sammy's murder, Katrina and the chaos that ensued had eroded that confidence, his feeling of security. Now he doubted. And second-guessed. Life, he'd learned, was fragile. The moment fleeting.

He thought about it a lot. One day life was as it should be; the next, turned upside down. A cop always lived with uncertainty, but this was different. Katrina had made it feel... global.

He and Tony signed the scene log, ducked under the tape and crossed to the group clustered around the grave.

Located six feet behind the tee box, under a large shade tree, Spencer saw that the crime-scene guys had gotten their shots and begun the excavation process. Elizabeth Walker crouched beside, watching intently.

The skeleton was, indeed, almost fully intact, positioned

faceup. Bits of what appeared to have been clothing clung to the mottled-looking bones.

"Hey, Terry," Spencer greeted the DIU detective, "how's it going?"

"Can't complain, though I mostly do, anyway." He smiled and shook his hand, then Tony's. "How about you?"

"Ditto, man. I'll tell Quentin I saw you."

"Hell no, you won't. Tell that no-good welcher he owes me a beer."

Spencer laughed. Quentin and Terry Landry had been partners before Quentin decided to quit the PD and go to law school. Now he was an assistant D.A. Truth was, you couldn't swing a dead cat in this town without hitting someone who had worked—or partied—with one of the Malone siblings.

Elizabeth Walker looked over her shoulder at him. An African-American who'd been a child in preintegrated New Orleans, she had a sharp eye for detail, a dry sense of humor and the no-nonsense air of a woman who had clawed her way up and out. "A Malone, God help us."

"Good to see you, too." He squatted beside her. "What do you think?"

"Definitely a woman." She indicated the pelvic bone. "See how short it is? How wide the pelvic bowl?"

"Age?"

"Young, not twenty-five. Her bones hadn't finished growing. I'll know more after I X-ray her back at the lab." She paused, then went on. "Judging by her color, she's been out here awhile. A couple years, I'd think."

"By out here, you mean exposed to the elements."

"Exactly." She pointed. "See how the bone is dry-looking, without the smooth ivory finish. And sort of a mottled gray and white. Bone is porous. If she'd been in the earth, she'd have taken on its color."

"Was she ever in the ground?"

"My best guess is yes, but in a shallow grave. The wind and rain have eroded the layer of soil and debris used to cover her. Maybe even Katrina's floodwater."

Spencer studied the victim. "She could have been here that long?"

"Absolutely."

Spencer looked up at Tony. "Shallow grave. Our guy could have been rushed."

Tony nodded. "Or not cared if she was found."

Spencer slipped on latex gloves and carefully brushed away some leaves and other debris. Scraps of fabric clung to her pelvic area. Panties, he guessed. Had she been wearing anything else?

The forensic anthropologist seemed to read his thoughts. "A synthetic," she said. "Nylon, probably. The elements do a quick number on natural fabrics like cotton and silk, but the synthetics can last years. She was dressed. Look here."

A zipper. Peeking out from leaves and pine straw. The garment it had fastened long gone.

"Can you tell me anything else?"

"She had breast implants. Unlike the real thing, they don't decompose."

"A forever upgrade," Tony murmured dryly. "What a selling point."

Elizabeth laughed. "Tell me about it."

"Is that it?" Spencer asked.

"Before I get her to the lab? Pretty much. Except for the missing right hand, there's no obvious traumas to the bones. And certainly nothing that could be the cause of death."

Missing hand? For a moment Spencer thought he had misheard her. His gaze went to her right arm, then down to where her hand should have been.

Should have been. But wasn't.

The serial killer dubbed the "Handyman" had never been found. Between lack of evidence and post-Katrina chaos, the investigation had gone nowhere and been closed.

Could this be one of his victims?

Excited, he looked up at Tony and saw by his expression that he was thinking the same thing.

"Scavenger could have taken off with it," Tony offered.

Elizabeth shook her head. "No way. Look at the bones, Detective. This was a clean cut. Like an amputation."

The three exchanged glances. "Damn interesting, to have a victim surface now. *If* these remains turn out to belong to one of the Handyman's victims."

"You think they won't?"

The forensic anthropologist followed them to their feet. "I suppose your top priority is determining whether one of those hands belonged to this woman?"

"How long?"

"Not very. We'll get her bagged and back to the lab. Bones are as unique as an individual. And they don't lie. If one of those hands belongs to her, we'll know."

"IDing her would be a home run. Having a known victim would open up a lot of investigative doors."

"I'll look for any kind of identifying bone trauma. That'll help. So will her dental work."

"With what's left, how close can you come to establishing when she died?"

"Not closer than I already have. Sorry. I'll make this a priority and call you when I know more."

Spencer thanked her and he and Tony started toward the golf cart. "If she was killed post-Katrina, the Handyman is here. And he's active."

"Detectives!" Elizabeth Walker called. "We found something."

They turned back, crossed to the tech holding the item in his gloved hands. He held it out.

An NOPD badge. Number 364.

Spencer stared at the badge, his heart thundering. He made a sound and was aware of the others looking his way. Of the seconds ticking past.

He knew that badge number. Knew it well.

"Slick? What is it?"

Spencer shifted his gaze to Tony. "We have one of our answers. She was killed before Katrina. Right before."

At his colleagues' blank looks, he added, "That badge belonged to Captain Sammy O'Shay."

The information hit with the force of a small bomb. For a moment, no one spoke.

Tony broke the silence first. "You're sure, absolutely sur—"

"Hell yes!"

Elizabeth cleared her throat. "How do you want to proceed, Detective?"

"I'll call Captain O'Shay. She'll want to come down here herself. She'll call the shots from there on."

Friday, April 20, 2007
3:00 p.m.

Patti held the badge in her gloved hands. They trembled slightly. Her chest hurt, as if she had been struck. The cool breeze rustled the leaves in the maple tree; one of the crime-scene techs shifted uncomfortably. Otherwise all were silent. Waiting. Giving her time.

She lifted her gaze, moved it around the circle. She saw sympathy. Shock and sadness.

And anger.

A cop had been killed. One of their own.

"I'm sorry, Aunt Patti," Spencer said softly, laying a hand on her shoulder.

"I'm not," she said, voice clear and strong. "He's already gone. This gives me an opportunity to nail the bastard who took him."

"What are you thinking?" he asked.

"That this changes everything. That it blows the 'killed by looters' theory to hell."

"Maybe."

"No maybe. Sammy stumbled upon the killer, most likely in the act or its aftermath. It got him killed."

"That's one explanation."

"You have another?"

"She could have killed him."

"Not likely."

"But possible."

She made a sound of frustration. "Anything's possible."

"The badge," Spencer continued, "could have ended up in the grave by—"

"Accident? Come on, Detective. It was found *under* her remains, not mixed in the debris around the grave. My guess is, the son of a bitch tossed Sammy's badge into the hole, then dumped the body on top."

"It could have gone down that way. No doubt. But I don't think we should close the door on other options."

"Other options?" she repeated, suddenly angry. The group went stone silent. "What are they? Right now, I have this. And I mean to pursue it."

6

Friday, April 20, 2007
7:10 p.m.

Much later, Patti sat at her desk. The department around her was mostly silent. Unless neck-deep in an investigation, NOPD detectives worked eight to five, so most of ISD had left for the day. The detectives all carried cell phones or pagers and understood that they were essentially on call 24/7.

She had no intention of packing up for the night—or the weekend. Finally she had a lead in Sammy's murder.

The two years that had passed hadn't dimmed her grief. People kept telling her "It'll get better" and "You'll move on."

But she knew better. Until she got justice for Sammy, she couldn't begin to let go.

Of her grief. Or her anger.

Her marriage and the NOPD had been her whole life. She felt as if she'd lost both. The department had let her down. Sammy had devoted his life to the NOPD. But when he'd been killed in the line of duty, their attempts at justice had been laughable. Their focus had been on the hurricane and their own future. The case had been closed. They'd moved on.

She hadn't moved on. And she wouldn't.

Now she had something.

Though, she had to admit she was having trouble wrapping her head around this. Sammy's badge found in a shallow grave in City Park, along with the skeletal remains of a young woman?

A young woman whose right hand had been severed.

She'd requested all the Handyman files. They contained damn little, considering this bastard had killed at least six women.

And a cop, she thought. Her husband.

She had promised herself she would bring his killer to justice. Until today, that promise had seemed damn near impossible to keep.

She needed that victim IDed. She needed something, some bit of evidence to link an individual to the case. She wouldn't rest until she found it.

"Aunt Patti?"

Spencer stood in her office doorway; she motioned him in, forcing a relaxed smile. "Ready for the weekend?" she asked him.

"Always." He crossed the room and sat in the chair opposite her desk. Although he smiled, she saw his concern. "Big day."

"Very."

"You're okay?"

"Absolutely."

"Have you eaten?"

She smiled at that. "I will. I promise."

He frowned and moved his gaze over her desk. "The Handyman files? Until we hear back from the coroner's offi—"

"I know. But I want to go over it all myself. Make certain nothing is missed."

"Tony and I are on this. Nothing's going to be missed."

"This is about me, not about you. Or my confidence in you."

He sat silently a moment, then leaned forward. "It's not going to get solved tonight. Nothing will be served by you staying here all night."

"It's what—" She glanced at her wall clock. "Just after seven. Hardly cause for concern."

"I'm worried about you, that's all."

"A waste of energy, I promise. Go home. Take Stacy out for dinner. Someplace nice." She wagged a finger at him. "That's not only your captain's orders, it's your godmother's as well."

That made him smile. He came around the desk, bent and kissed her cheek. "I'll do that."

He crossed to the door, stopped and looked back at her. "You'll be leaving behind me, right?"

"Absolutely."

Her smiled faded as he walked out the door.

God forgive her. It'd been a small lie. One meant to reassure.

She intended to sit here until she knew everything in these files by heart.

7

Friday, April 20, 2007
7:55 p.m.

Spencer let himself into his Riverbend cottage. He'd bought his Camaro from John Jr.—older brother number one—when John had gotten married, and this house from Quentin—older brother number two—when he'd gotten hitched. Since he was brother number three in the Malone lineup, he supposed it was his turn to "pass along."

Which was too bad. His brothers had damn good taste—he would miss the largesse.

He'd certainly been glad to have this place. Located at the Uptown bend of the Mississippi River, the Riverbend area had been among the twenty percent of the city left high and dry after Katrina.

He'd been host to a dozen family members after the storm. And to Stacy Killian, his girlfriend and fellow NOPD detective, whose City Park double had taken on four feet of water.

Stacy was the only one still with him.

Spencer stepped inside. "I'm home," he called.

"Back here."

He followed the sound of her voice and found her in front of the bathroom mirror, applying makeup. She wore a pair of snug-fitting, low-riding jeans and a small stretchy top that exposed a nearly indecent expanse of her flat belly.

"Looking good, Killian."

She met his gaze in the mirror and smiled. He saw that she had lined her eyes with a deep smoky color. "Glad you like."

"Oh, yeah. Not your usual look, but I could grow accustomed." He crooked his finger. "Come on over here and I'll show you."

She sauntered over and slid her arms around him. He nuzzled the side of her neck. "Never mind that I'm not going to let you out of the bedroom in that get-up, but...*damn.*"

"Sorry, stud." She rubbed herself against him, teasing. "It's for my new job."

He cocked an eyebrow, playing along. "New job? You've left DIU? Quit the force to move on?" Not so outrageous, considering when he met her she'd quit the Dallas force and moved to New Orleans to go to graduate school. And study English lit.

That hadn't lasted a semester.

Truth was, you either were a cop or you weren't—it wasn't something you could just give up. Like smoking. Or the bottle. There wasn't a twelve-step program for reformed cops.

Though most days, he thought there should be.

"Mmm," she said. "Moving on to the Bourbon Street Hustle."

The Hustle billed itself as a "gentleman's club." Skanky titty bar was a better description, one that catered to tourists, bikers and those who couldn't afford upscale clubs like Rick's Cabaret or Temptations.

Just a few years ago, Bourbon Street had been dotted with places like the Hustle, but those had become fewer as the high-end, luxurious clubs had appeared on the New Orleans scene. Folks who wouldn't be caught dead in a place like the Hustle felt comfortable frequenting this new breed of club.

Given what was left of the traditional Bourbon Street clubs, the Hustle wasn't bottom of the barrel, but damn close to it.

She kissed him, then stepped away. "Undercover gig. Starts tonight."

He was a cop, she was a cop. She had a job to do and could absolutely take care of herself.

But the thought of her down there, looking like *that,* being drooled over by a bunch of horny bastards… That he didn't like it would be an understatement.

He dropped his gaze to her chest. The tops of her breasts spilled out of her tight shirt.

She laughed at his expression. "Victoria's Secret, Wonderbra. Uncomfortable as hell." She crossed back to the mirror to admire her cleavage. "Bet these babies'll get me some major tips."

Not exactly what he wanted to hear. "I need a beer."

"Grab me a diet Coke. I'll be out in a minute."

She appeared as he was taking a swallow of his beer—and nearly choked on it. Her short blond hair had been transformed to a long auburn mane. Between the makeup and wig, he wouldn't recognize her in passing.

Which, of course, was the point.

"I've always wanted to be a redhead, now I've got the chance." She grinned and caught the can of soda he tossed her. "This is going to be fun."

She was liking this drug task force gig way too much.

Spencer forced himself to focus. He didn't want her to know he was feeling uncomfortable about this. It just wasn't cool. "What's the story?"

"We busted a small-time meth dealer. Turns out, he's the Hustle's regular bartender. He rolled right over, offered us the name of a big fish."

"And this fish is a regular patron."

"Comes in every night. Apparently he's got a regular girl there. I'm supposed to get to know her."

"Who's the guy?"

She popped the soda can's top. "Name's Marcus Gabrielle. Squeaky clean on paper. He's a commercial real estate broker. Married with two kids. Lives uptown."

"Wife know about the little hottie?"

"Doubt it." She took a swallow of the soft drink. "According to our informant he manufactures *and* distributes. We get him, we get his people on both sides of the process."

"Who else is in there with you?"

"Baxter. And Waldon. Baxter's tending bar with the guy we busted. Waldon's playing customer."

Rene Baxter was a solid cop, a small, wiry guy with one of those nondescript faces perfect for undercover work. Waldon was a big doofus who fancied himself an ace detective. And a ladies' man. Go figure.

"You'll be wired?"

"Of course, with the cavalry in a van around the corner."

Before he could ask anything else, she changed the subject. "I heard about City Park. About finding Uncle Sammy's shield in that grave. I'm sorry."

News about one of their own traveled fast. Spencer rolled the cold can between his palms. "Finding his badge in that grave…it blew me away."

"How's Patti?"

"I don't know." He frowned. "She said all the right things, but I'm worried she's…" He let the thought trail off.

"She's what?"

"When I left tonight, she was still there. Reviewing the Handyman files."

"And?"

"And Tony and I are on it. It was after hours. Until we hear back from the coroner's office, we're not even certain the Jane Doe is a Handyman victim."

He looked away, then back. "She won't even consider any other possibilities. In her mind, Sammy was killed by the Handyman. Period."

"If it dead ends, she will. This gives her a ball to run with."

"I know that, it's just…she hasn't been the same since Sammy was killed. I don't know, I can't put my finger on it. She's changed."

"It's going to take time," Stacy said softly. "For all of us."

He knew she referred not only to Sammy's murder, but the destruction and uncertainty Katrina had wrought.

Katrina had changed them all.

"You're right. Come here." He took the can from her hand and set it on the counter, then drew her against him. "I'll miss you tonight."

"I'll miss you, too." She kissed him, then eased away. "My shift starts at nine. I've got to go."

He pulled her back into his arms and held her close, a moment too long, a bit too tightly. When he released her, he saw the question in her eyes. "People with a lot to lose fight hard to hold on to it. Don't forget that, Stacy."

8

Friday, April 20, 2007
9:00 p.m.

When Stacy entered the Bourbon Street Hustle, Baxter was already in place. Their gazes met briefly as she approached the bar, then he returned his attention to mixing drinks. She shifted her gaze to the bartender working with him.

Ted Parrish, their informant. Tall, with long black hair and a goatee. He looked jumpy. It could be the position he was in— or he was cranked on his own product.

"I'm Brandi," she said, slipping into her persona. "The new girl."

"See Tonya," he said tightly, drawing a draft. "She's backstage. She'll tell you what you need to know."

Tonya Messinger, "talent" manager. "How do I get back there?"

"Right side of the stage. Dressing rooms and everything are there."

"Thanks!" she called, and headed in that direction, swinging her ass as she wound her way through tables and around groups of men clustered together. A guy with an awe-inspiring beer belly and a ruddy face made a grab for her. She shimmied away, teasingly wagging a finger at him. She figured her first choice of response—breaking his arm—might blow her cover.

Stacy had familiarized herself with the club's layout through photos. She now studied the interior, looking for details she might need later. The three-tier stage was the main attraction. The first tier was the largest and round, the other two basically "wings" jutting off the sides. Tables circled the stage; the ones closest to the stage were VIP tables.

The owners had done their best to conceal the club's rough edges and give the place an upscale feel: sophisticated, subdued lighting; white tablecloths on the tables; a flickering candle on each; velvet drapes around the stage.

The long bar occupied the far wall directly across from the stage, affording those who preferred a little distance a full view of the show.

As she understood it, there were a number of semiprivate and private areas for personal "performances." Call her suspicious but she'd wager tonight's tips that more than lap dancing went on in those rooms, most of it left of the law.

As she reached the backstage entrance, the house lights

dimmed, a strobe light started and pulsating music filled the club. A young woman strode out wearing sequins, feathers and scraps of fabric that would fit in the palms of her hands.

Yvette Borger. The girlfriend.

Twenty-two years old. Petite, with long, inky-black hair. Great body. Breasts too big for her petite frame.

Party pillows, Stacy thought in the slang tossed around the department. Made her own Victoria's Secret enhancement seem pretty lame.

Stacy watched her a moment, then ducked through the stage door.

She caught sight of Tonya right away, recognizing her from her photograph. She stood in the wings, watching Yvette's performance.

Stacy crossed to her. "Tonya?"

"Yes?" the woman responded.

"I'm Brandi. The new girl."

Tonya Messinger looked like she had been around the block a few times—and like someone you didn't want to cross. Stacy judged her age to be fifty, though her estimate could be off. Tobacco, alcohol and hard living all took their toll.

"You're late."

"Am I? I thought—"

The woman cut her off. "If your shift starts at nine, I want you here at eight-forty-five. You'll be punched in and at your station by start time. No excuses."

She eyed her, and Stacy had the feeling that in those few moments Tonya had calculated her age, weight and bust size.

"Sure you don't want to dance? We could use another girl and the tips are a lot better."

The Wonderbra wasn't quite that wonderful.

"Dancing's not my thing. I'm not very good at it."

Tonya laughed, the sound deep and raspy from a lifetime of smoking. "Honey, dancing's not what you need to succeed out there. Trust me, you've got the talent. Add some attitude and you'd be good to go."

Stacy pretended to be flattered. "Wow, thanks. I'll think about it."

"Do that. In the meantime, let's get you out on the floor."

While they headed back out front, Tonya gave her directions. "My job is to keep the girls in line. There's no drug use on my watch. No freebies for any reason. No catfights unless it's part of the show. That includes the wait staff."

She looked meaningfully at her, and Stacy nodded that she understood.

"Your job is twofold. Push the drinks. Try to up-sell with call brands. Buy me a drink is code for 'Let's party.' The girls make their money from tips—if you step on their toes, you'll regret it.

"Some of the girls drink, some don't. Whether they do or not, if the patron offers to buy a drink, he's charged. The girls will let you know ahead of time what they're drinking. Some like tonic water, some a soft drink or juice. If a patron pays for a cocktail, he wants to see her drinking it.

"Patrons will ask you to deliver messages, tips and little gifts. If you screw with that, you'll be sorry.

"In that vein," the older woman went on, "flirt. Be sexy. But if a patron comes on to you, you decline. Your job is pushing drinks, period. Got all that?"

Stacy said she did, and the next few hours passed in a blur of pats on her behind, suggestive comments and leering looks. Not that all the club's patrons were lecherous jerks. She had a table of folks visiting from Indiana. They'd never seen "anything like this before" and had stared, open-mouthed and slightly embarrassed. She'd also served a table of LSU guys—she'd carded them—who had been very respectful. Although it had been a breath of fresh air, being treated like someone's mother hadn't done much for her ego.

Waldon had arrived and sat at a table in her station. He seemed to be enjoying this assignment way too much, and when he leered at her, she "accidentally" spilled part of a drink on him to cool him off.

In that time, their suspect hadn't shown and the closest she'd gotten to Yvette was when the dancer came over to "party with" the LSU boys.

They hadn't had much money, and she had moved on.

Stacy finally got her opportunity late in the evening. Tonya gave her a note to deliver backstage to Yvette.

Stacy found her in her dressing area, reapplying her makeup. A cigarette burned in an ashtray on the vanity.

Stacy tapped on the door. "Tonya asked me to bring you this."

Yvette stared at the note, a frown wrinkling her brow.

Stacy watched her. "Is something wrong?"

Yvette tossed the note on the vanity top, her expression dismissive. "Just some freak. I get a lot of that."

"I'll bet. I mean, you're really good."

"You think so?"

The eagerness in her voice revealed just how young she was. Stacy lowered her voice so she wouldn't be heard by the others. "You've got the best act, hands down."

"What's your name?"

"Brandi."

"How do you like the job so far?"

Stacy shrugged. "It's okay. Tips have been pretty good."

"You want some advice?"

"Sure."

"Stay on Tonya's good side, 'cause she can be a real bitch. Play the game. It doesn't mean jack and you'll make lots more money."

"The game?"

"Yeah, you know. Play to the guys. Give 'em what they want." Yvette took a drag on her cigarette, then tamped it out. "Ted's a dog. He'll want to do you, so watch yourself. He'll offer crank, pills, booze...just stay clear."

"Sounds like you've got it all figured out."

"I've got to watch out for my own ass, you know? I'm not going to be in this dump forever. I've got plans."

Stacy wanted to ask what they were, wanted to ask if she had a special "guy." But she knew better. This had been a good first meeting. If she pushed too hard, too fast, the other woman would shut down.

"Well, thanks," she said, taking a step back. "I've got to get back out there."

Hours later, Stacy finished her shift and headed home. Marcus never appeared, and she hoped he hadn't been tipped or gotten spooked. By the end of the night Yvette had seemed annoyed, and Stacy wondered if it was because of the boyfriend's absence.

It'd been interesting watching the girls work. The way they turned it on and off. When performing for a customer, it was as if no one existed but him. The minute they walked away, it was all about the next guy.

It seemed like such a lie.

Or was it? The guys knew, right? They couldn't really think these girls were all turned on? It was just one big, hot fantasy.

Was that what guys wanted? Stacy wondered. A big, hot fantasy? Was that what Spencer wanted?

What *did* he want? They'd moved in together almost by accident. Because of Katrina. Because she'd needed a place to live and he'd had one.

And she had stayed. By a mutual, unspoken agreement. It'd been two years and she would have to say their feelings for each other had neither progressed nor deteriorated.

Inert. Is that how she would describe their relationship? She hoped not because thinking of it that way made her feel uncomfortable—and a bit ridiculous, as well.

How else should she describe it? They'd moved in together "almost by accident." They had stayed together by an "unspoken agreement."

He hadn't brought up marriage. He hadn't said he loved her.

And neither had she.

She stood in the bedroom doorway, watching him sleep. She had showered, washing away the stink of cigarettes and the layers of makeup, and changed into an oversize T-shirt. Was she waiting for Spencer to take the lead? she wondered. Did she want him to?

She wanted marriage, children. A normal life. Those longings had prompted her to try leaving police work behind, to try a fresh start in a brand-new city.

Instead, she'd gotten pulled back into police work—and she'd met Spencer. Become involved with him—and ended up in this almost-by-accident, unspoken-agreement relationship.

But how could she have a normal life when the future was so uncertain? Look at Sammy: wrong place, wrong time, and now Patti was a widow. Neither she nor Spencer were cut out to be anything but the cops they were. Was it fair to want children, to offer them such an uncertain future?

Stacy slipped into bed beside Spencer.

"How'd it go?" he mumbled.

"Okay. Suspect never showed."

He muttered something she couldn't make out.

She propped herself up on an elbow. "Malone, you ever pay for a lap dance?"

That woke him up. He rolled onto his side and looked at her. "Excuse me?"

"You ever go to those places, like the Hustle?"

"Have I ever?"

He looked a bit like someone who'd been awakened by an electrical shock.

"Yes," she said. "Have you ever? Just curious."

"Yeah, I've been in those places, hooted it up with the other guys. But paying some woman to grind herself against me… It's just not my thing."

"Is it the 'paying' part? The 'some woman' part…or—"

He cocked an eyebrow. "Or what? The 'a sexy woman all over me' part? Give me a break, Stacy. I've got wood just talking about it."

She smiled. "I think I can help with that."

"That so?"

"Mmm." She sat up, pulled off the T-shirt and tossed it on the floor. "I'm feeling generous tonight. I'm thinking I might just give you one for free."

9

Saturday, April 21, 2007
3:30 a.m.

Yvette sat curled up on the couch of her tiny French Quarter apartment. She had showered, washed her hair and scrubbed her face clean. She wore cotton pj's and SpongeBob Square-Pants slippers. She'd made herself a cup of hot chocolate, homemade with milk and Hershey's syrup—not that powdered crap. She knew she looked more the part of naive teenager than cynical stripper who'd seen it all—and then some.

Yvette had long since given up feeling embarrassed or ashamed over what she did for a living. What she had said to that new waitress, Brandi, had been the truth. She had no one to watch out for her—but her. She never had, even as a kid.

She'd survived because she was a fighter. And a realist. Tonight she'd made five hundred bucks. She'd make that tomorrow as well, maybe a little more.

So what if she had to grind herself against some guy's crotch or shake her tits for a bunch of horny strangers? She pulled down six-plus figures a year, much of it tax free— and the only investment she'd had to make was in her double-Ds.

Where else could a twenty-two-year-old with no skills, training or education make that kind of cash?

Nowhere. That was a fact. One she had learned the hard way.

Yvette sipped her chocolate, thoughts turning to Marcus. To his absence tonight. She frowned as she realized she had grown to expect him to be there each night. That she counted on it.

Not emotionally. She'd been kicked in the teeth enough times to have finally cured herself of falling for every guy who acted like he cared. Cured herself of stupidly trusting anyone who held out their hand in friendship.

She didn't love Marcus. She wasn't so stupid as that. Not only was he married, but he was beyond her. Too educated. Too rich. Too connected. The best she could hope for from Marcus was a good time and a lot of cash.

Yvette curled her fingers around the warm mug. Unlike most of the girls, she didn't blow her money. Not up her nose or on things like jewelry and clothes. With the help of a broker, she'd invested it. She had money invested in the market *and* a good, old-fashioned savings account.

She wasn't going to let anyone or anything beat her down—

not Marcus, a hurricane named Katrina or life itself. She'd been down that road with her daddy—and had vowed never again.

The memory came upon her so suddenly it took her breath. Blood. A growing pool of it. The sound of terror. Of hopelessness.

No! She wouldn't allow herself to go there. That belonged to another part of her life. To another person.

She meant to move forward. Only forward. Save enough to go to school. Buy a little house somewhere. Get a dog.

Have a happy life.

Her thoughts drifted to tonight's creepy note. From the freak who called himself the "Artist." It hadn't been the first note she had received from him. Nor had it been the first time a "fan" had written, professing their undying love and devotion. The job drew freaks, perverts and lonely guys in search of "true" love.

She set down her hot chocolate and reached for her backpack. She dug inside and pulled out the three notes.

She had received the first a week ago. Yvette opened it and reread the short, cryptic message.

I think you're the one. I can't be certain…am afraid to hope…I just pray I have finally found you, my sweet muse.
Yours, the Artist

It had been written on unlined journal paper. Or perhaps paper taken from a sketch tablet. The handwriting was spidery, in pencil. "Old person" handwriting.

The second had been delivered three days ago.

Tell me, do you long for love? True, undying and eternal love? For "the one" who will never leave you? I think you do. And it makes me love you all the more.

Yours, the Artist

She bit her lip to keep it from trembling. It was as if he had peeked inside her. It was what she had always wanted— undying and eternal love, someone who would love her forever, never leave her.

She shifted her attention to tonight's message. It had been written on a lovely sheet of Crane's stationery. In black ink. The envelope had been fixed with a wax seal. A blood-red *A*.

As I watched you last night, I realized you are, indeed, the one I've been waiting for. It has seemed ages since I've felt this rush, this well- spring of creativity… Of raw emotion.

Just know this, sweet muse, I love you. And someday…some perfect day, we will be to- gether. Forever.

Yours, the Artist

When would he make his next move? she wondered. Would he find the courage to approach her? To ante up for a "private performance"?

The prickly sense of unease surprised her. She tossed the note aside. Just another creep, she told herself firmly. One she would take more seriously if he'd bothered to tuck a twenty dollar bill into the envelope.

After all, "true love" didn't come free.

No, he wouldn't be approaching her for a private show. Freaks like him liked it better from a distance. They liked it cerebral. And when they got off, it was alone with their perverted thoughts.

10

Saturday, April 21, 2007
7:56 a.m.

The jangle of the phone dragged Spencer out of a deep sleep. He managed to reach it and bring the receiver to his ear without opening his eyes. "Yo."

"Wake up, Detective. I found something."

He cracked open his eyes. Squinting against the light, he looked at the clock. *Not quite eight.*

"Aunt Patti?"

"It's Captain O'Shay this morning. I'll pick you up in twenty minutes."

She hung up before Spencer could reply. Obviously she

knew him well enough to anticipate his attempt to wheedle a few more minutes out of her.

Spencer tossed down the phone and climbed out of bed.

"Bad news?" Stacy asked sleepily.

"Aunt Patti. She's on her way over."

Stacy murmured something that sounded like "Be careful," then burrowed deeper into her pillow. Spencer bent and kissed her, then headed for the shower.

Captain Patti O'Shay was nothing if not punctual. Exactly twenty minutes later, she pulled up in front of his house and tooted her horn. He stumbled out, "to-go" mug clutched in his hand.

After fastening his safety belt, he turned to her. "Want to tell me where we're going?"

She pulled away from the curb. "Quentin and Anna's."

His brother and sister-in-law's? Now she had his full attention. "I take it this isn't a social call?"

"Going through the Handyman files, I found something we missed last time. In one of the photos. See for yourself." She indicated the file folder lying on the dash.

He opened it. The folder contained photographs of the refrigerator where the hands had been discovered. She had circled something in the first photo, a small item affixed to the freezer door, nearly under the handle.

It'd been easy to miss because of its size, the location and because the duct tape that had been used to secure the unit half covered it.

"I made a blowup," Patti said without taking her eyes from the road.

He thumbed to the next photo. A promotional magnet, he saw. One for a suspense novel by local author Anna North.

His sister-in-law.

"Holy shit."

"My sentiments exactly."

"Anna's not going to like this."

An understatement, he knew. The only child of celebrities, Anna had been kidnapped as a child, her pinkie severed and sent to her family as a warning. She had escaped, but the ordeal had left her, understandably, traumatized. Not until she had become another maniac's target had she been able to conquer her fears.

That's how she had met Quentin; he had been the detective assigned to her case. They now lived with their young son in Mandeville, a bedroom community located across Lake Pontchartrain from New Orleans.

"We shouldn't have missed this," he said.

"No, we shouldn't have."

The months immediately following Katrina had been nightmarish; they'd been overwhelmed, stretched to near breaking. It had made them sloppy, a fact neither was proud of.

"Do they know we're coming?"

"I spoke with Quentin."

They fell silent once more. She glanced at Spencer. "He wasn't happy."

Another understatement. The Malone men took protecting

those they loved seriously. Having Anna threatened—or even the hint of a threat—would bring that streak out in him.

No doubt he was pacing like a caged lion right now.

That didn't prove to be the case. Thirty minutes later, as they pulled into Quentin and Anna's drive, Spencer saw that the couple were waiting on their wide front porch. Not only was Quentin sitting, Sam—their seventeen-month-old—was sprawled across his lap.

Anna stood as they climbed out of the car. Spencer adored his redheaded sister-in-law—and had from the moment he met her. How could he not? His brother had never been happier.

"Sam's asleep," she called, tone hushed. "Already played out, and it isn't even eight-thirty yet. And I wonder why I'm tired."

She said the last with a smile that showed that considering the source, she didn't mind the fatigue.

Spencer reached the porch and saw that the toddler was, indeed, asleep, his dark curls damp with sweat. Sam had been born days before Katrina struck. When they named him after Sammy, they'd had no idea how poignant that decision would become.

He embraced Anna, then greeted Quentin. "Yo, bro. Looking domestic."

All the Malone men were strongly built, with dark hair and blue eyes, but Quentin was unarguably the most classically handsome of them.

Quentin met his eyes. "I can still take you, little brother. If I were you, I wouldn't forget that."

"In your dreams, old man. I could—"

"For heaven's sake," Patti interrupted, "could you check the macho posturing long enough for me to get a look at the baby?"

Spencer stepped away and Quentin smiled sweetly at her. "Hello, Aunt Patti."

She bent and hugged him, then kissed Sam's head. "I saw him just last week, I swear he's grown since then."

"He has," Anna said. "Actually, we're thinking of nicknaming him Weed. I'll take him inside so we can talk."

She scooped him up and carried him into the house. The minute the door closed behind them, Quentin jumped to his feet, all but vibrating with pent-up energy.

"What's going on, Patti? And not just the 'official' bullshit story. The whole truth."

"As I explained on the phone, in studying photographs taken of the Handyman's refrigerator, we found—"

"One of Anna's promotional magnets. That I already know. How the hell did you miss it the first time around?"

Spencer laid a hand on his brother's arm. "Back off, Quent. We're doing everything we can."

"Back off? Anna having any connection to that madman, even one as flimsy as a free magnet, is not—"

"Spencer's right," Anna said from the doorway. "I'm not thrilled about this turn of events, but there's not much I can do about it. Except try to help them identify the refrigerator's owner."

He gazed at her a moment, then nodded tersely. Anna turned toward them. "So, what can I do?"

"Take a look."

Patti handed the file folder to Quentin. He studied the photos, jaw tight, then crossed to Anna and handed them to her.

"It's mine, all right." She handed the photos back. "*Dead of Night* was published in April 2005."

"How many of those magnets were distributed?"

"Twenty-five hundred. Give or take."

"All in the New Orleans area?"

"No. I gave them away at my book signings, through my Web site and to fans who wrote and requested one. In addition, I sent a stack to a number of my most supportive booksellers. For their customers."

"How many locally, do you think?"

"Five hundred, for sure. Maybe seven-fifty." Her voice shook slightly and Quentin put his arm around her.

"I know this makes you uncomfortable, Anna," Patti said. "I'm sorry."

"A psycho who severs his victims' hands does hit a little too close for comfort. But this isn't about me. It's about Sammy. And the girls who were murdered. I think I can handle it." Her eyes grew bright. "I loved Sammy, too."

Patti held her gaze a moment. "Thank you."

Spencer brought the focus back to the investigation. "Ever have a fan threaten you?"

"Just Ozzie."

"Osborne?"

At the mention of the rocker and erstwhile reality-TV-show figure, a ghost of a smile touched her mouth. "Hardly. A guy who axed his wife. Said he'd do the same to me."

Spencer arched his eyebrows in surprise. "And how, sister-in-law, did you meet him?"

"Fan mail from prison," Quentin said for her, voice tight.

"You get letters from prison?"

"Doesn't everyone?" When nobody laughed, she went on. "Yes, from both male and female cons. Since Ozzie, I don't even read them anymore. Refuse them and send them back unopened."

"Do you still have his?"

She shook her head and Quentin stepped in. "He was doing life without opportunity for parole. I took the letters to the proper officials. Mr. Oz's days of letter-writing to authors are over. Anna, it turns out, wasn't the only one."

"Any other readers, particularly local ones, who've made you uncomfortable?"

"Because of what I write, there's an occasional whack-job who comes up to me at a signing, but overwhelmingly everyone I meet is just a really nice person who likes to read scary books."

"Do you have a list of local fans' names and addresses?" Spencer asked.

"I do. I'll print a copy."

She headed inside and Quentin turned to them. "What next?"

"We run the names through the computer, see if we get any kind of a hit. We'll follow up from there."

"And if you don't get a hit?"

"We find another angle."

They fell silent a moment. From inside, they heard Sam waking up. Patti started for the door. "I'll go see if I can help Anna."

When she disappeared into the house, Quentin turned to Spencer. "How is she?"

"Patti? Not herself. Though finding this link to Sammy's murder seems to have given her direction."

"That's a good thing."

"Yeah, I guess."

For a long moment his brother simply gazed at him, then he nodded. "This couldn't have happened at a worse time. Anna's pregnant."

The news floored him, though Quentin and Anna hadn't made a secret of the fact they wanted another child—someday.

He hadn't realized that someday meant now. He playfully punched his brother's shoulder. "Way to go, stud. Big surprise."

"We just found out. We were waiting until she was through the first trimester to announce, just to be certain everything was okay."

Before Sam, Anna had lost a baby early in the first trimester. Unfortunately she and Quentin had shared their good news with everyone—then had to share the bad news as well. It'd been devastating for everyone involved.

"We've got several weeks to go, so I'd appreciate you keeping it under wraps."

"I'll try. But keeping a secret in the Malone family is damn near impossible. Personally, I think Mom's psychic."

"I'm going with John Jr.'s. theory that she's planted listening devices in our homes and vehicles."

"Works for me. But slightly more creepy than the psychic angle."

"How's Stacy?" Quentin asked, changing the subject.

"She's good." He frowned. "Has Mom said something?"

"Not that I know of. Why?"

"Just going with the conversation, man. You're the one who segued from psychic, snooping mothers to my relationship."

"And babies."

At what must have been his horrified expression, Quentin laughed. "What's the deal, little brother? You have commitment issues?"

"He's scared," Anna said, emerging from the house, Patti and Sam right behind her. She crossed to Spencer and handed him the list of names and addresses. "Stacy's great. If you don't get with it, you'll lose her."

"I agree," Patti said. "She's a good cop, too."

Spencer rolled his eyes. "Thanks for bringing this up, Quentin. I owe you."

He grinned. "Happy to help, Spence. After all, what are big brothers for?"

11

Saturday, April 21, 2007
1:00 p.m.

The Bon Temps Café served traditional Cajun-Creole fare, like jambalaya, crawfish etouffée and stuffed crabs. It was one of the many shiny new places that had opened post-the-Big-One, and although the food was excellent, Patti missed the slightly derelict atmosphere of the places that had been lost. What was it about ancient wiring and cracked lathe-and-plaster walls that she had found so appealing?

She took a table by the front windows so she could watch for her friend June Benson.

She and June had been friends for twenty years. They'd met in a support group for childless women who had either lost babies or were unable to conceive. Their situations had been similar—both had tragically miscarried and were then unable to conceive—and they had bonded despite the decade difference in their ages and their backgrounds.

Patti came from a hard-scrabble, working-class family of Irish immigrants. June's family could be described as New Orleans royalty. Descended from the original American planters to settle in "Nouvelle Orléans," the Benson family still owned the Garden District mansion built in 1856 by planter Jonathan Benson, still ruled Comus, the most elite and secretive of the Mardi Gras krewes, and served on the boards of the city's most high-profile philanthropic organizations.

Yet over the years the friendship had blossomed, then matured, carrying over to their extended families as well. The two families had shared in each other's celebrations of joy, times of grief—and everything in between.

After Sammy's murder, Patti had turned to June more than anyone else for comfort and support. June understood her completely. She had listened. Just listened. She hadn't tried to make it better, for nothing could have. Nor had the depths of Patti's despair frightened her.

Patti ordered an iced tea, then glanced at her watch, surprised at June's tardiness. Usually it was Patti rushing in, June already half finished with her tea.

At the blare of a horn, she looked up to see her friend dashing across St. Peter Street, forcing a cab driver to brake. June waved apologetically at the driver, reached the sidewalk, then ducked into the restaurant.

A moment later, she hurried to the table. "Sorry I'm late." She slid into the chair across the table from Patti. "Max got out and I had to chase him down. Then I couldn't find the key to my Club thingie."

Her auto anti-theft device. June only misplaced the key about once a week.

She waved to the waitress, who hurried over. She ordered herself an iced tea and the bread basket, then went on. "Max was almost to St. Charles Avenue before I got him."

A waiter brought a basket of fresh, hot French bread and whipped butter.

June tended toward extremes. She was either pin neat or totally disheveled. The picture of composure, or completely frazzled. She loved food and loathed exercise; fifty percent of the time she was on a diet, the other fifty on a binge.

Clearly today was a frazzled, flushed, binge day.

"And how did Max, the marvelous salt-and-pepper shih tzu, get out?" Patti asked as she watched the brunette slather butter on a piece of the bread.

"One guess."

"Riley," she said, referring to June's happy-go-lucky, much younger brother.

"Bingo. Left the door ajar." June laughed. "I swear, he's the least organized, most scattered—"

"Delightful, darling—"

"—mess of a young man. What was Mother thinking, having another child so late in life! Now I'm stuck with him."

Patti grinned. June adored Riley. He was born when she was

fifteen—she could have despised him. And from what she had told Patti, she had for years, secretly referring to him as "It" and "Thing."

June laughed about it now. How she had resented him. How jealous she had been of the attention her parents had lavished on him.

She had gone off to university and come home one Christmas break only to fall in love with the curly-haired, bright-eyed four-year-old.

"When is he going to grow up?" June asked, buttering another piece of bread. "He's twenty-seven."

"Maybe never. If you keep babying him."

"I do not baby him."

Their eyes met and they both laughed. "Okay, so I baby him a little."

Patti understood. She tended to exercise her maternal instincts on her nieces and nephews. For June it was more extreme. She had no one but Riley. Her parents were dead, her marriage had fallen apart early on.

"How's the gallery doing?" Patti asked, referring to Pieces, the Warehouse District art gallery June had opened in the fall and which Riley helped her run.

"It's going well, actually. Riley's recruited several really talented local artists, and we made enough last month to pay the bills *and* our salaries."

Without dipping into investments and trust funds. Neither June nor Riley had to worry about money, but June was too good a businesswoman not to.

"Can you keep a secret?" June asked, eyes twinkling. "Riley convinced Shauna to come on board."

Shauna was the baby of the Malone brood, but instead of joining the NOPD, she'd become an artist. And a damn good one at that.

"She asked him to keep it quiet until she notified her present representation, then she's going to tell the family herself."

It was so like June to share the news, anyway, then expect Patti to do what she couldn't.

"It must have taken some coaxing," Patti murmured as the waitress approached. "She was happy where she was."

The server took their order—a seafood salad for June and etouffée for Patti—then June went on, "You know Riley. Offered to take ten percent less commission for the first year. Plus, he appealed to their friendship."

Shauna and Riley were close in age, knew each other and had similar interests: art, music, dancing, good food. They had hung out together as teenagers and had remained good friends all these years. Shauna had even had a crush on the slightly older, good-looking Riley at one time.

June sighed. "I always wished they'd get together. They'd make a handsome couple."

"They still might. After all, they're both still single." Patti leaned forward. "Although I hear she's dating someone. An artist she met at an opening at the Contemporary Arts Center."

"You don't sound thrilled."

"I haven't met him."

June cocked an eyebrow. "Somebody did. And they're not thrilled."

"Colleen. Said he was moody and controlling."

"But we both know your sister can be a bit overprotective of her children."

"True." Patti changed the subject. "I have news. About Sammy."

June laid down her butter knife. "You have a suspect."

"Yes. And no." She cleared her throat. "Do you remember the killer the newspapers called the Handyman?"

"Vaguely. You never caught him."

Although June stated it as a simple fact, it stung like an admonition. "We didn't have much to go on," she said. "We do now."

For a moment, June stared at her. Then she shook her head. "But what does this have to do with Sammy? I thought the Handyman killed women?"

Patti explained about the find in City Park. "Sammy's badge was in the grave."

June gasped. "That can't... My God, Patti...this means—"

"That the Handyman killed Sammy."

The server arrived with their food. June gazed blankly at hers, then lifted her eyes to Patti. "Suddenly I'm not so hungry."

Patti reached across the table and covered her hand. "This doesn't change how he died. It doesn't make it worse or more painful."

"No?"

"No. But it does give me a lead. Finally." She smiled grimly. "I'm going to get him. And I'm going to make him pay."

June fell silent. They both picked at their food. Patti saw that her friend was upset.

"What?" she asked, pushing her own plate away.

"I'm worried about you."

"Now, there's something new."

June waved off the teasing sarcasm. "You act so tough, but I know——"

"The real me?"

"Yes."

"Tough exterior, soft, chewy center?" Patti teased.

"Yes. And it's not funny."

"I'm a police captain. Being soft is a liability."

June leaned forward. "I don't want you hurt any more than you already have been. First the heart attack, then Katrina and Sammy…"

"Thanks, but…I think closure is the only thing that'll stop the hurt."

June opened her mouth as if to argue her point, but closed it as Patti's cell phone buzzed. "Captain O'Shay."

"Aunt Patti. It's Spencer. We got a hit."

"Tell me."

"Ex-con. Did time for aggravated rape."

"Pick him up. I'm on my way."

12

Saturday, April 21, 2007
2:10 p.m.

By the time Patti arrived back at headquarters, the suspect had been picked up. Spencer met her outside the door to the interview room.

"That was quick," she said.

"Sent a couple of uniforms. He was climbing into his van when they pulled up. Name's Ben Franklin—" She cocked an eyebrow and he grinned. "I asked. No relation. Did time for aggravated rape and assault. Served seven of his ten years."

"How long's he been out?"

"Just over two years."

Timing worked with what they had so far. "And he's managed to keep his nose clean?"

"To fly under the radar," Spencer corrected. "The officer who picked him up saw some suspicious-looking items in his van. Half-dozen flat-screen TVs. Light fixtures."

He had her with the last. "Light fixtures?" she repeated.

"That's right. Chandeliers. Lots of sparkle. Officer White confronted Franklin about the items. Asked for receipts, which he couldn't produce."

"Big surprise. Have an inventory yet?"

"Working on it now." He motioned the room. "Maybe I should do this?"

"I'm not that *rusty,* Detective." She reached for the door. "You monitor."

Each interview room was outfitted with a video camera so interviews could be taped for later review or to be used as evidence in a trial. In addition, others could monitor the process from a room down the hall.

He caught her arm. "I don't think this arrangement is a good idea."

She looked at him, eyebrow cocked. "And why's that, Detective?"

"If we're going strictly by-the-book, you're too personally involved in the outcome of this interrogation."

"And you're not? Besides, who says we're going strictly by-the-book?"

He held her gaze a moment, then backed off. "Right. You're the captain."

Ignoring the disappointment in his voice, Patti stepped into the interview room. Ben Franklin was short and thick, with thinning hair and a deep tan. She figured he either frequented a tanning salon or got his color from a bottle. He probably thought it made him look young and vigorous; in her opinion, freaky landed a bit closer to accurate.

"Hello, Mr. Franklin. I'm Captain O'Shay."

He folded his arms across his wide chest and scowled at her.

"I need to ask you a few questions."

"I did nothing."

Of course not, sweetie. You're as pure as the driven snow. "You ever heard of a writer named Anna North?"

He eyed her suspiciously. "Who?"

"A local novelist. Writes mysteries."

Some emotion flickered across his features, then was gone. "Yeah. I've heard of her."

"You've read her books, haven't you?"

"What if I have?"

"Would you call yourself a fan?"

He shifted, looking uncomfortable. "Read her in the joint. Lots of time to read in the joint."

"Have you ever written the author?"

His gaze shifted slightly. "No."

"Gone to one of her book signings? Met her in person?"

"No."

"Any idea then how your name and address would have ended up on her personal fan list?"

"If you're suggesting I threatened her or anything, you're barkin' up the wrong tree."

"I'm not suggesting anything, Mr. Franklin. I'm just asking a few questions."

He shifted in his seat. "Okay, yeah. I wrote her once."

"Why?"

He squirmed, looking uncomfortable. "For advice. About becoming a writer myself." He met her eyes, the expression in his defiant. "I got a story to tell."

She took one of the magnets out of her pocket and tossed it onto the table in front of him. "Ever seen that before?"

He stared at it, frowning. "What is it?"

"A refrigerator magnet. For one of Anna North's books."

Clearly unimpressed, he shrugged and leaned back in his chair. "So?"

"You have one of those on your refrigerator? Ever?"

"Nah. I'm not much for that kind of crap."

"I hear you were doing a little shopping today."

"What's it to you?"

"Flat-screen TVs. Crystal chandeliers."

"That ain't against the law, is it?"

"Not if you can produce proof the items belong to you."

"I got canceled checks somewhere."

She eyed him, unsurprised. The "bad guys" always responded the same way—cheap attitude and lies. And perversely, she always enjoyed the show. Was taking twisted pleasure in watching suspects dig themselves into holes a character flaw? If so, nearly all cops had the same flaw.

"Where were you during Hurricane Katrina?"

Spencer slipped into the interview room. Patti glanced at him and he motioned her to the hallway.

Patti stood. "Why don't you take a moment to work on that answer."

She followed Spencer into the hall. "What's up?"

"Officer Lee finished searching Franklin's vehicle. He found this tucked under the driver's seat."

He handed her a plastic evidence bag. The bag held a gun. Standard issue Glock .45. The preferred weapon of the NOPD.

"The serial numbers have been filed off," Spencer said.

Glocks' serial numbers were found in three places: the right side of the slide, the right side of the barrel and the underside of the front of the frame. She turned the bag over and inspected the places the numbers should have been.

Should have been.

Removing a gun's serial number rendered it virtually untraceable.

Patti looked at Spencer; she saw from his expression that he was thinking the same thing as she.

Sammy had carried a Glock. It'd never been found. But they had retrieved a bullet from his body.

"I want ballistics done on—"

"I'll call the lab."

"Good. Keep me posted." She reentered the room and caught the suspect picking his nose. She sat and slid him the box of tissues. He had the decency to look embarrassed. "My colleague just informed me of something very interesting."

"Lucky you."

"Sorry I can't say the same about you." She leaned forward. "Tell me about the gun."

Under the tan he seemed to pale. "What gun?"

"The Glock. The one hidden under the driver's seat of your van. The one you filed the serial numbers off of."

"It's not mine."

That brought a smile to her face. "No? Then whose is it?"

"A friend."

"I need a name, Ben."

He pursed his lips, as if deciding whether or not to answer. She supposed he was doing a mental scan for someone to pin this on.

"What if I told you that gun had been used in a murder?"

She saw that she had gotten his attention by the way his expression altered. She could almost hear the *"Oh, shit, I'm totally fucked!"* running through his head.

"I wouldn't know anything about that," he said.

She laid her palms on the table. Her cell phone vibrated but she ignored it. "What if I told you it had been used to kill a cop?"

Now he looked ill. "I want a lawyer."

"Of course you do. You need one, Mr. Franklin. I can assure you of that."

"I found the piece."

"Where?"

"In City Park. It was half buried, folded up in a towel inside a black garbage bag. I tripped over it. I swear!"

City Park.Where Sammy's badge and the Jane Doe had been found.
"Where in the park?"

"The lagoon. The one by the art museum, along City Park Avenue."

A ways from where the badge had turned up. But considering the size of the city and where Sammy had been killed, suspiciously close.

"When was this?" she asked.

"A while ago."

"How long? Best guess."

"A year.Yeah, that's right. It was starting to get hot."

"You have the towel?"

"Please." He shifted. "Besides, it was a mess."

"A mess. What does that mean?"

"Stained."

"Blood?"

"Dunno. I tossed the towel and kept the piece. I've never fired it."

"Why'd you file the serials off?"

"I didn't!"

"Maybe because you knew the gun belonged to a cop?"

"No! I found it that way—"

"I guess you're just an all-around bad guy, aren't you, Ben? A rapist and now a cop killer."

"This is bullshit! I'm not saying another word until I have a lawyer."

Patti wanted to push more but knew better. Besides, until the ballistics report came back, she was operating on little more than wishful thinking.

"Then let's get you some representation, Mr. Franklin."

Patti pushed away from the table, stood and crossed to the door. There she stopped and looked back at him.

"You never told me, where were you during Hurricane Katrina?"

"Stuck on a fucking roof for three days. Where were you? Looting stores?"

"No, Mr. Franklin. I was rescuing assholes like you from rooftops."

13

Stacy sat slumped behind the wheel of her parked car, watching the house. Nice place. Very upscale. Garden District address.

Location. Location. Location. Wasn't that a Realtor's mantra, after all? Seemed Mr. Gabrielle followed his own advice.

She reviewed what she knew about the suspect—forty-six, married with two kids, successful businessman. Friend to the Audubon Zoo and the library.

Frequented titty bars—one in particular. Manufactured and distributed methamphetamine.

Not your typical Realtor.

Her cell phone vibrated; she saw it was Spencer.

"Yo," he said when she answered. "What's up?"

"Not much. Keeping an eye on Gabrielle's house. Figured I'd do a drive-by of some of the properties he's got for sale."

"This a solo recon?"

"With my captain's okay. How'd you know?"

"I know you, Killian. It's Saturday. You're working undercover all night. Where else would you be on your day off?"

"Are you suggesting I'm all work and no play?"

"Sorry, babe, but I call it as I see it."

"That's not what you said last night, *babe*."

"Don't be bringing that up. I'm in public."

She laughed softly. "What was Patti's big find?"

Spencer explained about the fridge magnet and visiting Quentin and Anna. "We got a big hit, right out of the gate. Ex-con. In possession of a Glock .45 with the serials removed."

"You're running ballistics?"

As no two weapons left identical impressions upon discharging, every spent bullet and casing carried a sort of "fingerprint." A technician would fire this gun into a box of thick gel, retrieve the bullet and compare its markings—or fingerprint—to the ones from the bullet taken from Sammy using an Integrated Ballistics Identification System machine.

"Could it be so easy?" Stacy asked. "After two years of not knowing?"

"Patti sure hopes so. She's overseeing it herself. Poor bastard," he added, referring to the ballistics expert. "He's going to have her hot breath on his neck until she gets an answer."

"Uh-oh," she said as the door to Gabrielle's home swung open. "There's activity."

"Meet me for a burger later? Shannon's at five?"

She agreed and hung up.

Marcus Gabrielle was a handsome man. Dark hair and eyes, nice build. Today dressed in tennis whites. The picture of health and personal success.

Stacy shifted her gaze to his wife. Blonde. Pretty. Looked to be considerably younger than Gabrielle, maybe ten years. They had two kids, a boy and girl. From the dossier, she knew them to be seven and nine. Cute. Appeared to be well behaved.

Stacy narrowed her eyes, studying the foursome. They were smiling, conversing with one another. Relaxed. Happy. The picture of the American dream.

American nightmare, more like.

They crossed to the Mercedes sedan parked in the drive. Gabrielle opened the car door for his wife; she kissed him, then slid into the vehicle. The kids piled into the back seat.

Stacy shook her head. Why would Gabrielle take the chance of messing that up?

Greed. Zero love for anyone but himself. Totally screwed value system. Same old story.

She still didn't get it.

Gabrielle watched until the Mercedes had turned right at the end of the block, then he headed to his own vehicle—a silver Porsche Boxster. He tossed his equipment bag in, then climbed behind the wheel.

A moment later, he rolled right past her without glancing her way. Stacy gave him a safe lead, then followed.

By the tennis gear, she assumed he would head to the New Orleans Country Club, where he was a member. Instead, he headed downtown and into the French Quarter.

Yvette was waiting on the corner of North Peters and Conti Street. Gabrielle drew to the curb and she hopped in.

So much for tennis at the club.

She was dressed in a simple print blouse and a pair of trousers. Sling-back pumps. A totally different girl from the one on the stage the night before.

Practicing to be a Realtor?

Now *that* was kinky.

The French Quarter was a crisscross of narrow, one-way streets. Stacy followed Gabrielle as best she could, at times forced to anticipate his next move. She managed to keep them in sight until he turned onto Rampart and a delivery truck cut her off, then stopped, blocking the narrow street.

By the time she made it onto South Rampart, Gabrielle and Yvette were long gone. She drove around the area for twenty minutes, in the hopes of spotting the Boxster, then gave up.

If they had been heading for a rendezvous, why had she been dressed so conservatively? Because it turned him on? Hardly, the guy was a strip club regular. Clearly he liked to play on the wild side.

She glanced at her watch. After four already. She had enough time to do drive-bys of a few of Gabrielle's listings and still meet Spencer at Shannon's by five. Tonight she would try to get some information out of Yvette.

14

Saturday, April 21, 2007
4:15 p.m.

Patti sat at the IBIS console while the device compared the striations on the bullet found in Sammy's body to the one they had test-fired into the box of gel.

They matched beautifully, leaving no doubt both bullets had been fired from the same weapon.

She gazed at the computer-enhanced images. She had him. At long last. Her husband's murderer. Most probably the Handyman killer as well.

Her feelings swung between elation and doubt. The elation she understood, but not the doubt. Ben Franklin did not seem a terribly menacing villain. More a low-level hood and all-around loser.

Which meant exactly nothing. Real life wasn't like Hollywood, where the bad guys screamed the part. The most vicious killer she'd ever busted had had the appearance and demeanor of a choirboy.

She sat back. She felt he had been telling the truth about his reason for contacting Anna. Sharing that had been too uncomfortable to have been a lie.

If he was Sammy's killer, if he had buried him and the woman there in City Park, would he have admitted being anywhere near there? Sure, he could simply be an extremely stupid thug. A lot of them were.

But she didn't want to spend time or energy on the wrong guy. She didn't want to celebrate prematurely.

She wanted *him*. Sammy's killer.

And she wouldn't rest until she was certain she had him.

"Good news?"

She glanced over her shoulder at Spencer and smiled grimly. "We may have him. Take a look."

He crossed and peered at the IBIS-enhanced images. A moment later, he straightened. "It's a good match."

"Yes."

"But you want more."

It wasn't a question; she answered, anyway. "What if Franklin did find the gun? The real killer buried the bodies, then disposed of the weapon."

"And got the hell out of town before Katrina struck."

"Yes."

"So, we find a connection between Franklin and the woman, and we've got him nailed. This might help." He handed her a legal-size manila envelope. "The analysis of the City Park Jane Doe. Elizabeth Walker dropped it off."

Excited, Patti opened the envelope and slid the report out. *Female. Caucasoid. Approximately twenty to twenty-five years old. Sixty-four inches tall. Hadn't given birth. An unusual number of broken bones. All old breaks. Probably the victim of childhood abuse. Badly overcrowded teeth.*

"She could have been strangled," Patti said. "Says here the hyoid bone was broken."

"Elizabeth mentioned that. Problem is, as young as the victim was, she can't say for certain."

Patti nodded. The hyoid bone was a horseshoe-shaped bone at the base of the skull that anchored the tongue in place. It started out in three pieces, not fully fusing until around age thirty-five.

Patti read on, through information she already knew from the crime scene, stopping when she found what she was seeking.

This victim belonged to the Handyman. The bones, the dismemberment point, fit perfectly.

It was official then—this young woman had been one of the Handyman's victims. Since Sammy's badge had been found in the grave with her, it could be assumed he had been one, too.

Spencer smiled. "You got to the good part."

She met his eyes. "This is our lucky day."

"Elizabeth suggested we send the skull over to Mackenzie at the FACES lab. It's in good shape, she thinks we could get a decent likeness."

Alison Mackenzie was a forensic sculptor with Louisiana State University's Forensic Anthropology and Computer Enhancement Services lab. Using standard data about tissue depths for a person's age, sex and race, along with the victim's skull, she re-created the dead's image in life. It was truly amazing how accurate some facial reconstructions turned out to be.

Of course, every Jane Doe didn't get such treatment. Forensic sculptors didn't grow on trees—and they didn't come cheap, either.

But this case was special. Not only were they dealing with a serial killer, but a cop killer as well.

"Next step, Captain?"

"We identify this victim. Then we link her to Franklin. Run a missing-persons search for anyone who fits this Jane Doe's description."

He arched his eyebrows. "A missing-persons search? From around the time of Katrina?"

It sounded like a sick joke. Eighty percent of the city had either evacuated or gone missing. At one point after the storm, the official "missing" toll had been over eleven thousand.

There were still people who couldn't be accounted for.

"Get the skull over to Mackenzie. Tell her it's a priority."

"You going to clear that with the brass?"

"This comes under ISD's jurisdiction and I'm ISD, Detective."

He didn't respond and she went on. "Fill Detective Sciame in. Tell him his weekend is ending early."

"And Franklin?"

"For now, we hold Mr. Franklin on unlawful possession of a firearm by a felon and possession of stolen goods."

15

Saturday, April 21, 2007
6:15 p.m.

The duplex occupied an overgrown lot on the deathly quiet Mid-city street. The double row of multifamily residences stood vacant, boarded over, FEMA's bright orange X a shot of startling color on each entryway—like door decorations from hell.

Before Katrina the rentals had housed low income families, hard-partying singles and those preferring to keep a low profile.

And one of those had been someone special. With special secrets. Secrets housed inside those walls.

My pretties. Mine. Gone now. Being kept by strangers. It's almost more than I can bear.

Yours to lose. Your fault. You left them behind.

Here! In our safe house. Stored as best as—

In a freezer? A monster storm on the way? You never even checked on them.

How could I? No one expected what happened. After the storm, the city was impassable, all routes in closed. Later, it wasn't safe. I could have been found out.

If you had cared enough, you would have found a way. Stop whining and start a new collection.

It's not a collection! You know nothing of inspiration. Of beauty. From the hands and heart flow eternal truth and beauty.

And from both spew ugliness and betrayal.

Stop it. Please. I can't take your bullying anymore.

Make it right, then. Do what you need to do to make it right.

16

Sunday, April 22, 2007
1:15 a.m.

Yvette worked to calm herself. She vibrated with anger. And with outrage.

Nobody gave her the run-around. Nobody stiffed her. Not even Marcus, the self-proclaimed owner of the universe.

She lit a cigarette and inhaled greedily, knowing the nicotine would calm her. She had played his blasted game, met his clients at the half dozen properties, let them in and waited for them to do their thing.

Whatever that was. Certainly not viewing commercial properties, though she didn't know squat about real estate.

But when it had come time to pay her, he had squeezed her ass and told her to be patient.

Bastard had promised her five hundred bucks. Just like the other times.

Then he came in tonight, with a group of his highfalutin cronies, and pretended she didn't exist.

Prick. He had sat back and laughed while one of the guys in his group tried to grab her tits. Big yuck.

Maybe what she needed was a little insurance policy. Before today, she had figured what she didn't know wouldn't hurt her. She had been a good girl, doing just as Marcus instructed, not particularly interested in the people she let into the properties or why they were there.

She'd wanted the money. That's what she had focused on.

No more. Next time she—

"Hey, Yvette."

She jerked around. Brandi stood in the doorway

"Got a special request. Table twelve." She held it out. "He sent a note."

Marcus. Time to send him a message.

"Tell him to go fuck himself."

Brandi made a sound of surprise. "But—"

"You heard me."

For a long moment, the other woman was silent. She still held out the note. "What if he complains to Tonya? She won't like this, Yvette."

"Know what? She can go fu—" Yvette bit the words off and yanked the piece of paper from Brandi's hand. She fumbled around the cluttered vanity top for a pen and came up with a red lip liner instead.

Smiling to herself, she scrawled *Go Fuck Yourself!* in red across the note.

"Here——" she shoved it at Brandi "——there's my answer."

"You're sure?" She nodded and the waitress backed toward the door. There she stopped. "Do you know him or something?"

"Or something." Yvette took a deep drag on the smoke. "Give him that. Now."

The waitress looked like she wanted to say more, to question her or argue, but simply left the dressing room.

Yvette waited for the fireworks to begin. Tonya ripping her a new one while she lectured about what was and wasn't acceptable. Marcus finding his way back here and slapping her around. Or another note delivered by Brandi, this one with a warning.

They didn't come. And when she went out for her last dance of the evening, she saw that Marcus had left.

Take that, chicken shit. Weasel.

The end of the night finally came and she clocked out. Tips had sucked, though she wasn't surprised. Most nights she enjoyed the game, was an active participant in it, but tonight she had simply been going through the motions.

And who was turned on by that?

She called "Good night" to her colleagues at the bar having a last drink, and let herself out the back door of the locked club.

Yvette walked home nearly every night, though she lived on the other side of the Quarter. She took the busiest route, often stopping at the Dungeon, a place open from midnight to 6:00 a.m. Sometimes one of the other girls accompanied her; once in a while she caught a lift home.

Truth was, living and working in the French Quarter eliminated the need for a car. Everything she needed was within walking distance.

She peeked out into the deserted alley. The door would automatically lock behind her, so before she shut it, she always checked the alley. With the exception of a few places, most notably Rampart Street near Armstrong Park, the Quarter was safe. At least for those who followed the basic rules of safety, like keeping to well-lit or busy streets.

This portion of the alley did not meet that criteria; however, twenty feet forward and a right turn did. The worst she'd encountered was the street person who occasionally made himself a home in a cardboard box near the Dumpster.

Antisocial and focused on their own survival, most of the homeless kept to themselves. This one broke the mold. One night he had trailed her home, hissing at her and making lewd comments. Finally she had thrown an empty beer bottle at him and he had taken off.

That was the thing about the Quarter. There wasn't a kind of freak that wasn't represented: men who dressed as women, women who dressed as men, horny bums, Goths, vamps, retards and all manner of delusional schizoids, most of them harmless.

She stepped into the alley. The door snapped shut behind her, the light dying with it.

"Hello, Yvette. I was waiting for you."

Marcus. She stopped and turned, searching the darkness. He stepped out of the shadows near the alley opening, blocking her exit.

"Have a good night?"

She hid her fear and tilted up her chin. "What do you care?"

He crossed to her. She saw that his eyes gleamed with a dangerous light. He stroked her cheek. "Don't ever do that to me again. You won't like what happens."

She knocked his hand away, furious. "Go back to your frigid country-club wife. Let her get you off!"

He leaned closer, voice low and deliberate. "Don't push me, Yvette. I own you."

Fear warred with fury. And pride. *Nobody owned her. Her life, her terms.*

She stiffened. "I want my money, Marcus. I want my five hundred bucks!"

He slid his left hand into her hair. The other went to her throat. "Is that what it's all about for you? The money?" He curled his fingers into her hair and yanked her head back. "Is it, sweetheart?"

Her eyes watered. It felt as if he was going to tear her hair out by the roots. If she struggled, he would. She didn't doubt that for a second.

"You promised," she whispered.

"You'll get it when I say. And until then, you'll do whatever I say. Got that?"

She said she did and he released her. She stumbled backward, hand going to her stinging scalp.

Bastard! She couldn't let him get away with it. She wouldn't.

"Maybe I should pay a little visit to the cops?" she shouted after him. "For that matter, your wife, too. I'm sure she'd be really interested in our little arrange—"

He was on her so quickly, she didn't have time to protect herself. The force of his body propelled her backward, against the damp brick wall. His hands went to her throat.

"Try it, bitch, and I'll cut out your heart."

He deepened the pressure. Yvette brought her hands to his, struggling to breathe. Dots of light danced before her eyes. Panicked, she wondered if he was going to kill her.

The door to the club opened; light spilled into the darkness. "Yvette? Are you there?"

Brandi! Thank God!

Unable to call out, she struggled against Marcus's grip. He released her and stepped back. "See you later, sweetheart," he said, then turned and walked away.

Yvette sank to her knees, sputtering and gasping for air.

A moment later Brandi was kneeling beside her, arm around her shoulders. "My God, are you okay?"

Yvette struggled to speak. She realized she was trembling. Her teeth began to chatter.

Brandi rubbed her back. "Was that the guy from tonight? The one you wouldn't dance for?"

Yvette nodded. "I thought he...was going...to kill me."

"I'm calling the cops."

Brandi started to stand; Yvette caught her arm, stopping her. "Don't," she croaked. "It'll only make things...worse."

"How can it be worse? He tried to kill you!"

"Just help me up. I'm okay."

Brandi hesitated a moment, then did as she asked. Unsteady on her feet, she took a deep, calming breath, acknowledging she was happy to be alive.

She sent a small smile to Brandi. "Thanks. If you hadn't…"

She let the thought trail off. Brandi jumped in quickly. "How about I give you a ride home?"

"I don't live that far. I can—"

"Walk? Get real. What if that creep is waiting for you?"

She had a point. And the truth was, at this moment she felt neither steady nor brave.

She and Brandi walked to the lot where Brandi had parked her car, a battered SUV. They climbed in and Yvette sagged back against the seat, exhausted.

"Where to?"

She gave directions, then closed her eyes. What had she been thinking? Challenging Marcus that way? Threatening him with the cops? Threatening to go to his wife?

"Right turn?"

She cracked open her eyes. "Yeah, right."

Several directions later, Brandi pulled the vehicle to a stop. "Here we are," she said.

Yvette grabbed the door handle, then hesitated, suddenly not wanting to be alone. "Thanks for the ride," she said.

"Anytime. If you change your mind about the cops—"

"I won't." Yvette opened the vehicle door, climbed halfway out, then glanced back. "I really appreciate…you know."

"No problem." Brandi smiled. "I'll watch to make sure you get in."

Yvette hesitated again, thinking of her dark, empty apartment. "You sure you're okay?"

She forced a breezy smile. "Yeah, I'm fine. See you around."

She slipped out of the vehicle and darted for the door.

17

Sunday, April 22, 2007
3:10 a.m.

Stacy watched Yvette dart toward the courtyard door. When she reached it, she stopped. But instead of stepping inside, she turned and jogged back to the SUV.

Stacy lowered the window. "What's up?"

"Are you hungry?"

"Are you kidding? I'm starving."

"Want to come in? I have to eat, too. We might as well do it together."

Yvette worked hard to be tough, to act like it all rolled off her, but Stacy saw she was shaken.

"Sounds like fun," she said. "Where can I park?"

Yvette indicated a "residents only" spot and watched as Stacy eased into it, then climbed out. Together they crossed to the building, a crumbling stucco-and-brick three-story, whose ironwork balconies reflected its Spanish influence. Yvette unlocked the door and they stepped inside.

Like most of the old buildings in the French Quarter, this one was built around a shady, central courtyard. In the days before air-conditioning, the courtyards served as cool city oases. They still did, only now as a place to escape the paved world beyond.

Each apartment opened out to the courtyard, the units accessed from shared staircases and covered walkways.

Yvette lived on the second floor. They made their way up the stairs and down the covered walkway. Stacy noted how quietly Yvette moved, as if doing her best not to disturb her sleeping neighbors. As they passed one of the units a dog began to bark.

A big one, judging by the size of its bark. Yvette winced; Stacy guessed this wasn't the first time she had awakened the beast. And most probably, the neighbors as well.

They reached Yvette's apartment—number twelve—and she let them in. Simultaneously she flipped on the lights and kicked off her shoes.

French Quarter living did not come cheap, even for a small place like this one. Stacy had learned that right away. Throw in the great courtyard and she'd bet Yvette paid twelve to fifteen hundred bucks a month.

Stacy moved her gaze over the room's interior. Charming and traditional. Lots of soft colors and fabrics, accented with feminine touches and the occasional startlingly modern painting or print.

"You've got a great place," she said, and crossed to study a large, crudely painted representation of a fairy. "This is wonderful. A little scary, but wonderful."

"I think so, too." Yvette came up beside her. "It's a local artist named Wren. I own another by him. It's in the bedroom. Come on, kitchen's this way."

Between the two rooms, Stacy noticed several more paintings. They didn't seem to be linked stylistically, so she asked Yvette what had drawn her to them.

"Don't know. They're all by local artists. Some I buy right out of studios here in the Quarter, some from galleries. A few from hawkers on Jackson Square."

She crossed to the refrigerator and opened it. "What do you want to eat?"

"What do you have?"

"Leftover pizza. Eggs. Milk." She slid open the crisper and made a face. "Something fuzzy."

She closed the fridge and crossed to a long, narrow cabinet. She peered inside. "Chocolate chip cookies—Famous Amos. Cereal. Popcorn."

She looked over her shoulder at Stacy. "I'm thinking popcorn and cocoa."

"Sounds like a plan."

Minutes later they were curled up on the couch, a giant bowl of popcorn between them and hands curled around the mugs of warm cocoa.

Stacy took a sip, then coughed. "Some strong cocoa."

"Added a little zip. Peppermint schnapps. The alcohol kills the effect of the caffeine. Do you like it?"

Stacy said she did and sipped again, glancing at the other woman. She saw several deep purple marks spotting her neck. "You're bruising."

"I am?" Yvette brought a hand to her throat. "How bad?"

Stacy fumbled in her purse and pulled out a compact with a mirror. She handed it to Yvette. "Take a look."

She did, silently. A moment later, she snapped the compact shut and handed it back.

"He's your boyfriend, isn't he?"

Instead of answering, she said, "He's not that bad."

"After what he did, I can't believe you're saying that. He's a pig."

"I egged him on. He's been good to me—"

"I *see* that."

"He's never done anything like that before."

"And if you're a good girl he won't again?" She shook her head. "A guy like that—"

"What do *you* know about Marcus?"

"He's married, for one. He was wearing a ring."

"Don't be stupid. Most of the guys I meet are. At least he doesn't pretend by taking it off."

"He put his hands on you. If I hadn't come looking for—"

"Why *did* you come looking for me?"

Because the surveillance team saw Gabrielle enter the alley and warned her.

"One of your tips," she said instead. "You know those funny radio guys who were in, slamming back Jell-O shots—"

"Walton and Johnson?"

"Yeah. They left you a tip, but I forgot to give it to you and…I thought I'd catch you leaving."

"An angel of mercy *and* honest." She reached for a handful of popcorn. "What the hell are you doing working at the Hustle?"

"I could ask you the same thing."

"The money."

"Ditto."

Yvette frowned, as if she didn't totally buy it, and Stacy leaned forward. "I was married for twelve years. Got hitched right out of high school. I didn't go to college, never worked. Barney wanted me home. Then the bastard up and leaves me with a bunch of debt and a kid to support."

"You have a kid?"

Shit. Now she had a kid. "A girl. She's eight."

"What's her name?"

"Sandi." *Brandi and Sandi.* Jeez.

But Yvette thought it was cute. "Do you have a picture?"

"Not with me. I don't like to bring personal stuff to work."

That, at least, wasn't a lie.

Stacy rummaged in her purse for the "tip" and pulled out a twenty dollar bill. "Here. Sorry about that."

Yvette stared at the bill. "Twenty bucks is all? From those rich guys? Keep it, you earned it."

Stacy frowned. "I helped you because you're my friend,

Yvette. And because it was the right thing to do. *Not* because I expected to be paid."

The younger woman gazed at her a moment, as though trying to decide if she was for real. Then she smiled. "Keep it, anyway. You've got a kid to take care of."

"Wow. Thanks." She stuffed the bill into her pocket. "Sorry if I was critical of Marcus. I guess I just don't get it."

She let the comment hang between them for several moments, offering Yvette a chance to explain. When she didn't, Stacy went on. "How long have you been seeing him?"

"Let's not talk about Marcus. Okay?"

"Sure. Sorry."

They fell silent a moment, then Stacy snapped her fingers. "I almost forgot! I saw you today. In the Quarter. I started across the street to say hello, but you got into a car before I could."

"Wasn't me."

"You sure? I was almost posi—"

"I said it wasn't me."

Stacy backed off. "Sure. Okay." She laughed. "I should've known. This chick was dressed like somebody's mama. Real frumpy."

"Not my style."

"Exactly."

Yvette finished her cocoa. "Ready for another? Or just a shot of schnapps?"

She shook her head. "I've got to drive, remember?"

"You could sleep over?" She took in Stacy's expression and

laughed. "I'm not gay. It just gets a little lonely around here. In the morning, we could go to the Coffeepot for brunch. They make the best Lost Bread in the city."

Lost Bread, Stacy had learned after moving down here, was New Orleans' version of French toast—made with day-old French bread. "I can't. I wish I could, but—"

"Because of Sandi," she said, disappointment clear in her voice.

"My mother's watching her, but I need to be there when she wakes up."

"Sure. Of course."

"I know! How about we meet for brunch tomorrow? Sandi's spending the day with her dad."

Yvette agreed, and a short time later, Stacy climbed into her Explorer. No sooner had she slammed the door behind her than her cell phone buzzed. It was Dan, one of the surveillance team.

"I appreciate you wrapping that up," he said. "I've been in this friggin' van so long, my ass's asleep. And the guys send their thanks for recruiting us for Sunday duty. We were hoping to spend the day in here, on top of each other."

"World's smallest violin. I tell you what, seeing it's so late, I'll de-wire myself. I promise to be really careful with your little toys."

"Your generosity overwhelms."

She laughed. "See you tomorrow, at one."

"One last thing, Killian. Your ex's name is *Barney?* Real smooth."

"At one," she repeated, and hung up to the sound of laughter.

18

Sunday, April 22, 2007
1:05 p.m.

When Stacy arrived, Yvette was already at a table in the light-dappled courtyard, sipping coffee and reading the *Times-Picayune*.

"Hey," Stacy said as she reached the table. "Sorry I'm late."

"You're not. I came early."

Stacy sat. "I don't know about you, but I'm fried this morning."

Yvette folded the section of the paper she'd been reading and laid it on top of the rest, which was at her feet. "I'm used to it."

"Just wait until you're thirty. How's your neck?"

"Sore. It hurts to swallow." She had draped a floral-print silk scarf around her neck to hide the bruises. "I got one of the girls to switch tonight for tomorrow night. I just don't feel up to dancing, you know?"

Stacy murmured that she did, and they fell silent.

The guys in the van would be happy to hear they had a twenty-four-hour reprieve. Yahoo. She, on the other hand, would prefer to keep the investigation moving forward.

The waitress took their orders—they both decided on the Lost Bread—filled their coffee cups, then left them alone.

"Have you...thought any more about what happened last night?"

"Should I have?"

Stacy shrugged and added cream to her coffee. "Thought you might like to talk. Sometimes it makes it better."

"I pushed his buttons. He snapped. I won't do it again."

She sipped the coffee, working to maintain a "girlfriends" kind of tone, chatty and intimate. "What do you know about his other life?"

Yvette narrowed her eyes. "Other life?"

"Away from the Hustle. You know."

"Actually, I snooped a bit." She leaned across the table, expression mischievous. "Borrowed a car and followed him."

Stacy's heart beat a little faster. She hoped the transmitter was working. "Really? What did you find out?"

"His wife is one of those uptight country-club types. The kind who think they're too good for the rest of the world. Especially types like me."

Stacy heard a note of little girl hurt in Yvette's voice, one she would vehemently deny. Obviously Yvette had been on the receiving end of that kind of thinking more than once.

"If she was so great, why would he need you?"

"Exactly!" Yvette beamed at her. "That's part of what set Marcus off last night. I threatened to tell her about us and to go to the——"

She bit the last back, though Stacy had a good idea she had been about to say "police."

She tried a gentle nudge. "Go to who?"

"The press if I had to."

"Maybe his wife holds the purse strings and that's why he stays with her."

Yvette shook her head. "I don't think so. He reps commercial property. Does real well. Besides, I don't really care if he stays with her or not. I just want to be paid what I'm owed."

Before Stacy could counter with another question, Yvette pointed to the paper. "I was reading about that body they found in City Park. They think that guy got her. The one who chops off his victims' hands."

"I heard about that. So creepy."

"I've got a theory on that."

"Yeah?"

"Know how they've never found any of his other victims? And how there's been no high-profile thing about girls going missing?" Yvette leaned forward. "They're working girls."

"You mean prostitutes."

"And girls like me."

"Could be he traveled around and that's why no other victims have turned up or been reported missing."

"Uh-uh." The waitress arrived with their French toast. Yvette dug in immediately, eating as if starved. Stacy followed more slowly, preparing how to steer the conversation back to Gabrielle.

"I've thought a lot about this," Yvette continued. "Nobody cares much about working girls. A lot of 'em either don't have families or their families don't know where they are."

It certainly wouldn't be the first time a serial killer had targeted prostitutes. But she couldn't tell her that.

Instead she nodded. "True."

"Can I tell you a secret?"

"Sure."

"I might know who that girl is. Or was." She lowered her voice even more. "My old roommate."

When she'd arranged this brunch, Stacy hadn't expected to get information about the Handyman. She imagined the expressions of the guys in the van. "How do you figure?"

"They think this girl was killed right before Katrina struck. That's when Kitten disappeared."

"So did about a million other New Orleanians." That number wasn't an exaggeration, and it represented eighty percent of the metro area's 1.3 million residents.

"But she never came back. Left all her stuff."

"I don't know, Yvette. Lots of folks did that."

Yvette looked irritated. "I've got a strong feeling about this, Brandi. I mean, we were both going to wait out the storm. We stocked up on water and junk food, then she disappears."

Yvette glanced over her shoulder, then back at Stacy. "I think he calls himself 'the Artist.'"

Now she had her. Stacy leaned forward. "Why?"

"She had this weird stalker. Sent her notes all the time. Called himself 'the Artist.' Real creepy dude."

"Did he threaten her?"

"She felt threatened. That's pretty much the same thing."

Not to the police. An overt threat always beat out an implied one. "Go to the cops. Tell them what you know and let them handle it."

"Right," she said sarcastically, "go to the cops. My good friends in blue."

"They're not all bad."

Yvette eyed her suspiciously. "They are if you're me. The cops and I have a history. None of it good."

She had a record. Solicitation. Resisting arrest. Possession.

And all that *after* her eighteenth birthday. Her run-ins with the law had started well before that.

"What are you going to do?"

She shrugged. "Nothing, I guess."

"But she was your friend. If he killed her…wouldn't you want him caught?" Stacy leaned forward. "Besides, if he's not caught, he might kill someone else."

"You tell 'em, then. I'll deny it all."

Arguing the point would do nothing but lose her Yvette's trust. So, she approached from another angle. "You still have her stuff?"

"Boxed up in the apartment. It's a real pain in the ass, too. She's not paying any rent and it's taking up half the second bedroom."

"Maybe you could go through it. See if there's an address or phone number, someone you could contact. At least then you'd know if she was okay."

"Yeah, maybe." She scraped the last piece of her toast through the well of syrup on her plate, then stuck the dripping bite in her mouth.

As if on cue, the waitress brought the check. Yvette grabbed it. "I've got it."

"You don't have—"

"You came to my rescue big-time last night. How 'bout we call us square now?"

Stacy agreed, and minutes later they exited the restaurant. The day was bright and warm, the humidity blessedly low. They stopped at the corner of St. Peter and Royal Street.

"My car's this way," Stacy said, pointing in the direction of Canal Street.

"I'm heading the other. Thanks for meeting me, it was fun."

"It was." Stacy smiled, started across the street, then stopped and looked back. "What was her name? Your roommate?"

"Kitten Sweet."

Kitten Sweet? Good God.

"You know, she probably ran off with some guy who offered her a ride out of town and didn't even think twice about leaving me behind and alone. Bitch is probably living someplace like Cleveland right now. I don't even know why I worried." With that, Yvette turned and headed down the street.

But Yvette *had* worried, Stacy could tell. For all her toughness, Stacy could see that the roommate's desertion had hurt.

Yvette Borger had been let down many times, and no matter what she told herself, it still hurt.

Kitten Sweet. Could she be dead? Could she be the woman found in City Park?

It seemed a bit of a long shot. Except for the stalker.

Her cell phone jangled. As expected, it was the surveillance team. "Hello, boys," she said. "You got all that?"

"Not a lot on our guy, but the *lagniappe* could be good."

Lagniappe was local vernacular for "A little something extra." It certainly worked in this case.

"Get me a transcript. I'll take it over to Captain O'Shay myself." She ended that call and dialed Spencer.

"Where are you?" she asked when he answered.

"Headquarters. Nothing like Sunday afternoon in the trenches."

"How about Aunt Patti?"

"She's on her way in."

"Stay put. I might have something on your City Park Jane Doe. I need to be de-wired first, then I'm on my way."

19

Patti couldn't stay still. First Franklin, now a possible ID of their Jane Doe. It was almost too good to be true. If the ID came through and they found a link between the woman and Franklin, she would have Sammy's killer. No doubts.

"How long's it been?" she asked Spencer.

"Twenty minutes."

"What's taking—"

"So long?" Stacy finished for her, hurrying into the office. "Have you tried navigating French Quarter traffic lately?"

"What do you have?" Patti asked.

She moved her gaze between her and Spencer. "Kitten Sweet. Working girl."

"Where'd you get the tip?"

"My undercover assignment. Said her roommate disappeared right before Katrina hit."

Stacy held up a hand, as if anticipating their reactions. "I know, it's a stretch. But Borger seemed adamant. And here's the kicker. She says Kitten was being stalked by some dude who called himself 'the Artist.' He sent her notes. She felt threatened."

"You were wired?"

"Of course. Dan's getting us a transcript." She moved her gaze between the two once more. "I suggested she go to the police. She refused. Not a lot of love lost there."

Spencer looked at Patti. "Can't call her in for questioning, it'll blow Stacy's cover."

Patti nodded. "We could pull her in for questioning on another matter. Bring her in on some bogus charge."

"Go fishing. Plant the idea of a trade. Something she might give up to get off the hook."

"And if she lawyers up, we're not only out of luck, we're in deep shit. Public Integrity Division sits around waiting for stuff like this to fall into their laps. Justifies their existence."

"She still has the roommate's stuff," Stacy offered. "I could nose around. It won't be quick, but since she's discussed Kitten's disappearance with me already, I can follow up."

Spencer grinned. "Pretend to be an amateur detective. Now, there's a stretch."

They'd met when Stacy had inserted herself, then a student

at the University of New Orleans, into one of Spencer's homicide investigations.

"Bite me, Malone." She turned back to Patti. "There might be something in Sweet's things that'll help ID her. Even if only her real name."

"What?" Spencer said, his tone dry. "You don't think Kitten Sweet's her real name?"

Patti ignored their bantering, thoughts racing. There was no way she could sit and wait for Stacy to find the opportunity to poke around. She intended to find out if Kitten Sweet was the break they'd been waiting for. If she had to do it without the sanction of the NOPD, so be it.

"Run it through the computer," Patti said. "See what you get. We'll go from there."

20

Monday, April 23, 2007
11:45 p.m.

The computer offered little. Kitten Sweet had been arrested several times, charged with solicitation, resisting arrest, and drunk and disorderly conduct. The woman's real name was Diana Burke, her last address listed Yvette Borger's Governor Nicholls Street apartment.

Although her records hadn't provided much information, they had confirmed Sweet *could* be their Jane Doe. She fit the physical profile: white, five foot four, twenty-one years old.

That was enough to convince Patti to move forward—with a plan that didn't include waiting for Stacy to finesse out answers. She wanted answers now.

The sooner they could link Franklin to the victim, the sooner they could tie this up. The tighter the knot, the stronger the case.

She wanted Franklin to fry. And she was willing to do whatever was necessary to make that happen.

Straight-arrow O'Shay could be bent.

She hadn't shared her thoughts with Spencer or Stacy. She didn't want them involved. She was the superior officer. She was acting alone. If the Public Integrity Division caught wind of this, she would go down.

But only her. That's the way she intended to keep it.

Patti parked her vehicle on Barracks Street, just down the block from Yvette Borger's apartment building. Yvette was working. She intended to slip in, do a bit of recon and slip back out. With any luck, she would find something the lab could use to tie Sweet to their Jane Doe.

She exited her vehicle and started toward the building. The door would be locked. Hopefully it wouldn't give her too much trouble.

In upholding the law, cops learned a lot about breaking it. Truth was, cops knew how to break the law better than most criminals. Because they had seen it all, what worked and what didn't. Of course, cops used that inside knowledge to catch the lawbreakers.

Except in certain, highly specialized situations.

Like this one.

She retrieved a small tool kit from her pocket, inserted a pippin file into the lock and manipulated it until a distinct click signaled success. She slipped the file back into the kit, the kit into her pocket.

Yvette lived in unit twelve. Patti scanned the building's setup—a central staircase on both sides of the courtyard, even numbers on her right, odds on her left. The door she had entered through appeared to be the only exit, as well.

She took the stairs to the second floor. She moved quickly and silently. Unfortunately not silently enough for the dog in number eight. He began to bark furiously.

A moment later, light spilled out of the unit immediately in front of her. A woman poked her head out. "Hey," she said.

"Hey," Patti responded.

The woman's gaze shifted, looking past her. Obviously wondering who she was here to see. And how she had gotten in.

"I'm visiting Yvette," she said. "Sorry I woke you."

"It's that stupid Samson. He barks at everything." She paused, frowning. "You're a friend of Yvette's?"

By her expression Patti could tell the woman didn't think she *looked* like a friend of Yvette's.

"I like to think of myself as her friend." Patti smiled. "Actually, I'm her mother. I'm here for the week."

She held her breath. Claiming to be such a high-profile relation was risky.

"Fun," the neighbor said. "She didn't tell me."

"It was a last-minute decision."

"I see the resemblance. I'm Nancy."

"Hi, Nancy. I'll take that as a big compliment. I forgot where she said she hid the key. Do you know?"

"In the planter. The one with the cherubs."

"Thanks!" She headed that way and looked back. Nancy still stood at her door, watching her. Patti found the key, waved goodbye and let herself into the apartment.

Inside, she paused to let out a pent-up breath. *Too close for comfort. Way too close.*

She flipped on the light—just in case the neighbor was still watching—then went in search of the boxes of Kitten Sweet's things.

Patti found them easily, just where Stacy said they would be, packed and stacked in the back bedroom. She began with the top box, methodically and carefully picking through it, then moved on to the second. The first two boxes held nothing but clothes and shoes. Patti had never seen so many halter tops and miniskirts in one place.

The third storage box contained letters, paperwork and photographs. Patti flipped through the photos. She recognized Sweet from her mug shot. Ditto for Borger. No one else jumped out.

She moved on to the paperwork. Letters from her family. Bills. Credit offers. Nothing that fit Stacy's description of the notes from the Artist.

Then she hit pay dirt. A manila envelope filled with Sweet's medical information, going back several years. Patti sifted through. Results of a pap smear from the woman's gynecologist. A local guy. A plastic surgeon's "paid-in-full" receipt for breast augmentation. A bill from a local dentist.

Bingo. If he had X-rays of Sweet's teeth, they could compare them to Jane Doe's.

She slipped the bill into her pocket, resealed the box and stood. She made certain the boxes looked just as she had found them, then turned off the lights and hurried out the front door.

As she turned to relock, Samson began barking. But not at her, she saw as she glanced that way.

Borger. Damn.

The woman saw her. "Hi," Patti called, waving.

She turned her attention to the door, pretending to be struggling with the lock, but actually relocking it.

"Can I help you?" Yvette asked. The young woman looked ill. Since she hadn't been due home for a couple of hours, Patti figured she had clocked out sick.

"I'm Nancy's mom," she said, praying Nancy didn't hear the commotion and take a peak out her door. "I'm here for the week. The key she gave me isn't working."

"I'm Yvette. That's my apartment. Nancy lives next door."

Patti pretended to be horrified. "Oh, my God…I'm so sorry. Please forgive me."

"No problem. If you don't mind…I'm not feeling so well."

"Sure." She backed away from the door. "I'm really sorry."

"Don't worry about it." Yvette unlocked her door. "Really, I…excuse me."

She ducked inside. Patti waited a moment, then turned and headed for the stairs. This time as she passed number eight, the dog didn't bark, a fact she gave thanks for. Maybe the beast could tell the difference between "coming" and "going."

She reached the stairs and descended, thoughts turning to what she had done. What she had taken wasn't evidence. Yvette

Borger wasn't a suspect in the investigation. The only thing she had jeopardized was her job.

She would deal with PID and the chief if Kitten Sweet IDed as their Jane Doe.

Truth was, her job didn't mean that much to her. Not anymore.

She cleared the courtyard and exited the building. There she stopped dead.

Spencer stood beside his Camaro, parked at the curb, leaning against the passenger side door. He grinned at her. "You're getting predictable, Patti O'Shay."

She couldn't help herself and smiled. "What tipped you?"

"Your 'We'll go from there.' Captain Patti O'Shay always knows how she wants to proceed. She always has a plan."

"I'll take that as a compliment. Does Stacy know?"

"Not unless she guessed. I suggest we keep it that way. How'd it go?"

"Except for a close call with Borger, great."

"Where's your car?" he asked.

"Up the block. In a tow zone."

"I'll drive you."

She agreed and they climbed in. He had pulled away from the curb before she glanced his way. "Hit the mother lode. Got the name and number of Sweet's dentist."

"Praying for X-rays?"

"And that his office was on high ground and the records survived the hurricane."

He pulled up alongside her vehicle. "Who's the coroner's forensic odontologist? Baker?"

"Last I checked." She opened the car door, stepped out and glanced back. "I want you out of this. I'll take it from here." He opened his mouth as if to argue; she held up a hand, cutting him off. "If anyone's getting burned, it's me."

He gazed at her a long moment, then nodded. "By the way, I have orders to make certain you're at Shannon's Tavern tomorrow night at seven. Sharp."

"John Jr.?"

"Who else? Planning a family thing for the opening of Shauna's one-person exhibit."

She nodded, but he stopped her before she could close the door. "Yo, Aunt Patti? Should I be worried about you?"

"In what way?"

"You're acting out of character. Scary out of character."

"If you're asking if I'm cracking up, I'm not. My priorities have changed, Spencer. They've changed big-time."

21

Tuesday, April 24, 2007
6:50 p.m.

Patti reached Shannon's just before seven. It'd been a good day. She had contacted Kitten Sweet's dentist; Dr. Thomas Mancuso did, indeed, have her dental X-rays. Within an hour of contacting him, she had a subpoena *duces tecum,* since privacy laws prevented him from just handing them over. By mid-afternoon, he had personally delivered them to her; she, in turn, had handed them to the coroner.

Word that a suspect in Sammy's murder had been apprehended had jackrabbited through the department. The stream of well-wishers had been almost constant and there had been a celebratory air to the day.

The toll of Katrina on the NOPD had been huge. The men and women of the force clearly considered the apprehension of Sammy's killer a personal victory. A step forward toward the future and away from the devastation wrought by the storm.

Patti parked her Camry and climbed out. Judging by the number of vehicles in the lot, the popular tavern looked particularly busy for a Tuesday night. She saw Spencer's Camaro and Quentin and Anna's minivan.

She wasn't the first to arrive.

Patti crossed to the tavern's front entrance and stepped inside. A round of applause stopped her in her tracks. She stood in the doorway, caught totally by surprise. A moment later, she was surrounded by well-wishers.

"Congratulations!"

"Way to go, Captain!"

"We got him, Patti. Justice served!"

A beer was shoved into her hand, the first of many. June and Riley Benson were there. June hugged her, tears in her eyes. Riley kissed her cheek and congratulated her. Spencer strolled over, a shit-eating grin spread across his face. Stacy was with him, John Jr. and Quentin trailing behind.

Spencer laughed. "Gotcha, Aunt Patti."

"I ought to decommission you."

"The chief's here, take it up with him."

As the time passed, the celebration grew louder. The entire Malone clan had turned out, all with their various mates. Patti finally had the occasion to meet Shauna's boyfriend, whom the family had described as tall, dark and sullen.

An apt description, Patti decided. He'd obviously bought into the whole "tortured artist" thing. But she could see why Shauna was attracted to him——he was incredibly handsome.

It was nearly eight o'clock before she finally had a chance to corner Spencer alone. She filled him in on the events of the day. "I think we have him," she said. "I had my doubts, you know that, but it's starting to feel right."

He hugged her. "You bet your ass it feels right. This SOB is going down. With everything we've got, linking him to the victim will be icing on the cake."

The crowd, most of whom were now two and a half sheets to the wind, began chanting "Song, song!" urging Riley to sing.

In his younger days, Riley had kept them all entertained by writing and singing silly songs about their lives that were a cross between satire, poetry and stand-up comedy.

He strummed his guitar.

"Bad guys beware, Patti O'Shay is there.
She won't sleep, she won't rest,
She'll arrest your butt when you least expect."

The crowd began to howl and he segued into a rendition of "For She's a Jolly Good Fellow."

That song led to several more. Patti made her way to the bar——this time for a cup of Shannon's strong coffee——aware of the assembled revelers' reaction to Riley. Tall, with a mop of curly hair and a boyish smile, Riley had charisma. Women flocked to him. Yet, he wasn't so good-looking that guys resented him. Patti continued to be surprised he was unattached.

Shauna joined her as Riley exited the small stage. Her niece had inherited the Malone family's dark hair and light eyes, though, like her mother, she was petite.

"What a waste of talent," Shauna said. "He could have been big."

Patti smiled at her niece. "Said he didn't have the drive."

"That makes sense. I mean, why should he?"

"What's that supposed to mean?"

She shrugged. "What does he need drive for? He's got the big-time silver spoon, instead."

"Do I hear a trace of bitterness?"

"Not at all. 'No drive' is just a nice way of saying he's too lazy, or too spoiled, to go for it."

Her words surprised Patti. Shauna and Riley had been really good friends.

"I still adore him," Shauna went on, as if reading her mind. "I'm thrilled to have signed with him. It's just… The waste of talent breaks my heart. And it's partly June's fault."

"June's fault? Riley is the one who refuses to grow up. She'd love for him to start standing on his own two—"

"Feet? Get real, Aunt Patti. She can't bear the thought of letting him go. Every time he's taken a real step toward making it on his own, she reels him back in. Her latest was buying the gallery."

"Obviously you've only heard his side of the story," Patti said, defending her friend. "I've been listening to June's side since their parents died eleven years ago. If he's spoiled, it's his parents who did it."

Shauna's boyfriend interrupted them. He looped an arm around her shoulders. "Ready to go, babe?"

"Rich, have you met my aunt?"

His gaze slid to her along with an easy smile that didn't feel quite genuine. "Yeah, earlier. Congrats again."

"Thank you."

He returned his attention to Shauna. "What do you say? Ready?"

"Not quite."

"That's cool. Do you mind catching a ride? I've got an early day tomorrow."

Shauna flushed, though with embarrassment or anger, Patti wasn't certain. "No problem, you go."

They watched him walk away, then Shauna turned to her. "Don't start. I've heard it all before."

"Maybe you should pay attention?"

"With all due respect, I'll tell you what I've told the rest of the family. Butt out."

Spencer and Quentin angled in. "Better than eat shit and die," Spencer said. "Though, man, is that guy a jerk."

Before the youngest Malone could respond, Shannon called, "Patti, my darlin', telephone!"

She made her way around the bar and took the receiver. "Patti O'Shay."

"Captain Patti O'Shay?"

She frowned. "Yes."

"Sammy O'Shay's widow?"

"Yes," she said, a prickly sensation at the back of her neck.

"FYI, you've got the wrong guy."

"Excuse me?"

"Franklin. He's not your guy."

The line went dead. She stood, holding the receiver to her ear, heart thundering, feeling as if a glass of cold water had just been tossed in her face.

She must have looked it, too, because Spencer and Quentin had come around the bar. "What's wrong?" Spencer asked.

She quickly told them, then turned back to Shannon. "Do you have Caller ID?"When he said he didn't, she tried another avenue. "Dial star 69."

He did, and she motioned to Spencer. "Run a check on this number—504-555-0314."

"Calling it in,"he said, and crossed to the entryway for quiet. Several moments later, he returned. "Pay phone. Canal Street, downtown."

"Send a cruiser."

"Already done."

"It could have been anybody," Quentin said. "Someone with an ax to grind against you."

"Or a crank," Spencer offered. "That we've arrested someone has been all over the news. This is somebody's idea of a sick joke."

"Not just anybody," she said. "Yes, the arrest was in the news. But the suspect's name wasn't mentioned."

"It was a friend of Franklin's. Trying to plant the seed of doubt."

"How did he know where to find me tonight?"

They fell silent at that, and she moved her gaze between them. She saw the moment their only remaining option became clear to them.

"Another cop," Quentin said. "It's got to be. Who've you pissed off, Aunt Patti?"

22

Wednesday, April 25, 2007
1:30 a.m.

Spencer eased to a stop in front of the Garden District mansion. Tony had already arrived, as had the coroner's representative. The first officers had cordoned off the scene.

A smattering of residents stood on their porches gawking, probably shaking in their Cole Haans and Manolo Blahniks, Spencer thought, as they acknowledged the horrible truth: money might be able to buy you a flood-free home in a ritzy neighborhood, but longevity was another story. When fate called, there wasn't a damn thing you could do about it.

Tonight that call had come in the form of a bullet.

Spencer signed in, then ducked under the police line. Tony

caught sight of him and ambled over. "Took you long enough, Slick."

"Kiss mine, Pasta Man." He motioned toward the victim. "What's his story?"

"One bullet to the back of his head as he was climbing out of his car."

"Poor bastard."

"Not any poor bastard," Tony said. "Marcus Gabrielle."

It took a moment for the name to register. When it did Spencer whistled. "Stacy's undercover suspect. She's going to be really pissed."

"So's her boss. Goodbye investigation."

"Think it's related to his extracurricular activities? Maybe somebody in his chain got wind of the investigation."

"It'd be my guess. Getting whacked is a consequence of being a bad boy."

Spencer moved his gaze slowly over the area, then crossed to Gabrielle. Other than the victim sprawled in a bloody mess on the driveway, nothing looked out of order.

He squatted beside the man, who lay on his back beside his vehicle, the center of his face blown away. The driver's-side door stood open; his car keys were still clenched in his right hand.

"Wallet missing?" he asked.

"Nope."

Spencer saw the gleam of gold at his wrist. After fitting on gloves, he eased aside the victim's bloodstained shirt cuff to get a look at it. A Rolex. With diamonds.

"A kick-ass piece of bling."

Tony indicated his left hand. "Check out the ring. This was no robbery."

What it looked like was an execution.

"Wife saw him last. Around 9:45." Tony scratched his head. "She could be the shooter, though she was pretty hysterical. Seemed legit."

"Somebody's with her now?"

"A neighbor and a uniform."

Spencer nodded. "You're sure he was getting *out* of the car? Look at the way his body landed. His left hand was on the handle, keys in his right. He opens the door, somebody from the street comes up to him, nails him from behind."

Tony nodded. "If he'd been climbing out of the car, he would have twisted the other way, fallen on his face."

Spencer stood, stepped around the body to inspect the inside of the vehicle. "If the wife had been welcoming him home with a bullet, seems she'd have gotten him front on. Brains would be splattered behind him, not in front."

"Brains have a way of doing that."

"You know it, Pasta Man."

"Rules out the wife being the shooter. Unless she was hiding in the bushes waiting for him, which would mean leaving the kids alone inside."

Spencer pulled off his gloves and stuffed them into his jacket pocket. "Shall we question the grieving widow?"

"We shall," Tony intoned. "After you, Slick."

They found the woman in the front parlor; she was a trim

blond sporting a huge diamond. Spencer placed her age somewhere between late twenties and early thirties.

"Mrs. Gabrielle," he said gently. "We need to ask you a few questions."

She nodded, looking a hairbreadth from falling apart. "This is our neighbor, Joe Williams."

The man stood and shook both their hands. Spencer always found it interesting the way people fell back on social niceties, even at a time like this.

"The kids are with my wife," the man said. "Next door." He sat back down. "Took them the back way so they wouldn't—"

See their daddy's brains splattered all over the driveway. Good choice.

Spencer thanked him, then turned back to the wife. "When did you last see your husband?"

"Sometime after nine but before ten. We had just gotten the children down."

"Can you be more specific about the time?"

She shredded the damp tissue she clutched in her hands. "It's a struggle to get them into bed… I know we should start at eight-thirty, but it's always nine."

Her tone had become at once defensive and pleading, as if she had to justify her parenting to him.

Tony stepped in. "I know just what you mean. I raised four of 'em. The weirdest thing about our empty nest is how quiet it is at 9:00 p.m."

"Go on," Spencer urged gently.

She looked gratefully at Tony. "It was nine-thirty, I think. Maybe even a little after."

"What happened then?"

"I said good night and told him to be——" Her voice cracked and her lips began to tremble.

"What, Mrs. Gabrielle?"

"I told him to be careful."

"He was going out."

"Yes."

"Where?"

She lowered her eyes, looking uncomfortable.

One moment passed, then another. Spencer tried again. "Your husband went out a lot at night, didn't he?"

She nodded, still not meeting his eyes.

"Do you know where he went?" When she didn't answer, he asked again. "Do you, Mrs. Gabrielle?"

"He was a good husband!" she cried. "A good father and provider! So what if he visited those clubs? It was business! The clients liked them. They wanted——"

She broke down sobbing. The neighbor glared at them, then awkwardly patted her back. Tony handed her the tissue box. She took it, whispering "Thanks."

"Your husband was a Realtor?" Spencer asked when she had composed herself again.

"Yes."

"Did he have any other business dealings that you know of?"

She lifted her gaze. "I don't understand."

"Did he have another source of income?"

She frowned, glanced at the neighbor, then back at him. "I don't know what you mean."

"Do you have full access to your finances, Mrs. Gabrielle?"

"Of course! I'm his—" Her face flooded with angry color. "Why are you asking about this? My husband's been killed. You should be asking...trying to find the animal who...who shot my husband!"

"We are," Tony said softly, "trust me, Mrs. Gabrielle. Do you know anyone who might have wished your husband harm?"

She shook her head. "No."

"Any business dealings gone bad? Fights with clients? Anything like that?"

"No." Her voice rose. "No."

Spencer shifted focus. "How did you discover that your husband had been shot?"

"Joe called. Told me the interior lights in Marcus's car were on. I knew that...couldn't be...so I—"

Went out to investigate. And found her husband in a pool of blood.

Spencer turned to the neighbor. "What time was that, Mr. Williams? When you noticed the lights?"

"Maybe 12:30, 12:45. Something like that."

"You usually up so late?"

He frowned slightly. "Not usually. I had horrible heartburn. I ate fried oysters. I love them, but they don't love me." He shifted his gaze between the detectives, working, Spencer thought, a bit too hard to appear innocent. "Went to the kitchen to get an antacid...saw the lights and called over."

"What happened next?"

"I heard Kim screaming and ran out to see what was wrong."

Spencer closed his notebook and stood. Tony followed

him to his feet. "Thank you, Mrs. Gabrielle. We'll be in touch."

"Wait!" She stood, swaying slightly on her feet. "What do I do now? I mean…what's next?"

Despite the fact that she was better off without her scumbag husband, she didn't know that and he felt sorry for her. "We'll contact you as soon as we know more. You'll be the first to hear. And I'm really sorry for your loss, ma'am."

They exited the home. While they had been inside, the crime-scene crew had arrived. The van's powerful scene lights lit up the area as if it were lunchtime. Presently the photographers were doing their thing.

Tony looked at him. "What do you think, Slick? Could she have pulled the trigger?"

"Anything's possible at this point, but I don't think so. From the way she reacted, she suspected the business her husband was up to at the Hustle was of the monkey variety. But she had chosen to look the other way."

"Because he was a good husband and provider."

"Bingo."

"What about his second career as drug kingpin?"

"*Alleged* drug kingpin," Spencer said dryly. "Clueless."

"I feel bad for her," Tony muttered. "Life's gonna suck bigtime for a while."

Spencer glanced at his watch, thinking of Stacy. Her gig at the Hustle should have ended thirty minutes ago. She would want to be here.

He flipped open his cell phone and dialed hers.

She answered right away. "Stacy Killian."

"It's me," he said. "Where are you?"

"St. Charles, crossing Poydras. Why?"

"You're going to want to make a stop on the way home."

"From the tone of your voice, I'm not picking up doughnuts."

"Gabrielle's dead," he said. "Shot to death in his driveway. We're at the scene."

"I'm on my way."

23

Wednesday, April 25, 2007
2:35 a.m.

Stacy stopped in front of Gabrielle's home, put the SUV into Park and climbed out. The crime-scene van was in place, scene lights turning night to day. She spotted the coroner's wagon and wondered which pathologist had pulled the lucky number tonight.

After signing the log, she ducked under the crime-scene tape and headed for Spencer and Tony.

Tony caught sight of her first. "Yo, Stacy. That's a new look for you, isn't it?"

"Yeah. You like it?"

"If I say yes, promise not to tell Betty?"

"Hell no, dirty old man."

He laughed. Spencer turned and smiled at her. "Killian."

Even though they made no secret of the fact that they were lovers and lived together, on the job they never acted like anything but colleagues and fellow detectives.

"Malone," she said, stopping beside them, "thanks for the heads-up." She shifted her attention to Gabrielle. Deputy Coroner Mitch Weiner, it seemed, had pulled the lucky number. He was squatted beside Gabrielle, examining the body.

"What's it looking like?" she asked.

Weiner glanced up. "Looks like a single shot. Back of the head."

"Robbery wasn't a motive," Spencer said. "Wallet and bling are still on him."

"More like an execution," Tony murmured.

"If Gabrielle was what he seemed to be, a successful, straight-arrow businessman, I might consider this a 'blood in' kill."

For several of the most notorious local gangs, the price to join was a kill. Just a random act of murder. Picking off someone like Gabrielle—wealthy, white, male—would earn the shooter extra glory.

"But knowing what I do about Gabrielle's unsavory sideline, my guess here is drug-related homicide."

Stacy nodded and flipped open her cell phone. "Has my captain been informed yet?"

"Not from us."

Knowing he would not want to wait until morning to hear the news, she dialed his cell. He answered, sounding grumpy.

Stacy enjoyed working for Captain Cooper. He had worked

his way up from a childhood in the Desire Housing Project. He was smart, fair but tough. Being a minority himself, he understood how tough a fight it was to overcome prejudice and earn equal respect in the world. Cooper had let her know from day one that he judged her on the quality of her work— and nothing else.

"It's Killian."

"Good news or bad?"

"Gabrielle's dead. Shot execution-style at his home. I'm at the scene."

"Son of a bitch. How'd you—"

"ISD notified me."

"Malone?"

"And Sciame. You want me to contact Baxter and Waldon?"

"Don't bother, there's nothing they can do tonight. We'll meet first thing, figure out where we go from here."

"Borger might know something."

"I want her brought in for questioning. Have a couple of uniforms drag her down to headquarters tomorrow morning."

"Requesting permission to conduct the interview."

"Granted. Operation's blown now." He coughed, the sound thick. "Tell Malone and Sciame we want in on every step of the investigation."

"You got it, Captain. Sorry I woke you."

"If you hadn't, I'd have kicked your ass."

He hung up; she closed her phone and turned to Spencer and Tony. "Captain Cooper wants full inclusion."

"No problem."

"I'm going to question Borger in the morning. I'm assuming you want in?"

"Absolutely."

"If anything else comes up tonight, let me know. I'm going to catch some shut-eye."

"I'll walk you to your car."

She and Spencer fell into step together. They didn't speak or touch as they made their way to the street where her SUV was parked. She unlocked the door, climbed in and looked up at him. "I'll see you at home."

"I shouldn't be too much longer."

"Good. I'll wait up."

Hand on the open door, he leaned toward her. "There's something I need to ask you."

She frowned at the seriousness of his tone. "Sure. Anything."

"I'm just wondering, with Gabrielle dead and the investigation blown…does this mean no more lap dances?"

24

Wednesday, April 25, 2007
9:20 a.m.

As planned, Stacy sent two uniforms to pick up Yvette and bring her in. The young woman hadn't been at all happy about it and had made a scene. Enough of one, in fact, that they'd had to cuff her to get her into the cruiser.

Stacy wondered if Yvette would recognize her right off or if it would take a moment or two. Either way, she figured it'd be ugly.

She took a deep breath, then opened the door and stepped into the interrogation room. At the sound, Yvette stopping pacing and swung to face her.

"Hello, Yvette," she said.

The young woman's expression transformed from angry to confused. "Brandi?"

"Detective Killian. Stacy Killian."

Confusion was replaced by understanding. "A cop? This is just wonderful. Fucking great."

"I'm sorry, Yvette. I was just doing my job."

"Right. Go to hell."

"Why don't you sit down? I have some bad news for you."

"I'll stand, thanks."

"Fine." Stacy crossed to the table, pulled out a chair and sat, facing the other woman. "Marcus Gabrielle is dead. He was shot last night outside his home."

Yvette blinked three times, her expression almost comically blank. "I don't under... Are you saying—"

"He was murdered. Getting into his car. Timing suggests he was on his way to see you at the Hustle."

Stacy could see she was digesting the information, sorting through her feelings, struggling to focus on what Stacy wanted from her. Yvette Borger was a smart girl; she would quickly focus on her own survival.

It didn't take more than a few moments. She crossed to the table, sat and faced Stacy. "I didn't have anything to do with Marcus getting killed. I couldn't have, I was at the Hustle. Just like you were."

"You were his girlfriend."

"So? I didn't want him dead."

"Not even after he tried to kill you?"

"I'd pissed him off. He was angry. We don't know that he

meant to——" Her expression shifted to one of realization. "You were undercover because of Marcus."

"Yes."

"And Saturday night someone on your team alerted you that he was in the alley."

"Yes."

"You get off lying to people?"

"I may have saved your life." Stacy leaned toward her. "Do you know what Marcus was into?"

"Yeah. Strippers and real estate."

"He manufactured and distributed meth. You helped him."

Something flickered behind her eyes. "You're crazy."

"Really? What were you doing for him on Saturday, April 21?"

"I don't know what you're talking about."

"He picked you up on the corner of North Peters and Conti Street. I saw you. You were dressed like a frump. Remember?"

When she still didn't respond, Stacy tapped the file folder she had laid on the table in front of her. "Marcus was up to his ass in some very bad shit. You were an accomplice. I was undercover at the Hustle to get to know you, Yvette. Not Marcus."

It bordered the truth, not that she would feel guilty if it had been an outright lie. Yvette had aligned herself with a criminal; she had done it for profit. Peel away all the "poor kid" crap and those were the facts, the hard truth.

"I had nothing to do with that!" Yvette said. "I just opened up properties for him. That's all."

"You made deliveries?"

"No. I met clients, opened doors and waited."

"For what?"

"To lock up again."

Stacy frowned. "What were they doing there? Picking something up? Or delivering?"

She shrugged. "I don't know. Marcus paid me to do a job, I didn't ask any questions."

"How much did he pay you?"

She hesitated. "Five hundred dollars."

"Every Saturday?"

"Not always Saturday. Some Sundays. Weekdays, too."

"To lock and unlock a door? That's it?" When she nodded, Stacy cocked an eyebrow in disbelief. "And you had no idea what these people you met were doing?"

"None."

"And you never snooped?"

"Never."

"I'm sure you'll understand why I find that hard to swallow."

"That's your problem, isn't it?"

"No, Yvette, I think it's yours."

"You're really good at what you do, you know? I thought you were my friend."

Stacy ignored the quiver of hurt in the other woman's voice. Yvette Borger, she decided, was an accomplished actress. "You go to the same properties all the time? Or different ones?"

"Different ones, though I saw a couple of the places several times."

"What about the people you met?"

"Repeats. Every week or two. Can I go now?"

"How long did you perform this service for him?"

She thought a moment. "Six months, give or take."

"That's a lot of money."

"You wanting a kickback?"

"I like you, Yvette. I do. I hate that I had to deceive you, but it was my job. If you help me, I'll help you. Tell me everything you know about Marcus's drug business and I'll do what I can to keep you from being charged."

"This is such bullshit!"

"We'll want you to look at mug shots, see if you can pick anybody out." Stacy ignored the way Yvette glowered at her. "And if we need it, we'll expect your help revisiting the properties."

"I don't have time for this."

"You don't have a choice, actually. Sorry."

Of course, she wasn't sorry at all. An angry flush flooded Yvette's face. As she opened her mouth, as if to retort, Spencer poked his head into the room.

"This a good time?"

Stacy waved him in. They had discussed this beforehand. She would question the stripper about Marcus, then Spencer would step in and question her about her roommate. Patti would watch from the viewing room down the hall.

"I'm Detective Malone," he said to Yvette, taking a seat across from her. "How are you today?"

"Confused," she answered, angry sarcasm gone, replaced by a little-girl-lost, damsel-in-distress quiver that set Stacy's teeth on edge. "I have no idea why I'm here."

"Didn't Detective Killian tell you about Marcus Gabrielle's murder?"

"Yes. But like I told her, I had nothing to do with that. How could I have? I was dancing last night."

Yvette's whole demeanor had changed. Her face had become soft and trusting, her eyes luminescent pools of innocence. She actually batted her eyelashes at him.

Stacy wanted to puke, not so much irritated by Yvette's attempt to influence Spencer with her feminine wiles as by Spencer's obvious reaction to them. This young woman knew how to use the gifts God had given her.

Men could be so stupid.

"He was your boyfriend, was he not?"

"A good customer. He liked me, tipped me very well."

"You saw him outside the Hustle?"

"Occasionally. He paid me to help him with his real estate business. I opened up properties, things like that."

Things like that, indeed. Stacy stood. "It looks like you have things under control, Detective Malone. I'm going to grab a cup of coffee."

Stacy exited the interview room and went to join Patti. The older woman sat alone in the viewing room.

"She's good," Patti said, not taking her eyes from the monitor.

"Tell me about it."

Patti chuckled. "He's only human. And a male one at that."

Before Stacy could respond, Spencer began. "I understand from Detective Killian that you may have some information for us about a murder."

"I already told you, I was dancing last night. The first I heard about Marcus—"

"Not Marcus. Your former roommate, Kitten Sweet."

"What about her?"

Stacy had to hand it to her, she was a damn convincing liar.

"You have reason to believe Kitten Sweet is the Jane Doe found in City Park."

"I thought she might be." Yvette shrugged. "She disappeared around the same time. It could have happened."

Spencer frowned slightly. "You told Detective Killian that Kitten had been receiving love letters—"

"No," she interrupted, her voice suddenly sharp. "I told a cocktail waitress named Brandi."

He didn't miss a beat. "That she had a stalker. That she had received threatening letters from someone who called himself the Artist."

"I made that up." She tossed her hair. "She didn't believe me, so I embellished. It made a good story."

Stacy glanced at Patti. The other woman was frowning.

"So you're saying Kitten Sweet wasn't being stalked? She didn't have a anonymous admirer who called himself the Artist?"

"That is what I'm saying." She leaned forward in a way that emphasized her cleavage. "I shouldn't have fibbed. I wanted her to believe me. I wanted to have something exciting and important to say."

She dropped her gaze, then returned it to his, the expression in her eyes pleading. "It's a character flaw, one I'm not proud of."

For the second time, Stacy wanted to gag. To his credit, Spencer seemed unmoved by her wrenching confession.

"Have you ever seen this man before?" he asked.

He slid a photograph—of Franklin, Stacy knew—across the table.

The woman glanced at it, then quickly away. "No."

"Are you certain?"

"Positive."

Patti glanced at Stacy. "She's lying."

Stacy nodded. The reply had rung false in its quickness, the way she had shifted her gaze away while answering.

But why lie about this? Out of fear? Spite? Or simply the desire to get the hell out, as quickly as possible?

"You lied before," Spencer said, "maybe you're lying now?"

"I embellished," she corrected. "And not to the cops—at least I didn't think she was a cop."

"You always tell the police the truth?"

"Yes."

She said it with such earnestness, Stacy laughed out loud, then stood. Obviously it was time for the "bad cop" to take another whack at her.

"Go get her," Patti muttered as she exited the room.

A moment later, she rejoined Malone and Yvette.

He glanced at her. "How was your coffee, Detective?"

"A little weak."

"Weak? I find that hard to believe."

"True. It's usually overcooked."

Neither of them were talking about coffee. Malone grinned

and pushed away from the table. "If you remember something else or want to reevaluate anything you said to me, give me a call."

He held out his card, which she took with a smile. "If you need me, Detective, you know where to find me."

When the door clicked shut behind him, Yvette looked at Stacy. "He's cute."

"If you go for that type." Stacy opened her folder, flipped through. "The people you met at the proper—"

"He have a girlfriend?"

Stacy narrowed her eyes. "Yes, I think he does."

"Is it serious?"

"Very."

"She have a ring?"

The question hit Stacy hard. She supposed a ring was the difference between "available" and "not."

Just what were she and Spencer?

"You have his number," she said. "Call and ask him."

"I just might do that."

Have a ball. "These people you met at the properties, they ever introduce themselves?"

"Never. We didn't speak."

"Did they ever leave with something they hadn't arrived with?"

"And vice versa."

"Like what?"

She shrugged. "Dunno. Didn't ask."

"I think we're going to have to hold you."

"For what? You have nothing."

"You're the closest thing we have to 'something.' Give me somewhere else to look, I'll see what I can do."

"I liked you better as Brandi."

"I'll bet you did." Stacy smiled slightly and stood. "I'll see that you get your phone call."

"He had a partner," she said quickly. "Seems to me, if Marcus was using his commercial listings as drop-offs or pickup points, his partner would be in on it."

"Drop-offs or pickup points," Stacy repeated. "Did I say that's what was going on?"

Yvette glared at her. "It's pretty obvious, isn't it?"

"Name?"

"Ramone."

"Ramone what?"

"No clue. Marcus never said, I didn't ask."

"Tell me about him."

"I don't know much. I met him once."

"Where?"

"The Hustle."

"You dance for him?"

She shook her head. "He didn't like the scene. Seemed anxious to get out. I figured he was gay."

Stacy frowned. "If a man doesn't get off on your brand of entertainment, he's gay?"

A small smile curved Yvette's mouth. "Pretty much."

Irritated, both with Yvette and herself, she refocused on Gabrielle's partner. "Ramone ever take you to one of the properties? Or arrange to meet you? Anything like that?"

"No. Like I said, I met him once. Marcus called him his 'partner.' That's all I know." Her stomach growled loudly. "Can I go now? Your gofer boys dragged me down here before breakfast."

Stacy nodded and stood. "We'll be in touch. I'll get somebody to drive you home."

"Don't bother. I need the fresh air."

Stacy set one of her business cards on the table. "If you think of anything, give me a call."

"Like that's going to happen."

Yvette left the card on the table, stood and walked away.

Stacy watched her go, then joined Spencer in the viewing room. Patti had gone, but Captain Cooper and Baxter had taken her place.

"I've filled them in," Spencer said. "Captain O'Shay's handing it back to you guys. This is clearly DIU's territory."

Stacy nodded. "I agree."

"Obviously Gabrielle was using his commercial listings as pickup and drop-off points."

"Drugs and money."

"He used Borger as a way to cover his own ass. If there'd been a bust—"

"Or a dissatisfied customer."

"—she would be the one in the line of fire."

"That's why he paid her so much. Big risks, big money. That's the way it works."

"What's with this Ramone?" Captain Cooper asked. "Why didn't we know he had a partner?"

"If he's a real estate partner, he was totally behind the scenes. He didn't come up in any of our searches."

"Check him out. Could be this Ramone decided he no longer needed a partner."

"That's what my money's on," Baxter offered. "Good old-fashioned greed."

"When that's done, I want Borger to look through the mug books. And run a list of all Gabrielle's listings. I want every one of them searched. Get a warrant."

As they began to file out, Captain Cooper stopped Stacy. "And Killian, let Baxter deal with Borger. I think a man'll have better luck with her."

That's just what was irritating the crap out of her.

To the sound of her partner's snickers, she agreed.

25

Wednesday, April 25, 2007
3:40 p.m.

Halfway across the French Quarter, Yvette regretted having declined the ride home. Heat radiated off the pavement in shimmering waves; her pits were soaked and her feet blistered. The "barely there" sandals she had slipped into before the cops escorted her out of her apartment hadn't been designed for hikes in the heat.

Damn cops. Dirty lying pigs. They're the ones who should be dragged from their homes and interrogated. She thought of Brandi—make that *Detective Killian*—and felt the all-too-familiar feelings of betrayal and hurt rise up in her chest.

She forced them back, defiantly. So what? She'd hardly known the chick. No skin off her nose.

Marcus was dead.

She stopped cold, the finality of that hitting her. She struggled to breathe, the humid air suddenly suffocating.

She hadn't loved him. Truth was, she hadn't even liked him. He had been a cheat. And a liar. A vicious prick who had nearly strangled her to make a point.

But his murder hit too close to home.

Cool air blasted her as a couple exited a restaurant called Big Bubba's. She stopped, looked longingly at the poster in the window—a fried shrimp po'boy and frosted mug of beer—then ducked inside.

She took a seat at the counter and ordered a half shrimp sandwich and a real Coke. Sugar. Caffeine. Calories. The real thing.

The waitress set the Coke and a straw in front of her. She peeled away the wrapper, dropped the straw into the drink and took a long sip, thoughts turning once again to Marcus.

She could play Little-Miss-Innocent for the cops, but she had known Marcus was up to something illegal. Of course she had. Otherwise he wouldn't have paid her so much.

She had suspected drugs, the obvious choice. But she hadn't asked questions or snooped. She figured the less she knew, the better off she would be. The healthier, too.

Methamphetamine. Horrible shit. She didn't touch the stuff. It turned people into cranked-up, paranoiac freaks.

The kind of people who dealt in things like meth wouldn't think twice about icing a stripper to insure her silence.

Yvette noisily sucked down the last of the soft drink and ordered another. The waitress brought it and her sandwich; she dug in, thoughts racing.

Marcus still owed her five hundred bucks.

It occurred to her that she should feel bad about thinking that, but she didn't. Marcus had brought this on himself. Not that she wished him dead, but it was hard to feel bad about the death of a really rotten human being.

Some people would think the same if she was killed.

The truth of that hit her hard. Her bite of sandwich lodged in her throat and tears filled her eyes.

What would they say? "Just another dead stripper" or "The whore had it coming"?

She forced herself to swallow. Crying was for losers and babies. Hadn't her dad told her that? As he'd belittled her to the point of tears? Every so often he would reach over and pinch her hard. "You'll thank me someday," he'd say. "You'll be tough."

She didn't want to be this person anymore.

Why'd she lie about the Artist sending letters to Kitten? Why'd she make up that story about her roommate?

Because she had wanted to impress, to look important or smart or interesting. To be anything but what she was.

And what about the partner named Ramone? To deflect attention. To give Detective Killian another tail to chase.

She reached into her pocket for the card the handsome detective had given her. *Detective Spencer Malone.*

She stared at the card, his name. A guy like that would never go for a woman like her. She'd seen it in his eyes. She had flirted; he had humored her.

She *had* recognized Franklin. He came into the Hustle sometimes. She'd seen him trolling for hookers.

What had he done? Did it have something to do with Marcus? Drugs? Or the City Park Jane Doe?

She'd lied about that, too. Because she'd been afraid. She hadn't wanted any part of recognizing Franklin. Getting involved was dangerous.

She always had a reason, didn't she? Always had an excuse, a justification for her behavior, one that made it okay.

"You need anything else, darlin'?"

She blinked at the woman, then shook her head. "Just the check."

In no time at all, Yvette was back out on the street. The sky had turned cloudy and the air had cooled slightly. Her feet still hurt, but with home just a few blocks away, she could make it.

From unbearable to simply miserable.

Yvette pushed that worry aside and darted across Ursuline Street, taking the shortest route home. Within minutes, she reached her building, unlocked the courtyard door and ducked inside. She breathed a sigh of relief—the shady courtyard felt ten degrees cooler than the street outside its walls.

She slipped out of her sandals, and the flagstone was cool and damp against the bottoms of her feet. Carrying the shoes, she limped toward the stairs.

The majority of the building's other residents held traditional nine to five jobs. The courtyard was empty save for Miss Alma and her yippy Pomeranian, Sissy. The old saying about a dog and their owner growing to look alike proved true in this case. Both were ancient with pointy noses and bug eyes. Yvette had long suspected that Miss Alma dyed her hair to match Sissy's cinnamon-colored fur; she knew for a fact the woman brought the dog to the beauty parlor with her.

"Hello, Miss Alma," she said, ignoring Sissy's growl.

"Afternoon, dear. Sissy, shush. She does that to everyone, but she wouldn't hurt a flea."

Unless the flea came within range. "I know, Miss Alma. Enjoy the rest of your afternoon."

Yvette climbed the stairs, reached the second floor. Nancy was out watering her plants. As she passed apartment eight, the pug that lived there began to bark.

Yvette jumped, same as she always did, and shouted for him to "Shut up!"

"Hey, Yvette!" Nancy called. "Wouldn't you just love to have that dog muzzled?"

"You know it's true," she answered. "Every night he barks his stupid head off when I come home, wakes everybody up. Can you believe Bob and Ray complained to *me* about it? Like I should change my schedule, so their monkey-faced dog doesn't wake them up."

"What'cha gonna do?" She dumped the last of the watering can on her begonias. "Say, I hope you and your mom are having a good time."

Yvette frowned. "What?"

"You and your mom, I hope you're having fun." She glanced at Yvette. "She seems nice."

"My mother's dead."

Her friend's face went slack with surprise. "But...we met the other night."

Yvette shook her head. "What made you think this person was my mother?"

"She told me she was. It was late...you were working. Samson started barking and I—" She bit her words back, obviously upset. "I told her where your key was. She said you'd told her but she'd forgotten."

Yvette fought to steady her voice. "You told a stranger where I keep my spare key?"

"I'm really, really sorry. But she seemed so nice. So... motherly."

Yvette remembered leaving work early because of menstrual cramps, finding the woman standing at her door. Yvette struggled to remember what she had looked like, the words they had exchanged.

"I'm Nancy's mom. I'm here for the week. The key she gave me isn't working."

Yvette looked at Nancy. "Was *your* mother here this week?" Her neighbor didn't need to reply, Yvette saw the answer on her face.

"What night did this happen?"

The other woman thought a moment, then confirmed what Yvette already knew.

Monday night.

"What did she look like?" Yvette asked.

"Like she could be your mom. I even told her how much like her you looked."

"Short, reddish hair? Medium height and trim? Wearing a dark jacket and slacks?"

Nancy's eyes widened in surprise. "Yes. How did you—"

"She tricked me, too." Yvette quickly explained, then asked, "You haven't seen her since, have you?"

Nancy shook her head and hugged herself. "This is so creepy. Who do you think she was?"

"I don't know, but I intend to find out." After warning her neighbor to keep watch, she headed for her apartment.

She checked the cherub planter; the spare key was gone. Had she interrupted the woman *before* she'd been inside her apartment? Or after?

Yvette swallowed past the sudden, suffocating fear that rose up in her. She hadn't for a minute sensed that something was wrong. That a stranger had been in her home, touching her things.

In a strange way, that scared her most of all.

This person, whoever she was, still had the key.

Yvette's knees went weak. She forced herself to cross to her door, unlock it and step into her apartment. And sensed immediately that something wasn't right.

Of course she did. In all probability, she would "sense" something out of order for a long time to come.

She slid her gaze toward the doorway to the kitchen, then the short hall that led to the two bedrooms. Her heart began to pound.

"Hello," she called out, though she hadn't a clue why. Did she think a whack-job intruder was going to answer?

"Yo, babe, I'm here. C'mon back!"

Perversely, she didn't find the silence comforting. A bold answer would give her the chance to run like hell. She moved her gaze slowly over the room. Nothing looked out of order. Nothing looked different from when she had left—been dragged out—that morning.

Her tips.

She hurried toward the kitchen. She kept her stash in a plastic bag in a cleaned, empty ice cream carton in the freezer. She reached the unit, opened the freezer.

The carton was there, the bag of money inside. She quickly counted it and found that none had been taken.

Breathing a sigh of relief, she replaced the carton, shut the freezer door and turned.

Thumbtacked to the back of her kitchen door was a note.

I did it for you.
Yours always, the Artist

Yvette stared at the message, her hands beginning to shake. Did what for her? Broke into her apartment?

Then she knew. A cry rose to her throat. She brought a hand to her mouth to hold it back.

Marcus.

Her admirer had killed him. For her.

26

Wednesday, April 25, 2007
4:45 p.m.

Patti looked at the forensic odontologist's report, bitterly disappointed. The dental records proved that Kitten Sweet was *not* their Jane Doe.

It changed nothing. Franklin was still in jail, charged with theft and felony possession of a firearm. He wasn't going anywhere.

But it left them with nothing—no new angle to investigate, nothing new to tie Franklin to Sammy's murder and the Handyman victims.

She had broken the law, the very thing she had sworn to uphold. She had involved one of her detectives, put both their careers on the line. And for what?

"You've got the wrong guy."

She had managed to put that call out of her mind, managed to convince herself it'd been some crank. Somebody with an ax to grind with her, which wasn't such a far-fetched concept.

Chief Howard had appointed her to the post-Katrina tribunal to judge officers who had gone AWOL during and after the storm. When an officer took an oath, it was to serve the public, no matter what. Some of the stories had broken her heart, but where did you draw the line? "Protect and Serve" meant just that, even when it was *really* inconvenient.

Patti picked up the list of names she'd assembled and scanned them. The officers ranged from first-year rookies to veterans with twenty-five years under their belt. She read through the names, able to picture each and every one. Could one of them be this angry at her?

What happened if she assumed the caller's claim was legit? They had the wrong guy. Just as Franklin claimed, he had found the gun in City Park. It fit. Sammy stumbles upon the Handyman and his victim. The Handyman manages to get Sammy's gun, kills him with it, dumps both victims in the park, then disposes of the weapon as quickly as possible.

Right there at the park.

So who made the call?

Someone who'd known about the gathering at Shannon's. A cop? Someone connected to a cop or the force?

"You don't look happy."

Patti glanced up. Spencer stood in her office doorway. "I'm not. Take a look."

She slid the report across the desk. He strode over, picked it up and scanned the information.

Tony ambled into the office. "Who died?"

Spencer handed him the findings. Tony read it, then handed it back. "So much for that anonymous tip."

Patti worked to keep her disappointment from showing. Spencer had lied to his partner about how they'd gotten Kitten Sweet's name as the possible Jane Doe. She hadn't asked him to, but hated that she had put him in the position of having to choose between them.

"Did the search of Franklin's apartment turn up anything?" she asked.

"More stolen merch," Spencer replied. "And a truly amazing collection of adult magazines. Nothing bizarre, just straight nudie shots."

"Checked the freezer," Tony offered. "Hamburger meat and Eskimo Pies, no hands or other body parts. No saws, clippers or anything else that could be used to sever a human hand."

"What about a computer?"

"Nope. The answering machine was clear and his only mail was a stack of bills and advertising circulars. Can you believe somebody was offering him a MasterCard? Go figure."

Dammit. She stood and crossed to her single window. She gazed out at the brilliant spring day. "Franklin's not our guy."

"With all due respect, Captain," Tony said, "he had the gun. He placed himself at the scene."

She turned and faced them. "Placing himself at the scene is circumstantial."

Spencer and Tony exchanged glances. Spencer spoke first. "The old rule of thumb about somebody who looks guilty, being guilty, usually proves true. It certainly fits in this case. The gun is strong physical evidence connecting him to the grave and the victims in it. The man is a convicted rapist. He's also a thief and a liar."

She rubbed the bridge of her nose. "I have to be sure. One hundred percent positive."

"What can we do?"

"Find me a victim. If I can link Franklin to just one of the Handyman victims, even a weak link, I'll be satisfied."

"Captain O'Shay, could I have a word?"

The chief of police stood in her doorway. She smiled and waved him in. "Of course, Chief. The detectives and I were just finishing."

He greeted both detectives. "How's your dad's retirement going, Spencer?"

"Not bored with fishing yet."

Spencer's dad—Patti's brother-in-law—had been career NOPD. He'd never risen above the rank of detective, but that had been okay with him. He'd simply loved the work. He'd retired a year ago. Hurricane Katrina and Sammy's death had been catalysts for the decision.

As the two detectives exited the office, Patti told them to keep her posted, then turned to her boss. "What can I do for you, Chief Howard?"

He ignored her question and asked one of his own. "How are you, Patti?"

Something in his tone raised her hackles. "I'm very well, thank you."

"I'm sorry I haven't been by before this. Hell of a thing, uncovering Sammy's badge that way."

"To tell you the truth, I'm relieved. To finally know what went down and have a trail to follow."

"Seems to me the trail's led you to your guy. Congratulations."

She frowned slightly. Chief Howard never did anything without intent. A simple "Congratulations" was anything but simple. So why was he here?

"Thank you, Chief, but I'm not certain we do."

His eyebrows shot up. "That surprises me, Captain. I've reviewed the case and think it's strong."

"True. But until we have a legitimate tie between Franklin and one of the Handyman's victims, it's not ironclad."

Chief Howard was quiet a moment. "I'm distressed to hear you say that."

"I'm sorry, sir. That's the way I see it."

"Patti," he said softly, "you have to trust the process. If he's charged, tried and found guilty, you'll have to accept it."

"I don't know if I can do that."

His cell phone buzzed; he checked the display, then slipped it back into his pocket. "Perhaps this case is too close? I could turn it over to someone else? After the stress of Sammy's death, no one would think less—"

"That's absolutely not necessary," she said. "I'm in charge of ISD, this case and the investigation. Franklin's been charged and is being held on the theft and weapons charge. We have time to dig."

"True, if you feel you have the manpower."

Which meant he didn't.

Wrap it up, move on.

"Give me a little more time. The forensic sculptor is working on a facial reconstruction now. It should be ready within a couple of days. We'll publicize the image, see if anyone recognizes her."

"Agreed. Anything else?"

He knew about the dental records. Probably the call she had gotten at Shannon's, as well. Little slipped by Chief Howard. That's the way he ran his department.

"We got a tip about a missing young woman. Had the forensic odontologist compare her dental records with Jane Doe's teeth. They didn't match."

He nodded. Obviously this was not news. And luckily, he didn't ask about the source of the "tip."

"Anything else?"

"An anonymous call to me. At Shannon's."

"The night of the surprise party." The chief had made a brief appearance, then left.

"Yes, the caller said we 'had the wrong guy.'"

"And you believe this person? He presented you with proof?"

"I'm not discounting anything at this point."

"Admirable, Captain." He glanced at his watch, then looked at her again. "The public will be reassured to know this monster's been caught."

"Not if he proves to be the wrong monster."

He frowned. "We'll be making certain that doesn't happen, won't we, Captain O'Shay?"

He had officially put her on notice. The clock was ticking on this investigation. The chief wanted her to build the case against Franklin, not continue to look for suspects.

"Yes, sir. Understood."

As he walked away, she acknowledged that for the first time in her career, she wasn't sure she could follow a direct order.

27

Saturday, April 28, 2007
1:15 a.m.

The Hustle was jumping, even by Friday night standards. It was the first weekend of Jazz Fest—next to Mardi Gras, the city's biggest tourist draw—and the tips and booze were flowing.

Yvette figured she might break her personal record, despite the fact she was jumpy, distracted and barely going through the motions.

The last two days had been the longest of her life. She had spent them looking over her shoulder, searching every shadow and thinking about Marcus's murder.

I did it for you.

Yours always, the Artist.

After discovering the note, she had been frozen with fear. Panic had followed. She hadn't known what to do, who to call. She had no one. No family or close friends, no husband or boyfriend.

Not the police. Not them.

She had no one to depend on but herself.

She had considered packing up, taking off. To hell with her apartment and this crummy job.

But she had run before. Once upon a time, she had lived in fear. Of her father. The street. Helplessness. Hopelessness. She'd promised herself she'd never live that way again, never run away. It's why she had refused to evacuate for Katrina. If she stood up to that bitch, she figured she could stand up to anything.

So she'd had her locks changed. Made a couple of inquiries to alarm companies. Thought about buying a gun, then rejected the idea.

In the meantime, it had been quiet. No more anonymous notes. No more break-ins. Maybe it was over.

"Hi, Yvette," Tonya said, poking her head into the dressing room, which was really not much more than a screened-off enclosure. "Almost time. I've got a note for you." Tonya handed her the sealed envelope. "See you in six."

Yvette opened the envelope, pulled out the note. Paper fluttered to the floor. No, she saw. Not paper. Money.

Five one hundred dollar bills.

She stared at them, heart beating heavily, then shifted her gaze to the note.

Here's what he owed you.

A cry flew to her throat; she jumped to her feet and ran after Tonya. "Wait!" she called. "Tonya!"

The woman stopped and turned.

"Who gave you this?"

"Some guy."

"Where? What table?"

"At the bar."

"Show me."

Tonya glanced at her watch and frowned. "You're up in—"

"I know when I'm up, dammit! Point him out, it's important!"

The woman hesitated a moment more, then motioned Yvette to follow her. They exited the backstage area and moved around the tables until they had a clear view of the bar.

She clutched Tonya's arm. "Where is he?"

"I don't see him... He must have gone."

"He can't have. Please, look again."

She did, then shook her head. "What's going on, Yvette?"

She shook her head, fear choking her. "He...I can't...I..."

Tonya squeezed her hand. "I'll get Jenny to dance for you. Go to your dressing room and calm down. I'll be right there."

Yvette nodded and hurried backstage. Inside the small enclosure, she stopped. The one hundred dollar bills were scattered on the floor, just where they had fallen.

Five hundred dollars. The money Marcus had owed her.

How had the Artist known? She hadn't told anyone.

Goose bumps crawled up her arms. She moved her gaze over the small, cluttered enclosure. Had he been here?

Tonya interrupted her thoughts. "Are those one hundred dollar bills?"

Yvette met her startled gaze and nodded.

"Where did you...? Were they in that note I delivered?"

"Yes."

"My God."

Yvette bent and collected the bills. Her hands shook. She slipped them back into the envelope, wondering what the hell she should do now.

"You want to talk about this?"

Yvette looked at her. "What did the guy look like?"

"Average, I guess. Kind of nondescript. Harmless."

That was only slightly reassuring. "Does he come in a lot?"

Tonya furrowed her brow. "I know I've seen him before. But always at the bar. He's the kind of guy you just don't...notice."

The woman paused. "Do you think...surely you don't think he's...dangerous?"

Yvette bit her lip, and Tonya caught her breath. "Tell me what's going on. Start at the beginning."

So Yvette did, beginning with the first note he'd sent her, sharing how a woman had deceived a neighbor into giving her a key. "I thought he was harmless, just another one of those guys. You know, the really sad, lonely ones."

"Go on."

"Then Marcus was killed." Tonya wasn't surprised at the news. The police had questioned all the employees of the Hustle about Marcus and his associates. "Apparently he was into some pretty serious shit."

"Meth manufacture and distribution."

Yvette widened her eyes. "How did you—"

"Know? Honey, I know everything that goes on around here. If not immediately, soon after."

"So you knew Brandi was a cop?"

"Not at first. Knew something wasn't right about that one. Also knew she was Ted's 'hire.' I stayed after him until he told me what was going on. Stupid shit."

When Marcus had turned up dead, Ted had lost his leverage with the cops and was now in jail.

"Tonya, can I ask you a question?"

"Sure, hon."

"Do you believe in God?"

The woman screwed up her face in thought. "Don't know. I guess so. Why?"

"I never thought much about it, but after Katrina, I figured there was a God and that He wanted me to live."

Yvette realized she had closed her hand around the bills, crumpling them, and eased her grip. "I thought it was a good thing, like I was going to do something big or…important. Really turn it around and be somebody. But now—"

She cleared her throat, forced out the thought that had been nagging at her since she realized the Artist had killed Marcus. "What if He wanted me to live for this? As a catalyst for Marcus getting whacked? Or to make me a victim instead of someone who's a better person?"

For a long moment, Tonya was quiet. "I don't think it works

that way. And you know what, if it did, He'd be a pretty crappy God."

If Tonya had been a priest or a preacher, the thought might be comforting. But coming from a broken-down, hard-drinking ex-exotic dancer, Yvette wasn't reassured at all.

28

Saturday, April 28, 2007
3:30 a.m.

The screech of his cell phone dragged Spencer from the depths of sleep. He fumbled for the device, managing to find it and answer without opening his eyes.

"Malone here."

"*Detective* Malone?"

The voice on the other end was female, sounded young—and scared. "Yeah. Who's this?"

"Yvette Borger."

That woke him up. "Ms. Borger?" Stacy rolled onto her side and looked at him in question. "What—"

"I know who killed Marcus," she said, voice cracking. "And now he's after me."

"Where are you?"

"Paulie's Place."

"That little hole-in-the-wall next to the Dungeon?"

She said it was and he climbed out of bed. "Stay put. I'll be right there."

Stacy sat up. "What's the deal?"

"She says she knows who killed Marcus. And that he's after her."

"I'm coming along."

"I expected you would. Gabrielle belongs to DIU."

"Damn right. So why'd she call you?" she asked, throwing back the covers.

He stopped in the doorway to the john and grinned back at her. "Because she thinks I'm cute."

"I don't trust her."

"No joke," he said, then ducked into the john to relieve himself. When he stepped out, Stacy was dressed and waiting. She took his place, reappearing moments later. He saw that she had brushed her hair.

"What did you mean by that?" she asked as they headed for the front door.

"It's obvious you don't trust her. Yvette Borger trades on her looks and sexuality. And you just don't get that."

Stacy stopped, frowned at him. "I get that."

"I mean—" He opened the door for her. "It's so opposite to who you are, you're automatically suspicious."

"She thinks you can be manipulated."

"With her feminine wiles."

"You're okay with that?"

They crossed the porch, heading for Spencer's car. He unlocked it and they slid inside. "I understand it."

"So you're saying you trust her?"

He started the engine, pulled away from the curb. "She's mostly full of shit. But it's not personal. Not for me." He glanced at her. "She sounded genuinely scared."

"That could be an act."

"Then why call me?" She arched her eyebrows and he laughed. "In the middle of the night? Come on."

"She asked if you had a girlfriend. I told her I thought so."

"You're not certain?"

She ignored his question. "She asked if it was serious."

He eased through a yellow light, heading down Carrollton Avenue toward the interstate. "So?"

"So…is it?"

"What do you think?"

"That's a cop-out and you—" She shook her head and looked away. After a moment, she looked back at him. "What are we doing, Spencer?"

"Driving to the Quarter in the middle of the night to question an informant."

"You know what I mean. What are *we* doing?"

He didn't have an answer, which, frankly, scared the crap out of him. It just seemed wrong. They had been together, exclusively, for two years, and had lived together a good part of that time.

Shouldn't he know, in either his heart or his gut, how he felt? What he wanted, long term?

"You tell me, Stacy. Where are we going?"

"I don't know," she said softly. "I'm starting to think I really don't have a clue."

They fell silent and remained that way for the rest of the drive. They reached Paulie's Place, located on Toulouse Street. He parked the Camaro illegally, flipped down his visor with his NOPD identification and climbed out.

They crossed the sidewalk and entered the lounge. Yvette was sitting at the bar, an untouched beer in front of her. She saw him first, then Stacy. To her credit, her expression altered only slightly.

She slid off the bar stool and stood waiting. Her gaze, he noticed, jumped around and she kept clasping and unclasping her hands.

Truth was, she looked terrified. If she was faking it, she should give up dancing and head to Hollywood.

Of course, being authentically terrified only meant she believed her own story. She could still be as nutty as a Christmas fruitcake.

"Are you all right?" he asked.

She nodded. "Thank you for... I'm sorry, I know it's late."

"Let's go outside so we can talk."

She didn't need to be coaxed. She dug four dollars out of her pocket, deposited it on the bar and grabbed her backpack. "Thanks, Jackie," she called to the burly bartender.

The street outside was mostly empty. Nearly all the bars and clubs were closed, staff and patrons alike grabbing some shut-eye before the new day.

"Are you cold?" he asked her. "We could sit in the car."

She shook her head. "I need a cigarette."

She retrieved her pack of smokes, then fumbled to light one, her hands shaking badly.

"Allow me," he said.

She shot him a grateful look and handed him the matches.

A moment later, the paper and tobacco caught and she inhaled deeply.

Spencer gave her a moment, then murmured, "You say you know who killed Marcus?"

"I do." She sucked on the cigarette. "But you won't believe me."

"Give us a try," Stacy said softly. "You might be surprised."

"I doubt that, but okay." She tilted her chin up defiantly. "The Artist."

Stacy's eyebrows shot up. "The guy you made up?"

"I told you you wouldn't believe me."

Spencer stepped in. "Cut us some slack, Yvette. Just a couple of days ago you told us the Artist didn't exist."

She drew on the cigarette again. "I made up his connection to Kitten, but he exists."

"Go on."

"I've been getting these…love notes. They're signed the Artist."

"How many have you gotten?"

She thought a moment. "Five, including the one tonight." She paused as if expecting a question, then went on. "I didn't think much about them until…until the day I learned about Marcus."

She cleared her throat. "I just figured he was some lonely-hearts-club geek until the day you questioned me about Marcus. When I got home, and he'd left me a note. It was inside, tacked to the back of my kitchen door."

"He was in your apartment?" Spencer said. "He broke in?"

"Yes." She dropped the smoke, then ground it out with the toe of her strappy stiletto. "The note said 'I did it for you.'"

"Did what?"

"Killed Marcus."

"Did he say that? Specifically?"

"No, but what else could it be?"

Spencer glanced at Stacy. Although her expression was neutral, he knew she was having a hard time buying any of this. She wasn't alone.

"Ms. Borger," Spencer said gently. "It could have been anything. He jacked off, took a bottle of pills, kicked his dog—"

"No!" she said, cutting him off. "Tonight he was in the club! He had Tonya deliver this."

She dug into her backpack and pulled out a wad of bills and a card. "It's five hundred dollars."

When they didn't respond, she made a sound of frustration. "Marcus owed me that amount. The last time I did that side job for him, he stiffed me."

She looked directly at Stacy for the first time. "That's what we were arguing about in the alley that night. When he tried to choke me. Look."

She handed the note to Spencer, who read it aloud. "Here's the money he owed you."

He handed it to Stacy. She read it and frowned. "This one isn't signed."

"That can't be." She took it, her expression falling. "I guess I just knew...I mean, he's signed everything else the 'Artist.' I swear!"

"Do you have the other notes?" Spencer asked.

"Not with me, but I saved them. They're at my apartment."

"Let's go get them."

None of them spoke during the short drive. When they climbed out in front of her building, Spencer saw that light glimmered ever so faintly on the horizon.

It was going to be a long damn day.

She unlocked the street entrance and they filed into the courtyard. They followed her upstairs. Two doors from hers a dog began to bark, a cross between a yap and a howl. Spencer felt sorry for the poor bastards the beast woke up.

She let them in, flipped the light switch just inside the door, but didn't make a move into the apartment.

"Yvette?" he said.

She looked at him. "Since he's been in here, it takes me a while to get up the courage to... I know it's silly, but—"

"It's not silly. We'll check it out."

Within a couple of minutes, they had searched the small apartment and determined it empty.

"Thanks," she said. "I had the locks changed... I forgot to tell you that part. About the woman."

"The woman?" Spencer repeated, frowning.

"Yes. I came home the other night and found a woman at my door. She claimed to be my neighbor Nancy's mother. Said the key Nancy gave her didn't work."

"Maybe she *was* Nancy's mom?" Stacy offered.

"She wasn't. That same night, she told Nancy she was *my* mother. That's how she got inside. Nancy told her where I keep my spare key."

Spencer frowned. "What night was this?"

"Monday. I came home early. Cramps."

Patti's close call.

He caught Stacy looking at him quizzically, and he refocused. "Could the Artist be a woman?"

Yvette opened her mouth as if to form an automatic no, but shook her head instead. "I just assumed it was a man. I mean, it's mostly guys who, you know, hang around the Hustle and stuff. Besides, Tonya said a guy gave her the letter to give to me tonight."

"Tonya?"

"Manages the Hustle's talent and wait staff," Stacy offered. Then to Yvette, she said, "Why don't you get us the letters?"

"They're in the bedroom. I'll be right back."

When she left them alone, Stacy turned to him. "What's the deal, Malone?"

"What do you mean?"

"When Yvette told you about the woman who claimed to be her mother, you got a funny look on your face."

"Did I?"

She cocked an eyebrow. "Don't give me that innocent crap. You're hiding somethi—"

"They're gone."

They turned. The young woman stood in the doorway, wild-eyed and pale. "They were here, I swear. He must have taken them."

"Show us."

She led them to her bedroom, pointed to the nightstand, its single drawer standing open. "I had them in there."

"Are you certain you didn't move them?"

"I'm sure. They were there. All of them!"

"Tell me about Ramone," Stacy said.

"What? Who—"

"Ramone?" she said again. "Marcus's partner. The one you told me about."

When she hesitated, Stacy answered for her. "Let me guess, you made him up."

"I didn't make this up!"

"What about the photograph Detective Malone showed you? You recognized him, didn't you?"

"Yes! I've seen him around the club. He hits on the girls. So what?"

"If that's the case, why'd you lie?"

"Because I was pissed. Because I didn't want to get involved. Because someone like me doesn't help the cops."

"Give me a reason why we should believe you now."

"Because it's true." She hugged herself. "It's all true. The letters. The money. The woman breaking in."

Her voice took on a desperate tone and she moved her gaze between them. "He killed Marcus. I know he did!"

"We're not saying he didn't," Spencer said gently. "We're not denying any of this is true. But we need something to work with. Some proof that what you're telling us is true."

"Screw you." She spit the words at them. "I should have known not to go to you for help."

"Put yourself in our shoes, Ms. Borger. What would you believe?"

"Get out! If you're not going to help me, just get the hell out!"

They didn't argue or try to reason with her and a couple of minutes later they were on the street. Truth was, without more from her, there was little they could do.

"Well, that was interesting," Stacy said. "What do you think? Is she a liar or just plain nuts?"

"Part of what she told us was true."

She stopped and looked at him. "Which part?"

"The woman." He unlocked the Camaro and opened the door, but didn't make a move to get in. "It was Patti."

After dropping that bomb, he climbed into the car. Stacy followed a moment later. Once she was buckled in, she turned to him, expression incredulous. "What do you mean, it was Patti?"

"She wanted something to tie Yvette's roommate to the Jane Doe. But she couldn't blow your cover, and she refused to wait."

"So she broke in?"

"Yes."

Stacy was quiet a moment, as if processing the information. When she spoke, he heard the disappointment in her voice. "I can't believe you were involved in this, Spencer. If PID catches wind—"

"I didn't have any part of it. Aunt Patti didn't tell me what she was up to."

"You guessed."

"Yes." He started the car and eased away from the curb. "I confronted her with it."

Traffic was nonexistent. He had cleared the French Quarter and crossed Canal Street within a couple of minutes—a trip that could take twenty minutes when the Quarter was jamming.

They were jumping on the expressway before Stacy spoke again. "Did she find anything?"

"Name of the roommate's dentist. But before you get too excited, yes, the dentist had X-rays, and no, they didn't match our Jane Doe's."

"She broke the law for nothing."

"If you can call peace of mind nothing."

"That's such crap, Spencer. And you know it."

"She's the captain."

"And she's losing it, dammit!"

They fell silent. "What are you going to do?" he asked finally.

"You've put me in a very awkward position."

"I'm sorry. Considering the circumstances, I felt I had to tell you."

"I won't lie. If I'm asked, I'll tell what I know."

"Fair enough." He exited onto Carrollton Avenue, heading toward the river. "But nobody's going to ask."

29

Saturday, April 28, 2007
6:35 a.m.

Stacy couldn't sleep, couldn't shut off her mind. Like a hamster on a wheel, her thoughts went round and round, replaying the events of the night, the things she had learned.

Captain Patti O'Shay had broken the law. Spencer had known she was doing it. He'd felt no remorse, then or now.

And he'd kept it from her. So effectively, she hadn't even suspected.

Stacy was uncertain which revelation had rocked her more—his secret-keeping or her total obliviousness to it.

How could she trust him? And how could a relationship

flourish amid secrets and lies? A healthy relationship required total honesty, which led to complete trust.

Like the best cop partnerships. You never wondered if your partner had your back. If you wondered, you were dead.

Spencer snored softly beside her. Not an unpleasant sound. Comforting. Familiar.

She rolled onto her side and gazed at him. No wonder neither of them had a clue where they were going. How could they?

"Why're you staring at me?" he asked, not opening his eyes.

"I'm not."

He cracked them open. "Liar."

She leaned over and kissed him. "Go back to sleep. I'm getting up."

"Crazy woman."

Tell me about it.

She slipped out of bed and pulled a sweatshirt on over her cotton pj's.

"Stacy?"

She stopped at the door and looked back. "Yeah?"

"Marry me."

She stared at him, quite literally dumbstruck. Several seconds ticked by before she found her voice. "You didn't just say—"

"I did. Marry me."

Just last night they had agreed they didn't know where their relationship was going. "You've caught me by surprise, Spencer. Why are you asking me...now?"

"Dunno. Think 'bout it, okay?"

She nodded and backed out of the room, gently closing the door behind her.

Like most girls, she had daydreamed about the day the man she loved would propose marriage. The fantasy included bended knee, candlelight, music and the promise of undying love—not to mention a ring.

Somehow "Dunno," a sweatshirt and pj's didn't cut it.

She started the coffee and went out for the paper. The day looked to be pretty damn spectacular: blue sky, puffy clouds, low humidity. Of course, in New Orleans the weather had been known to turn on a dime.

When she returned with the paper, the coffee was already burbling its last. Spencer stood at the counter, leaning against it for support, staring at the coffeemaker.

"You're up."

"Smelled the brew. Couldn't resist."

She cocked an eyebrow. Interesting. Fresh-brewed coffee seemed to be able to do what his unanswered question could not—propel him out of bed.

So much for his being on pins and needles. It was only a decision about the rest of their lives.

He poured himself a cup of coffee, sweetened it, shuffled across to the table and plopped onto a chair. "What d'you have t'day?"

"Baxter and I are touring Gabrielle's listings. See if we missed anything. We're bringing a canine unit with us."

The dogs were trained to indicate on all types of narcotics. In fact, their olfactory glands were so sensitive, they could pinpoint areas where drugs had been stored, even when they were no longer there and in amounts as miniscule as parts per billion.

"Smart." He sipped the coffee. "Gabrielle's records offer any leads?"

"He's the one who was smart. His appointment book, PDA and computer were all clean. The lab's performing forensics on his cell phone."

The ordinary cell phone user didn't realize that cell phones retained information even after being deleted or wiped. Mobile Electronic Forensics, which used specially designed software to retrieve stored data, was fast becoming a major player in crime investigation. Invaluable information such as contact lists, numbers called and duration of those calls, text messages sent or received, as well as pictures, movies and even customized rings tones, could all be lifted. There was even software that could read multiple languages, such as Arabic and Chinese.

"But so far," she continued, "we've got nothing to tie him to either end of the meth process except the word of the bartender."

"And his getting gunned down in his Uptown driveway on a school night," he added, yawning. "Want to go for bagels?"

"I can't believe you're thinking about food."

"I'm hungry."

"By any chance, do you remember dropping a bomb on me a few minutes ago? The 'M' bomb?"

"I do. Seems to me, the bomb's in your court."

"Don't you think we should talk about this?"

"If you want to. But in the end it's either yes or no."

"You drive me crazy!" She folded her arms across her chest. "Flipping nuts."

He took a sip of his coffee, a smile tugging at his mouth. "Reason enough to say yes. It's not every day you can agree to spend the rest of your life with someone who sends you off your rocker."

That was the closest she was going to get to her romantic fantasy: being sent off a rocker instead of over the moon. Some girls had all the luck.

Something in her expression sobered him. "I am who I am, Stacy."

And so was she. "No," she said softly. "I won't marry you."

His expression didn't change. He simply nodded. "Do you want to move out?"

"Is that what this is about, Spencer? You could have just asked me to go."

He frowned. "That's not why I asked."

"Then why did you?" She held up a hand. "And don't tell me you don't know. I'm not accepting that."

"We talked last night about where our relationship was going. This morning, getting married just seemed the thing to do."

"The thing to do?"

"That it was time. You know, to—"

"Shit or get off the pot?"

"I wouldn't have put it that way, but yes."

This proposal had just gone from bad to worse. "Maybe I will move out."

"Stacy, I didn't mean—"

"Yeah, you did." She pressed her lips together a moment,

using the time to focus her thoughts. "You're right, Spencer. Maybe it's time we faced the fact that this isn't going anywhere and moved on."

He didn't respond. She crossed to the doorway, stopped and looked back at him. He sat unmoving, gaze fixed on a point somewhere past her. She wondered if he hurt at all. If he, like she, felt as if someone had reached inside her chest and now held her heart in a vice grip.

Somehow, she thought not.

She let out a long breath. "It might take me a couple of weeks to find a place. I'll start looking right away."

30

Saturday, April 28, 2007
11:15 a.m.

Yvette had provided a list of thirty addresses she had "opened" for Gabrielle since the first of the year. Luckily, she'd written down the addresses in her day-runner—a practice Gabrielle surely would not have approved of.

There had been additional addresses the previous year, but she'd tossed her 2006 planner and without it they all ran together in her mind. Stacy had acquired a full list of all Gabrielle's listings, but wouldn't resort to those unless Yvette's proved a bust.

Rene Baxter, Stacy's partner in this investigation, had offered to drive, and she had jumped at the offer. They had warrants for each address and an agent from Gabrielle's office had agreed to accompany them, serving as the property owners' representation.

Rene was following the agent's chamois-colored Camry. Buster, a seventy-five-pound drug-sniffing yellow Lab and his handler, Bob, were following them in the K-9 cruiser. B & B— as the two were known around the NOPD.

They had crossed Poydras Street and were heading into what was called the Warehouse District.

"When I was a kid, this entire area was empty warehouses. Pretty much urban blight. Now look. High-priced condos and trendy clubs."

And restaurants, Stacy saw. Art galleries. Very hip.

"A condo there—" Baxter pointed to a three-story building "—can cost a half a million bucks. How screwed up is that?"

Stacy didn't comment and he angled her a glance. "You're quiet today."

Preoccupied with the turn her life had taken this morning. "Just tired," she fibbed.

"Hungry?"

She glanced at him. "Grumpy or Bashful or Doc?"

He laughed at her reference to the Seven Dwarfs from Snow White. "I'm going to need some lunch pretty soon."

"We just started."

"Yeah, but we started really close to lunchtime."

She smiled. Small and wiry, not an ounce overweight, Rene Baxter was an eating machine. Where he put it, she had no clue. "Let's do this one and another, then we'll break."

"Agreed. Tacos, chicken or burgers?"

"I'm sure Buster'd be happy with any of those, but I'm thinking tacos."

"Can take the girl out of Texas but can't take Texas out of the girl."

"You know it, partner."

The Camry pulled to a stop in front of a three-story brick building. A big For Sale—Gabrielle Realty sign was propped up in the front window. Rene eased into the spot behind it, and they all climbed out.

Buster strained slightly against his lead, obviously anxious to get started. After all, this was what he had been trained for. For Buster, this was the juice.

You go, big boy.

The Realtor unlocked the door and they filed in. Stacy moved her gaze over the space. It appeared to have most recently been a restaurant or club.

Bob unleashed Buster, who began to do his thing. She watched the dog as he began his search, sniffing, totally focused. When he picked up on a scent, he would "alert." There were two types of alerts, she had learned. The passive, in which the dog would sit, and the aggressive, where he would scratch.

"He's found something," Bob said. A moment later, the animal began pawing at an air-conditioning vent.

Obviously, Buster was a scratcher.

Stacy and Rene hurried over. The vent was located in the hallway that led to the bathrooms. The vent cover proved to be loose, and they removed it easily. Stacy eased out the air filter, which was filthy.

"Flashlight," Stacy said. Bob handed her one and she directed the beam around the small space. "Empty."

"Now," Bob said. "But I promise you, there were drugs in there at least once."

"How'd you do that?" Rene asked. "How'd you know he'd found something before he did?"

Bob laughed and scratched Buster's head. "His breathing. It changed."

Stacy's cell phone vibrated; she separated from the group and answered. It was Spencer.

"Hey," he said.

"Hey to you."

"How's it going?"

"Pretty great. Buster just got excited."

"Where are you?"

"Used to be a supper club. On South Peters, in the Warehouse District."

He was silent, and she cleared her throat. "What's up?"

"I don't want you to move out."

She tightened her grip on the phone. "I can't talk about this right now."

"I know. I just…I wanted you to know that."

"Thanks," she said softly. "We'll talk later."

Stacy ended the call and slipped the device back into its holster. The moment she did, it vibrated. She unclipped it and saw from the caller ID, it was Spencer again.

"Yo," she said.

"What was the name of the club?"

"Don't know, signage is gone. Why?"

"Curious more than anything. Ask Baxter if he knows."

She did. Rene looked momentarily perplexed, then grinned. "The Cosmopolitan," he said. "Was the hot place for about a year. Sported a bar made out of ice."

She relayed the information; Spencer whistled. "That place belonged to Aunt Patti's friend June. And her brother Riley. They shut it down after Katrina. Didn't know they'd decided to sell."

"Bet they didn't know their listing agent was a drug dealer. I might need to question them. Got a number?"

He gave it to her and hung up.

While she had been on the phone, Buster had searched the rest of the space—and come up empty.

"Next address?" Stacy asked, eager to move on.

Rene must have been eager as well; he agreed with no mention of tacos at all.

Three and a half hours later, they had visited fifteen of the thirty addresses—and Buster had alerted at every one of them.

They had Gabrielle now. He had been using his listings as drop-off and pickup points for his meth business. The storage place had been the same in every one—an air-conditioning vent.

Rather ingenious, Stacy thought, using vacant commercial properties. A "Realtor" meets "prospective buyers." No chance of neighbors becoming suspicious at the comings and goings of strangers.

Just another real estate showing.

Too bad Gabrielle was dead. She would have loved busting him.

Too bad for Borger, too. At present she was their only link to Gabrielle's drug trade.

As she and Baxter wolfed down Mexican fast food, they decided to split up. He would continue on with Buster and Bob while she would start questioning property owners, mostly as a formality.

Beginning with Patti's friends, the Bensons. Curiously, they owned three of the properties on Yvette's list.

As a courtesy, she notified Patti.

"I'll bet they're at the gallery," she said. "Pieces. On Julia Street. If you don't mind, I'll meet you there."

"No problem at all. I'm leaving now."

Patti was waiting in her car when Stacy arrived. Stacy climbed out of her SUV and together they crossed to the gallery's double glass doors and stepped inside.

The current exhibition was of large, vigorously executed paintings, their subject matter highly abstracted portraits and landscapes. Like the art galleries she had visited before—and there had been many as her sister, Jane, was an artist—the interior was spare, the walls white, the floors muted. In this case, stained, scored concrete.

Nothing about the interior would distract, clash or interfere with the artwork.

June stood behind an elegant writing desk located between the two viewing rooms. She was on the phone. When she spotted them, her face lit up. "I've got to go. I'll call you back."

"Patti!" she cried, hurrying over. "What a surprise!"

She hugged Patti, then turned to her with a warm smile. "Stacy, it's good to see you again."

Stacy returned the smile. "Likewise."

The woman shifted her gaze back to Patti expectantly. "Please tell me you've finally decided to add some color to your walls? Something other than Jazz Fest and Mardi Gras posters?"

"Like there's enough for real art in my civil servant's salary."

"I'd make you a deal."

"I'm sure you would. One I still couldn't afford."

Stacy stepped in. "Actually, we're here to question you about a couple pieces of property you and Riley have for sale. Three, to be exact."

Riley burst out of the back, cell phone clutched in his hand. "June! I sold that piece to—" He saw them and stopped, a huge smile spreading across his face. "Aunt Patti, what a nice surprise."

He kissed her cheek, then turned to Stacy and grinned. "I didn't know you were an art lover, Stacy."

"I'd better be. If I wasn't, my sister'd be pretty pissed at me."

"Your sister?"

"Jane."

He stared at her a moment, looking stunned. "*Jane Killian's* your sister?"

"I thought you knew."

His face took on an expression of delight. "My God, I love her work. She's a genius!"

Stacy laughed. There was a time that statement would have

bothered her. Her and Jane's relationship had come a long way in the past couple of years.

All it had taken was a maniac trying to kill Jane—and damn near succeeding.

"I'll tell her you said so."

"Does she have local representation?"

He reminded her a bit of Buster, big and enthusiastic, nearly quivering over the possibility of a "find."

He caught her hand. "We're having an opening Saturday night. I'd love it if you came."

"Riley!" June admonished him. "Stop flirting with her. She's spoken for."

"No ring," he teased, smile widening. "I can flirt if I want."

It occurred to her that this was the second time in recent days someone had made a similar comment—*no ring, no commitment.*

"I apologize for my brother's exuberance," June said, scowling at her sibling.

"Please, don't apologize. He's right. I'm not wearing a ring."

Patti's mouth dropped and June looked distraught. Stacy cleared her throat. "That didn't come out quite the way I planned. I only meant that Riley didn't do anything wrong."

"Thank you," he said with exaggerated solemnity. "So, will you come Saturday?"

"It's Shauna's show, isn't it? Spencer and I will be here along with the rest of the Malone clan."

He sighed dramatically and released her hands. "The Malones get all the best ones. Always have."

"Oh, stop it," June scolded. "Patti and Stacy are here on official business. Let them do their jobs."

Instead of being chastened, he looked delighted. "By all means, don't let me stand in the way of justice."

Patti grabbed the opening. "You have three pieces of commercial property for sale, listed with Gabrielle Realty. Is that correct?"

"It is," June answered. "After Katrina, we decided to divest of some of our holdings. The businesses were all devastated by the storm. We lost tenants, had to fight with insurance companies, deal with repairs and all that entailed."

"We decided it wasn't worth it," Riley offered. "Life's too short."

"Why did you choose to list with Marcus Gabrielle?"

She looked uncomfortable. "I read about his murder. It was...horrible. Shot down like that, in his own driveway."

She rubbed her arms. "I thought this city was over that. I thought Katrina had taught us all something."

Dream on. Unfortunately, the criminal element was never "changed" for long. In fact, murders were significantly up, though mostly turf wars between rival gangs.

June sighed. "He was a good customer of ours. A true patron of the arts. When we decided to sell the properties, we chose to return the favor."

"I liked him," Riley offered. "He seemed like a good guy."

Stacy didn't disabuse him of the notion, though she found it almost funny. The "good guy" cheated on his wife, physically bullied his girlfriend and manufactured and distributed meth.

Stacy stepped in. "Did he ever come in with people you'd describe as unsavory? Or whom you were surprised to see him with?"

"No," June replied. "He mostly came alone. Or with his wife."

"No one else?"

"And once with that agent of his. What was her name?" She looked at her brother.

"Trudy," he answered, "short gray hair."

The same agent who had escorted them to the properties today.

"What's this all about?" June asked, as if suddenly questioning their visit and interview.

"Just following every lead," Stacy said smoothly.

"Any suspects?" Riley asked.

"We're working on it."

"I've thought of his wife and kids so often in the past few days," June murmured. "Such a tragedy."

The gallery phone jangled; Riley excused himself to answer it.

"If you think of anything, June, please call."

"I will, of course." She walked them to the gallery entrance. "We're still on for brunch tomorrow?" she asked Patti when they reached it.

"Absolutely. You still making eggs Sardou?"

She said she was. From inside, Riley called for his sister. "See you Saturday," she said, then ducked back into the gallery.

As the late afternoon sunshine spilled over them, Patti looked at Stacy. "Want to tell me what's going on?"

"What do you mean?"

"You and Spencer."

"Nothing's going on."

"Are you fighting?"

Stacy shook her head. "With all due respect, Patti, I think that's a little personal."

"Not in this family."

She was right. There was no worry of dysfunctional secrets or deeply harbored hurts in the Malone family. They pretty much laid it all out for everyone to see.

"We're not fighting," she said. "But we are talking about me getting my own place."

"It finally happened. We all told him it would if he didn't commit. We warned him he'd lose you."

Well, that explained his proposal. Family pressure. Screws applied and turned.

"You've got it all wrong, Patti. He asked me to marry him. I said no."

The older woman looked confused. "But you and he—"

"He doesn't love me," Stacy said softly. "And I want someone who does. I think I deserve that."

Patti's cell phone buzzed, cutting her off. Sending Stacy an apologetic glance, she answered. "Captain O'Shay."

Stacy watched as Patti listened, her expression sharpening. "Thank you for letting me know. I'm coming now."

She snapped the phone closed and looked at Stacy. "That was Alison Mackenzie from FACES. The City Park Jane Doe's facial reconstruction is complete."

31

Saturday, April 28, 2007
8:45 p.m.

By the time Yvette clocked in that night, she had worked up a fierce case of righteous indignation. Of course Detectives Malone and Killian hadn't believed her. If a teacher, nurse or librarian had presented them with the same story, they would have jumped right on it. But a stripper? Oh no, with her they needed "proof."

Typical cops.

What had she been thinking, turning to them? How could she have hoped they would protect her?

When had the cops, or anybody else, ever protected her?

The one calling himself the Artist had killed Marcus. He was obsessed with her, had been in her home several times. He had killed Marcus "for her."

If Detectives Malone and Killian wanted proof, she'd get it for them.

She didn't know why it was suddenly so important that they believe her, that she prove she was right, but it was.

Tonya poked her head into Yvette's dressing area. "Just checking on you. Everything okay?"

Yvette smiled grimly. "I haven't heard from him again, if that's what you're wondering."

"He hasn't been in, either, but I'm on the lookout. If he shows tonight, I'll know it."

"If he does, let me know right away."

Tonya nodded. "I was thinking, I've seen him in here before this. Before the storm."

Yvette had landed the job at the Hustle after Katrina. The Hustle was one of the first clubs to reopen—and they had needed girls. Besides, it had been a nice step up for her.

"He liked another girl," Tonya said.

A lump formed in Yvette's throat. "Who?"

"Jessica Skye. She was real popular. Blond. Blue-eyed. Great body."

Yvette felt cold suddenly. She rubbed her arms. "Where'd she go?"

"Quit. Evacuated for the storm."

"She ever say anything about some guy creeping her out?"

"Not a thing."

Tonya started out the door, then stopped and looked back. "If he comes in tonight, what are you going to do?"

"I don't know. Get a look at him for sure."

"The thing about this guy is, he doesn't look scary. He's kind of dumpy. Smallish. Wears thick, clunky glasses. You know, like Clark Kent or pre-spider-bite Peter Parker."

Yvette nodded and thanked the woman. Alone again, she turned back to the mirror to finish applying makeup.

Only two of the girls presently working the Hustle— Autumn and Gia—had been here before the storm.

Yvette wondered if they would remember Jessica, and if they did, whether she had said anything about an admirer who called himself the Artist.

Both of the other women were working tonight, so she planned to speak to them before their shifts ended.

The rest of the evening crawled by. Yvette now understood what it meant to be on pins and needles. She felt as if her every nerve was on the alert, waiting for Tonya to signal that "he" was here. As she danced, her thoughts were consumed with him. Was he watching her? Planning his next move? Sensing her fear, getting off on it?

Tonya's signal never came. A part of her had been relieved, another part frustrated. She wanted to see him for herself, look into his eyes and know what she was dealing with.

Tonight she would have to content herself with talking to Gia and Autumn. She caught Gia first, sitting at the bar after closing.

Yvette took the stool next to hers. "Hi, Gia."

"Hey, Vette," the woman responded, her voice a soft, deep drawl. "You had a good night?"

"Not my best, but decent. How about you?"

"Same. Beats the hell out of what I'd make at Dillard's," she said, referring to a local department store chain.

"Got a question about a girl who danced here before Katrina. Jessica Skye. You remember her?"

"Sure, Jess was a sweetie."

"You ever hear from her?"

"Nope. She left for the storm. That's the last I heard from her." She lit a cigarette and took a long drag. "Why?"

"I'm getting letters from this dude who calls himself the Artist. Tonya's thinking he used to request Jessica a lot."

"Tonya said that?"

Yvette nodded. "I wondered if he sent her the same kind of letters."

"She never mentioned it to me. We didn't have that kind of relationship."

"She never said anything about being stalked, creeped out or anything?"

"Sorry."

"She have a boyfriend?"

"Not that I know of. Hard to do what we do and have a real relationship." Gia took a last drag on her smoke, then drained her cocktail. "I'm beat. See you tomorrow."

As she stood to go, Yvette touched her arm. "Autumn still around?"

"She took off already." The woman frowned slightly, then leaned her head toward Yvette's. "Word of advice?"

Yvette turned slightly and met her eyes. She nodded.

"I wouldn't trust Tonya farther than I could throw her. She's in it for Tonya. Always."

Long after the other woman walked away, Yvette sat at the bar, nursing her drink, the things Gia had said ringing in her head.

I wouldn't trust Tonya farther than I could throw her. Hard to do what we do and have a real relationship.

And not just a romantic one but any relationship. She didn't have any friends. Not real friends, anyway. The kind you trusted and turned to for understanding and support. No family. No boyfriend.

She thought of Marcus and wanted to laugh. There'd been no affection there, no respect. The attraction for her had been money, for him sex. Or something like it.

The guys she met were either already in a relationship and looking for some action on the side, or were freaks, like her buddy the Artist.

And if a regular Joe stumbled in here, he wouldn't want someone like her.

What's your girlfriend do? She's a dancer down at the Hustle.

And if the guy was proud of that—or worse, turned on by it—he was a creep. If he approved of what she did because of the money, he was a pimp and a creep.

Problem was, for a woman who made a living shaking her tits and ass, she had some pretty conservative ideas about love.

But maybe they all did. They operated outside the mainstream but longed to live—and love—inside it.

Tonya took the stool next to hers. "You talked to Gia."

It wasn't a question. Yvette answered, anyway. "She remembered Jessica, but Jessica never mentioned the Artist or receiving any creepy letters."

"What about Autumn?"

"I missed her."

"She's dancing tomorrow night." Tonya stood. "C'mon. I'll give you a lift home."

Yvette hesitated.

I wouldn't trust Tonya farther than I could throw her.

She opened her mouth to ask why the woman was being so nice to her, then shut it, question unspoken. Fact was, she needed someone to trust—and nobody else was available.

32

Sunday, April 29, 2007
Noon

Yvette hadn't slept well. She had tossed and turned, troubled by nightmares of faceless women running for their lives. In each dream, when they'd had nowhere left to run, Yvette had realized *she* was the woman. And that she was going to die.

Thunder rumbled in the dark sky outside her kitchen window. It had been raining since long before daybreak. The weather certainly wasn't lightening her mood.

The front intercom sounded. Yvette answered.

"It's Tonya." The woman's voice shook. "Can I come up?"

"I'll buzz you in."

The woman was winded and wet when she reached Yvette's apartment. She clutched part of a newspaper to her chest. "You have anything to drink?"

"Juice or cof—"

"Something stronger. Bloody Mary?"

"No tomato juice. Screwdriver?"

Tonya collapsed onto one of the kitchen chairs. "Make it strong."

Yvette did, quickly adding vodka to a glass of orange juice. She set it on the table in front of Tonya, then took a seat across from her.

The woman picked up the glass, gulped down half the drink, then carefully laid the newspaper on the table, facing Yvette.

It was the Metro Section. Yvette looked at the newspaper, no clue as to what Tonya wanted her to see.

Tonya reached across the table and tapped the paper. "That's her. Jessica, the girl I told you about."

Yvette stared at the image. Not a photograph. A police artist's rendering, in clay. She scanned the paragraph that described the woman. The police were trying to identify the "Jane Doe" and asking the public for help.

Yvette dragged her gaze from the image to look at Tonya once more. "Are you sure?"

"Absolutely. I'm so freaked out."

"But that means she's—"

"Dead." Tonya drained the drink. She held up the empty glass. "Mind if I refill?"

She told her to help herself, though it seemed obvious the one she had just guzzled hadn't been her first. Did she always drink like this, or was she that rattled?

Tonya mixed the drink, then looked back at Yvette. "And not just dead, murdered. Otherwise they wouldn't be trying to ID her."

Yvette stared at her a moment, the reason Tonya had rushed over here sinking in. "Oh, my God," she said. "You don't think he...that the Artist killed her, do you?"

"Maybe. He liked her. She disappeared. And you think he killed Marcus."

Yvette felt ill. "You're sure it's her?"

Tonya nodded. "Read the description. It fits her to a T. Age, height—"

"But lots of women—"

"No. Read that again. Jessica had really crooked teeth. She hardly ever smiled because of them. They make a point of mentioning them."

Tonya sipped the drink, expression intent. "She was beautiful except for those teeth. She talked about getting braces but was afraid they'd turn the guys off."

Yvette pushed the paper away, unable to look at the representation a moment longer. She realized she was shaking. And that she was scared.

"What do we do now? Go to the police?" Even as she asked the question, she wondered if Tonya's word would be enough to convince them.

The other woman's response seemed to echo her thoughts.

"We need proof that the creep writing you those letters was also writing Jess."

"How do we do that?"

"You talk to Autumn tonight, and I'll do a little snooping."

33

Saturday, May 5, 2007
8:25 p.m.

It'd been a quiet week. Blessedly so. No notes or packages from the Artist. No mysterious women claiming to be somebody's mother stealing keys or breaking in.

Yvette wondered if the reconstruction in the paper had scared him off. If he had, indeed, murdered Jessica Skye, maybe knowing she had been found and that the police were investigating had made him decide to take off.

She hadn't exactly lowered her guard, but she had relaxed it.

She'd spoken to Autumn. The dancer remembered Jess, but like Gia, didn't recall her saying she had a freaky fan or that she was feeling threatened or uncomfortable about anything.

Autumn hadn't heard from the other dancer since Katrina, but figured she'd blown out of town as Katrina blew in. Like just about everyone else in the Big Easy.

Yvette had shown her the likeness from the newspaper, but Autumn had been less certain it was Jessica. The description fit, but she remembered Jess being much prettier.

Yvette had vowed to put all thoughts of the Artist aside for the evening. She had taken a day shift so she could have the night off. It was the last Art Walk of the season, when the galleries throughout the art district coordinated their show openings, serving wine and cheese to art lovers who strolled from one exhibit to the next.

Yvette loved Art Walks. She loved the diversity of the crowd, from the young and old, rich and poor, traditional to pretty damn whacked—and everything in between. The only common thread between them, an appreciation for the arts.

And she totally got off sipping wine with strangers and pretending to be someone she wasn't—sophisticated and smart.

Yvette left the Gallery 1-1-1 and started toward Pieces. She walked with a couple she had been chatting to about the previous gallery's exhibit of Katrina-inspired monoprints.

She acknowledged to herself that she'd had too much to drink. Her head buzzed pleasurably and her feet felt light as air. She parted from the other couple and made her way into Pieces.

Works by Shauna M.

The paintings were big, bold and energetic. Yvette decided right off that she wanted to buy one, though it would have to be a small one—she was simply running out of wall space.

She caught sight of the featured artist, who was easy to pick out as she was surrounded by admirers. Yvette tilted her head. Pretty and petite, with dark hair and a brilliant smile, Shauna M. didn't look that much older than her.

Yvette gazed at the other woman, a pinch of envy in the pit of her gut. She used to draw a lot. When she was supposed to be listening to her teachers. When her parents left her alone. After her mother's accident, to escape her sorrow—and her fear.

She had dreamed of being an artist one day.

It would have been a stupid thing for her to pursue. She didn't have the talent. Her drawings had been little more than childish doodles. When she'd made the mistake of sharing her dream, her father had told her so. To spare her the pain of wishful thinking, he'd said.

It hurt to remember. How pitying he had been. And how amused. He had teased her for years afterward.

Swallowing hard, Yvette shifted her gaze. A man was with Shauna M., his hand possessively on her shoulder. He was intensely handsome, with dark hair and eyes. Angular, chiseled face. An artist himself, she would bet. He had the "look."

She wanted that, Yvette acknowledged. To be Shauna M. To have what she had—the show, the accolades, the guy.

Suddenly the man turned his head. His dark gaze seemed to search her out. They stared at each other. She felt her face flood with color. As if reading her thoughts, his lips lifted in a mocking smile.

Embarrassed, she turned quickly away, pretending to look

for someone. She spotted the bar and started for it. Halfway there, she heard a voice she recognized.

Detective Killian.

Yvette stopped and turned in the direction of the voice. The woman stood not twelve feet from her. Detective Malone was with her. They seemed to be admiring a painting. Seemed to be. Could they be following her? But why would they be?

She studied them. They stood close, too close for colleagues. While she watched, Malone laid a hand on the small of Killian's back, the gesture familiar and intimate.

They were a couple, she realized. For all she knew, they could be husband and wife.

For all she knew.

Everything Brandi had told her had been a lie.

The pleasure drained from what remained of her evening. To hell with this. She was out of here. She'd go have a drink where she fit in, with people like her.

She turned and nearly ran into the dark-haired man who'd been at Shauna M.'s side. He caught her arms to steady her. "Whoa. Sorry about that."

"It really was my fault. Sorry."

He smiled, revealing beautiful, perfectly aligned white teeth. She couldn't help but think of Jessica Skye.

"She hardly ever smiled because of them."

"Rich Ruston," he said, holding out his hand.

She took it. "Yvette Borger."

"You like the show, Yvette?"

"Very much." She ignored the butterflies in her stomach. "Are you a friend of the artist?" she asked.

"I am. Are you?"

"Just an art lover."

"Not an artist?"

She hesitated, then replied that she wasn't, wishing with all her heart that she could answer differently. "You are, though."

"I am." He smiled again. "How did you know?"

"I just did."

"Can I get you a glass of wine?"

"Thank you. White."

He returned a moment later with two plastic cups, one red and the other white. He handed her the chardonnay. She took a sip.

"Would you like to see my favorite piece in the show?" he asked.

He led her across the gallery. She felt unsteady on her feet and concentrated on putting one foot in front of the other. How many glasses of wine had she had?

They stopped in front of the small piece, not more than ten inches square. She sipped the wine again. And again. Someone jostled her; wine sloshed over the rim of her cup.

She turned and blinked.

The woman was here, the one who had claimed to be both her and Nancy's mother. The woman who had used those lies to gain access to her apartment.

"…a jewel," he was saying. "Powerful and intimate."

Head buzzing, she watched as the woman crossed to Malone and Killian and hugged them.

Hugged them?

What was going on? A cop conspiracy? Were they playing a game with her?

"What is it?" he asked as she swayed against him. He cupped her elbow. "Are you all right?"

"That woman," she managed. "I recognize—"

She brought a hand to her head.

"Yvette? Are you... Perhaps you should si—"

"Fi...jus'a bi'too much wi—"

The buzz in her head became a roar. Her knees went weak, then gave out.

Her world went black.

34

Saturday, May 5, 2007
9:00 p.m.

When Yvette came to, she lay on the floor, a half dozen people staring down at her. She blinked, confused. She'd been talking to that cute guy...Rich... She'd seen the woman...the one who—

"Yvette? Are you all right?"

That came from Detective Malone. She looked at him, focusing. Vision clearing. Detective Killian knelt beside him.

She didn't answer, moving her gaze over the cluster of faces. Rich's wasn't among them. Neither was the woman's.

"You fainted," the detective said.

"I saw her," she said. "She was here."

"Who?"

"The woman who broke into my apartment."

The two detectives exchanged glances, then turned toward a kind-looking woman hovering nearby. "June, let's give her some air."

The woman nodded, then shooed everyone off.

"She *was* here," Yvette said again, struggling to get up. "You're letting her—"

Then she remembered the woman hugging them both. "You know her!"

"Calm down—"

"You hugged her!" She struggled to her feet, feeling light-headed. "What is this, some weird cop game?"

Her voice rose. She realized her shirt and pants were wet. When she'd fainted, she had spilled the remainder of her wine on herself.

Detective Killian took a step forward, hand out. "Take it easy, Yvette. You've had a shock."

"You're damn right I've had a shock!" She backed up. "Get away from me, liars."

She knew she sounded like a crazy person but didn't care.

The woman named June laid a hand on the detective's arm. "You're upsetting her more," she said softly. "Let me take care of this."

They backed off, and she stepped forward. "My name's June Benson. This is my brother, Riley." She indicated a tall, curly-haired man. "We own this gallery. Can I do something to help you?"

Yvette became aware of the number of people still in the gallery, of them looking at her. Of the artist's horrified expression. Heat stung her cheeks. "Keep them away from me. Please."

"Done." She smiled reassuringly. "How about a glass of water or a Coke?"

"Thank you. A Coke."

June Benson led her into a back room of the gallery that looked to serve as an employee lounge.

"Sit down. Please."

Yvette did, grateful.

"Are you all right?"

She nodded.

"Have you fainted before?"

"No, I…no."

"Do you have any idea why you did tonight?"

Yvette frowned. "I'd probably had too much wine, but…this has never—"

"Have you eaten?"

"Enough. Cheese and crackers on the Art Walk. A bowl of cereal before I left home."

"What were you doing before you fainted?"

"Talking to Rich Ruston. He brought me a glass of wine."

"Really?" She frowned. "Could he have slipped something in it?"

"He could have, but why would—"

Stupid. She knew why. A date-rape drug. She was an easy mark. Woman alone. Already tipsy.

Why had she thought an art opening would be any safer than a bar?

Riley Benson appeared in the doorway. He looked concerned. "You okay?"

"Yes, thanks. Sorry for making such a scene."

"Don't worry about it. It wasn't your fault." He shifted his gaze to June. "Nell Nolan from the *Times-Picayune* is asking for you. Wants a quote."

"Nell Nolan? The social-scene writer?"

"The very one. With a photographer."

"Can't you—"

"You're much better at those sound bites than I am." When she hesitated a moment more, he waved her on. "I'll stay."

She agreed, though she didn't look thrilled. "I'll be back. Drink that Coke. The sugar will help."

"She's sweet," Yvette said.

"As pie," he responded, though something in his tone led her to believe he didn't agree. No doubt Big Sister didn't hesitate to break Little Brother's balls whenever she thought he needed it.

"I should go," she said. "I feel fine now."

"Finish your drink first. Let the crowd thin a bit more."

So they didn't stare at her when she left.

Tears stung her eyes at his kindness. Silly to be affected that way, she supposed. But the truth was, people usually weren't all that kind to her.

"Did you like the show?"

"What I saw of it, yes."

"Shauna's a friend. I've known her since we were kids. She's really talented."

Not knowing how to respond, she sipped her soft drink.

"What do you do?"

"I'm a dancer."

"Cool." He smiled at her and she decided he had one of the nicest smiles she'd ever seen. Really warm. Cute. He even had a dimple in his right cheek.

"They say all the creative arts are intertwined. Writing, music, dance, visual arts."

"I used to love to draw."

"There you go."

She didn't have the heart to tell him her "creative art" involved taking off her clothes; no sense spoiling his perfectly good theory.

"It's gotten quiet," she murmured.

"I'll take a peek."

He stood, crossed to the door and looked out. He grinned back at her. "A few stragglers. Nell's looking the other way."

She returned his smile and stood. "Thanks."

"I'll walk you to your car."

"I cabbed."

"Then I'll drive you home."

"I've already taken too much of your time."

"It's no trouble. After all, you nearly died in my gallery."

She laughed at that. "If you insist, but it's really not—"

"I do insist."

They exited the gallery back room. June stood talking with

Shauna and a tall thin man who sported a goatee and a spiral-bound notebook.

Shauna saw them, excused herself and crossed to them. She smiled at Yvette. "Are you okay?"

Her face heated. "I'm fine. I'm so sorry for disrupting your show. I don't know what happened."

The artist's smile looked a little stiff. "It's not your fault. Really."

"I like your work, by the way. It's great."

"Thanks. I'm—"

"Shauna?" June joined them. "Why don't you see Robert to the door. He may have another question or two."

"Art critic for the *T-P*," June said as Shauna walked away. She turned her gaze on Yvette. "You're feeling better?"

"She is," Riley said, answering for her. "She doesn't have a car, so I'm going to drive her home."

The woman frowned slightly. Yvette jumped in. "I don't want to cause any more troub—"

"It's no trouble," he said. "Trouble would be waiting an hour for a cab. After all, this *is* post-Katrina New Orleans."

June didn't respond, though Yvette could tell she wasn't happy about the turn of events. Yvette thanked her again and left with Riley.

He led her across the street to a small, private parking lot. Using a remote, he opened the electronic gate, then led her to his vehicle, a sleek, black Infiniti sedan.

He helped her in, then went around to the driver's side. "Where to?" he asked.

"Not far. Dauphine and Governor Nicholls. In the French Quarter."

He looked disappointed and she drew her eyebrows together. "What?"

"I was hoping you lived clear across town."

Yvette steeled herself against the warmth that stole over her at his flirting and changed the subject. "Your sister didn't want you to do this. I could tell."

"She's a bit overprotective."

"She thinks you need to be protected from me?"

He laughed. "You're right. Let me amend that. She's a bit controlling."

"But nice." She leaned back in her seat. The leather was pure luxury.

"We're fifteen years apart. And since both our parents were dead by my sixteenth birthday, she was stuck raising me. I guess she's earned the right to be controlling."

"I guess she has."

"You want to get something to eat?"

She looked at him in surprise. "Okay."

"Camellia Grill's open late."

She said that sounded great and ten minutes later they were seated across from each other in a booth, hungrily considering menu choices.

After they'd ordered, she said, "Shauna was angry at me."

"She wasn't."

"How do you know? She looked—"

"A little pissed. She was. But not at you. Her boyfriend. The guy you were talking to when you went down."

"Rich?"

"Yeah, Rich."

His tone made it clear he didn't have a high opinion of the other man. They fell silent a moment. Finally Yvette cleared her throat. "He came up to me. I didn't approach him."

"I know. I saw."

She gazed into her coffee, wondering if he had seen the way she had looked at Shauna—with yearning to have the things she had. With envy.

"You didn't do anything wrong, you know," he said softly, breaking the silence.

"I knew he was with her, but I let him bring me a drink and—"

"He's a dog, Yvette. Not a nice guy. I've told Shauna that. Tonight she saw it for herself."

"I'm sorry."

"For what?" He frowned. "You say that a lot."

"Don't judge by tonight. I had reason to."

"I disagree."

She ignored that and reached for her water. "Besides, I'm sorry for her. I've been there. It hurts."

"Yeah, it does."

They fell silent. Yvette sipped her water and Riley gazed out the window. "What was all that about? With Spencer and Stacy?"

"Who?"

"The detectives. Spencer Malone and Stacy Killian."

"You know them?"

"Sure. They're old friends. Well, Spencer is. He's Shauna's brother."

The "M." Now she got it. Great.

"How do *you* know them?" he asked.

"A guy I knew was murdered. They questioned me."

"About the murder?" His eyebrows shot up. "They don't think you had any—"

"Anything to do with it?" She shook her head. "No, nothing like that. I occasionally showed real estate for him. They wanted names of business partners, stuff like that."

"You're talking about Marcus Gabrielle, aren't you?"

She felt the blood drain from her face. "How did you know?"

"They questioned June and me. Gabrielle was listing some property for us. We knew him because he was one of our clients."

"Small town."

"And a lot smaller since the storm."

The waitress brought their food, big plates of greasy hash browns with onions and peppers, covered in cheese. He had two fried eggs and toast with his.

As they dug in, he asked, "So what was the deal? At the gallery you said something about seeing the woman who broke into your apartment?"

Yvette considered telling him she'd been confused, but decided on the truth instead.

She trusted him, though she didn't know why. There was just something about him that inspired it.

She laid down her fork and leaned toward him. "A woman claiming to be my mother tricked my neighbor into giving her a key to my apartment. I caught the woman just as she was leaving, though I didn't realize it."

She quickly filled in the details, then added, "She was at your gallery tonight. She hugged Spencer and Stacy."

"What did she look like?"

"Medium height and trim. Short reddish hair. Fiftyish."

He took a forkful of the potatoes, expression thoughtful as he chewed and swallowed. "You're talking about Aunt Patti. You have to be."

"Aunt Patti?" she repeated, feeling as if she had been sucker-punched.

"She's not really my aunt. She and June are practically lifelong friends. She's Spencer's aunt and also his captain."

"She's a *cop?*"

He smiled at her incredulous tone. "A highly respected and, I might add, somewhat feared captain."

What the hell was going on? What were they up to?

"There's no way she broke into your apartment," Riley added.

"It was her, I know it."

He shrugged. "The Patti O'Shay I know lives and dies by the book, though I could ask June—"

"No, don't." She shook her head. "In fact, forget I said anything. You're probably right. I'd had too much wine and wasn't thinking clearly."

He leaned forward. "So how are you going to find the woman who sneaked into your apartment?"

She already had. Captain Patti O'Shay was in for a very big surprise.

"I don't know," she answered. "Maybe I never will and that's okay."

"Be careful, Yvette. There are some crazy, dangerous people out there."

And their being cops made them even more dangerous.

"I will," she promised. "Believe me, I will."

Sunday, May 6, 2007
9:25 a.m.

Sunday, May 6, 2007
9:25 a.m.

Yvette awakened feeling really good. Refreshed. Happy. She smiled and stretched, thinking of Riley and the weird events of the night before.

She had invited him up. They had talked until late. Talked—and nothing else.

He hadn't expected sex. Hadn't pushed or pouted when she didn't initiate.

Though he *had* kissed her when they said goodbye. It'd been long and deep—and had totally turned her on.

She wanted to let herself like him. Wanted to trust all her

first impressions of him: that he was genuine and kind, a true gentleman. That he really liked her.

Don't be an idiot, Yvette. Too good to be true is just that—too good to be true.

Yvette climbed out of bed and headed to the bathroom to brush her teeth. That done, she went to the kitchen for a Coke. She popped the can's top and took a long swallow of the sweet, fizzy drink.

Breakfast of champions. Her personal power drink.

She saw that the message light on her cell phone was blinking, snatched up the device and checked the ID. Tonya's number, she saw. She had called the night before. After 1:00 a.m. Yvette dialed voice mail, then punched in her password.

"It's me. He was here tonight. I've got a plan. Call me on my cell as soon as you get this. Bye."

Yvette deleted the message, then dialed the woman back. The call rolled into voice mail, which didn't surprise her. Anything before noon was early for someone who worked until 2:00 a.m.

"Hi, Tonya," Yvette said. "Got your message. What did you do? How did he react when he learned I wasn't there? Call me."

She pocketed the phone, then shuffled to the living room and plopped onto the couch. She sipped her drink, recalling what Riley had told her: The woman who had broken into her apartment was a cop. A captain.

Captain Patti O'Shay. Spencer Malone's aunt.

What had she been up to? Did it have something to do with Marcus and their investigation into his drug business?

She tried Tonya once more, unsurprised when voice mail picked up again. "I forgot to mention, I have stuff to tell you, too. I know the identity of the woman who broke into my place. She's a cop! Call me."

She ended the call, thoughts returning to Riley. She really did like him. And for today, if she wanted to delude herself that he felt the same about her, she would. And have a great time doing it, too.

She leapt to her feet, deciding to start right away.

Yvette enjoyed her day. She shopped at the French Market, poked in and out of stores on Royal Street, enjoyed beignets and coffee at Café du Monde. All the while, she kept her cell phone close, waiting for Tonya to call and hoping Riley would.

She was disappointed on both counts.

She didn't stress too much about Tonya's lack of response. She would see her at the Hustle tonight. But she had so badly wanted Riley to call. She had thought after that kiss, he would.

He had found out what kind of dancer she was.

It would have been easy. A call to his friends Killian and Malone. She wouldn't hear from him again, she realized. She might as well move on now.

Even as she told herself it was no big deal, she acknowledged that it hurt.

In the hopes of having time to talk to Tonya, Yvette arrived at the Hustle thirty minutes early. "Hi, Dante," she said, greeting the bleached-blond steroid-bloated bouncer.

"Hey, Vette."

"Tonya here?"

"Haven't seen her."

"Really?" She glanced at her watch. Tonya was always here by now. "That's weird."

"I might've missed her. Check the time clock."

She did and discovered the other woman had not clocked in. An uneasy feeling plucked at her. Tonya had left an urgent-sounding message, asking Yvette to call her back ASAP, then disappeared. Why would she do that?

She wouldn't.

Something was wrong.

Yvette shook the thought off. Marcus's murder and this whole Artist thing was getting to her. Causing her imagination to run wild.

Tonya was late. It happened. She'd show. And have a perfectly reasonable explanation.

Yvette decided she would feel pretty silly, especially if she called and left *another* message.

She did, anyway. Then another and another. With each message left—and each hour that crawled past—her panic became more acute.

At closing, Tonya was still MIA. No notice to the club that she wouldn't be in. No claim of illness or anything else.

She just hadn't come in.

Something was wrong. Something had happened to her.

The Artist. He had been in the club the night before. Had Tonya confronted him? Followed him? Asked him about Jessica?

What did she do now?

Yvette realized she was trembling and hugged herself. She would wait until morning, she decided. See if Tonya called back. And if she didn't, she would decide what to do from there.

36

Monday, May 7, 2007
10:00 a.m.

Yvette waited as long as she could before calling a cab. Tonya owned a condo near City Park on Bayou St. John, with a balcony that overlooked the waterway. Pre-Katrina the property had been way out of her league. Tonya had snapped it up post-Katrina for a fraction of its pre-storm value.

Yvette knew all this because the woman had bragged about it at the time.

If Tonya wasn't there, she hadn't a clue how she would get in.

Luck seemed to be on her side when the driver dropped her off; Tonya's orange VW Beetle sat in a parking spot directly in front of the building.

Yvette hurried to the lobby call box. She found Tonya's name and rang for her. And got a busy signal. Relief washed over her. She had worried over nothing. Tonya would have a good explanation. She was sick, tired or both. She had decided the Hustle sucked and had taken a job elsewhere.

Yvette was going to kick Tonya's ass for making her worry like this.

Yvette rang again. And again got a busy signal. As she hung up, a man and woman, in a heated discussion about someone named Tim, exited. Yvette grabbed the door a moment before it snapped shut.

She located Tonya's unit and knocked. When the woman didn't answer, she knocked again.

"Tonya, it's me! Yvette."

Still no answer.

With a glance in either direction, Yvette tried the door. It was locked. She squatted and checked under the welcome mat for a key. When that proved futile, she tried the unit next door.

A little old man with stoop shoulders and white hair answered. Yvette decided he was ninety if he was a day.

"Hi," she said. "I'm a friend of Tonya's. Have you seen her?"

He shook his head. "Haven't heard her, either. Been quiet as a mouse." He smiled at her, though his gaze fixed on her chest. "'Course, when I take my hearing aid out, I couldn't hear the end of the world."

"She didn't show up for work and I'm pretty worried."

"Did you try the door?"

"It's locked. But her car's out front."

The wizened neighbor frowned. "I don't like the sound of that. She could need help."

"Exactly."

"I could get you a little look-see inside," he said proudly. "No problem."

"You could?" She batted her lashes at him. "That'd be swell."

He puffed up. "You just wait there."

A moment later, he reappeared with a key. "Tonya gave me a spare. To check on things when she's gone, take deliveries, stuff like that. I'm sure she wouldn't mind."

Yvette was sure, too.

"I help several of the neighbors this way." He shuffled across to her door. "You know, dear, this isn't exactly legal."

Flatly illegal was more like it.

"But since you're so worried about her—"

She leaned toward him to offer him a better view of her cleavage. "Thank you *so* much. You're a lifesaver."

Within moments he had the door open. "I'll wait right here," he offered. "Keep an eye out."

She thanked him and peaked inside the condo. "Tonya," she called. "It's Yvette."

She stepped inside. At first glance, nothing appeared out of place. Just the normal clutter of living. Tonya was neither a neat freak nor a slob.

Yvette called out again, cautiously making her way into the condo. She moved from living room to kitchen, from kitchen to first bedroom. Obviously a guest room. Pin-neat. Empty closet.

She made her way to the second bedroom. This one was noticeably larger than the other—and obviously occupied. Bed was unmade. Silky pajamas in a vivid coral color lay in a heap on the floor. Closet stuffed with clothes.

No blood. No body.

Thank God.

Taking a deep breath, she turned and started for the adjoining bath. The last place to search. The door was closed. With each step her heart beat faster, harder. She reached the door, grabbed the knob and twisted.

It eased open. She sucked in a sharp breath—for courage— and entered the room.

And found it empty.

Her relief was immediate and tangible, a physical wave that made her knees go weak. She crossed to the commode, lowered the lid and sank onto it, dropping her head into her hands.

Thank God…thank God. She had been certain she would find Tonya dead, in a pool of blood. Or at least signs of a desperate struggle.

Talk about a vivid imagination. The Artist was getting to her, making her jumpy, irrational.

"Everything okay in there?" the neighbor called, sounding anxious.

"Fine," she called back. "I'm on my way out."

Yvette got to her feet and headed for the front door, feeling a bit ridiculous. She and Tonya would have a good laugh about this—

She stopped, realization hitting her.

Tonya was still MIA.

So, where was she?

She turned and hurried back to the bathroom. Toothbrush and paste on the counter, cosmetics strewn about. Comb. Brush. Hairspray. A travel-size jewelry case, open, earrings and bracelets spilling out. Vehicle parked out front.

She could have taken a cab, but to where? Not the airport or train station, for she hadn't packed stuff for a trip. There was no way she'd have left without makeup and jewelry.

"Miss?" The neighbor stood in the doorway, looking at her strangely. "What's wrong?"

"I don't know," she answered, voice trembling. "But something is."

"Can I help?"

Yvette giggled, the sound nervous, high-pitched. She heard how she sounded—at the very least, bubbleheaded, at the worst, unhinged.

"I don't..." She clasped her hands together and met his concerned gaze. "I don't know what to do next."

37

Monday, May 7, 2007
11:25 a.m.

The neighbor—whose name she had learned over coffee was Bill—had helped her calm down and focus. She had briefly explained the situation; he had agreed it was troubling. If she was worried about her friend, she should go to the police. He had been adamant about that. And about the fact that every hour that passed made the possibility of helping Tonya, if she was in danger, more remote.

So here she stood at the information desk at police headquarters, asking for Captain Patti O'Shay.

She had decided to approach the woman for two reasons. First, she had something to hold over the woman's head, something to compel her to help. Second, she had told Detectives Malone and Killian about the Artist and they hadn't believed her. She had no confidence Tonya's disappearance would change that.

It was a bold move, she knew. And stupid, considering that all she really knew about the woman was that she had illegally entered her apartment. Who knew, perhaps *she* was the Artist? Captain O'Shay would not appreciate being blackmailed into helping her.

This could go badly—very. But she was willing to take the chance.

"I have information about one of her investigations," she told the desk officer. "The Handyman murders."

"The detectives on *that* case—"

"I won't speak to anyone but her."

The officer studied her a moment, eyes narrowed. "ID."

Shit. She should have anticipated this. She had planned to give a false name, afraid the captain would refuse to see her.

She dug her driver's license out of her wallet and slid it across the counter to him. He studied it a moment, then her. Finally he slid her a clipboard. "Sign in, Ms. Borger. I'll see if she's available."

Fingers crossed, she waited. She fully expected to be turned away or shuffled to another officer, so when, seconds later, he directed her to the elevators, she had to work to hide her surprise.

"Third floor. Captain O'Shay will meet you there."

Yvette followed his instructions, fighting back the nerves settled in her stomach. She was playing with potential fire here, confronting a police captain. Calling her out.

She didn't have much choice.

The elevator doors slid open. Captain Patti O'Shay stood waiting for her. "Ms. Borger. This is unexpected."

Yvette smiled, feigning confidence. "I'm sure it is. We need to talk. Privately."

The older woman nodded and motioned for Yvette to follow her. They didn't speak again until they had reached her office and she had shut the door. "Have a seat, Ms. Borger."

Yvette did, crossing her legs. "Let's not play around, I know what you did."

The captain didn't blink. "Really? And what would that be?"

"You tricked my neighbor into telling you where I keep a spare key to my apartment and you used it. I would call that illegally entering. When I caught you leaving, you used the same story. Unfortunate timing, wasn't it? For you, anyway."

"What do you want?"

Clever, moving the conversation forward without admitting to a thing.

"I could make a lot of trouble for you. I saw you. My neighbor Nancy saw you."

"Yes," she agreed, "you could. So what do you want?"

"First, I want to know why. Why my apartment? What were you looking for?"

"Information about your former roommate."

Yvette wasn't certain what she had expected, but it wasn't that. "Kitten?"

"Yes. You told Detective Killian you believed she was the City Park Jane Doe. I have a special interest in that case."

Yvette battled differing emotions—relief, anger, the desire
to punish the woman for making her afraid.

"If I'd called you in for questioning—"

"You would've blown 'Brandi's' cover."

She inclined her head slightly "Time was of the essence."

"Which makes it all right?"

"Hardly. Justifiable, at the time. To me."

Typical cop. The rights of people like her were completely expendable.

"I could fry you over this. I should."

"Have a ball." Patti leaned slightly forward. "What you don't
seem to understand, Ms. Borger, is that I have very little to lose.
So little, in fact, I'd chance it again to nail that bastard."

Welcome to the club. She understood having nothing to lose.
She had felt that way her whole life.

"You want something from me," the woman said.

"Yes. Your help." Captain O'Shay arched her eyebrows in
question; Yvette forged ahead. "My boss from the Hustle is
missing. I think she's in trouble."

"And you need me to…?"

"Sound the alarm. Find her. Save her."

"Have you filed a missing-persons report?"

"No! This isn't—" She changed tack. "Did Detective Malone
tell you about the Artist?"

"The letter-writing stalker you made up?"

"But I didn't make him up! He's been writing me…stalking
me. When I told that story about Kitten, he'd sent me a few
notes. I just…used him in my story. But now…I'm afraid." She
paused. "I think he killed Marcus."

"Gabrielle?"

"Yes. For me." She explained about coming home and finding his note. "It said, 'I did it for you.' He didn't sign it, but I know it was from him."

The other woman frowned. "And you relayed this to Detectives Malone and Killian?"

"Yes. They didn't believe me."

"They thought you were conning them."

"Why would I? Why create this—" She bit the words back because, of course, she had done exactly that before. To the captain's credit, she said nothing.

"Now I think he's killed Tonya. That's my boss, Tonya Messinger. She was trying to help me."

Captain O'Shay folded her hands on the desk but said nothing, her gaze fixed intently on Yvette.

"Tonya manages all the girls at the Hustle. The talent and the wait staff." She clasped her hands together. "Like I said, she was helping me."

"How so?"

"I told her about the Artist. His notes, how he broke into my apartment. She saw his note, the money—"

The captain cut her off. "Perhaps you should start at the beginning, Ms. Borger?"

So she did, sharing everything up to Tonya's recognizing Jessica. "She remembered that the guy writing me used to like another girl—" Yvette reached into her purse, retrieved the newspaper image of Jane Doe and laid the clipping on the desk in front of her. "*That* girl."

"My God," Captain O'Shay muttered. "You know who she is?"

"Yes. But first, I want your word you'll help me."

"You've got it. Name?"

"Jessica Skye. She danced at the Hustle. Disappeared with Katrina."

"She ever mention this Artist? Weird notes? Anything?"

Yvette shook her head. "She never said anything to Tonya. I asked the two girls who worked with Jessica, but she didn't say anything to them, either."

"You didn't know Jessica?"

She shook her head. "I didn't dance there before Katrina."

"So you didn't recognize her yourself?"

"No. Tonya did."

"What about the other girls at the Hustle? Did they ID her photo?"

"They weren't positive. But Tonya was absolutely certain it was her."

"The same Tonya who's missing now?"

Yvette stiffened. "I know what you're thinking and it's not true."

"What am I thinking, Ms. Borger?"

"That I'm full of shit. That I'm lying."

"Are you?" she asked calmly.

"No! Tonya was going to nose around. Alert me when the Artist came around."

"And did he?"

"Yes. The night I was at the Art Walk. She left a message on my cell phone. She wanted me to call her, she had an idea."

"What was it?"

"Don't know. I called her back, a bunch of times, but haven't heard a word since."

"Do you have the message?"

"I deleted it. I didn't know I'd need it." She realized her hands were sweating and rubbed them on her jeans. "She didn't show up for work Sunday night so this morning I visited her condo."

"And?"

Yvette swallowed past the lump that had formed in her throat. "Her car was there. Her stuff. But she...wasn't."

Captain O'Shay stood and went to stand at the single small window. She stared out several moments, expression thoughtful.

After what seemed an eternity to Yvette, she turned and faced her once more. "I have a question for you."

"Okay."

"Are you scared?" When Yvette gazed blankly at her, she went on. "You come in wanting my help. For your friend. What about you? If what you're telling me is true, a murderer has become obsessed with you."

A murderer has become obsessed with you.

Yvette went cold. She realized she had been so consumed with finding Tonya, so worried about her, she hadn't paused to consider just how much danger she might be in.

She could be next.

The woman was watching her intently, no doubt able to read her thoughts, the resulting fear, in her expression.

"He's worshipping you from afar. But he's privy to the intimate details of your life. Where you work and live. Who your friends are. Who your lover was. Probably the route you take home, your entire schedule."

"Why are you trying to frighten me?" Yvette asked, voice shaking.

"Just spelling it out. Giving you a little wake-up call."

Yvette stiffened her spine. "Will you help me?"

"Yes, though I need some time to think this through. To make a plan."

"How long?"

"The end of today."

"How do I know your plan isn't to eliminate me as soon as I'm out of here?"

The woman smiled at that. "I guess you'll just have to trust me."

"Tell me again why I should?"

"Because you don't really have a choice, Ms. Borger. You need me."

38

Monday, May 7, 2007
12:45 p.m.

Patti sat at her desk. What she had said to Yvette Borger had been true—the young woman needed her. But she, ISD captain and career NOPD, needed her just as much. Maybe more.

She wanted the Handyman that badly.

Not the Handyman, per se, but Sammy's killer. So badly she could taste it.

Borger had given her no proof. Nothing but her word to go on.

She believed her. Ironically. After a lifetime of analytically weighing evidence, objectively assessing witnesses and suspects, she was throwing it all away. Putting her trust in a known liar.

That's why Spencer hadn't bought Yvette's tale—she had fabricated the original story about Kitten. When Marcus Gabrielle had been killed, she had created a fictitious "business partner." Then she had approached them with the Artist again, without witnesses or proof.

Toss in a record and an admitted dislike for cops, only an idiot would take her at her word.

Captain Patti O'Shay, at your service.

She considered going to the chief, laying it all out for him, asking him to give her a chance. But if he refused, she was screwed.

And he would refuse. Chief Howard liked Franklin. She couldn't blame him. The guy was an ex-con; he'd been caught with the murder weapon in his possession. Unless she presented him with something really compelling, Chief Howard would not be swayed.

She had to go this one alone. That included leaving Spencer out of it.

Time to put all her ducks in a row.

First, a detective to question the two dancers who had known Jessica Skye. She had called the Hustle and obtained the necessary information from the general manager.

Standing, she crossed to her door and peered out to see who was available. As she did, Tony Sciame ambled across her line of vision, a Taco Bell bag clutched in his left hand.

"Detective Sciame, could I have a minute? Feel free to bring your lunch."

"Sure, Captain." He followed her into her office and plopped onto a chair. The smell of spicy meat and grease filled the air. "Mind if I eat?" he asked.

"Please do."

She watched as he pulled out a soft taco and took a huge bite. Messy things. Beef and sauce oozed out the ends and onto his fingers. He didn't seem to mind and took another bite, gaze on hers, waiting.

"I want you to question these two women, Gia Stiles and Autumn Wind."

She slid the women's data across her desk. "That's their home information. They're both dancers at the Hustle. Apparently they knew a fellow dancer, Jessica Skye. I have reason to believe Ms. Skye is our City Park Jane Doe."

Tony nodded, crumpled the now-empty taco wrapper, stuffed it into the bag, then helped himself to another.

"That it?" he asked.

"See what else you can dig up on Skye. Previous addresses. Friends. Lovers. Family members."

He made quick work of the second taco, wiped his fingers on a napkin, then retrieved his spiral notebook from his shirt pocket and plucked a pen from the holder on her desk. He jotted down what she had said so far, then looked back up at her.

"Track down her doctor and dentist. Her dental records would be a home run. Get back to me ASAP."

"You want me to call Spencer in on this?"

"Not necessary this time, Detective."

He returned his gaze to hers. He had been a cop long enough to read between the lines and know something was up. And long enough to understand that if she wanted him to know what that was, she would tell him.

He stood. "I'll be in touch."

"You do that, Detective. And shut the door behind you, please."

When he had, she picked up the phone and dialed the number Yvette Borger had left for her.

"Yvette," she said when the young woman answered. "Captain O'Shay."

"Yes?"

The word sounded breathless, hopeful.

"I'm going to help you."

Complete silence followed. Patti frowned. "Ms. Borger? Are you still there?"

"Yes. I...I'm just surprised."

"Surprised? Even with the threat of exposure you dangled over my head?"

"You're a cop," she said simply. "A captain. I figured my threat was pretty lame."

That said a lot about her opinion of police officers.

None of it good.

"Can you get me into Tonya's apartment?" she asked.

"I think so. The neighbor has a key. He let me in."

"Good." Patti glanced at her watch. "Meet me there at two."

When Patti arrived, Yvette was waiting for her. The other woman looked nervous.

"Thanks for doing this," Yvette said.

"I hope it turns out to be mutually beneficial." They started toward the condo complex's front entrance. "What can you tell me about this neighbor?"

"Lives in the unit next to Tonya. When she didn't respond to my knocking, I tried his door."

"What's his name?"

"Bill. I don't know his last name."

"Know anything else about him? Could he be involved in her disappearance?"

"I don't think so. He's really old."

Patti didn't have much confidence in Yvette's assessment. After all, at Yvette's age, "really old" was a lot younger than at hers.

"He's got a thing for boobs," she went on. "I don't think he ever took his eyes off mine."

Patti nearly choked on a laugh. She had to hand it to the other woman, she didn't mince words.

They made their way into the building and to Bill's condo. He answered their ring and Patti saw right away she hadn't given Yvette's observational skills enough credit. The man was ninety if he was a day.

He smiled at Yvette. "You came back to see me. And brought a friend. How nice."

"Captain O'Shay," Patti said, displaying her shield. "I'm helping Ms. Borger out with her situation."

"Bill Young."

"Good to meet you, Bill. I understand you let Ms. Borger into her friend's apartment this morning."

"I did. Tonya gave me a spare key for deliveries and such."

This definitely fell under the "and such" category.

"Ms. Borger is concerned about her friend. I thought I'd take a look around."

If he found her request unusual, he didn't show it. "Hold on, I'll get the key."

After he unlocked the condo for them, Patti found the interior to be just as Yvette had described, lived-in but orderly. Nothing jumped out as out of sync.

Until she reached the kitchen. A pink jeweled heart key ring lay on the counter by the phone. Patti picked it up.

"Do you recognize this as hers?"

Yvette frowned. "No. But it could be. She really likes pink."

Patti thumbed through the keys. There were six of them. Several looked like run-of-the-mill house keys, and one was a new-fangled key fob, complete with remote lock buttons and a pop-out key.

Very nifty.

She looked at Yvette. "What kind of vehicle does your friend drive?"

"Orange VW Beetle. It's out front."

Patti turned over the fob; the blue-and-white VW logo jumped out at her. She held it up for Yvette to see.

"Maybe those are her spare keys?" she said, tone hopeful.

"Maybe. But most people have spare keys, not rings. Also, most cars come with one remote locking device, not two."

Patti returned her attention to the surroundings, scanning the countertops, dining table and chairs. She went to the pantry and peeked inside, then pulled out any drawers big enough to hold a woman's handbag.

No handbag.

Interesting. The woman took her purse but left her keys.

"What are you thinking?" Yvette asked.

Patti shook her head and crossed to the woman's message machine. The message light blinked; she hit Play. Yvette's voice filled the quiet.

"Got your message. What did you do? How did he react when he learned I wasn't there? Call me."

The machine beeped; the next message played. Again it was Yvette's voice she heard. *"I forgot to mention, I have stuff to tell you, too. I know the identity of the woman who broke into my place. She's a cop! Call me."*

Several more followed and with each Yvette's voice became noticeably more worried. The last was followed by a half dozen hang-ups, then the machine clicked off.

Patti looked at Yvette. The younger woman tilted up her chin. "I told you I called her."

"Yes, you did."

Pen in hand, she scrolled through the numbers. All but one were the same. She jotted it down, then motioned to Yvette. "I've seen enough. Let's take a look at her car."

They did, though nothing new and amazing jumped out at them. Patti returned the keys, relocked the woman's door and thanked Bill. He looked disappointed when they refused tea, but still promised to let Yvette know if he saw Tonya—or anybody suspicious hanging around her condo.

"What next?" Yvette asked when they had exited the building.

"I'm going to dig a bit. I need you to sit tight."

"For how long?"

"Don't know," she replied. "Not long. Where's your car?"

She indicated a pink Cadillac, circa 1970s. Patti looked at her, eyebrow cocked. "That's not a car, it's a boat. A big, pink boat."

Yvette laughed. "I borrowed it from Miss Alma. She lives in my building. She was a Mary Kay cosmetics super sales person or something in 1974. It's her pride and joy."

"And she let you borrow it?"

"Promised I'd pick up dog biscuits for her Pomeranian, Sissy. Sissy is the one thing she loves more than the car."

Patti sort of understood that. "I'll get back to you."

"Promise?"

"Yes, promise." She started for her own vehicle, then stopped and looked back. "Don't hesitate to call, no matter the time of day…or night. And don't take any chances. If you're right about this Artist guy, you're in a very dangerous position."

39

Monday, May 7, 2007
8:45 p.m.

Silence. Only the wind snaking through dead branches and the crackle of debris underfoot.

A wasteland. Of death. And hopelessness.

All that effort, for what? She's not worthy.

No. It's not true. I believe in her.

That's what you said about the last one, remember? Cheap whore. She broke your heart.

Stop! It was the other one's fault. Cheap and coarse. Nosing around. Asking questions. Causing her to doubt.

You're a fool. A blind fool.

Only for love. What's more worthy than that?

Insure she loves you, then. Give her an incentive.

An incentive. Of course. That's what she needs. To remind her what's important. To whom her heart belongs.

Then she won't stray.

40

Tuesday, May 8, 2007
8:40 a.m.

Tony Sciame tapped on her partially open door. "Captain?"

She waved him in. "What did you get?"

He lowered himself into the chair across from her desk. "Spoke with both those dancers from the Hustle. Neither definitively IDed Skye as being our Jane Doe. Said she 'could' be. And 'maybe' was. But they directed me to where she had lived."

"Any luck?"

"Talked to the landlord. He remembered her well. Tossed all her stuff after the storm, though he was very quick to assure me he did it by the book, waited the mandated forty-five days. Even paid to store it after he re-rented her place."

"He ever hear from her?"

"Never."

"He ID her from the photo?"

"Another 'not sure.'" Tony cleared his throat. "From what he said, her stuff was pretty crappy. Could be she didn't bother retrieving any of it, just moved on."

"And it could be she's dead."

"Yeah," he agreed. "Could be."

"Any luck tracking down her doctor?"

"Believe it or not, yes. It was on file at the Hustle. Dr. Nathan Geist. I tried him, left a message with his nurse."

"Contact him at home if you have to. Get back to me tonight, even if you can't reach him."

"You got it, Captain."

He started back out. She stopped him halfway through the door. "Detective?"

"Yeah?"

"For now, I'd like to keep this between just you and me."

He cocked an eyebrow in question.

"In good time," she said to his silent query. "I'm not at liberty to discuss it just yet."

He nodded but didn't comment. As soon as he was out the door, she dialed Stacy's captain at the Sixth. "Captain Cooper," she said when he answered. "Patti O'Shay."

"Captain O'Shay," he said in his deep, booming voice. "Heard you had some good news recently. Congratulations. Sammy was a hell of a guy."

A sudden flood of tears filled her eyes, surprising her. "Yes," she said, working to speak normally around them, "he was."

"What can I do for you?"

"We might have a link to the Handyman case. Through the Hustle."

"I'll be damned."

"Going to plant one of my team down there." *Unofficially. Her own personal investigator.*

"You want the contact info?"

"It'd save me time."

He rattled off the name of the owner and general manager and their numbers. They chatted a moment more, then said goodbye.

Five minutes later, she had spoken to the Hustle's owner. He had been none too pleased to learn his business was once again a target of police attention, but had agreed to allow undercover officers in his establishment. He had passed her to the Hustle's general manager to work out the details.

From him, she had learned that Tonya had not yet been replaced. Until that moment, anyway.

As of that moment, Patti was the Hustle's new wait staff and talent manager.

As she ended the call, her cell phone vibrated. "Captain Patti O'Shay."

"It's me. Yvette."

She sounded shaky. Patti frowned. "What's wrong?"

"He was here," she said. "In my apartment. While I was sleeping!"

"How do you know he was there?"

"He left me a note. On my bathroom vanity."

"What'd it say? Exactly."

Patti heard the crackle of paper. "'When will you realize you don't need anyone but me? What will it take to prove my love to you?'"

"Is that all?" Patti asked quietly.

"No, he—" Her voice cracked. "A locket. With a photo of Tonya in it."

Patti glanced at her watch. "I'll be right there."

41

Tuesday, May 8, 2007
10:30 a.m.

Yvette grabbed her smokes, purse and keys and headed out front to wait for Patti O'Shay. That bastard had been in her home. Somehow he had gotten in. Again.

She hadn't heard a thing.

The courtyard was empty. Even old Miss Alma and her dog, Sissy, were absent. Yvette hurried through and stumbled out into the bright, clear day.

Thank God…thank God…

She breathed deeply. It smelled like the Quarter, of fresh-baked goodies, exhaust from the constant stream of vehicles passing her building, and…possibilities.

She was alive.

He could have killed her. He had been in her apartment. Perhaps had even stood beside her bed and gazed down at her as she slept.

When will you realize you don't need anyone but me?

Trembling, Yvette fumbled to get a cigarette from her pack, hands shaking so badly she dropped the pack twice. Finally she had one, lit it and inhaled deeply.

The smoke calmed her somewhat. Tonya was dead. She didn't have to see a body to know it was true. Somehow he had realized Tonya could ID him—to her or the police—and he'd killed her.

Tears burned her eyes. She had hardly known the woman. Until a few days ago, she hadn't even liked her much. But Tonya had put herself out there for her, tried to help.

She had been killed because of it.

She drew on the cigarette, her mind racing. What should she do? Stay? Or go?

Run. As fast as you can. Don't look back.

The slam of a car door drew her attention. Patti O'Shay had arrived and was crossing the street, coming toward her.

"Those things'll kill you, you know," she said as she neared, indicating the cigarette.

Yvette blew out a stream of smoke. "Not if the Artist gets me first."

"He won't," Patti said simply. "I won't let him."

Yvette wished she could believe her. She wished she had the confidence in Captain O'Shay that she'd had even twenty-four hours ago. She put out the smoke and indicated her apartment building.

"I didn't want to be up there alone."

"I understand."

"Did you bring the note and locket?"

She nodded and dug them out of her pocket. She held them out. Patti picked up the note first, by the edges, opened it and read. Then she reached for the necklace.

It did, indeed, hold a picture of the woman. She stared at it, frowning.

"What?" Yvette asked.

"You ever see her wear this?"

She scrunched up her face in thought. "No."

"Do you find it at all odd that a woman would wear a locket with her own picture in it?"

Yvette stared at her, shaken. Confused. "But if he left it, doesn't that mean it's hers?"

"Could be. Don't you find it strange?"

"Yes," she whispered. "So if it's not Tonya's, whose—"

"Let's not speculate on that right now. I need to examine your apartment."

They entered the building and made their way to the second floor. As they neared Samson's apartment, the unit's door flew open and Ray rushed out, wild-eyed and unkempt looking. From inside came the sound of sobbing.

"Did you hear anything?" he cried.

"Ray? What's wro—"

"Did you see someone?" He grabbed her arm. "Last night? When you got home from work?"

His grip on her arm hurt, and Yvette pulled away. "I didn't work. I turned in early."

"Somebody poisoned Samson! They fed him hamburger with antifreeze in it."

Yvette went cold. She brought a hand to her mouth. *The Artist. Dear God.*

She shook her head in denial. "But how? Samson's always inside or with you and Bob."

"We don't know." His voice rose. "We were out overnight. We got home and found hi… It was…horrible."

"Are you certain he didn't just get into—"

"Antifreeze?" His voice was disbelieving. "The vet confirmed it. We've called the police, but so far no one's come."

"I'm a police officer," Patti said. "Maybe I can help."

He looked at her in surprise, as if only just realizing she was standing there.

"Were your doors and windows locked?" Patti asked.

"Yes. I mean, I think so."

"I could check them, if you'd like?"

"Thank God!" He grabbed her hand and pulled her inside, calling out to his partner. "Bob, this is a police officer! She's going to help us!"

The other man sat slumped on the pretty chaise, his expression the picture of grief. He looked up at Patti. "Who would do such a thing? And why?" He held out a framed photograph of the pug. "Who could harm such a sweet animal?"

Yvette had always thought Samson pretty much the ugliest dog on earth. But otherwise he'd been sweet-tempered—all bark but no bite. Unlike Miss Alma's adorable Pom, who pretty much scared the crap out of her.

She swallowed hard, hurting for them. They adored Samson, treated him like their baby.

While Ray and Patti checked the windows, she went and sat by Bob, putting her arm around him. "How is he? Is he—"

"Alive?" he choked out. "Yes. But he's really sick. Dr. Morgan said it was a good thing we found him when we did—"

He began to cry again, and Yvette awkwardly patted his back. She wondered what it would be like to love someone—or something—that way. What it would be like to be loved that way.

Was that the way the Artist loved her?

A trembling sensation settled in the pit of her gut. For one dizzying moment she imagined succumbing. Allowing herself to be consumed by his terrifying brand of devotion.

Would she finally know how it felt to be loved?

Ray and Patti returned. "Windows were locked from the inside," Patti said. "No signs of forced entry around the door. Are you certain the door was locked?"

"Yes," Ray said emphatically.

Patti looked at the other man. When he didn't agree, Ray made a sound of disbelief. "Bob, you didn't...you and I have talked about this before!"

"I know. I'm sorry." He wrung his hands and shifted his gaze to Patti, then Yvette, his expression pleading.

"I didn't think locking up was such a big deal. Because of the courtyard door and…and because of Samson. I figured, of all the apartments, why would someone choose to break into ours?"

"Was anything taken?" Patti asked.

"Nothing. Everything looked just as we left it except—"

"Samson," Ray finished, flushing. "A neighbor did it. Because of the barking. We'd had complaints, but—"

"Who could be so vile?" Bob asked. "So cruel?"

The Artist. He did it to quiet Samson. To shut him up. So he could terrorize her without detection.

Yvette stood, legs rubbery. "I don't feel so good."

She made it to her apartment before she lost it. She threw up, aware of Patti O'Shay hovering in the doorway behind her.

"Are you all right?" she asked when she had stopped.

"No." Yvette stood, crossed to the sink and rinsed her mouth out. Then she looked at Patti. "Hell no."

She realized she was shivering and grabbed her robe from the hook on the back of the door. She slipped into it, then looked at Patti. "The Artist poisoned Samson. To shut him up."

"I think so, too."

"I couldn't tell them."

"No."

"I want to sit down."

She headed into the living room and sat on the couch. A moment later, Patti handed her a cold washcloth. "How about something to drink?"

"Coke. There's some in the fridge."

Several moments later, Patti handed the can to her.

"You're being so nice to me," she said.

"Why wouldn't I be?"

She shrugged and sipped the sweet drink. "Why would you be? You don't know me. I'm nobody to you."

Patti frowned at her, as if she had said something puzzling. "You were sick. Of course I helped you."

"Human decency demanded it?"

If she heard cynicism in her voice, Patti O'Shay didn't show it. "Yes."

Right. Like that happened every day. "Look, I appreciate you coming down here to help me. I really appreciate you listening and taking me seriously."

"But?"

"But I don't need your help anymore. Samson sealed the deal."

"What deal is that, Yvette?"

"I'm out of here. Gone. No notice to the Hustle or anybody else."

"And you think that'll solve the problem?"

"Duh. The bastard won't be able to find me."

"It might solve *your* problem," she corrected. "What about the next girl?"

"I'm supposed to care about the 'next' girl?"

"Don't you?"

At the older woman's tone, Yvette flushed. "Don't give me that goody-goody crap. Because of me, Tonya was killed. Samson was poisoned. Seems it's damn dangerous to be anywhere around me. I'd be worried if I were you."

"I'm not scared. And I'm not going to run."

"Big brave cop. Bully for you."

She stood, went to her bedroom and knelt beside the bed. From underneath, she dragged a large suitcase. She opened it and inside was another, smaller one.

"Running solves nothing."

"Says you." She laid them side by side on the bed. "Seems to me it'll keep me alive."

She went to her dresser, opened the top drawer and scooped out the contents.

"Do you really think you can run from him?"

"I can try."

"He's obsessed with you. He's twisted. A true psychopath. He won't allow anyone or anything to get in the way of what he wants. Including you."

"That makes no sense."

"Do you think a madman like this ever makes sense? Everything he's done, he's justified to himself."

"*You're* in his way now," she said defiantly. "Aren't you scared?"

"I'm angry. And determined to stop him from hurting you or anybody else. To bring him to justice."

"I'm not like you," she said. "I'm scared. And I've had enough."

She yanked open the second dresser drawer and rifled through its contents, tossing aside all but her favorites.

"If you stay, I promise you round-the-clock protection."

"Sure you would."

"I'd do it myself."

"What's in it for me besides possibly getting killed?"

"What do you want out of it?"

A new life. A way to wipe the slate clean and start over from scratch.

Instead, she said, "What can you afford?"

"How about doing it to catch a murderer? To stop this freak from hurting someone else?"

"Put my life on the line to save some stranger?"

"Basically, yes."

"I'm outta here."

"How does fifty thousand dollars sound?"

Yvette stopped packing. She looked at the other woman. "You have fifty thousand dollars?"

"I do. Part of an insurance payoff."

"I'll want to see a bank statement. Current."

"No problem."

Yvette narrowed her eyes. "Half up front."

"Ten percent."

"Twenty," she countered. "And protection—24/7."

"You've got it." Patti held out her hand. "Deal?"

Yvette stared at her outstretched hand. She'd get ten thousand, up front. If it got too crazy, she could take off.

Ten grand richer.

"Deal," she said, and clasped Patti's hand. "But I have one question I need answered first."

"Then ask it."

"Why's it so important to you that you catch this Handyman guy?"

The woman's expression tightened, becoming fierce. "Because he killed my husband."

42

Tuesday, May 8, 2007
12:15 p.m.

Patti set her plan into motion. She had promised Yvette
twenty-four-hour protection, and there was only one way to
keep that promise—to personally provide that protection.

To do that she had to be independent of the NOPD. The
chief of police, stand-up guy though he was, would not allow
one of his captains to launch her own personal investigation.

Chief Howard was a solid cop. An African-American born
and raised in New Orleans, he was passionate about the community and a strong supporter of his sworn officers. That said,
he didn't coddle and always expected one hundred and ten
percent.

Patti had called ahead; he was expecting her. His secretary had notified him that she had arrived.

"Go in, Captain O'Shay," the woman said. "He's ready for you."

Patti thanked her, then took a deep breath. She had made a deal that would cost her her nest egg.

And most likely her career, as well.

If it led to Sammy's killer, it would be worth it.

"Chief?" she said, tapping on his door, then stepping into his office. "Thanks for making time for me."

He smiled. "I always have time for you, Captain."

"I'm requesting a leave of absence."

He didn't blink and she wondered if he had been expecting this. She certainly wouldn't be the first ranking officer since Katrina who had requested leave. And considering her personal circumstances, it was more surprising that she hadn't requested one before now.

"May I ask why?"

"I need a break. Sammy's death, the aftermath of the storm, it all took more of a toll on me than I realized."

"Until now."

"Yes."

He studied her a long moment. "Odd choice of timing. You have a suspect in jail."

She could use Franklin's arrest to justify her timing, explain that with relief had come emotional exhaustion, but she just wasn't that good a storyteller. And even if she was, she suspected he would see through her.

She looked him straight in the eyes. "I still have strong doubts Franklin's the one."

"You can try to convince me of that."

Not from inside the rule book. "I don't have anything to convince you with, Chief. I'm going on my gut here."

"When?" he asked, not challenging her opinion, moving forward instead.

"Effective as soon as I have a chance to notify my team. I'm shooting for the end of the day."

"How long?"

"A month at least. Not that much considering the events of the past two years."

"Can't do without you a month. Two weeks."

If he got wind of what she was up to, she doubted he'd want her back at all. "Three."

"Done." His cell phone vibrated; he glanced at the display but didn't pick up. "Who's your ranking detective?"

"Sciame."

The chief nodded. "Good cop. Steady. You think he's up to filling your shoes in your absence?"

"Absolutely."

"Make it happen, Captain O'Shay."

He answered his cell, signaling an end to their meeting. Patti exited the office, her mood vacillating between exhilaration and despair.

There was no backing out now. She was neck deep in it.

Patti made her announcement at the end of the day. Minutes before, she had informed Tony Sciame. He stood beside her now, ready to take over.

When she had finished, complete silence ensued. She moved her gaze over the faces of the men and women under her command. Their expressions ranged from surprise to sympathy to anxiety.

She settled her gaze regretfully on Spencer. He looked hurt that she hadn't included him, tipped him beforehand. She should have; their relationship warranted it.

Not this time, Spencer. This time she had to go it alone.

"Are there any questions?" she asked.

A detective notorious for cracking wise broke the silence. "Have you lost your friggin' mind, Captain? Leaving Sciame in charge? Can our budget support that many doughnuts?"

"Kiss my ass, Chuckles," Tony shot back. "Then show a little respect for your superiors."

Grinning, "Chuckles" flipped Tony the bird while a ripple of laughter moved through the group.

Patti hid the fact that she appreciated the two detectives breaking the tension. "I have complete confidence in Detective Sciame. I wouldn't leave him in charge if I didn't. In addition, he and I will communicate daily about new and ongoing investigations." She smiled slightly. "I'm taking time off, not moving to Siberia. Any other questions?"

There weren't, and moments later the group broke up. Patti hurried toward her office. She had a number of details to take care of before meeting with Tony to officially hand over the reins.

Spencer met her at her office door. "What the hell's going on?"

"I told you. And everyone else."

"What you told us was bullshit."

"I'm sorry you feel that way, Spencer. But you can't possibly understand what I've been through—"

"Save the canned speeches for the chief. This move has nothing to do with Uncle Sammy's murder."

"Are you calling me a liar, Detective Malone?"

"Just calling your bluff."

"That's where you're wrong." She met his gaze evenly. "This is about Sammy's murder. Excuse me, I have a number of loose ends to tie up before I go today."

"How about the truth, Aunt Patti?" he said, voice lowered. "Don't you think I deserve that much?"

His words were like a kick in the gut. She ignored the feeling, the urge to bring him in. That would be wrong, selfish of her. Keeping him out of it was for his own good.

"I have nothing more to say about this, Detective. I'm sorry."

She said the last, really meaning it. Hoping he heard—and believed—the regret in her tone.

She turned to retreat into her office; he caught her arm, stopping her.

"Why was Yvette Borger in to see you Monday?"

She looked back at her nephew. "Excuse me, *Detective?*"

"You heard me, *Captain.* Yvette Borger was in to see you on Monday. Why?"

She narrowed her eyes. "Questions like that of a ranking officer are not career builders."

"Screw the career," he said softly. "This is personal."

"Yvette Borger has nothing to do with my decision."

Which, in essence, was true. This was about Sammy. About catching his killer.

"She's a liar, Aunt Patti. Pathological. Don't get pulled into her games. Don't let her—"

"I'm sorry, Spencer," she said softly, "I don't have the time right now."

She stepped into her office and closed the door, shutting him out for good.

43

Tuesday, May 8, 2007
1:45 p.m.

Yvette packed her suitcase. Per Patti's instructions, she included everything she would need for a week. She was moving in with Captain Patti O'Shay. Twenty-four/seven protection meant just that—they lived, worked and relaxed together.

In that vein, Patti had arranged with the Hustle's owner to take Tonya's place. She felt their best bet to nail the Artist was through the club. Because it was a public place, she also believed Yvette would be in the least danger there.

Truly weird. Yvette Borger playing nice with a cop.

As she zipped her suitcase shut, it occurred to her she could still run. Chuck the money and take off. She had enough socked away to live comfortably until she could find another gig. Atlanta was a big, anonymous city. Lots of nightlife. She could easily find a job and a place to live there.

Fifty thousand dollars.

Enough to start a new life. Go to college. Learn a real trade—one she could actually practice with her clothes on.

Patti had promised to bring the deposit. She had also promised to bring proof she had the remainder of the money.

Yvette thought of how the woman had answered her question of why catching the Handyman mattered so much to her.

"He killed my husband."

Patti O'Shay wanted to catch him. And she was willing to do whatever necessary to make it happen—even to the tune of a fifty thousand dollar payoff.

Patti O'Shay was a police captain. She no doubt made a decent salary, but she wasn't rich. Fifty thousand dollars would represent a hefty sum.

The insurance payoff on her husband's death.

The realization left Yvette weak-kneed. She sat on the bed, next to the big suitcase. Patti O'Shay had loved her husband that much. So much she would offer up fifty grand to nail his killer.

There had to be a catch. She couldn't imagine anyone actually doing that. It was unreal. Nobody did that kind of thing anymore. Did they?

No. She would get the ten grand, but no more. Patti O'Shay would screw her out of the rest.

After all, how could Yvette collect?

She couldn't. The woman was a cop. She could squash Yvette like a bug.

She pictured her neighbors' grief. Remembered Ray's anguished cry: *"Who could be so vile? So cruel?"*

What the hell was she thinking? This monster had poisoned Samson and killed Marcus. If Patti was correct and he was the Handyman, he had murdered six women and a police captain. And now he had his sights on her.

Go. Run. Don't look back.

With a sudden sense of urgency, Yvette leapt to her feet. She finished fastening the suitcase and rolled it out to the door. As she reached it, her intercom buzzed.

She froze. Could it be Patti already?

If it was, she'd play along. Take the deposit, go through the motions. And when the opportunity presented itself, she would take off.

She answered the intercom. "I'm ready," she said.

"That sounds interesting. Must be my lucky day."

"Riley!" she said, recognizing his voice. "I thought you were someone else."

"Darn it."

She smiled. With everything that had happened since Saturday night, she had hardly thought of him. Now, hearing his voice, she remembered how much she had liked him. "What's up?"

"I forgot to get your number. So here I am. Can I come up?"

She hesitated. If Patti showed up while he was here, she would have some quick explaining to do.

"Yvette?"

"I'll buzz you in."

A couple of minutes later, he was at her door. He smiled when she swung it open. "Hey there."

"Hey to you."

"I was hoping you'd be here. I—" His gaze shifted to her suitcases, then he looked at her. "Where're you going?"

Damn. "To...stay with a friend. Just a little R and R, that's all."

He looked disappointed. "I was going to see if you wanted to get together tonight."

"I've got to work."

"I thought you were visiting a friend?"

"I am," she said quickly. "She lives across the lake. On the north shore. Has a pool."

He grinned. "A vacation from the city. I totally get that. How about after?"

"Pardon?"

"After you're done working? You and me? Food. Fun. Flirting."

She felt herself flush, something she hadn't done in years. God, she liked him. "It'll be really late."

"How late?"

"Too late to go out. I'm a...cocktail waitress."

"A dancing cocktail waitress?"

She'd forgotten she'd told him she was a dancer.

"Can't make a living dancing, so I push drinks in between dancing gigs."

"Where do you work? I'll stop by for a drink."

"No! My boss gets really bitchy about that."

His smile seemed to freeze, and he took a step back. "Sure. Okay. Sorry I bothered you."

"You didn't! I really want to get together. Tonight just doesn't work."

"How about Thursday night?"

"This Thursday?"

"I'm playing at Tipitina's. I'd love it if you came to hear me."

He looked so eager. And she wanted to. Really, really wanted to.

She thought of Patti.

Fifty thousand dollars. Enough to start a new life. One she didn't have to lie about.

"I'll have to get off work. Not always easy."

"If not this Thursday, how about next? It's a regular gig— six to eight."

Six to eight was doable. But how would she ditch Patti?

"Will you come?" he asked

"I didn't know you were a musician," she said, evading his question.

"I dabble. Will you?"

"I'll try."

"Promise?"

She did and he bent and kissed her cheek. "I'll call you."

A moment later, he was out the door and walking away. She realized she hadn't given him her cell number and yanked the door open again.

"Riley, wait!"

He stopped, turned. She hurried toward him. "You forgot again."

"Forgot—"

"My phone number. Got a pen?"

He did, in his jacket pocket. He held it out. "But I don't have any paper."

She took the pen. "I don't need it."

She caught his hand, turned it over and jotted her cell phone number in his palm.

He stared at it a moment, looking startled. Then he laughed. "Okay, then. Got it."

She turned to walk away; this time he stopped her. "What?" she asked.

"My pen."

"Sorry." She held it out. He took it, then grabbed her hand. He flipped it palm up and jotted down his number.

She met his gaze, surprised.

"Now we're even." He walked away, not glancing back until he had reached the stairs. "Thursday night," he called, "six to eight."

Then he disappeared from view.

44

Tuesday, May 8, 2007
4:10 p.m.

Patti had grown up in the Bywater area of the city. When she and Sammy married, they'd bought a Creole cottage not far from her childhood home.

They had lovingly restored that cottage, planning to move to a larger home when they started a family. But the babies never came, so they'd spent the rest of their marriage in their newlywed cottage.

Located just down river from the French Quarter, Bywater was a solid, middle-class neighborhood. Neither as historic nor upscale as its nearest residential neighbor, the Faubourg Marigny, it had boasted an active and committed resident community and had begun to experience a sort of renaissance—before Katrina hit.

Floodwaters had battered the neighborhood—and permanently changed its dynamic. Some residents had rebuilt. Some had sold and moved on. And some remained indecisive still, two years out. Those properties sat, cleaned, gutted and boarded over, a terrible reminder of the past.

More horrible for Patti than for most. A daily reminder of her personal loss, an a.m. and p.m. kick in the gut.

"Nice place," Yvette said, dropping her purse on the overstuffed couch.

"Thanks."

"Didn't you flood here?"

"We did." Water had breached the west side of the Industrial Canal, inundating all but the properties closest to the Mississippi. Her and Sammy's cottage sat closer to the river than others in the neighborhood. "But only twelve inches. We were lucky."

Lucky. Only twelve inches of water in her home. Only her husband murdered. Life altered forever.

"You rebuilt, anyway."

"Where else was I going to go? My life is here."

Yvette gazed at her, brow furrowed in thought. As if studying an alien life form.

How did you explain family, roots and history to a twenty-two- year-old who, as far as she could tell, didn't even own a pet? Instead, she asked Yvette about herself. "Why are you still here?"

She shrugged. "The French Quarter was high and dry. I was able to move up to the Hustle. I figured, why start over?"

In a way, they'd stayed for the same reason.

"I thought we should set some ground rules," Patti said.

"Ground rules?" she repeated, arching her eyebrows. "Like what? Being in bed by ten, up by nine? No smoking?"

"This arrangement is to keep you safe. To that end, we stick together. Where you go, I go. And vice versa."

"The bathroom?" Yvette folded her arms across her chest. "Do you watch me pee? Shower? I've never been under house arrest before."

"You'll have your own bathroom. And your own bedroom, as well. I suggest you sleep with your door open. I also insist you keep the window locked. You do what I say. Always."

"Isn't this going to be fun? Just like a girlfriend sleepover."

Patti frowned at her sarcasm. "You don't seem to grasp the seriousness of this situation."

"Oh, I grasp it all right. There's a maniac out there who's killing people. And for some reason, he's become obsessed with me. Lucky me."

Patti cocked an eyebrow at the "Oh, well" simplicity of the response. It seemed to her that Yvette didn't have a clue how fragile life was—or how fleeting it could be.

And that death, when it came, was quite final.

She tried another approach. "This is a business arrangement. I'm paying you a lot of money to follow my rules. If you choose not to, legally I can't stop you. But I can't protect you then, either. And you'll have negated our deal. Ultimately it's your choice."

Yvette held her gaze for a long moment, then nodded.

"Good. Your bedroom is the second room on the right. Maybe you want to get settled in?"

She said she did and started in that direction. Patti called out, stopping her. "And Yvette?" The young woman looked back at her. "No smoking in the house."

45

Thursday, May 10, 2007
12:15 p.m.

Stacy stood in the doorway of the tidy little kitchen, gazing down at what had once been a woman named Alma Maytree. A neighbor had called, worried over the incessant yapping of the woman's dog—and because they hadn't seen "Miss Alma" in several days.

Miss Alma had been eighty-two years old. A sweet old lady who had loved her baby—as she'd called her dog, Sissy—and had been kind to all her neighbors. Even the ones who didn't deserve it.

The neighbor who'd contacted the police had feared she'd had a heart attack. Or fallen and been unable to get up.

It was much worse than that.

Someone had bashed in the right side of her head. She had fallen face first onto the white tile floor, leaving quite a mess. She wore a baby-blue chenille robe and slippers. What looked like a floral nightgown peeked out from underneath. A cast-iron frying pan lay on the floor, only inches from the body.

"The old 'iron skillet to the head' method. Works every time," Baxter said.

Stacy glanced at him. "No question about the murder weapon, that's for certain."

"I haven't seen one of those in ages." Rene snapped on latex gloves. "My grandmother cooked with nothing but. Brings back memories."

"She ever hit you in the head with one?"

He grinned. "It would explain a lot, wouldn't it? But no, she just thought about it. A lot."

The first officer had cordoned off the area around the apartment's entrance. A dozen or so of the building's tenants clustered just beyond, staring and whispering. One of them had offered to take care of Sissy, an offer Stacy had jumped on. A couple of officers were in the process of questioning them and their neighbors.

"Any luck finding an apartment?" Rene asked, squatting down beside the victim.

Stacy followed suit. She had made the mistake of inquiring about an apartment to several of her fellow officers. Suddenly everybody knew her business.

"One I'd want to live in? Not hardly."

"Want to talk about it?"

"Hardly."

"If you ask me—"

"I'm not."

"—maybe you should tough it out with Malone? He's a jerk, but he's okay."

"That makes no sense at all, you know that."

"I'm a guy. It makes perfect sense."

"Could we please give Miss Alma here our full attention? I think she deserves it."

"She'd dead, Killian. I don't think she knows the difference."

She ignored him. "Pan was definitely the weapon." She indicated the blood, hair and other matter, probably bits of flesh and bone, clinging to its right side and bottom.

"He didn't hit her square."

"He was taller. Right-handed, obviously." A left-handed killer, striking from behind, would have struck the victim on the left.

"How do you figure he was taller?"

Stacy stood and crossed to the large cabinet closest to the oven. She opened it and, as she expected, found Alma Maytree's pots and pans. She selected one of a similar size to the one on the floor.

She motioned one of the crime techs over, a woman several inches shorter than she. "Stand right there."

Stacy stood about an arm's length behind her, and swung at her head, stopping right before she made contact.

Her arm made a natural arc downward, hand tipping slightly

thumb up. She repeated the motion. Each time the same part of the pan would have connected with the tech's head in about the same spot.

Stacy thanked the tech, who hadn't even flinched, and shifted her attention to the scene. Nothing was out of place except the body and frying pan. She hadn't yet searched the rest of the apartment, but from what she had seen so far, it looked to be in the same condition.

It appeared Miss Alma had been making tea. Kettle of water on the stove. Teapot and tea bags on the counter. Two cups, empty, waiting to be filled.

Two cups. Not one.

Whoever did this, Miss Alma had trusted. She had thought of her, or him, as a friend. Had invited them in. Turned her back to them. Then wham!

But why?

"Judging by the robe and slippers," Baxter said, "I'm guessing it was either early morning or approaching bedtime."

Stacy crossed to the trash can, lifted off its top and looked inside.

Baxter followed her, peering over her shoulder. "You can tell a lot about people by their garbage."

And sometimes, what time of day it is.

"I mean," Baxter went on, "who would think this sweet old lady would enjoy Cajun Fire Cracklings?"

"Where do you see Cajun Cracklings?"

"I don't. I'm just saying, who would?"

"You drove your mother crazy, didn't you?"

He grinned. "Looks to me like Miss Alma had had dinner."

Stacy nodded. The remnants of a chicken-and-rice dinner was sitting squarely on top of the debris. "And a friend came to call."

"Some friend," he muttered. He crossed to the refrigerator and opened it, peering inside.

"Anything out of whack there?"

"Nope."

Frowning, Stacy replaced the can's lid. "Remember Yvette Borger?"

"The exotic dancer who was diddling Marcus Gabrielle?"

Stacy nodded. "She lives in this building."

"No kidding? Think there's a connection to Gabrielle here?"

"Seems unlikely, but I don't like coincidences."

The coroner's representative arrived. He took one look at Alma Maytree and shook his head. "Kids and geriatrics. There's just something extra heinous about it. You know what I mean?"

Stacy did. Both children and the elderly were helpless to defend themselves.

He fitted on gloves and knelt by the body. "This looks pretty cut and dried," he murmured. "But if this job's taught me anything, it's not to take things at face value."

He carefully inspected her hands and arms. "No defensive wounds. Nails look clean."

"How long's she been dead?"

"A couple days, give or take. I'll see if I can get any closer back at the lab, but establishing time of death this far out is far from exact."

True. The longer a person was dead, the more difficult it was to pinpoint when they'd died.

"Do your thing," Stacy said. "We'll look around."

The apartment's furnishings ran toward fussy. Lots of antique lace, silk flowers and chintz. Not a pillow out of place in the living room. The bed was made. No discarded clothes on the floor, laid across a chair or hanging on a bathroom hook. The only true clutter in the entire place was on the bathroom vanity.

Lotions, creams, perfumes, lipsticks. Stacy picked up one small tub. "Age Erase—rehydrates, rejuvenates and reduces the visible signs of aging."

"Hope springs eternal," Baxter murmured, picking up another cream and reading the label. "Even at eighty-something."

"Two," Stacy offered. "I think it's sweet."

And really sad, considering.

They returned to the kitchen. The evidence team was collecting the garbage from the can under the sink.

"Be really careful not to jostle that," Stacy said. "The layering of the debris could help us establish TOD."

"Gotcha, Detective."

"How's it coming, Mitch?"

He'd already bagged her hands and feet. Next step would be loading her into a body bag and transporting her to the morgue. The process was done as cleanly as possible to avoid loss or contamination of evidence.

The man looked up. "What you see is what you get, is my guess."

"When will we hear from you?"

"Couple days. I've got several ahead of her." He held up a hand as if to ward off any wheedling. "I gotta have a life, my wife insists on it."

She smiled slightly and unclipped her cell phone. "As always, we appreciate your dedication."

She dialed Spencer's cell. "It's me," she said when he answered. "Thought you'd want to know, I've got a stiff at Yvette Borger's apartment building."

46

Thursday, May 10, 2007
1:25 p.m.

When Patti's cell phone buzzed, she and Yvette were hunting down friends and coworkers of Jessica Skye. It was Spencer. "I thought you'd be interested. One of Yvette's neighbors got whacked."

"Who?" she asked.

"Alma Maytree. Took a frying pan to the side of her head."

Alma Maytree. The name sounded familiar. Had Yvette mentioned her?

"When?"

"Don't know. I'm heading there now. You'll have to come out of retirement to find out."

She shut her phone, veered into the left lane, then used the neutral-ground crossover to execute a U-turn.

"What's up?" Yvette asked.

"We're heading back to the house."

Yvette yawned. "Why?"

"I'm dropping you off."

That got her attention, something that had been pretty damn difficult to manage.

"And leaving me? Alone?"

"There's been a murder. I need to go to the scene. I can't bring you."

"Isn't that against 'the rules'?"

"I don't have a choice." She glanced at her. "You don't have to look so damn smug."

"Sorry. Can't help myself."

She sounded anything but sorry, and Patti gritted her teeth. As the hours had passed with no contact from the Artist, Yvette had grown more rebellious—not that she had been particularly accommodating to begin with. She was bored. At once surly and self-righteous. Prickly. She didn't get the point of Patti's rules and never missed an opportunity to diss them.

Patti could put up with that—and a lot more—if it led to Sammy's killer. *If.*

Could this dead neighbor have anything to do with her case? Alma Maytree. She wanted to ask Yvette if she knew her, but feared Yvette would put two and two together and realize the woman was dead. And Patti was uncertain how she would react. She could panic, then run.

Patti couldn't chance it. Instead, she would gather the facts, assess the situation, then decide. Could be this murder was unrelated to Yvette or the Artist.

One coincidence was tough enough to swallow. But three?

Marcus Gabrielle had been murdered. Samson had been poisoned. And now a woman named Alma Maytree was dead.

Patti made the turn onto Piety Street. Moments later, she pulled up in front of her cottage.

"I'll let myself in." Yvette held her hand out for the key.

Patti removed her house key from the ring but didn't hand it over. "I shouldn't be gone long. Lock the door and don't let anyone in."

"Yes, Mom."

Patti gazed at her for a long moment. "You do understand how much danger you're in?"

"If I say yes, will you give me the key?"

When Patti glared at her, she laughed. "I'm just playing with you. Yes, I understand how much danger I'm in. And how serious this is. And how important it is to follow your rules."

Knowing a snow job when she heard it, Patti dropped the key into her hand, then watched as Yvette jogged up the walk, unlocked the door and disappeared inside without a backward glance.

Patti sat a moment, struggling with the need to tiptoe up the walk and double-check that she had relocked the door. Or to circle the block, then peek in the windows to see what Yvette was up to.

Was this how a parent felt when faced with giving their adolescents some freedom? Anxious about them screwing up? Hopeful they wouldn't, torn between being suspicious and wanting to trust?

Yvette was an adult. She earned her living dancing in a strip club. She lived on her own. Made her own choices, day in and out. But damn, she acted like a kid. Like a silly, self-absorbed teenager.

Patti gazed at the house a moment more, then pulled away from the curb, heading toward the French Quarter.

Within minutes, she pulled up to the uniformed officer re-directing traffic at Yvette's corner. She held up her shield and he waved her through.

She parked, climbed out and strode to the building's entrance. She greeted the officer stationed there, entered and followed the crime-scene tape to the victim, who had lived on the first floor.

Patti reached the woman's apartment, signed the log and ducked under the barricade. The complex was crawling with NOPD and crime-scene techs, each focused on their job.

It never ceased to amaze her how so many people could cram into one space and carry out their individual and detailed tasks with such precision.

But they did, crime after crime.

She wound her way through them until she reached the heart of the crime scene: the victim. Spencer had already arrived. He stood beside Stacy, Baxter and Deputy Coroner Mitch Weiner. They were deep in a discussion about the Saints' picks in the recent NFL draft.

"Hello, Mitch," she said. "Detectives."

"We've been waiting for you," the deputy coroner replied. "Malone figured you'd want a look before we packed her up."

"I appreciate that."

She studied the body, taking in the scene, the position of the victim, the frying pan.

"Done," she said, and turned back to the group. "What've you got?"

Stacy answered first. "Blow to the head killed her. No defensive wounds. No other injuries detected."

Mitch stepped in. "My guess is, she's been dead a few days. I'll know more after the autopsy."

"Any suspects?"

"Not yet. The neighbors we've spoken with say she was universally liked."

Stacy stepped in. "We believe she knew her attacker. She let him into her apartment after she had prepared for bed."

"How do you know it's a him?" Patti asked.

"Pardon?"

"An older woman. She's in a robe. Preparing tea before bed. Would she let a man into her apartment?"

"Not just any man," Baxter murmured. "A close relative."

"A neighbor, maybe. A good friend. Someone very non-threatening."

"Police officer," Mitch tossed in. "Priest."

They fell silent. The coroner's reps loaded the body into a bag. After telling them he'd be in touch, Mitch left with the body.

Patti turned to Spencer and Stacy. "The question is, does this have anything to do with Yvette Borger?"

Spencer cocked an eyebrow. "Why would it?"

"Two nights ago the Artist paid a midnight visit to Yvette. He managed to enter her house, leave her a note and exit without waking her. She found the note the next morning."

"Or so she says."

Patti ignored Spencer's sarcasm and continued. "That same night, her neighbor's pug, Samson, was poisoned. And now Alma Maytree is dead, quite possibly killed the same night."

"And you believe her?"

She frowned at the challenge in her nephew's voice. "I do."

"So much so that you've taken a leave of absence from your job and, in my opinion, your senses, to help her. Have you lost your friggin' mind?"

Several people glanced their way. Patti motioned for the door. "Why don't we take this conversation outside, Detective?"

They filed out of the apartment, Stacy with them. When they'd found a quiet corner of the courtyard, Spencer faced her. "I don't give a flip if the woman's a total psycho. Except now, she's messing with someone I care about."

"I appreciate your concern, Spencer. I love you, too. But I don't need protecting."

"She has no proof. She manufactured the letters. Manufactured the Artist. For attention. She gets her jollies from it."

"She didn't manufacture Alma Maytree. Didn't manufacture Samson being poisoned."

"How do you know *she* didn't kill Alma Maytree? And poison Samson?"

"Why? What's her motive?"

"How about she's just plain crazy?"

Stacy stepped in. "Is it so far-fetched, Patti? Maybe she killed Gabrielle, too. Or had him killed? Because he stiffed her. Or because he tried to kill her. She trusted him, he betrayed her."

"There's more," Patti said. "Yvette came to me for help. Her friend from the Hustle, Tonya Messing—"

"Her friend?" Stacy interrupted. "They were anything but friends when I was there working undercover. Yvette called her a 'bitch.' Her word, not mine."

"Apparently when you and Spencer refused to help her, she turned to Tonya. Now Tonya's missing."

"Missing?"

"Tonya had recognized our Jane Doe from the paper, as a former dancer from the Hustle. Jessica Skye. Disappeared with the storm." She leaned forward. "She also recognized the guy sending the notes to Yvette as having been interested in Jessica."

"And they began their own little investigation."

"Yes. When Tonya went missing, Yvette came to me."

"Has anyone else corroborated Skye being the Jane Doe?"

"Not yet, no."

"Not another dancer at the club?"

When she indicated none had, the two detectives exchanged glances. Spencer spoke first. "Don't you see what's happening here? Tonya's the only one who can positively ID Skye and suddenly she's 'missing.' When Stacy and I went to her apartment to see all of the Artist's letters, they were suddenly gone. She's pathological, Aunt Patti."

"I agree, Captain," Stacy said. "Aligning yourself too closely with her would be a mistake."

Too late.

Patti gazed at the pair, torn. Spencer and Stacy were good cops. With good instincts. But she had to go with her own instincts.

"I'm not changing course. I can't. If what she said is true, the Artist is the Handyman. And she's my connection to him."

"If," Spencer said, voice tight.

"I took Tonya's place at the Hustle. And moved Yvette in with me. For her own protection."

For a full three seconds, Spencer simply gaped at her. When he spoke, the words exploded from him. "That's the most lame-brained, boneheaded scheme—"

"Don't overstep your bounds, Detective. I'm still your superior officer."

"Then act like it, for God's sake!"

Stacy laid a hand on Spencer's arm. "And you're doing all this with the chief's blessing?"

"He doesn't know anything about it. Officially, I'm on leave."

Stacy made a sound of distress. "I beg you, reconsider. You're not thinking clearly. You're still grieving. Between that and the stress of—"

"My thinking is crystal clear. I know exactly what I'm doing."

"Throwing away your career?" Spencer demanded. "Are you prepared for that?"

"Absolutely."

"Let me ask you, Aunt Patti, how did you get Little Miss Scamalot to accept your offer? Out of the goodness of her heart? Because she wanted to help you catch a killer?"

"Yes."

She had hesitated before answering, a fraction of a second only, but enough to tip off Spencer. "Collaborating with Borger only two days and already lying. That's not the Patti O'Shay I know and respect."

It had been a lie, of course. And a poor one.

"You wouldn't understand."

"Try me. What did you offer her?"

"Money."

"Now, there's a surprise. How much?"

"That's between me and Yvette."

Spencer gazed at her a long moment, jaw tight. "Then I want in," he said. "If for no other reason than to watch your back."

"No. Absolutely not. Jeopardizing my career is one thing, jeopardizing yours is another."

He opened his mouth as if to argue but she cut him off. "Detectives, I think you have a scene to finish processing. And I've got a leave to continue. Excuse me."

She turned and walked away, aware of their concern, Spencer's frustration.

She didn't blame them. If either of them had made the same decisions, she would have been damn concerned indeed.

47

Thursday, May 10, 2007
5:15 p.m.

Yvette paced and checked her watch. She had hung around Patti's house all afternoon, itching to get out. She was bored. Irritated. It'd been two days and the Artist hadn't shown himself.

Maybe he had moved on? Found a new girl to go all "whack job" over. Maybe she had gotten lucky and a tree had fallen on him. Or he'd been hit by a truck.

She thought of Patti. The woman's hands had trembled when she'd handed her the check for ten grand. In that moment, Yvette had realized how important this was to her. How huge an investment.

And in that moment, guilt had plucked at her.

She had taken the money, anyway.

Her cell phone dinged, announcing the arrival of a text message.

Please Come. Tips. 6:00. R.

Yvette reread the message. She wanted to go. She didn't have to be at the Hustle until nine, which would give her plenty of time to go by Tipitina's.

If Patti could break the rules, why couldn't she?

Decision made, she checked her watch again and called a cab. Patti would be really pissed when she found out. And if she didn't get out before the woman returned, she'd stop her.

Bossy, worrywart.

The cab arrived as she was zipping her sexiest jeans. She slipped into a pair of low-heeled sandals, grabbed her purse and darted out to the cab.

A local landmark, Tipitina's had featured some big names over the years but was known mostly for showcasing local and regional music. Located in the Quarter, it had been spared the worst of Katrina's sucker punch.

The taxi dropped her in front of the club. Yvette paid the driver and headed inside. It was early for a place like Tip's, but there looked to be a fair-size crowd, anyway.

Riley spotted her the moment she walked in. His set hadn't begun yet, and he hurried over to her. "You came. This is so cool."

"I can't stay too long. I have to work."

"I'm just glad you're here." He caught her hands. "I wrote a song for you."

She felt herself flush with pleasure. "You did?"

"I wasn't going to sing it unless you came tonight."

"I'm glad I did."

"Me, too." He bent and kissed her. Just the briefest of touches, his mouth to hers. She felt the contact to the tips of her toes.

"I've got to get up there. Clap for me, okay?"

He returned to the stage. She got a Coke and perched on a tall stool. His was a simple style: an acoustic guitar, a piano, Southern ballads about love and heartbreak, faith and family. He had a smoky voice, achingly accessible.

What, she wondered, was he doing managing an art gallery?

When he sang "her" song, he looked right at her. Into her. She felt hot. Light-headed and giddy. The words, the moment, wrapped around her—and she fell in love with him.

No one had ever accused her of being smart.

"Hello."

She glanced at the woman who had come to stand beside her. She recognized her, though she wasn't sure from where. "Hi."

"June Benson," the woman said. "Riley's sister."

"That's right." Yvette smiled. "I knew I'd seen you before." She motioned the stage. "He's good."

"I think so, too."

"He told me y'all are really close."

"We are." She paused to sip her drink. "Riley's been talking a lot about you."

"He has?"

"Mmm." She shifted her gaze to the stage, expression ferocious. "My brother is...impetuous. He acts before he thinks. Wears his heart on his sleeve. I wanted you to know that."

"I don't understand what you mean."

She returned her gaze to Yvette, looking her straight in the eyes. "He's easily hurt. That's what I'm trying to tell you."

"Why would you think I'd hurt him?"

"I know who you are. The kind of dancer you are. And that you're definitely not a 'cocktail waitress.'"

Yvette felt as if she had been punched. "How did you—"

"Spencer Malone told me. That night at the gallery."

"I see."

"Do you?" The woman leaned toward her. "I love my brother and don't want to see his heart broken. That's all."

Yvette struggled to keep how deeply June's words hurt from showing. "And a woman like me would break his heart. Is that right? Because I'm trash? A whore?"

"I didn't say that."

"You didn't have to."

Riley's first set ended and he bounded over. "You guys are talking. That's so great."

"We are getting to know each other," June murmured.

"Didn't I tell you? Isn't she the best?" He beamed at his sister, then turned to Yvette. "Did you like your song?"

She had. Liked it—and him—too much. It'd been a nice fantasy while it lasted.

"Yes," she whispered, standing. "I've got to go. Sorry."

She ducked past him and hurried toward the club entrance. He caught up with her.

"What gives? Did June say something to you?"

"That she didn't want you hurt."

"She's overprotective. More like my mother than my sister sometimes." He smiled. "She didn't mean anything by it."

"Yes, she did. She thinks I'm a—" She bit the words back, dangerously near tears. She wouldn't cry. Not now. Not ever again.

"A what? You misunderstood her, she's a really sweet—"

"I'm not who you think I am."

His eyebrows shot up. "Your name's not Yvette Borger?"

She lifted her chin. "I'm not a cocktail waitress. I'm a stripper," she said as harshly as she could. "At the Hustle. I do three sets a night and make damn good money. I get extra for lap dances and still more for 'private' lap dances. That's why your sister thinks I'll hurt you. Because I'm no good."

He didn't reply, and she wrenched her arm free. "I have to go."

As she walked away, Yvette realized what hurt the most was that he didn't try to stop her.

But she wasn't surprised.

48

Thursday, May 10, 2007
9:25 p.m.

Yvette didn't bother calling a cab. Despite the warm, humid night, she was cold. What an idiot she was. For allowing herself to be drawn into a fantasy. Her own little fairy tale, which didn't have a damn thing to do with real life.

She paused to fire up a cigarette, then continued toward the Hustle. Nobody said life was going to be fair. Nobody promised it'd be easy, that people would be nice.

"The Golden Rule is for losers. To get anywhere in this world, you've got to watch out for number one."

Just two of the pearls her old man had doled out, particularly with a belly full of beer.

She'd remembered those nuggets of wisdom when, at sixteen, she'd hit him over the head with the coffeepot, emptied his wallet and run. It'd been the last time she'd seen him, though she had heard he'd survived. That he still worked for the Greenwood, Mississippi, post office.

She reached the Hustle and ducked inside. Dante the bouncer grinned at her. "You're late, sweet cheeks."

"Shit happens."

He shook his head. "Fine by me. Tell that to the Sarge. That one's strung way too tight."

Patti. No doubt freaking out. Afraid she had lost her "deposit."

"She can kiss my ass."

"Can I?"

He leered at her; she flipped him the bird and made her way backstage. Patti was there, pacing. She saw Yvette and stopped, expression tight.

"Where the hell were you?"

Yvette met her gaze insolently. "I went to see a friend."

"Without telling me. We had an agreement—"

"You broke the rules first."

"Grow up."

"I don't need your lectures." Yvette turned and flounced into her dressing room.

Patti followed. "Actually, I think you do. You came to me for help, remember?"

"Don't pull that crap with me. You need me. More than I need you."

"Are you so certain about that? I seem to remember you

being pretty scared. Pretty certain that the Artist had killed your friend. Or was that another of your fabrications?"

Angry, Yvette folded her arms across her chest. "Screw off! I have a life."

"The question is, do you want to keep it?"

She jerked her chin up. "I think he's packed up his saw and moved on."

"What makes you think that?"

"We haven't seen or heard from him. My moving in with you spooked him."

Patti laughed. "You think a freak who's killed some nine people is going to get spooked by me?"

"You're a cop. You carry a gun."

"And you're an irresponsible child."

"Screw this. And you."

Yvette strode across to the vanity and began stuffing her things into a tote bag.

"Where do you think you're going to go?"

"Anywhere else but here. I don't need you or this crappy job."

"Alma Maytree is dead."

Yvette froze. She turned slowly and looked at Patti. "What did you say?"

"Alma Maytree is dead. That's where I went this afternoon. Somebody killed her."

"Oh, my God."

"Two nights ago or so. Bashed in the side of her head with a frying pan."

Her father, out cold. Blood trickling from his head. Pooling on the speckled Formica floor.

She shook her head. "Why would anyone hurt Miss Alma? She was the sweetest, most gentle person. Nice to everybody."

"This happened two nights ago, Yvette."

For a full three seconds, she stared dumbly at Patti. Then she understood.

The Artist.

"He did this, didn't he?"

"We can't jump to conclusions. It might have nothing to do with him."

"But you think it does?"

"Yes."

"But…why?" she cried. "Why would he hurt her? I don't understand!"

"The same reason he poisoned Samson. To get to you."

Yvette brought a hand to her mouth and sank to the floor. "I'm going to be sick."

Patti snatched up the trash can and brought it to her. Yvette bent over it and retched up the horror of the past weeks, the disappointments of a lifetime, the fear that held her in its grip.

When she'd finished, Patti handed her a damp towel and a bottle of water.

"Do you get it now, Yvette? Do you see what you're dealing with? Why I set up all those stupid rules?"

Yvette thought of Miss Alma, her sweet nature, how much she had loved her yappy Pomeranian. She pictured Riley, imagined a life with someone like him. A good life. With children and a home. The fairy tale.

"I don't want to die," she whispered.

"Then you need to do what I say. This isn't a game."

Or she could run. Take the money and get the hell out of New Orleans.

Yvette stood, legs wobbly, and crossed to her chair. She sank onto it and reached for her handbag and cigarettes. Her hands shook so badly, she could hardly light one.

When she had, she pulled greedily on it. After a moment, calmer, she said, "This is crazy. Insane."

"Yes, it is."

"I shouldn't be here. I should go."

"He hurt your friend. A sweet old lady who couldn't fight back. He poisoned a defenseless animal. Killed six other women, that we know of."

"And your husband."

"Yes. And my husband. Don't let him get away with it, Yvette. Help me get him."

Yvette stared at her. The moments ticked past. The cigarette had burned down to the filter. With a yelp of pain, she stamped it out.

"Help me," Patti said. "Please."

Finger stinging, vision blurred by tears, Yvette said she would.

49

Monday, May 14, 2007
6:30 a.m.

Stacy stepped out of the bathroom, fully dressed. The Alma Maytree murder was not adding up for her. As of last evening, every tenant in the building—except Yvette Borger—had been questioned either by her, Baxter or one of the assisting officers.

No one had seen anything. No one had noticed anyone who looked like they didn't belong. Building residents uniformly agreed that people got through the locked gate by piggyback-ing in with someone else legitimately coming or going.

Before Miss Alma's murder no one had believed it to be a huge issue; they now did.

But why slip in, bash in an old lady's head and leave with nothing to show for it?

She'd accessed the woman's financials: a little pension plan from a lifetime at the American Can Company, social security. But no big life insurance policy for some distant relative to kill for.

And distant relatives were all she had. A great-niece in Chicago. A nephew in Birmingham. His kids.

They'd been horrified to hear of the murder.

Besides questioning Borger, she intended to query anyone she hadn't spoken to personally.

Stacy crossed to the bed and bent to kiss a still sleeping Spencer goodbye. As she did, he grabbed her wrist and pulled her down on top of him.

"Where do you think you're going?" he asked, his voice a sleepy drawl.

"To do a little digging into the Maytree murder."

"Sounds boring. Stay and play with me instead." He tightened his arms around her. "Pretty please. I'll make it worth your while."

She knew he would. He always did. She regretfully wriggled away. "Can't. Made an appointment with Maytree's landlord."

He propped himself up on an elbow. "All work and no play, Killian."

"Tell me about it." She kissed him again. "Call me later."

When she reached the door, he called her name, stopping her. She looked back.

"I don't want you to go."

Something in his tone and expression told her he wasn't referring to this morning's trip.

He was talking about her leaving for good.

"We'll talk later."

"You said that a couple weeks ago."

She had, then avoided the conversation. But so had he. Until now.

"What are you afraid of, Stacy?"

"I'm not afraid."

"Do you want to move out?"

She gazed at him, then shook her head. "No."

"Then don't. Stay."

"Sometimes it's not about what you want."

"That must be girl-speak because I don't get it."

"Call me later. Okay?"

She ducked out of the bedroom before he could say more. What *was* she afraid of? she wondered, filling a travel mug with coffee, then heading out to her car. Being hurt? Or was it more complicated than that?

More complicated. A lot more.

Not wanting to pursue that particular train of thought, she climbed into the SUV and started it up. She had arranged to meet the landlord early, so he could let her in. She wouldn't make any friends by interrupting Monday-morning routines, but that didn't bother her.

What Patti had said kept plucking at her. That the Artist had visited Yvette the same night Alma Maytree had been murdered and Ray Wilkins and Bob Simmons's pug had been poisoned.

She had tried to broach the subject with Spencer; he'd refused to discuss it.

She intended to talk to the dog owners first. The assisting officer had interviewed them, but they'd said nothing about their dog having been poisoned. Of course, there could be a number of reasons for that, including the fact the officer hadn't had a reason to ask.

She had one now.

Fifteen minutes later, she stood at the door to apartment eight. She knocked loudly, hoping to be heard above the continual bark of a very upset dog.

Samson. Obviously recovered.

One of the men answered the door. He was medium height and trim. Dark hair threaded with gray. Dressed and pressed. She placed him somewhere between forty and fifty.

She held up her shield. "Detective Killian. NOPD. I need to ask you a few questions about your neighbor, Alma Maytree. And your dog."

The man looked over his shoulder. "Ray, get out here! Police."

Another man stumbled out of the kitchen, coffee mug clutched in his hand and hair sticking out in six different directions. He wore rumpled shorts and a faded T-shirt. The contrast between the two was dramatic.

"Ray, this is Detective Killian," he said. "She's here about Miss Alma. And Samson."

"Forgive the way I look, I had a rough night." Ray waved her inside. "You want coffee?"

"Thanks, no. I power-guzzled a cup on the way here."

He nodded his understanding and directed them to their

charmingly decorated living room. Samson trailed behind, snuffling and snorting.

Stacy sat on the velvet-covered chair; the dog flopped down at her feet.

She motioned to the animal. "He seems to have made a full recovery."

"You know about his being poisoned?" Ray said.

"Captain O'Shay informed me."

"Yvette's friend?" She nodded and he went on. "He's doing okay, though I wouldn't say he's fully recovered. Poor baby."

At that, the "baby" lifted his head and looked at his master. Ray smiled and clucked at him; the animal stood, trotted over and allowed his master to scoop him up and set him on his lap. With his pushed-in face, she decided, Samson was so ugly he was cute.

"Any idea who did it?" she asked.

They shook their heads in unison. "We didn't pursue it. He pulled through and after what happened to Miss Alma—"

"We just didn't."

"I understand you were out the night it happened."

Bob nodded, looking miserable. "Overnight trip to the Mississippi Gulf Coast casinos. Saw a show, lost a few bucks, drank too much. Typical getaway."

"What do you do, Bob?"

"Loan officer. Gulf Coast Bank. You know, the bank that makes pigs fly."

She smiled slightly, thinking of the local bank's very funny ads featuring pigs flying over the Superdome. She turned to his partner. "How about you, Ray?"

"I have a dog-grooming business. Ray's Perfect Pups."

"Here in the Quarter?"

"Yes."

Bill frowned. "May I ask why that's important?"

Before she could reply, her cell phone vibrated. She excused herself and answered. "Detective Killian."

"Hi, Detective. This is Jamie from the lab. Got something interesting for you on the Maytree murder."

"Shoot."

"Guess what we found on her robe? Dog fur."

"Not so blown away. She had a Pomeranian."

"Goldish-orange fur. Found lots of that. This was definitely canine, but a different breed. And a different color. Black and white."

"She spent a lot of time in the courtyard with Sissy. No doubt other animals and their owners use that courtyard."

"The only place we found it was on her robe, in front, lapel area. Only two strands. Killer may have carried it inside with him, transferred it to the victim."

Stacy narrowed her eyes in thought. Now, that *was* interesting. "I want to know what breed those strands are from."

"Under way. It'll take a little time."

"Thanks, Jamie. Keep me posted."

She flipped her phone shut and returned to the couple. "By any chance, did Alma Maytree have a key to your apartment?"

Bob's face went slack with surprise. "Yes. She helped with Samson sometimes. When we were gone."

"Like overnight trips to the Gulf Coast?"

"Yes, she…" His words trailed off as he filled in the blanks. She saw the moment it all made sense. "Oh, my God, you don't think… The person who poisoned Samson—"

Ray jumped in. "Killed Miss Alma?"

Stacy ignored that question, asking another of her own. "Ray, did Miss Alma bring Sissy to you for grooming?"

"She did. I groomed Sissy for free…in exchange for Miss Alma helping us out with Sam—"

His eyes welled with tears. "She was such a sweetheart, how could anyone…hurt her?"

Stacy stood. "I don't know. But I intend to find out."

As soon as Stacy cleared Yvette's building, she dialed Patti's cell phone. The woman picked up right away.

"It's Stacy. Where are you?"

"At the house. What's up?"

"I have news. Regarding the Maytree murder. Be there in ten."

Ten became fifteen because of a garbage truck. Patti was waiting at the door when Stacy pulled up. She hurried up the walk to meet her.

Without speaking, they went inside. Stacy followed Patti to the kitchen. There, the woman shoved a mug of coffee into her hands, then poured one for herself.

"Where's Yvette?"

"Sleeping."

"You look like you could use some."

"I haven't quite grasped the concept of 'work half the night, sleep till noon.' What do you have?"

"Heard from the lab this morning. Found plenty of Sissy's

fur on Miss Alma's robe. Also picked up two strands from another breed."

"Just two?"

"On her robe. Definitely canine."

"Killer brought it in, transferred it to the robe."

"It's possible."

"Anyone in the building have a pet that fits that description?"

"Don't know yet. That's the first thing I'm going to find out when I leave here. The lab's working to identify the breed."

Before Patti could comment, Stacy went on. "Miss Alma had a key to Bob and Ray's apartment."

"Samson's owners."

"Yes. She helped them out when they were gone. In exchange, Ray groomed Sissy for free."

Patti sipped her coffee, brow furrowed in thought. "Let's assume Miss Alma's murder, Samson's poisoning and the Artist's nocturnal visit are all related. Why kill the old lady and poison the dog?"

"Kill the old lady to get the key—"

"To poison the dog—"

"To keep him quiet—"

"So he can make his visit to Yvette without waking the entire apartment complex."

"Bingo." Stacy set her coffee cup on the counter. "The killer knew Alma Maytree had a key to that apartment."

"How?"

"And how did he know he could get to Samson when he did?"

"What's *she* doing here?"

Stacy turned to the kitchen doorway. Yvette stood there, looking absolutely wrecked. Stacy smiled. "Hello, Yvette."

She didn't return the greeting. "I repeat, what's she doing here?"

"Helping," Patti answered. "Be nice."

Stacy fought back a grin. Patti sounded like a scolding mother.

The young woman glared. "Helping? You thought I was full of shit, remember?"

"Maybe now I think you're not as full of it as before."

"Gee, thanks." She shuffled to the fridge, opened it and retrieved a Coke.

Stacy turned back to Patti. "Any sign of the Artist yet?"

"No. Not since Yvette moved in here. Almost a week."

"One big thing's changed," Stacy said.

Patti nodded. "She's not in her apartment."

"Exactly. I've got a plan. Yvette moves back into her apartment. With a roommate. A friend she made at the Hustle."

Yvette popped the can's top. "I suppose you have someone in mind?"

"A cocktail waitress named Brandi."

"No way."

"I don't really think this is up to you."

The younger woman jerked her chin up. "That's where you're wrong. It is most definitely up to me."

"As I understand it," Stacy said softly, "you're in it for the money. Throwing me into the mix doesn't change that."

Her face flooded with angry color. "I can change my mind if I want. And I will."

Patti stepped between them. "I agree with Yvette. Thanks for the offer, but I'm not going to jeopardize your career."

"I appreciate your concern, but the department has no say in where I live. Or how I spend my off hours."

That wasn't quite true. NOPD officers had a code of conduct to live by, but what she was proposing was neither illegal nor would it dishonor her badge.

"I'll have a gun," Stacy continued. "And a badge. He won't be able to resist paying another midnight visit. When he does, I take him down."

"Spencer will have my hide," Patti said.

Yvette's jaw dropped. "You're not actually consid—"

Stacy cut her off. "He'll get over it. What do you think?"

"I'm thinking I've got to be crazy, but it just might work."

50

Monday, May 14, 2007
5:45 p.m.

Stacy packed enough of her things to make her move-in look authentic. Making frequent trips back to the Riverbend house might arouse suspicion. The Artist could be watching Yvette's building. Hell, he could be one of her neighbors.

She, Patti and Yvette had planned it all out. Brandi would move in tonight. Stacy had instructed Yvette to make a big deal out of it. Tell everyone that she had been staying with a friend because she was so freaked out about what happened to Miss Alma and Samson.

Tell them that's the reason for a roommate. Introduce Brandi around. Make it look normal.

Yvette hadn't been happy, but they hadn't given her an option. This was the new deal. Period.

"Something you want to tell me, Killian?"

Spencer.

She looked over her shoulder at him. *Dual-purpose move. This would give them a little time and space. To sort it out. Decide what they wanted.*

She forced a carefree smile. "Hi, hon."

"You never call me that."

She didn't. Damn. "I have news."

His gaze slid to the suitcases. "Apparently."

"I've found a temporary place to live."

"Good thing I came home when I did."

"I wasn't going to leave without telling you."

"Right." He slipped his hands into his pockets. "That's the way it looks."

"It's work-related. But it'll give us some breathing room. Test a separation."

"Test a separation," he repeated. "I think that's all bullshit."

"So we agree to disagree. Lots of couples do."

"What's the case?"

She hesitated. "I said work-related. Not necessarily an active case."

"More bullshit, Stacy. What are you trying to hide?"

Trying not to rub salt in the wound. "I'm not hiding anything. Brandi's back. She's moving in with Yvette."

At his shocked expression, she tipped her hands palms up. "I think there's something there, Spencer."

Quickly, before he could argue, she filled him in. She began with the crime lab calling, learning about the key, then how she had connected the dots and gone to Patti with her offer.

"Patti's tossing away her career and you're going to help? I can't believe this."

"There's something there," she said again. "And while I'm there, I can watch Patti's back."

"I know what's there. A liar and a cheat. And a woman whose decisions are being motivated by grief. What's your excuse?"

"What are you most upset about? The fact I think we need a break? Or that I'm buying into Yvette's story?"

"This is ridiculous."

"In your opinion."

He left the room. She watched him go, then returned to her packing, half expecting to hear the front door slam and the Camaro roar to life.

She didn't, and let out a shaky breath. Well, that had gone well. *Not.*

She wanted to stay with him. But she wanted him to *need* her to stay. If he had made one real plea, shown a hint of real emotion, she would have let him know that.

But he hadn't.

Which was symptomatic of their relationship.

She finished packing, then headed to the bathroom for her transformation. Fifteen minutes later, she went in search of Spencer. He sat on the front porch, drinking a beer.

She stepped outside. "Will you help me get my bags into the car?"

He laughed, the sound short and brutal. "Sure."

He brought the suitcases out, loaded them into her Explorer, then shut the hatch.

"See you around, Killian."

"Spencer, I—" She touched his arm. "I handled this badly. I'm sorry, I—"

He shook off her hand. "I have an answer to that question you asked me earlier. Truth is, I'm more upset about you helping Patti than you moving out."

She took an involuntary step back, hurt to her core. Tears stung her eyes, and she blinked quickly against them. She would not allow him to see how deeply he had cut her.

"Right. I'm glad we're on the same page." She went around to the driver's side and opened the door. "I'll make arrangements for the rest of my stuff."

"No hurry. Whenever."

"Great." She climbed into the vehicle. "See you around."

"Absolutely."

She started the Explorer and drove off. When she reached the end of the block, she glanced in the rearview mirror. He stood in the street, watching her go, expression set. Feeling as if she had a thousand-pound weight sitting on her chest, she drove on.

Stacy made it to Patti's without incident, her cell phone tellingly silent. She had hoped he would think about what he had said, realize he hadn't meant it and call her back.

As it stood now, they were through.

She pulled into the drive and climbed out. Patti was waiting. She looked anxious.

"Everything all right?" Patti asked.

"Sure. Why wouldn't it be?"

The woman arched her eyebrows. "Name starts with an S—for stubborn."

"It's over." She held up a hand to ward off any argument from the other woman. "He was more upset about my involvement in this than with my leaving."

"That sounds like wounded male pride to me. I'm sure he'll—"

Stacy cut her off. "It's time for us to move on. And it's been coming for a while." She shifted the conversation to Yvette. "Is she ready?"

"Ready. But not happy."

"Tough shit."

"She's really young," Patti said softly. "She hasn't had an easy life."

"You actually *like* her?"

"I understand her."

At the sound of a door slamming, they turned. Yvette stalked into the foyer, lugging a suitcase.

She dropped it with a thud at Stacy's feet. "I'm not doing this again. I'm returning to my apartment and that's where I'm going to stay."

Stacy rolled her eyes. Arrogance was unattractive enough when it was attached to true talent or brilliance. Attached to childishness, it was just plain irritating. When would Yvette realize this was as much to save her as to catch Sammy's killer?

"Play nice," Patti said. "I'll see you at the Hustle tomorrow night."

"Whatever."

She strode to the SUV, leaving the suitcase for Stacy to bring. Stacy gritted her teeth. *If the Artist showed, maybe she should let him scare the crap out of the little witch.*

After telling Patti goodbye, she headed to the Explorer, then climbed into the driver's seat.

"What about my suitcase?" Yvette said.

"Your arms aren't broken."

The younger woman glared at her. Stacy smiled. "It's not my stuff, I don't care if we leave it behind."

With a huff, Yvette threw open the door and went to retrieve her case. After she had stowed it in back, she climbed back in, steaming.

Stacy glanced at Yvette. "You just can't see that we're inconveniencing ourselves for you?"

"Whatever." She slammed her car door. "NOPD must not pay much. This is a pretty crappy ride."

"I have other priorities."

"Like what?"

"Saving for the future, for one." Yvette didn't respond and Stacy added, "You probably think that's pretty boring."

"Actually, I don't." She looked at her. "What does your boyfriend think about this?"

Stacy pulled away from the curb, heading back into the French Quarter. "My boyfriend?"

"Detective Malone. I know you live with him."

"So?"

"So what does he think about you moving in with me?"

"He's not happy. Not that it's any of your business."

"Be careful or he'll find someone who does make him happy."

"Relationships aren't so black and white."

She smiled snidely. "That's what girls like you tell themselves."

"Really? And girls like you think a real relationship is a lap dance and a really good tip."

"Screw you."

They didn't speak again until they had entered her apartment building's courtyard. Then they made a lot of commotion, lugging Brandi's suitcases, giggling like girlfriends on a new adventure. Along the way, Yvette introduced "Brandi" to a half-dozen neighbors, repeating the roommate story with the ease of an accomplished actress—or liar.

Once inside the apartment, both dropped all pretense of friendliness. "I'll take your bedroom," Stacy said.

"I don't think so. That's my bed and I'm sleeping in it."

"If your Artist pal decides to visit tonight, he'll creep into your bedroom. Not the guest room. Which sort of defeats the purpose of my being here, now, doesn't it?"

"Well, I'm not changing the sheets," Yvette snapped, dragging her bag to the second bedroom. "You want clean sheets, you do it yourself."

Stacy had wanted them. After making up the bed and partially unpacking, she met Yvette in the kitchen. They decided on Chinese takeout for dinner. After it was delivered, they ate it with chopsticks in front of the TV, then both turned in for the night—all without exchanging anything but the most basic niceties. "Pass the rice" and "Could you turn up the volume" had been the conversational highlights of the evening.

Yvette's bed was comfortable, the apartment quiet. Still, Stacy couldn't sleep. She tossed and turned, thoughts racing. She longed to call Spencer. Just to hear his voice. In the hopes that he longed to hear hers, too.

From the front of the apartment came the sound of a door opening. A telltale click, a gentle whoosh.

Stacy retrieved her Glock and cleared the bed without making a sound. Weapon out, she inched her way down the hall. She checked Yvette's room first.

Her bed was empty.

Firming her grip on the Glock, she started forward, pausing every couple of steps to listen. *Silence.*

The kitchen was empty. But not the front room.

Yvette. Standing at the open door, smoking.

"What are you doing?"

The younger woman jumped, startled, then spun around. "You scared the shit out of me!"

Stacy lowered her weapon. "Nice mouth."

"Fuck off. Better?"

"I suggest you close the door. That isn't safe."

"I wanted a smoke."

"Then do it at a window."

She scowled, bent and put the cigarette out in a large potted palm. "You're so bossy."

"It's my job. It'll help keep you alive."

She stepped inside, closed and locked the door. "How'd you know I was up?"

"I heard you." At her surprised expression, Stacy added, "Also part of my job."

She decided not to share that she'd been unable to sleep. Let the woman think she had a super-spidey sense of hearing.

"Mind if I get a glass of milk?"

"Help yourself. But give it the sniff test first."

"Thanks." Stacy headed to the kitchen; Yvette followed. She laid her weapon on the counter, opened the refrigerator and took out the carton.

After checking the date, she sniffed. Confident it hadn't soured, she poured herself a cup, then warmed it in the microwave.

"You don't put anything in it?"

She shook her head. "My mother used to give me warm milk when—"

"When what?"

When she couldn't sleep. When she couldn't get the sound of Jane's screams out of her head.

"At night sometimes. Heating the milk brings out the natural sugar in it, so it tastes sweet. You should try it."

Yvette poured a cup, heated it and sipped. She made a face. "It's okay. Needs some Hershey's. Or whiskey."

Stacy laughed. "That's one way to get to sleep."

"Why couldn't you sleep sometimes? When you were a kid?"

"My sister Jane was in a really horrible accident and almost died. She was with me. I was older, I felt responsible."

Yvette took another sip. "What kind of an accident?"

"Hit by a boater while swimming. The prop—" She bit the words *"chewed up her face and nearly decapitated her"* back. "She's good now. Really good."

"You're close?"

"Very."

"I don't have any family."

"None?"

It seemed to Stacy she hesitated slightly before saying no. Could be "no family" was more a statement of principle than fact.

"Sorry I scared you earlier. Cops move quietly."

"S'okay. I shouldn't have opened the door like that. I guess that was stupid."

Stacy curled her hands around the warm mug. "Can I ask you a question?"

Yvette shrugged. "I guess."

"Why are you doing this? Hanging around, maybe putting yourself in danger. You could have taken off."

"Patti's paying me."

She said it so casually, as if it was totally no big deal. "Obviously you think that's okay?"

"Obviously you don't. I'm not ashamed."

"Maybe you should be?"

Yvette flushed, but not with embarrassment, Stacy suspected. With anger. "Screw the goody-goody crap. I'm putting my life on the line to help her. Besides, the money was her idea, not mine."

"You could have refused it."

"Why would I have done that?"

"Because the Handyman murdered her husband. She's grieving. It makes her vulnerable."

"To people like me."

"Yes."

"From where I'm standing, people like you are a lot more dangerous. At least I'm honest about my motives."

"This is stupid." Stacy dumped the last of her milk in the sink. "I'm going to bed."

She didn't get far. "Why're you really here?" Yvette called. "Afraid I'm going to run off with her ten grand?"

The amount knocked the wind out of Stacy. "She's paying you ten thousand dollars?"

"Fifty. Ten's the deposit."

Stacy gazed at the young woman, her dislike of her so strong she felt ill. "That money's part of her husband's life insurance payoff."

"And it's hers to spend as she chooses."

Stacy shook her head. "You make me sick."

Yvette stiffened. "I'm being paid for performing a service. She made the offer, I took it."

"Performing a service. That's what you do, right? It's at the heart of all your relationships, your every move. I was going to apologize for what I said about life being all about money for you. Now I see just how accurate that comment was."

51

Wednesday, May 16, 2007
8:05 a.m.

Patti worked to shake out the mental cobwebs. She sat at her kitchen table, cup of coffee and the *Times-Picayune* on the table in front of her.

Still no Artist. Not at Yvette's apartment, not at the Hustle. She was beginning to think Yvette was right: he had gotten spooked and had taken off.

Her cell phone vibrated. She saw from the display that it was Stacy. "What's up?" she answered.

"The brat refuses to get up."

"Did you try shooting her in the butt?"

"Very funny. Should I douse her with a glass of cold water? I've got to head in."

Patti dragged a hand through her hair. "Leave her. I'll clean up and head over there and collect Sleeping Beauty."

"Wrong story. This one's more like Beauty and the Beast. Guess who's the Beast?"

Patti laughed. "All quiet last night?"

"Yes. You?"

"No Artist."

"Thoughts?"

"It's too early to think, I'll check in later."

Patti hung up. Yvette had grown more difficult to manage by the day. She believed the Artist had lost interest. No longer afraid, the young woman was all attitude and no gratitude.

If Patti didn't want this guy so desperately, she'd cut Yvette loose. She had lied to her chief and the men and women under her command. She had alienated Spencer and now driven a wedge between him and Stacy. And for what?

Her cell phone went off again, but this time it wasn't Stacy. It was June.

"I'm at your front door," she said. "I come bearing gifts."

"I'll be right there."

A moment later, she swung open the door. June held a napkin-covered basket. "I went crazy baking. Save me from myself?"

"You're an angel of mercy, you know that?"

She stepped aside so her friend could enter. "Why didn't you ring the bell?"

"I was afraid you might be sleeping. I know your new hours are…different."

Patti cut her an amused glance. "Who've you been talking to?"

"Spencer."

Big surprise. "Come on, I've got coffee."

June followed her to the kitchen. Patti got out plates and napkins, filled a mug for June and freshened her own.

Muffins, Patti saw as they sat down. Big, fat banana-nut muffins.

Heaven on earth.

June made pretty much the best muffins on the planet. They were so good, for a time she had considered marketing them. She could have been the Mrs. Fields of muffins. But then the low-carb craze had come along, and she'd abandoned the idea.

"So what Spencer told me is true."

Patti dug in. "What'd he tell you?"

"That you asked for a leave of absence to try to track down Sammy's killer yourself. That you've lost hold of your senses. That you've now involved Stacy in it. He's quite worried."

"And he called you and asked if you would try to talk some sense into me."

"Pretty much. What's going on?"

"I haven't lost my mind, if you're worried."

June smiled and peeled away a muffin's paper liner. "Prove it."

"Yes, I've taken a leave of absence. I don't think that in itself is so shocking. As for tracking down Sammy's killer, I've had doubts about Franklin. The department does not. While I'm footloose and fancy free, I thought I'd investigate a few leads."

"Now, venturing into the 'lost it' category. That's not who Patti O'Shay is."

Patti looked away, then back. "I'm not so certain I know who Patti O'Shay is anymore."

"It's natural for you to feel this way." June reached across the table and covered Patti's hand with her own. "After what you've been through."

"Now, I've inserted a wedge between Spencer and Stacy."

"He said she moved out. That they were through."

Patti nodded. "How'd he sound?"

"Miserable." June took a sip of her coffee. "Personally, I say good for her. It's about time."

"How can you say that?"

"Has he not been stringing her along? Taking her for granted? Men wield all the power in relationships. Seems like she's taking some back." She reached for her muffin. "Again, I say good for her."

June had said things like that before. Patti felt bad for her. Several failed romances and a short, disastrous marriage had left her wary of men, cynical about relationships and the balance of power between the sexes.

Patti's experience had been so different—mutual respect, give and take, collaboration.

"You're not the only one who's lost their mind," June continued. "Riley seems to have taken leave of his senses as well."

"How so?"

"He's besotted with that dancer. Yvette—"

"Borger?"

She nodded. "He does this, gets all head-over-heels stupid about some woman, then when it doesn't work out, he mopes around for weeks. Then suddenly—"

"—is head-over-heels over another one?"

"Exactly." June sighed. "She came to see him play the other night."

"What night?"

"Last Thursday."

The night she disappeared. So that's where she'd gone.

"Why does he keep falling for women like her?"

"What do you mean, women like her?"

"You know what I mean. Strippers, party girls. Why can't he fall for someone like Shauna?"

"Yvette's okay," Patti said, realizing she was defending the woman to yet another person in her life, this time her oldest friend. "She hasn't had it easy."

"Who has?" June shot back. "You didn't see me drop out, resort to drugs or turning tricks."

Patti stiffened, offended. "As far as either of us know, she has turned to neither drugs nor prostitution."

"Lap dancing is—"

"A way for a young, uneducated woman to make a good living. Not all of us have a fat inheritance to fall back on. I respect her for doing as well as she has."

June flushed. Patti squeezed her hand. "We can agree to disagree. Right?"

"Sure. I——" She cleared her throat. "Forgive me. I sounded just awful then, didn't I? Like one of those snobs Mother used to play bridge with. Always looking down their noses at somebody. I guess the Good Lord knew what He was doing when He didn't give me children."

"That's just nonsense. You have Riley. You've been watching out for him most of his life. And he's turned out wonderfully."

Patti was shocked to see June's eyes fill with tears. "I've screwed him up. Made him too dependent. Emasculated him."

"Emasculated? June, that's just not true. You've been a wonderful sister."

"I worry about him. About the way he sometimes broods. He'll withdraw from me, become almost secreti——" She bit the thought back. "He'll be fine."

"Exactly. He'll be fine."

"Thank you." June caught her hand again, holding it tightly. "You're my best friend, Patti."

"You're my best friend, too. Twenty years now."

"We were such babies when we met."

Patti laughed. "*You* were such a baby. Remember, I've got ten years on you."

June didn't smile. "I don't know if I could have managed all the curves and bumps without you. And I mean that."

Tears stung Patti's eyes. "Now you're just getting maudlin. And you're making me that way, too."

June released her hand, then wiped a tear from her cheek. "Must be premenopausal."

"Been there, done that, it sucked." Patti's cell phone

vibrated. She saw that it was headquarters, sent June an apologetic glance and picked up. "Captain O'Shay."

"Patti, it's Tony. Thought you'd want in on this. Looks like we have another Handyman victim."

52

Wednesday, May 16, 2007
9:20 a.m.

The lower Ninth ward had been one of the hardest hit by Katrina. Water had topped the levees in some areas by more than twelve feet. Rebuilding here had been at best sporadic. The current population of this parish stood at about twenty-five percent its pre-hurricane population. It was a tragic wasteland—but a smart place to dump a body.

Patti picked her way around the piles of building debris, slick from the previous night's rain. She ducked under the scene tape, aware of the crime techs arriving behind her. The press wouldn't be far behind once word leaked that the Handyman had struck again.

Spencer and Tony stood beside the badly decomposed victim. They looked her way as Patti approached. Spencer didn't smile.

"Hey, Captain," Tony said, holding out a jar of Vicks VapoRub.

She took it and applied a smear under her nose; it helped mitigate the stench of the corpse. "Detectives. What've we got?"

She could see the basics already: female, white, quite dead.

"Found by a couple of sightseers on a 'disaster tour.' Saw more than they wanted to, that's for damn certain."

"ID?"

"Nope."

"Cause of death?"

"To be confirmed by autopsy, but she was shot in the chest. Twice."

Patti frowned. "That's not the Handyman's MO."

"True. But that is."

She followed the direction of his gaze. *Right hand missing.*

"No sign of the hand?" she asked.

"Nope. That's not to say a dog or wild animal couldn't have carried it off, but there's no doubt it was 'removed' first."

Patti fitted on latex gloves and squatted beside the victim. When dumped, the victim had been fully dressed. Like her body, the garments had begun to deteriorate in the hot, humid air. Patti moved her gaze over her, starting with her head, forcing herself to go slowly. Long, bleached-blond hair—she'd needed to have her roots done. Dangly earrings, flashy. Two necklaces, both gold. She had indeed been drilled in the chest. Point of entry for both: her left side.

Patti lowered her gaze. Wearing thong panties and low-cut blue jeans. "No sexual assault is my guess."

"But maybe sex. Then a ride and bang bang, tomorrow never comes."

She nodded. Wouldn't be the first time some guy got rid of his honey after enjoying himself one last time.

But was that the Handyman's way?

Until now, they'd never had enough of a victim to know.

Patti shifted her gaze. Left hand intact. Long, square-tip nails, most probably synthetics. Red polish. Half dozen bangle bracelets adorning the wrist.

"Hello, friends."

Deputy Coroner Ray Hollister had pulled this one. Lucky him.

He looked at the victim, then scowled up at the sunny sky. "Nobody can convince me global warming doesn't exist. It's too damn hot for May."

As if on cue, they simultaneously murmured their agreement. He slipped into his gloves. "Somebody want to fill me in?"

Patti did, quickly. He nodded

He examined the victim's left hand. "No defensive wounds. Nails all intact. Bet they'll come back clean."

"Means she didn't fight," Spencer said.

"Most probably didn't see it coming." The coroner frowned, studying the wound. "Interesting entry point," he said. "Her left side. Gun was quite close to the victim when fired. Notice the tattooing."

Sure enough, a telltale "tattoo" circled each wound. Upon discharge, particles of burned gunpowder and primer exploded from a gun's barrel, depositing on both shooter and victim. Much could be learned from the amount and patterning of the particles, including the angle and distance of the shooter. The tighter the circle, the closer the gun.

"First shot," he said, pointing to the smallest circle. "Second," he continued, indicating the other.

Patti agreed. "We'll need to take a good look at the bullet's trajectory."

"Wonder why he didn't shoot her in the head," Tony murmured.

"Maybe he thought it was too messy," Spencer offered. "Or too visible."

Patti nodded. "What if they were in a car? He's driving, has a gun tucked in a handy position—"

"Pardon the pun."

"—and squeezes off a shot before she knows what's happening."

"No big mess for the world to see."

"The shot doesn't kill her. She slumps in her seat, he rips off another one."

"It does the trick, if not immediately, soon enough. He drives on. Nobody notices a thing."

The coroner carefully examined the other entry point, then glanced up at her. "From what I'm seeing, your scenario could work, Captain. But so could others."

Lucky them. "How long's she been dead?"

"My 'in the field' guess, four or five days. It's been hot.

We've had a couple good rains and she's totally exposed. Give me some light."

Spencer directed his penlight beam to the spot the coroner indicated—one of the wounds. The light revealed a squirming world of activity—bugs, doing their part in the decomposition dance.

"Ultimately the insects will tell the tale."

The lab's entomologist would collect samples of the insect life on the corpse and provide an estimated time frame based on the stage of growth or development of the larvae.

"*A Bug's Life,*" Tony quipped. "I'll never look at that kid's movie in quite the same way."

"What about the missing hand, Ray?"

"Gone," he deadpanned.

"We need to know if this is the work of the Handyman. Can you compare this sample to the originals?"

"I'll do the best I can, though I specialize in flesh, not bones." He suddenly looked impatient. "Mind if I get to it? I'm about to get sunstroke."

He didn't wait for an answer, simply set about his business.

Patti looked at Tony. "Get Elizabeth Walker. I want her to compare this victim's severed wrist bone with the samples found in the Katrina refrigerator. ASAP."

She shifted her gaze to Spencer. "We need a name. The sooner we ID her, the sooner we—"

"I think I can help there," the coroner said.

They looked down at the man, crouched beside the body.

Very carefully he eased a gloved finger under one of the woman's necklaces and lifted it away from her shirt.

The sun caught on the gold pendant. Gold twisted into curving, ornate letters. They spelled *Tonya*.

53

Spencer looked at Patti. "What? You know who this is?"

"Tonya Messinger. It has to be. Yvette's friend, the one she said was missing."

She hadn't been fabricating.

"Tonya who?" Tony asked.

Patti ignored him and looked at her watch, expression concerned. "I've got to go. Keep me posted. Every detail."

"Go?" Tony frowned. "Captain, with all due respect, this is too big for you to step back from now."

"I agree," Spencer said. "Seems to me you need to call an end to your *leave*. I suspect full support will be available now."

Tony looked at Spencer. "Support for what?"

He went on as if Tony hadn't spoken. "If this really is the work of the Handyman, Franklin's off that particular hook. And you know what that means."

The chief would be out his jailed suspect. And be anxious to land another.

It changed everything.

"I'll think about it," Patti said. "Yvette's still the best lead we have. And I made a promise to keep her safe."

"We can do that better as a team than you can alone."

"Keep who safe?" Tony asked, confused.

"Like I said, I'll think about it."

Patti started off; Spencer stopped her. "I'm going to need to question her."

She looked over her shoulder at him. "Yes, you will. I'll make certain she's available."

He watched her walk away, then turned back to Tony. "I suppose you'd like me to cut the crap and tell you what's going on."

"I'd appreciate it, Slick. Now would be good."

Spencer filled in Tony as best he could, skimming over facts that would prove troublesome for Patti. If Tony suspected he was still being partially bullshitted—which he probably did— he was a good-enough friend not to say so.

When he'd finished, Tony said, "You need to question Borger."

"Absolutely."

"Mind if I ride shotgun?"

"It'll be like old times."

They left the scene to the techs and coroner's reps. Once buckled into the Camaro, Spencer dialed Patti. "Tony and I are on our way. Where are you?"

"Yvette's apartment," she answered.

"Twenty minutes," he said, then hung up.

He dialed Elizabeth Walker next. "Big news. We've got ourselves a new Handyman victim. Or what appears to be one of the Handyman's."

"You want me to evaluate the amputation?"

"Give the lady a gold star. When can you be here?"

"Three hours. That's the best I can do."

"Call me when you're thirty minutes out. I'll meet you."

He hung up and Tony sent him an amused glance. "What did we do before cell phones?"

"Don't know, man. Lived like animals."

Tony chuckled. "Speaking of you being an animal, have you called Stacy yet?"

"Patti probably did."

"Way to weenie out. She should hear it from you."

He hadn't spoken to her since she moved out, a fact Tony was aware of. "What about my manly pride? My dignity and—"

"Jackass stupidity? Seems a bit of crow-eating might be in order."

Spencer scowled at him. "You suck, you know that?"

Tony laughed. "Just my opinion, Slick."

Grumbling to himself, Spencer opened his phone and dialed Stacy. "Hey," he said when she answered.

"Back at you," she replied.

"I wanted to let you know, looks like you and Patti were right. Tonya Messinger turned up dead today."

"Where?"

"Lower Ninth. Shot twice. Right hand severed." He heard her sharply indrawn breath. "Yeah, things just got freaky. I'm on my way to interview Yvette. Patti's with her."

"What are Patti's plans?"

"Don't know yet. What're yours?"

"What do you hope they'll be?"

Spencer angled a glance at Tony, who saw it and grinned.

"Tell her you love her," Tony said. "That you're a jackass and want her back."

"Is that Tony?" she asked.

"Yeah," he answered. "Being a jerk. I'll keep you posted."

Patti buzzed them into the courtyard, then met them outside Yvette's door. "What's the latest?" she asked before they even cleared the threshold.

"Talked to Elizabeth Walker. She's on her way. Asked her to call me when she was close. I'll meet her at the morgue. The techs are finishing processing the scene now. They're giving this top priority."

"Good. Anything else?"

They shook their heads, and she led them into the living room. There, they found Yvette huddled in a corner on her couch.

"Hello, Yvette," Spencer said. She didn't reply and he introduced Tony. "This is Detective Sciame."

She flicked her gaze over him, then went back to staring at the wall.

"I'm sorry," Spencer went on. "I know she was your friend."

"I told you," she said, meeting his eyes, tone accusing. "You didn't believe me."

"No," he admitted, "I didn't. But I do now."

"You called me a liar, Detective."

"I did. I'm sorry."

"Sorry *so* doesn't cover it."

"I understand. I need your help, anyway."

"Fine." She drew her knees tighter to her chest. "What do you want to know?"

"Everything about the Artist."

"You mean all the stuff I already told you and you didn't believe?"

"Pretty much."

She looked frustrated but did as he asked. Everything she told him, he had heard before. It began when she received a love note from someone calling himself the Artist. She received four in all, one containing five hundred dollars—the exact amount of money Marcus owed her.

"Tonya delivered the note. She saw the money and I confided what was going on. She recognized Jessica from the picture in the paper and also remembered that some guy had sent similar notes to her."

Patti stepped in. "Tonya was already missing when I came on board. Judging by what we saw today, she was most probably already dead."

Yvette brought her hands to her face. He saw that they trembled. "It's my fault," she said. "She tried to help me. Now she's dead."

"It's not your fault. You didn't kill her."

"I wish I could believe...if she hadn't agreed to help me—"

"But she did," Patti said firmly. "Let's not let this bastard get away with it."

"When's the last time you heard from the Artist?"

"Tuesday the eighth I woke up and found a note he'd left."

"In your apartment?"

"Yes. And a locket."

"A locket?" he repeated, frowning.

"Tonya's. Her picture was in it."

"Just hers?"

"Yes."

Spencer and Tony exchanged glances.

"I know that's weird, but maybe she broke up with some guy, got rid of his picture, but kept the necklace."

Spencer frowned slightly and looked at Patti. "Tuesday the eighth. Wasn't that the date you began your leave?"

She said it was, and he turned back to Yvette. "And you haven't seen or heard from him since?"

Patti answered for her. "No. Not here or through the club. I have the locket and note."

"I don't feel so good," Yvette said, jumping to her feet.

They watched her hurry from the room. Spencer glanced at Patti, saw her concern. "She okay?" he asked.

"She does that a lot. It's starting to worry me."

"What about security tapes from the Hustle?" Tony looked from Patti to Spencer. "Could be our guy's pictured—"

"Already been down that road," Patti said. "They flip 'em every thirty-six hours. Besides, Tonya was the only one who knew what this guy looked like."

"And she's dead."

"What's our next move?" Tony asked.

"Twenty-four-hour protection for Yvette," Patti answered. "We get Captain Cooper's okay to make Stacy's living arrangement here official. Get a team to Messinger's condo. I want it searched, pull out all the bells and whistles. We also need a positive ID on Messinger. See who you can find. Family, boyfriend—"

"Borger."

"Too involved."

"She might have a record," Tony offered. "That'd put her prints on file."

"Check it out, ASAP. If so, talk to Hollister. See if he can get a couple good prints from her."

Spencer looked at Tony, who grinned.

She glowered at them. "What?"

"Kinda bossy for a person on leave—"

"—a person who's too stressed—"

"—dare we say overwhelmed—"

"—to perform her duties."

"Can it, clowns. Captain Patti O'Shay is officially back in the saddle."

54

Wednesday, May 16, 2007
2:00 p.m.

Spencer stood in the doorway to Patti's office, watching her. With a series of phone calls, she had spoken to the chief and was officially back in charge of ISD, had arranged round-the-clock protection for Yvette, gotten Stacy "officially" installed as Yvette's roommate and ordered an investigative team, which included Tony, to Messinger's condo.

She was, quite simply, amazing.

"Glad to be back under your command," he said. "Even if I'm pissed at you."

"Sorry, but I had to play it the way I did."

"You didn't trust me."

"I'd trust you with my life. But I won't jeopardize your career."

"That's not for you to decide."

She smiled slightly. "And that, Detective, is bullshit. I'm your immediate ranking officer and your aunt. I would never take advantage of my position that way."

"I'm still pissed."

"I can live with that."

His cell phone went off, keeping him from retorting. "Detective Malone."

"It's Elizabeth Walker. I'm thirty minutes out."

"Great, I'll meet you at the morgue."

The morgue had not been built with comfort in mind. No warm, fuzzies here. Just stainless-steel tables and work stations, cold tile floors and refrigerated cadaver drawers.

The job brought Spencer here way more than he liked. Frankly, even after all these years on the force, the place still gave him the creeps.

He and Elizabeth arrived at the same time. "Thanks for dropping everything and coming in," Spencer said, falling into step with her. "We've waited a long time for another crack at this guy."

"Fill me in."

"Woman. Dead four or five days. Shot. Right hand MIA."

They entered the building and crossed to the attendant. Though the woman recognized them, she asked for ID.

"Here to examine the Jane Doe brought in today," he said.

"Which one?"

"Lower Ninth ward."

She nodded. "Sign in. I'll tell Chris you're on your way."

In his twenties, Chris was tall, thin and pale. His communication skills ranked up there with those of a rock, and Spencer decided he spent way too much time with dead people.

"She's right here."

The process was extremely efficient. Chris rolled the examining table into the refrigerated room where the bodies were stored on stainless-steel, racked trays. The trays rested on rollers and the shelving was totally adjustable, which allowed the bodies to be stacked, basically, one on top of another.

As they watched, Chris raised the table until it was the same height as the fourth shelf, then rolled the tray out onto it.

On the tray lay Jane Doe's remains, zipped nice and neat into a black body bag.

"Where do you want her?"

"Under the lights, please," Elizabeth answered.

She snapped on gloves, crossed to the table and adjusted the surgical lamp. "Before I left, I took a minute to review my findings on the City Park Jane Doe and the original samples. I brought my notes and photos. Let's see what we've got."

She unzipped the bag. Her expression didn't change; her attention went immediately to the amputation site.

He left her to work and wandered over to where Chris sat inputting data in a computer. "Kind of quiet down here."

"Deadly dull," he shot back, snickering at his own joke.

Autopsy room humor.

"Detective?" Elizabeth motioned him over. "You're not going

to like me very much. But there's a good chance this is the work of a different killer."

He had called her for confirmation, thought they would get it and move forward with the investigation. Instead, he was left feeling as if the rug had been yanked from under his feet—again.

"Talk to me," he said, hearing the frustration in his own voice.

"First, this killer used a much less effective tool. Maybe a small garden saw or even some sort of kitchen utensil."

"He was in a situation where he had to use what was available." Even as he offered the explanation, he discounted it. The Handyman had planned his acts carefully, not leaving things like tools to chance. That much had been obvious.

Elizabeth went on, expression sympathetic. "This cutter was obviously uncertain of himself. Look here." Adjusting the light and magnifier, she used clamp tweezers to draw what was left of the tissue away from the bone. "See those marks on the bone? They're false starts."

"In your opinion."

She lifted her gaze. "My expert opinion. Yes."

"What else?"

"The amputation shows no skill, the cutter just sawed and hacked away. The City Park Jane Doe's was slick, very professional."

Spencer frowned. "A couple of the original samples displayed the same unskilled cuts. Could be he's gotten rusty in the past couple of years? That along with not having his usual quality equipment, could account for the clumsiness, couldn't it?"

"It might," she conceded. "But here's the kicker. I think this killer's left-handed, not right."

This just got worse and worse.

"Sorry, Detective, just calling it as I see it."

"Show me."

She retrieved seven photos from her briefcase and spread them out on the nearest work station. "Here are photos from all the previous victims. These first three represent the ones we assumed were the Handyman's earliest attempts. Notice the false starts."

"Just like this victim."

"Yes, but with one difference. Do you see it?"

He studied the images, frowning. "You're the expert, you tell me."

"Here, the cutter pulls the saw from left to right. That's evidenced by the depth of the cut, where it starts and how it finishes. Let's look at today's victim again."

Spencer saw what she meant right away. "Dammit!"

"Sorry. Really, I am."

He searched for an explanation. "Could this be bogus?"

"I don't understand."

"Could he have used his left hand even though he was right-handed?"

"That would certainly explain some of the clumsiness. But why?"

"To throw us off. To make us question whether he was the Real McCoy or not."

"Anything's possible, Detective. Although I think it's a stretch. On many levels."

"Such as?"

"Keeping in mind that my specialty is bones, not behavior, the human animal is one who falls back on the automatic or innate.

"Being right-handed or left-handed is innate. The killer would need an incredible amount of control to consciously use his 'wrong' hand, especially during a time of elevated adrenaline or excitement."

She was right. In addition, serial killers were creatures of ritual. The Handyman took his victim's right hand. He would do it exactly the same way each time, refining the ritual as he went. The act, the way he played it out, was meaningful to him—emotionally and intellectually. Often sexually gratifying as well.

So what now? It didn't mean Tonya hadn't been a victim of the Handyman, but it certainly wasn't the slam dunk they had expected.

"When can you have an official finding?"

"I'll coordinate with Ray. Certainly within the next couple of days."

He nodded. "Until then, can we keep this between us?"

"Absolutely." She frowned slightly. "What's going on?"

"I'm not sure. But this is an especially sensitive case, and I want to make certain all my ducks are in a row before I present anything to the brass."

Elizabeth agreed and stayed behind to catch up with the pathologist; Spencer headed to his car. As he slid into the Camaro his phone vibrated. It was Tony.

"Pasta Man," he said. "I was just going to call you."

"Great minds, Slick. Got news. Jessica Skye's family has been located. Small town in Alabama. Daphne. They've not heard from her since before Katrina."

"Have they tried to find her?"

"Got the sense that wasn't high on their priority list. Apparently Jessica and her family weren't on great terms, though her mother sounded really shook up when I asked if she'd be willing to look at a photo, see if she thought it was her daughter."

The forensic sculptor's reconstruction.

"She agreed to do it?"

"She did. I contacted the Daphne PD," Tony went on. "Promised me they'd do the honors as soon as they received a jpeg image of the reconstruction."

"I'm heading in now, I'll do it. You got a name?"

"Detective Fields. You want the number?"

"I'll look it up. How's the condo search coming?"

"Progressing. So far, nothing's jumped up and bit me in the ass. The techs are applying Luminol now."

The chemical mixture, when sprayed on areas where blood was suspected but not seen, reacted with iron in the hemoglobin and fluoresced. Many a criminal thought he had expertly mopped up the scene of the crime, only to be tripped up by Luminol.

"By the way, there's a photo of Messinger on her bathroom vanity wearing the Tonya necklace."

"It'll do until we can get a positive ID. I have news, too. Messinger may not have been killed by the Handyman."

"You're shitting me, right?"

"Wish I was. Dr. Walker found some major differences between the old amputations and this new one. The most stunning, she believes the original samples were made by a right-handed killer, this one a left-handed."

"You going to tell the captain this happy news?"

"Actually, I was going to let you."

"Fat chance, Slick. You're family, she won't kill you."

Before Spencer could argue the truth of that, Tony hung up.

55

Wednesday, May 16, 2007
6:35 p.m.

Yvette bent over her bathroom sink and splashed her face with cold water. It snapped her out of the fog she had been in since Patti told her.

Tonya was dead. Murdered. In her heart, Yvette had known it all along. But now it was real.

He shot her. Twice.

And removed her right hand. His trademark.

She straightened. Gazed into the mirror.

Her fault. Tonya was dead because of her.

She stared at herself, suddenly light-headed. Her knees went to rubber and she clutched the vanity for support. She breathed deeply through her nose, exhaling through her mouth. Letting go. Of the guilt. The fear.

Her life had spun completely out of control, her with it. Morphing her into a person she was afraid to know.

"You okay?" Stacy called softly, tapping on the bathroom door.

Anger surged up in her. She fisted her fingers. "No, I'm not okay! I'm pissed. At you. At your stupid boyfriend. If you'd done something right away when I told you about the Artist, Tonya would be alive."

"You don't know that. He may have targeted—"

"I turned to Tonya for help...and now she's—" Yvette fought the urge to cry. "It's your fault, not mine. You hear me? Your fault!"

The other woman didn't respond. The seconds ticked awkwardly past. Yvette went to the door, rested her palms and forehead against it. "Say something, dammit!"

"I'm sorry, Yvette." She said it softly, her voice thick. "I really am."

"Sorry doesn't mean jack!"

Make the hurt go away. Make this nightmare end.

Stacy cleared her throat. "If you...need anything, let me know. I'll be right out here."

Yvette squeezed her eyes shut against the need that welled up inside her. For comfort. Companionship. The urge to spill her guts and pour out her heart.

"Just leave me alone," she said instead, harshly. "Go away! I don't want you h—"

To her horror, the words choked off on a sob. A terrible, broken sound.

Biting back another, she crossed to the commode, flipped down the lid and sat. She curved her arms around herself and rocked back and forth.

What to do? What to do? She was losing it.

On the vanity counter, her cell phone pinged, announcing the arrival of a text message. She gazed at the device a moment, then reached for it. Hands shaking, she retrieved the message.

i miss u
pls dont b mad

He didn't identify himself; he didn't have to.

Riley.

Yvette reread the message, heart beating heavily. It seemed forever since she'd stormed out of Tipitina's, pride wounded and heart broken.

In light of today's news, her actions seemed childish and melodramatic. She wished she could take them back. Wished she could rewind to last Thursday night and stand up to June Benson.

Stand up for herself. Her feelings.

Maybe she could do it now?

She hit reply and typed:

i miss u 2

Holding her breath, she sent it. A moment later, her phone pinged. He'd responded! She eagerly read:

meet me tnite moonwlk

She wanted to, badly. To tell him how she felt, what his sister had done. How it had hurt. And ask if they still had a chance.

And she wanted to do it without a chaperone. How could she get rid of Stacy?

If you need anything, let me know.

She needed something, all right. Quickly, she typed a reply.

when

He answered almost instantaneously:

now

Smiling to herself, she typed:

ok wait 4 me

Yvette knew she had to come up with something urgent enough to propel Stacy from her post. Something that couldn't be put off or ordered in.

She mentally thumbed though her choices: food, drink, reading material. Then she knew. Something every woman understood.

Smiling to herself, she got to her feet, went to the vanity

cabinet. From it she retrieved an almost full box of tampons. She dug some tissues out of the waste basket, dumped the box's contents in, then covered it with the used tissues.

Box in hand, she went to the bathroom door, peeked out. From where she stood, she had a straight view into the living room. The detective sat on the couch, reading a magazine.

"Stacy?"

The woman looked over at her. It occurred to Yvette that Stacy's expression seemed off; she ignored the thought and moved her plan forward.

"I've got a problem." She held up the empty box. "I just started."

"You don't have any?"

She shook her head. "There's a drugstore up the block and around the corner. Royal Pharmacy."

"Does the store deliver?"

"Not that I know of." Yvette mustered what she hoped was distress. "I flow kind of… It's going to get messy fast."

Stacy made a face and stood. "Where's the store?"

"Up one block, take a left. It's right there."

"Dead-bolt and security chain the door. Don't open for anyone. *Anyone.* Got that?"

Yvette nodded and scurried out of the bathroom, joining the other woman at the door. "And Stacy?" When the woman looked back at her she sent her a weak smile. "Thanks."

The moment she had closed and locked the door, she raced back to the bathroom. She rinsed her face again, ran a brush through her hair, then applied mascara, blush and lip gloss.

Snatching up her purse, she tiptoed to the door and peered out the peephole. The coast looked clear and she carefully eased the door open, half expecting the other woman to jump out with an "Aha!"

She didn't. Nor was she anywhere in sight.

Yvette slipped out, locking the door behind her. Not glancing back, she hurried to meet Riley.

The Moon Walk was a scenic boardwalk along the Mississippi River, across from Jackson Square. Just steps from the water, it had been named for Mayor "Moon" Landrieu.

Yvette dropped a dollar in a street musician's hat; he acknowledged without missing a note of "Blue Moon." He wasn't very good, but she figured he had to make a living—and the living for French Quarter street performers had been lean since Katrina.

She hurried up the ramp that led to the observation deck and promenade. She saw him right away, pacing, expression distraught.

"Riley!"

He stopped and turned, broke into a broad smile and strode to her. He caught her hands. "You came. I'd begun to lose hope."

"I said I'd be here."

He searched her gaze. "Since the other night, I've been by your apartment several times. You never answered your bell."

"Why didn't you call?"

"Figured you wouldn't answer." He tightened his fingers on hers. "June told me what she said to you. That's not what I'm about, Yvette. I promise."

"What she said really hurt."

"She's overprotective."

Yvette firmed her resolve to stick up for herself. "What she said was just plain mean. She judged me without knowing anything about me."

"She's just crazy sometimes. Don't hold it against me. Please?"

He tightened his hands on hers. "I like you, Yvette. And it doesn't matter to me what you do for a living. No, that's wrong. It does, but I still want to be with you. Whether you're a waitress or a stripper doesn't change that fact."

She gazed at him. *Could it be?* Was he simply accepting what she did as a fact of her life? Neither condemning her stripping nor turned on by it?

"What are you thinking?" he asked.

"That you're too good to be true."

"I'm not." He drew her against his chest. "I'm real. And I'm here."

She stood on tiptoes, lifting her face to his. "So am I," she whispered.

He kissed her. Once, then again and again. Deep, drugging kisses. Ones that left her wanting him naked. Wanting her naked against him.

"Get a room, why don'tcha?"

That came along with snickers from a group of teenagers. Riley pulled away, faced flushed and out of breath. "Do you trust me?"

"Trust you? Why—"

"I want to show you something."

"What?"

"It'll ruin the surprise."

"Where?"

"Not far."

When she hesitated, he held out his hand. "Do you trust me?" he asked again.

Did she? With everything going on, she shouldn't. After all, what did she really know about Riley Benson?

She shouldn't, but she did. She prayed she wasn't making another mistake. That she wouldn't have her heart broken again.

She laid her hand in his. "Yes," she said simply. "I trust you."

56

Wednesday, May 16, 2007
9:45 p.m.

Stacy paced. The lying little sneak had conned her. And she had fallen for it, hook, line and sinker. She wasn't certain whether she was more pissed off or embarrassed.

She'd had to call Patti and tell her she'd been duped. By now the rest of the team knew. By morning most of the department would be in on the joke—the one played on her.

She had to admit a bit of grudging respect for the woman. She'd come up with the one thing that would propel her to leave Yvette unsupervised. For twelve minutes. Twelve stinking minutes.

She'd gotten back and Yvette had been gone. She would have worried she'd been snatched by the Handyman, but while searching for her keys, Nancy had popped her head out and informed her she had seen Yvette leave—alone and smiling.

Stacy bet she had been smiling. Congratulating herself on outsmarting her archenemy, the hapless Detective Killian. Never mind that the archenemy was around to protect her from a madman.

How could such a bright girl be so stupid?

All this to meet a guy. Stacy had come to that conclusion after performing a quick search of the apartment. It didn't appear Yvette had taken anything but her purse, and she had left makeup strewn on the vanity counter.

Patti hadn't bought "the guy" angle. She feared that Yvette had decided to cut and run. And that on her own, Yvette would be an easy target.

The captain had sentenced Stacy to "stay put." She needed Stacy at the apartment in case Yvette returned or the Artist showed. So here she was, pacing and stewing, while the rest of the team actively searched for the dancer.

She dialed Rene. "Anything?" she asked when he answered.

"Nada."

"She never showed at the Hustle?"

"Sorry."

"Shit. Keep me posted."

Frustrated, she snapped her cell phone shut, tossed it onto the couch and continued pacing. If Yvette had bolted, Stacy's stupidity had jeopardized the investigation.

But if the Artist had gotten Yvette, Stacy's stupidity would have jeopardized the young woman's life.

"If you'd done something right away, when I told you about the Artist, Tonya would be alive. It's your fault she's dead, not mine. Your fault!"

The words hurt. And the possibility that they were even partly true was too horrible to contemplate. They'd had good reason to doubt Yvette, but that didn't change how Stacy felt now, knowing a woman was dead.

At the tap on the door, she all but lunged for it, hoping Yvette had returned.

She hadn't. Instead, Spencer stood on the other side, a Starbucks grande cup in his hand and a shit-eating grin on his face.

She swung open the door. "I hate this job."

"I know you do." He held out the cup. "Nothing a triple mocha with whip won't cure."

It hit her then, like a lightning bolt.

She loved him. She was *in love* with him.

He made her laugh when nothing was funny. Made her smile when smiling was the last thing on her mind. And he made her feel connected. To the job. This city.

To life.

That's why she had been so hurt by his flippant proposal. She didn't want "comfortable." She didn't want him to just settle for her because they got along well or his family loved her.

She needed him to love her back.

"You okay?" he asked. "You look funny suddenly."

"I'm fine." She took the cup. "C'mon in. Keep me from killing myself."

He made a sympathetic noise. "She pulled the tampon routine on you. I would have reacted the same way."

"Promise?"

"Are you kidding? Us guys are total wimps about that kind of girlie stuff." He glanced at her. "Kitchen's to the right?"

She said it was, then watched, amused, as he wandered that way, then starting nosing around.

She shook her head when he opened the freezer and peered inside. "Hungry, Malone? Or looking for body parts?"

"You never know." He poked through the scant contents before selecting a carton of ice cream.

Blue Bell. Rocky Road.

"Just so you know, most women, especially right before their period, eat ice cream directly out of the carto—"

Not ice cream, she saw. Money. Lots of it.

Spencer counted it. "There's three thousand bucks here."

"She didn't bolt, then. It would have been too easy to take the cash."

He nodded, rewrapped the money and replaced it and the carton. He moved on to the cabinets. "There may be a problem with the Handyman angle and Messinger's death."

She waited, knowing he didn't expect a response.

"Elizabeth Walker doesn't think the same person performed the amputations. In fact—" He reached the sink, peeked into the cabinet below. "In her expert opinion, the Handyman's right-handed. And Messinger's killer was left-handed. Yvette have a car?"

"Not that I know of. Why?"

"Antifreeze." He held up the gallon jug. "Know anything else it's used for?"

"Poisoning loud dogs?"

"Bingo. And remember, Samson was poisoned the same night Miss Alma was killed and Yvette had her last visit from the Artist."

"Her supposed visit from the Artist."

Stacy suddenly remembered her first night staying here with Yvette, pictured her using the chopsticks. "Did you say left-handed?"

"Yeah, why?"

"Yvette's left-handed."

"Are you certain?"

"Pretty damn." She paused. "You know, without a search warrant, anything you find is inadmissible."

"That's why I'm not finding anything." He closed the cabinet door. "Don't say anything to Patti just yet. I'm going to do a bit of research, see what I come up with."

"There's something I haven't told you. It's about Patti. She promised Yvette fifty thousand dollars if she'd stay and help her catch the guy. Ten grand of it up front."

A deep, angry flush crept from his neck to his hairline. "Part of Sammy's life insurance money. A big part. Son of a bitch."

"I'm really sorry, Spencer."

He took two steps toward her, caught her by the upper arms and pulled her against him. "You and I," he said, "have unfinshed business. Personal business. Unfortunately it'll have to wait."

He kissed her, then released her. A moment later, he was gone. Leaving her with even more to stew about.

57

Thursday, May 17, 2007
1:30 a.m.

Some believed that new life could be found in the waters of baptism. That water cleansed the soul.

But water could also destroy. Overwhelm everything in its path. Leaving behind nothing but stinking, rotting waste.

It could burn. Strip flesh from bones.

Stop punishing yourself! It's not your fault. It's hers.

No. Please, no. She's the one. She has to be. Pure. Sinless. My perfect muse.

Turn off the water. Step out of the shower.

A rush of cool air. Goose bumps. Shudders of relief. And agony.

She is just like the others. A cheap, faithless whore.

A sound resounded off the walls. Of despair. Hollow and hopeless.

Cross to the mirror. Wipe away the fog. What do you see?

A distorted image. A stranger. A lost soul.

No! She threw your love and trust back in your face. But unlike the other whores, she had help.

Yes. Yes. Fellow betrayers. Their fault.

Punish her. Punish them. Make them all pay the price for your pain.

58

Thursday, May 17, 2007
8:35 a.m.

Spencer sat at his desk, a cup of cooling coffee in front of him. He'd drunk too many cups already, and a dull headache throbbed at the base of his skull.

He had left Stacy last night and come directly here. He spent the time since tracking down the story of Yvette Borger's life, then had carefully fitted those pieces with the various parts of this investigative puzzle.

A picture had begun to emerge. One of a troubled young woman with many secrets.

Yvette's real name was Carrie Sue Borger. She came from Greenwood, Mississippi, a small town in the heart of the Delta.

An only child, her mother had died in a fall when Yvette was nine. The girl's relationship with the Greenwood PD started the next year. She'd been picked up a dozen times between then and her sixteenth birthday.

At sixteen, she'd worked briefly at the local Waffle House, then disappeared, apparently having decided to leave both Greenwood and her dad behind. The really interesting part of the story came here: before she left home, she hit her father in the head with a coffeepot and left him for dead.

But Vic Borger hadn't died. He'd called the cops on his only child but she had been long gone.

"How long've you been here, Slick?"

Spencer lifted his gaze to his partner. "Most of the night."

"You look it."

"Thanks." Spencer cocked an eyebrow. "Three doughnuts, Pasta Man?"

"One's for you. Heard you'd been burning the midnight oil and thought a little sustenance might be in order."

Tony handed him a doughnut and napkin, which Spencer accepted. He took a big bite, only realizing then how hungry he was. Too bad he was eating the nutritional equivalent of crap.

Tony settled on the edge of his desk and started in on his pastry. "Heard 'bout last night," he said, mouth full. "Borger gave Stacy the slip."

Spencer smiled involuntarily. "Stacy's really pissed."

"Borger better watch out. That girl's got a temper."

"Tell me about it."

"I got a positive ID on our Jane Doe."

"Jessica Skye?"

His friend polished off the first doughnut, started on the second and nodded.

"I'll be damned. Who from?"

"Her mother. IDed her from the photo of the facial reconstruction. Daphne PD said it seemed legit. Woman broke down sobbing."

He popped the last bite into his mouth, chewed and swallowed. "We're working on securing dental records now, just to be certain."

What did that bring to the party? Did it give weight to Yvette's claims? Or make her look more guilty?

"A couple of the dancers from the Hustle recognized Franklin. He was a regular before the storm. Since Katrina he's been in a few times."

Another thing Yvette had lied about. And a solid connection between Franklin and a known Handyman victim.

"Patti know any of this yet?"

"Just found out myself." He dusted his fingers on a napkin, then tossed it in the trash. "Got one more thing. One of Messinger's neighbors saw her drive off with a woman that Sunday. A woman with long, dark hair."

Spencer saw by Tony's expression that he was thinking the same thing: *Yvette had long, dark hair.*

"She's certain it was that Sunday?"

"Absolutely. She was returning from mass, thought about the fact Messinger never went to church. Said a little prayer for her eternal soul."

"Thoughtful. What kind of car?"

"Couldn't recall. A sedan. Nondescript."

"A dark-haired woman. The witness give you anything more than that?"

"This witness was no spring chicken. Personally, I think we're lucky she gave us that much. I'm not certain which was worse, her memory or her eyesight. She agreed to come in for a photo lineup. I suggest we see what we get and use her as a last resort or icing on the cake."

Spencer pushed away from the desk and stood. "It's meeting time."

Tony followed him to his feet. "I prefer Miller time."

"We're going to need a beer after the captain hears everything I've got to say."

They found Patti in her office, on the phone. She waved them in. "Stay put. If Borger shows, call me and bring her downtown."

She ended the call and looked at them. "I've got a unit outside Yvette's building. Frankly it doesn't look good. She's been gone more than twelve hours. She skipped out on Stacy around 6:00 p.m. and no one's heard a word from her since. What do you have?"

Tony began. He filled her in on the positive ID and the witness who claimed to have seen Tonya drive off with a dark-haired woman.

"In addition, two of the Hustle's dancers called Franklin a prestorm regular."

Spencer took over. "That's very good news, Captain. A known victim with a substantiated connection to Franklin."

"Franklin can't be our man now. While he's been locked up, the Handyman gave us an eighth victim. Tonya Messinger."

"Maybe not." Spencer cleared his throat. "Based on her preliminary comparisons of the original samples to Messinger, Elizabeth Walker believes this latest victim is the work of a different killer."

Patti folded her hands on the desk in front of her. It was the only outward sign that his words had affected her.

He went on, explaining about the amateurishness of the amputation and finishing with the anthropologist's opinion that the first killer was right-handed, the second left-handed.

"Why am I just hearing about this?" She moved her gaze between him and Tony.

Spencer spoke up. "I didn't want to sound the alarm. Once alerted, you would have had to act on the news. Besides, it was Dr. Walker's preliminary conclusion and isn't definitive."

"Exactly, Detective. Anything else you need to tell me?"

He cleared his throat for the second time, a fact that didn't escape her. "Something's not right about Yvette Borger's story. There're things that just don't add up for me."

"This is the same tune you've been playing, Detective. If you don't have anything new—"

"I think I do. Hear me out."

She sat back. "Go on."

"The minute you got on board with Yvette, all communication from the Artist stopped. Have you asked yourself why?"

He didn't expect her to answer and went on. "Because she couldn't fabricate anymore. With your and Stacy's 24/7 protection, she was never alone."

He leaned forward. "She has no real proof of his existence. The person who positively IDed Jessica Skye and could supposedly ID the Artist is dead. The murderer attempted to make it appear like the Handyman had struck again, however our bone expert doubts the authenticity of that.

"I did a little research," he continued. "Yvette Borger's real name is Carrie Sue Borger. She's from Greenwood, Mississippi, dropped out of high school at sixteen after being in and out of trouble for a couple years, then skipped town.

"Not a new story, but hers has a twist. Before she left, she bashed in her old man's head, then left him for dead. With a coffeepot. In the kitchen."

"Sounds like a game of Clue," Tony interjected. "Colonel Mustard, in the kitchen, with the candlestick."

Spencer sent the other man an impatient glance. "If you remember, Alma Maytree's killer whacked her in the head with an iron skillet."

Tony stepped in again. "And as I mentioned earlier, we have a witness who claims that on the last day of her life, Tonya Messinger drove off with a woman with long, dark hair."

"What exactly are you proposing?" Patti asked, looking directly at Spencer.

"That Ben Franklin is, in fact, the Handyman killer. Sammy caught him in the act, and he shot him dead. And Yvette Borger is a pathological liar and a murderer."

"And Marcus Gabrielle?"

"Killed because of his drug connections."

"And her motive for all this?"

"I don't know yet," he admitted. "For attention. To get away with taking out Tonya. Because she's crazy."

"She had opportunity," Tony added. "She had means."

"And everything you have is circumstantial or speculative."

"Not quite all. Antifreeze."

"Excuse me?"

"Under Yvette's kitchen sink. The neighbor's dog—"

"Samson."

"—was poisoned with antifreeze. Yvette doesn't own a car and I can't imagine a reason to have a gallon of it under her sink."

For several moments, Patti was silent. Spencer sensed her struggle to come to grips with what he was saying. She didn't want it to be true.

When she finally spoke, her voice betrayed none of that conflict. "Interesting theory, Detective. I have several problems with it. The first, currently Yvette is missing. She could have bolted. Or for all we know, the Handyman has her."

"She sneaked out to meet a guy."

"You hope."

"She didn't bolt. Not without her $3,000 cash-stash."

"First antifreeze, now a stash? Detective, am I to assume you performed an unauthorized search on Ms. Borger's apartment?"

"Stacy was looking for a snack. Yvette had the cash tucked in an ice cream carton."

Tony looked at him. "What kind?"

"Rocky Road. Blue Bell."

He nodded. "Good choice."

Patti scowled. "Has it occurred to either of you cowboys that the guy she went to meet was her admirer the Artist? Aka, the Handyman?"

"And has it occurred to you, Aunt Patti, that her admirer is a figment of her twisted psyche?"

"Why are you so intent on discounting her?"

"Why are you so intent on not?"

They stared at one another. "Tony," Patti said after a moment, not breaking eye contact, "would you give us a minute alone?"

"No problem, Captain." He heaved himself out of the chair and ambled for the door.

When it clicked shut behind his partner, Spencer leaned toward her. "Why can't you accept that Franklin really may have killed Sammy? Why can't you just accept it and let go?"

"I just…can't."

"You know what I think, Aunt Patti? That if you accept that Franklin killed him, you've got to move on. You've got to let go of Sammy."

She looked as if he had stuck a knife in her heart. He went on, anyway. "This whole thing with Yvette was a way of keeping him in your life. At the forefront of your every action. You were even willing to throw away your career and nest egg to do it."

Her lips trembled. Tears pooled in her eyes but didn't spill over. It broke his heart. "I loved him, too," he said softly. "We all did."

"But he wasn't your whole life."

"He wasn't yours, either." At her expression, he said it again. "He wasn't, Aunt Patti."

Her desk phone jangled, interrupting the moment. She answered, voice thick. "Captain O'Shay." She listened a moment, eyebrows furrowing. "When?"

After another moment of silence, she nodded. "Have them set her up in an interview room. I'm on my way there."

She hung up, looked at him. "You were right. Yvette Borger's very much alive. She's been picked up. They're bringing her in."

"Request permission to question her."

"Granted. But I get first crack at her."

59

Thursday, May 17, 2007
9:50 a.m.

Patti entered the interview room. She had let Yvette wait and worry, using the minutes to compose herself. To prepare her words. School her demeanor.

Now, she realized, she shouldn't have bothered. She was about to toss her calculated approach right out the window.

"Hello, Yvette."

The young woman turned to face her. "I'm sorry," she said.

"For what?" Patti crossed to the table and took the seat directly across from Yvette.

"Sneaking out that way."

"I worried you were dead. That the Artist had gotten you."

She shifted slightly in her seat. "He didn't."

"Quite obviously." Patti cocked her head, studying the young woman. "What was so important that you were willing to risk your life for it?"

"I was meeting someone."

Just as Stacy and Spencer had concluded. "I thought you were a smart girl. I see I was wrong."

"I'm not stupid."

"Really? There's a madman after you and you're sneaking out to meet some guy—"

"Not 'some' guy. Someone special."

"Let me guess," Patti said. "Riley Benson."

Her mouth dropped with surprise and Patti smiled, though without pleasure. "That's who you gave me the slip for last time. June told me."

Yvette met her gaze, as if in challenge. "Did she tell you she doesn't think I'm good enough for him? She told me."

"This isn't about June. Or Riley. You're not a teenager. And this isn't playtime."

"I know it's serious. It's just—"

"Your friend is dead. You could be next."

"Stop trying to scare me."

"You need to be scared. Maybe you'll use some of those smarts you insist God gave you."

Yvette fisted her fingers. "Why do you have to ruin everything!"

"I'm not your parent. Grow up."

"No, you're my employer, aren't you? But just because you paid me to hang around doesn't mean you own me."

Patti leaned forward, surprised at the force of her own anger. It took all her control to keep her tone even, her voice low and clear. "Why *aren't* you scared, Yvette?"

"I don't know what you mean."

"You're not acting like you believe your own story."

"That's just dumb."

"Alma Maytree was hit in the head with a frying pan."

"So?"

"You hit your father in the head with a coffeepot. Didn't you...Carrie Sue?"

Yvette went white. "You know about that?"

"We know."

"I didn't kill him."

"But you wanted to."

That came from Spencer, who had entered the room, Tony with him. Yvette looked at them, expression registering surprise, then fear.

"That's not true."

"Your father thought it was."

"My old man's a son of a bitch who—"

"Deserved to die?" Spencer asked.

"Who can go straight to hell," she finished.

"Maybe he has. He's dead, did you know?"

She hadn't known, Patti saw by Yvette's expression. She also saw that the girl wasn't upset by the news.

"What does *he* have to do with anything?"

"That Sunday you say you couldn't reach Tonya, a neighbor saw her drive off with a woman with long, dark hair."

"What?"

Spencer repeated himself, then asked, "Where were you that Sunday?"

"I called her several times. Patti heard the calls." She looked at Patti. "Right?"

"I did. But you made those calls from a mobile phone."

"So? What difference does that..."

She let the words trail off. Getting it, Patti saw by her expression. Cell calls could be made from anywhere. Even from beside the very person you were dialing. Even when that person was dead.

Of course, cell phone records couldn't pinpoint exact location but they could verify vicinity by establishing which towers the calls travelled through.

"I repeat," Spencer said, "that Sunday, where were you?"

She shifted uncomfortably in her seat. "In the morning I hung out around the apartment. Then I went to the Quarter. Spent the afternoon shopping."

"Did you meet anyone?"

"No."

"Run into a friend? Stop into a shop where they know you?"

"No."

"How about at your apartment? Did you speak with any of your neighbors?"

She shook her head, expression stricken.

"Is there *anyone* who can verify your story?"

"I don't think... I was alone. All day."

"What about the night Miss Alma was killed and Samson poisoned? Monday, May 7."

"I have most Mondays off. I was home. I went to bed early. Slept all night."

"That's it?"

She looked pleadingly at Patti. "The Artist broke in that night. He could have killed me, but—"

"He didn't, did he, Yvette?"

"He left me a note and locket pendant. With Tonya's picture in it."

"Why do you think he didn't kill you?" Patti asked, surprised by her own ferocity, by the way the words seemed to explode out of her.

Yvette clasped her hands together. "I don't know. How could I? Maybe because he...he loves me?"

"We want to believe you, kid," Tony said, tone fatherly. "I want to. Problem is—"

"You're so full of shit," Spencer said. "You're a liar and an opportunist."

"I'm not! I—I want a lawyer."

"Sure. Call one when you get home."

"Home? I don't understand."

"We're not keeping you, Carrie Sue. You're not under arrest."

"But what about—"

"NOPD protection?" Patti asked. "You've got it. If you still want it?"

"Of course I still want it!" she cried, jumping to her feet. "Are you nuts? The Artist exists! He's after me!"

"Okay then, an officer will accompany you home. He or another officer will be assigned to protect you."

Yvette looked confused. "So I can go?"

"Absolutely." Patti turned to Tony. "Detective Sciame, will you accompany Ms. Borger downstairs?"

"Sure, Captain." He understood what he was to do: accompany her downstairs, hand her off to a patrol unit who would bring her home, then stay to "protect" her.

Tony stood and smiled at the young woman. "Ready?"

When the door snapped shut behind them, Patti turned to Spencer. "I want a search warrant for her apartment. You know what we're looking for—anything to link her to the murders of Messinger and Maytree."

"Got it, Captain." He stood. "You coming?"

"In a minute. You go on."

He frowned slightly, as if he found her behavior bizarre, but did as she requested.

For a long time Patti sat in the empty interview room. She rubbed the back of her neck, working at the knots of tension. She was having difficulty wrapping her mind around this. She trusted Spencer. And Tony. Everything they said made sense. The evidence against Yvette's version of the truth was piling up.

So why couldn't she fully buy into it? Why couldn't she accept Franklin as Sammy's killer? Why did she want to grasp at far-fetched straws instead?

"If you accept that Franklin killed him, you've got to move on. Let go of Sammy."

"This whole thing with Yvette was a way of keeping him in your life."

The words hurt terribly.

They hurt because they were true.

Tears burned her eyes; a lump formed in her throat. She didn't want to let Sammy go. She wasn't ready for a life without him.

Patti lifted her gaze to the ceiling, swallowing hard. Spencer had been right about Yvette being alive. Maybe he was right about all of it—Yvette Borger was not only a liar and scam artist, but a murderer as well.

The judge would approve the warrant. They already "unofficially" knew of one suspicious item they'd find: the gallon of antifreeze. A car-rental receipt for the weekend Tonya disappeared would be a home run. A gun. Bloodstained garments.

"Aunt Patti?" She looked up. Spencer had poked his head into the interview room. "You okay?"

"I'm fine."

He frowned. "It's been a half an hour."

"I didn't know I was on the clock."

"The request is on the way to Judge Boudreaux."

"He's good about acting quickly. Let me know when you have it."

"You want in?"

"Don't think so. Spencer?" When he met her eyes, she said, "You were right. About Sammy. I didn't want to let go. I still don't."

He came to her side, laid a hand on her shoulder and squeezed. "I know."

Tears swamped her. Fighting them, she covered his hand with hers. "And Spencer?"

He met her eyes. "Yeah?"

"Thanks."

60

Thursday, May 17, 2007
1:10 p.m.

Yvette paced her living room, emotions swinging between fury and terror. They were trying to pin Miss Alma's murder on her. As if she could ever hurt that sweet old lady. And Tonya. The only person willing to help her.

It was bullshit! Absolute bullshit! They were questioning *her*? Suspecting *her*? While a maniac roamed free?

They'd found out about Carrie Sue.

She stopped pacing, brought a hand to her throat, feeling like she might throw up. Carrie Sue had been a pathetic victim. The day she walked away from Greenwood, Carrie Sue had died—and Yvette had been born.

The kitchen floor. The pool of blood.

Yvette breathed deeply through her nose, struggling against the nausea. She would not be sick. Her father had deserved what he got. Hell, he'd deserved worse.

But Miss Alma had never hurt anybody.

Outside her door sat a cop. For her own "protection." Right. More like, to make certain she didn't bolt for real this time.

Cops were all alike. She'd been stupid to trust Patti O'Shay. Stupid to think the woman would actually follow through on her promises.

Patti had never meant to protect Yvette. That had been a sham. She had used Yvette as bait to catch her husband's killer. Now they were trying to pin these murders on her. Or at least creating a big umbrella of suspicion over her. But why?

Patti O'Shay had what she needed. And now she wanted out of paying Yvette the money she had promised her.

Was that what this was all about? Money?

She should have run. She could still. Take the ten grand and run like hell. Away from New Orleans. Make a new life somewhere else.

Riley.

She thought of the night before, how magical and perfect it had been. He had taken her to the gallery. To the show they had been unpacking in the back room. Big, bold paintings. Organic and blatantly sexual.

Riley had wanted her to see them because they reminded him of her.

Swept away with emotion, they had made love, surrounded

by the exquisite works of art. They had fallen asleep in each other's arms, only to awake and make love again.

She had finally met a man she could love and one she believed could love her. And now this. It wasn't fair.

"Life isn't fair. Get used to it, girl."

She brought her hands to her ears, trying to shut out her father's voice. To get him out of her head. To stop his pounding and pounding at her.

"Ms. Borger? Police!"

She dropped her hand and swung toward her door. *The cop stationed out front.* "Yes?"

"People here to see you."

Yvette went to the door and opened it. Stacy and a man she didn't recognize stood there, two uniformed officers behind them.

"Hello, Yvette," Stacy said.

"My good friend Brandi," she said sarcastically. "What a surprise."

"Thanks for making me look like a jerk last night."

"My pleasure."

"Mine, too. Now." Stacy shoved a piece of paper into her hands. "Search warrant."

Yvette looked at it, stunned. She saw her name, her address. "I don't understand."

"A judge granted us the right to search your apartment."

"Why? For what?"

"Evidence in the murders of Alma Maytree and Tonya Messinger."

"That's crazy!"

"The law requires that you or your legal representative be on the premises for the search."

"Legal representative?"

"Lawyer."

"I don't have one."

"Then you may wait here or follow us. It's your choice. Either way, we'll present you with a list of everything we take."

"I want a lawyer."

"You may have one, of course. Call one. But we have the right to search your property now, lawyer present or not."

So Yvette trailed them around the apartment, biting back sounds of distress as they went through her things. Touching, examining. Sometimes quietly discussing an item between themselves.

Yvette hugged herself, feeling violated. Sick to her stomach. She wondered if she would ever feel comfortable in her home again.

They had begun with the living room, then went on to the bedrooms and bath. Digging through her vanity drawers, they found her contraceptive jelly and a clutch of condoms. Young Officer Guidry glanced at her from the corners of his eyes; she stiffened her spine and lifted her chin.

She could imagine what he thought of her. What he thought she was.

Whore. Hooker.

He could think what he wanted; she knew better.

Stacy and her cop crew saved the kitchen for last. It wasn't until they entered the room that she remembered her cache of tip money. Heart in her throat, she watched as they began to search the refrigerator, then freezer.

They checked each carton, container and box. What, she wondered, a bubble of hysteria rising up in her, were they looking for? Tonya's hand?

She held her breath as Stacy removed the Rocky Road carton, opened it and retrieved the plastic bag of cash. Light-headed, Yvette watched Stacy unwrap, then count it.

The police could call it evidence and confiscate it.

Goodbye three thousand bucks.

Stacy glanced at her in question.

"My tip money," she whispered.

Stacy nodded and folded the aluminum foil around the cash, then tucked it back into the Rocky Road carton. "You might want to rethink the hiding place. It's not as clever as you imagine."

Finished with the freezer, they moved on to the sink area. Stacy knelt in front of the cabinet below and began shuffling through the bottles, jugs and cans of cleaning supplies.

Again, it looked as if she was searching for something specific.

Stacy pulled out a gallon jug. Yvette didn't recognize it and frowned. "What is that?"

"You don't know? It's antifreeze."

"That's not mine."

"Then what's it doing here?"

"I don't know! I don't even know what antifreeze is."

"Then it's not a problem."

"But—"

She brought a hand to her head, dizzy.

"Are you all right?" Officer Guidry asked.

"I need to…I'm going to go sit down."

He followed her into the living room. She sank onto the couch and dropped her head into her hands.

"Can I get you something?" he asked.

She shook her head, thoughts racing. Antifreeze? How had it ended up in her cabinet? And why were the cops interested—

Samson. "The vet said he was poisoned. Antifreeze."

"We're done."

She looked up, vision blurry. Stacy held out a sheet of paper. "That's a list of everything we took. I need you to check the list, then sign it. I'll leave you a signed copy, as well, to share with your lawyer."

Lawyer?

She blinked and took the list, scanned it. Credit card receipts. One of her old T-shirts. Some photographs. Her day-planner. Journal. The antifreeze.

Not much. A weird collection of seemingly unrelated things.

She signed the paper; they gave her a copy. She walked them to the door, then locked it behind them. She brought her shaking hands to her face. How could this be happening? She was the victim, not the perpetrator.

Cops could do anything they wanted.

They had probably planted the stuff themselves.

Of course. Stacy living here. Patti in and out. Spencer, too, she'd bet. They had keys.

Why were they doing this to her? And what of the Artist? He was real. He'd killed Jessica Skye. He would kill her, as well.

Dizzy with fear, she crossed to the couch and sat. She put her head between her knees and breathed slowly and deeply, in through her nose and out her mouth.

Let the fear go. Be calm and think...think. How to get out of this?

She had to give them the slip. Get out of town. But how?

Officer Guidry was standing watch right outside her door. She had given them permission to station him there. For her "protection."

If she withdrew that permission, they'd suspect she meant to take off—and they would be all over her.

She wasn't under arrest. They couldn't stop her from going to work. Or anywhere else.

So Officer Guidry would accompany her to work tonight. Just like they'd planned. Only she had plans of her own.

She would show them. They thought they had outsmarted her. Trapped her in whatever sick game they were playing.

Think again, Captain Patti O'Shay.

Her best chance for escape was the Hustle. Lots of people and distractions, several entrances and exits. She would go right after a dance, with just the clothes on her back—and her cache of tip money.

She got to her feet, clearheaded now. Revitalized. She remembered feeling this way when she had finally resolved to leave Greenwood. And again, right before Katrina hit. That time, she had made the decision to stay, to fight back. To stand up and shout "Take that, bitch!"

This was a different kind of F-you, but just as liberating. Just as exhilarating.

Yvette began to pace. She would need to empty her bank accounts and operate on a cash-only basis, at least for a while. Otherwise they could track her through her financial transactions.

She could get out of the Quarter easily, but she would need to get out of the city. Quickly. As soon as they realized she'd bolted, they would converge on both the bus and rail stations. And renting a vehicle would be too risky.

Riley. She had no one else.

His cell number was in her day-planner, which the police had confiscated. Her cell phone, she realized. He had text-messaged her; it'd be saved there.

She scrambled for her phone, found his number and dialed.

It dumped immediately to voice mail. Afraid to leave a message, she ended the call.

What now? She could call the gallery....

What if his sister answered? June couldn't know she'd contacted Riley. She would run right to her good buddy Captain O'Shay.

Lie. If June answered, pretend to be someone else.

Hands shaking she retrieved the phone book, dialed Pieces. Sure enough, June answered.

"Riley Benson, please." Yvette worked to keep the tremor out of her voice.

"May I tell him who's calling and what this is in reference to?"

Pick a name. A reason for calling. The new show. The paintings that had surrounded them while they made love.

"Tell him Ellen St. James is calling. About the Avery piece I was interested in."

"You must be the lawyer," June said warmly. "Congratulations on your new practice."

"Thank you. I'm very excited."

"You can't go wrong with an Avery. He's very talented, and I predict his work will escalate in value."

"Just what Riley assured me. Is he in?"

"He is. Hold, please."

A moment later he came on the line. "This is Riley Benson."

She heard the question in his voice. She spoke quickly. "Riley, it's me, Yvette. Don't let on it's me, please. I need your help."

"Yes, Ellen. It's a fabulous piece. One of my personal favorites."

She said a silent thank-you, then continued, "I've got to get out of town," she continued. "There's this guy…he's crazy… he's threatened to hurt me. I'm afraid."

"Hold please, Ellen."

Yvette heard him talking to his sister, assuring her he could handle the gallery while she ran an errand.

A moment later, he came back to her. "Go to the police," he said, voice low, fierce-sounding. "They'll protect you."

"They won't. I already tried them and they didn't believe me."

"I'll talk to Aunt Pat—"

"No! Please, Riley. I need *you*. I have no one else."

"This is nuts. I'll protect you. Come here and—"

"I can't." A sob rose in her throat. "He'll hurt you and I…I couldn't bear that."

"Then tell me how I can help."

"I'm going to slip out of the Hustle tonight. Will you meet me? Give me a ride out of town?"

"Where to?"

"I don't know. I haven't figured that out yet."

"Yvette—"

"Please, Riley. Please help me."

For an agonizing moment, he was silent. Then he sighed. "Okay. *If* you'll promise to tell me everything when I pick you up."

A cry of relief flew to her lips. "I will, I promise. Come at eleven-forty-five. Meet me at the corner of Dauphine and Bienville. Don't freak out if I'm a little late. I'm going to need to finish my number, make everything look normal."

He agreed to be there, to wait as long as it took. "One last thing. Don't tell anyone, Riley. *Anyone.* It's important."

When he didn't reply, she begged. "If you care at all about me, you'll promise. Not even your sister."

"All right, but this doesn't feel right."

Her vision blurred with tears. It didn't feel right to her, either. Her entire freaking life didn't feel right. "I wanted to tell you…how much last night meant to me."

"Then don't go. Yvette, ple—"

She realized she was crying and hung up before she totally lost it.

61

Thursday, May 17, 2007
10:00 p.m.

Yvette had everything in place. Riley would be waiting for her when she finished her last dance around midnight. She had stashed a set of clothes near the alley exit. She had hidden her wallet and tip money with the clothes.

Everything else, she left behind.

It hurt, but she would get over it. She had done it before.

She would complete her number, but instead of heading to her dressing area, she would head for the exit. Grab her garments and go, dressing in the alley as she made her escape.

Her bank accounts had proved a problem. She couldn't close them without alerting Patti and company to what she was up to. So she had written a check to Riley. She would give it to him, beg him to cash it, then bring her the money. He was wealthy. Twenty or so thousand dollars wouldn't be a great temptation to him.

By the time Patti realized Riley's part in the plan and went to him for information, she would be long gone. And any information he could offer would be useless.

Provided he didn't screw her. If he did, it wouldn't be the first time she'd been betrayed. It would just hurt more than the others.

The "new Tonya" ducked her head into Yvette's dressing room. "You're on in ten."

Yvette thanked her and fired up a cigarette. She had left a note for her landlord, asking him to store her things and with it, a check for a thousand bucks to cover the cost of a storage unit and hiring someone to pack and haul it there. He was a good guy. She was fairly confident he'd do it.

But would she ever be back to collect?

Her art collection. She hated leaving it behind. Each was like a brilliantly colored piece of her.

Yes, Yvette silently vowed. She would.

She glanced at the clock. *Time to go.*

She said one quick, silent prayer, then exited the dressing room. "Wish me luck," she called to Officer Guidry, wiggling her fingers in a flirty goodbye.

He did, his ears turning pink.

Minutes later, she was on stage. Though the music was familiar and her movements routine, it took all her concentration to focus on them. She had no idea how many other NOPD officers were planted in and around the club tonight, but she would bet there were several.

Where were they? she wondered, searching the crowd while she danced. The big guy with the florid complexion? The one in the cowboy hat? And what of the Artist? Was he here, watching and laughing, playing them all for fools?

Her gaze settled on a man she recognized—Rich Ruston. The guy from Pieces gallery, Shauna Malone's boyfriend. She had been talking to him when she fainted. He was alone. Sitting near the front.

He saw her gaze on him and he smiled. Something about the curving of his mouth made her blood run cold.

Had he come to see her? Or was his being here a coincidence?

Her heart pounded, but not from the dance. Not from exertion.

She swung right. Her gaze landed on another man, another familiar face. He wagged his tongue lewdly at her.

She had to get out of here.

She spun again, her gaze searching for Rich Ruston.

He was gone.

Her number ended. She made her way into the audience, playing her part as best she could, mind on the clock. Counting the minutes until she could sneak away. Worrying about Riley. Wondering whether he would be waiting, as he promised.

The guy with the wagging tongue requested a private dance. On her way to meet him, she took a detour. Her clothes were

right where she left them, in the trash can by the alley exit. So
was her wallet and money. Her flip-flops.

With an involuntary sound of relief, she snatched them up
and ducked out into the dark alley.

62

Friday, May 18, 2007
12:50 a.m.

The call awakened Patti, though she hadn't been sleeping deeply. She brought the receiver to her ear. "O'Shay."

It was Spencer. "Borger's gone."

That brought her fully awake; she sat up. "How the hell did she manage... We had a half-dozen officers stationed in the club!"

"Seems she ducked out after her set. Never returned to her dressing room."

"Where are you?"

"At the scene."

Patti climbed out of bed. "I'm on my way."

She made the drive to the French Quarter club in ten minutes and met Spencer at the front entrance. "Any news?"

"Nada."

She turned toward Officer Guidry. "Have you done a complete search?"

"As best we could. When the club closes, we'll search again. Until then we've got people stationed at every exit."

"You didn't before?"

The young cop turned red. "Who would have thought she'd leave naked?"

"She didn't, Officer."

"But she finished her set in nothing but a G-string!"

"Are you telling me you believe Yvette Borger is wandering the French Quarter in a G-string?" She sent him a withering look. "She managed to hide clothes near an exit. Probably money, too. Somebody should have anticipated this."

She turned back to Spencer. "Tell me you've sent a unit to her apartment."

"Better than that. Stacy and Rene."

"Good. I want everybody to stay in place. Carefully check anyone who exits. Once the club closes, I want it searched. Every storage closet and air vent. Understood?"

The chastened officer scurried off to spread the word.

Patti looked at Spencer. "You've personally searched her dressing room?"

"I have. Her purse is still there, minus her wallet. She's one smart cookie, no doubt about that."

No doubt at all.

"Her timing says it all, in my opinion."

Patti wanted to defend her. Other reasons for her disappearance sprang to her lips: she was running from the Artist, this was another of her romantic rendezvous, she enjoyed the challenge of giving them the slip and had made it a sort of contest.

She didn't utter them. The fact was, Yvette looked damn guilty.

How could she have been so wrong about her?

"Captain O'Shay? There's someone here I think you might want to speak to."

She turned. Officer Guidry stood in the dressing room doorway, another man behind him. Guidry stepped aside and she saw who it was.

"Riley?"

"Aunt Patti! Oh, my God, something *has* happened to her!"

He looked panicked. His mop of curly hair stuck straight out in several places, as if he had been nervously running his hands through it. "Happened to whom, Riley?"

"Yvette. She asked me to meet her. At 11:45. I waited but—"

"Slow down, start at the beginning."

He took a deep breath. "She called this afternoon. She said she was in trouble."

"What kind of trouble?"

"She said this guy was hounding her. Threatening her. She needed my help." He flexed his fingers. "She needed to get out of town. I offered to call you, but she said you wouldn't help."

"She asked you to meet her here?"

"No. The corner of Dauphine and Bienville. But she didn't show up."

Patti glanced at her watch—*1:40*. "At 11:45? And you're just looking for her now?"

"She told me she might be late. Made me promise to wait."

Spencer cleared his throat. "So where is she?"

"I don't know." He lifted his gaze, expression stricken. "I waited. I had the right corner, I wrote it down!"

Patti frowned. "Do you have your cell phone?"

He nodded. "I tried to call her. She didn't answer."

"Try again now."

She watched as he dialed, saw the hope in his expression turn to despair. He held out the phone; she heard Yvette's voice message.

"I think Yvette may be in some very serious trouble," Patti said. "I want you to go back to that corner and wait, just in case. If she shows, call me." She handed him her card. "It's important, Riley."

He nodded again and stood. "Okay, Aunt Patti. You'll call me if you find her?"

"I will. Absolutely. Officer Guidry will take your number in case I need to reach you."

Spencer's cell rang. He excused himself to answer.

"If you need anything, Riley, call me."

A moment later, Spencer returned. "That was Stacy. Yvette's gone, all right. Took her tip stash and left a note for her landlord, asking him to store her stuff."

"So why didn't she catch her ride out of town?"

"Another smokescreen? She knew Riley would sound the alarm. Fuel our fear of option number two."

Option number two. The one Patti didn't want to think about.

The Artist.

63

The search of the club proved futile. Riley spent most of the night in his vehicle and had also come up empty.

Yvette had vanished.

Patti had returned to the department and put out an all-radio alert for Yvette. At morning roll call her photo had been distributed to all patrol units. If she showed her face on the street, she would be picked up.

"She's fine, Aunt Patti. The fox outfoxed us, that's all."

She focused on Spencer, standing in her office doorway. "I hope so. The alternative is damn grim."

Yvette in the grasp of a madman.

"It's not your fault. None of it."

"That's not the way it feels."

"The self-blame game will get you nowhere fast."

"Are you advising *me*, Boo?"

He grinned at the use of her childhood nickname for him. "In the mood for some good news?"

"Are you kidding?" She forced a harsh laugh. "You're looking at a desperate woman."

"Stacy's moving back in. Tonight."

"You call that good news?" The thought passed her lips before she could stop it.

He looked startled. "You don't?"

"I adore Stacy, you know that. It's just...she's not the problem. You are."

He looked so shocked, she felt a moment of pity for him. "I'm sorry, Spencer. But until you figure out what I mean by that, her moving back in isn't such great news. And she won't be staying long. Do you hear what I'm saying?"

"Mail, Captain."

She motioned Dora, the ISD receptionist, into her office. The woman set a stack of mail on Patti's desk and turned to leave. "Hi, Spencer, baby. You had a call. Somebody named Rich Ruston. Said it was important."

"He leave a number?"

"Yes, indeed, sugar. It's on your desk."

Patti began thumbing through the mail. She stopped at a cream-colored envelope. Crane's stationery. Addressed to Captain Patti O'Shay.

"Rich Ruston, Shauna's pain-in-the-ass boyfriend," Spence said aloud. "I wonder what he wan—"

Secured with a wax seal, bright red, in an ornate letter A She opened the envelope, read the short message.

Now you begin to regret your interference.
The Artist

"Captain?"

She lifted her gaze to Spencer's. "It seems I've made mysel an enemy."

He strode across to her; she handed him the note card. He read it, then met her eyes. "Yvette?"

"She disappears and suddenly the Artist reappears. With a hard-on toward me. Oddly coincidental, I think."

"What do you want me to do?"

"Get it to the lab, ASAP. And get me the number for the Greenwood PD."

Moments later she was on the phone with Chief Butler o the GPD. He was an old-timer, with a thick drawl and an old fashioned, mannerly way. It'd been a long time since anothe officer had called her "ma'am."

"Thanks for taking the time to speak with me, Chief Butler I'm in need of additional information about Carrie Sue Borger Anything you can tell me might help."

"Happy to try," he drawled. "Sweet little thing back when. My first recollection of Carrie Sue was the night her mama died. Little darlin' was cowerin' in the corner, her eyes the size of half dollars."

"How'd her mother die?"

"Fell down the back stairs, broke her neck. Little Carrie Sue witnessed the fall." He paused. "I suppose I shouldn't speculate this way, but what the hell, maybe it'll help. Always had my suspicions Carrie Sue's mama had some help goin' down those stairs. Couldn't prove it, though. Coroner classified it accidental and that was that."

"You interviewed Carrie Sue?"

"Yup. If she saw anything, she wasn't talkin'. Could've been too scared to talk. Her daddy was no damn good. Ornery. Soured on life. After her mama passed, everybody worried about Carrie Sue bein' brung up by him. Nothin' we could do about. She was his kin."

"There were no outward signs of abuse?" Patti asked, feeling sorry for the youngster.

"Emotional, maybe. Nobody was real surprised when she started runnin' wild."

"What about the assault charge against Carrie Sue?"

"As far as I'm concerned, Vic Borger deserved that knock on the head. Probably more than that. He came in, forced me to file the charge, but I didn't put much effort into pursuing it."

"And her father? He's—"

"Dead," he finished for her. "Passed away a year or so ago. Whatever case we might have had died with him."

He had little else to tell her. She'd had no other family, few friends, and as far as he knew, hadn't been back to Greenwood since she left.

"If she does happen into town, will you let me know?"

"Happy to. Has Carrie Sue gotten herself into trouble down there?"

"She has, Chief Butler. Though I'll be honest, at this point I'm not quite sure what kind."

She ended the call and flipped open her inter-department directory. She found the name she was looking for: Dr. Lucia Gonzales.

Lucia was the department's forensic psychologist. She was a post-Katrina hire, a bright, young Latino woman who had come from Texas to help the traumatized after the storm and had fallen in love with the struggling city.

When she decided to stay, Patti figured she either had no innate sense of self-preservation, zero common sense or simply couldn't resist fighting for the underdog. But whatever her psychological motivations, Patti was damn glad they had her on board.

"Captain Patti O'Shay," she said when the woman answered. "ISD."

"Yes, Captain. How are you?"

Not a polite, empty greeting. A real inquiry into Patti's state of mind and emotions. After Sammy's murder, she had spent many hours on the doctor's couch.

"I'd need more than this phone call for that, Lucia. I wanted to discuss a suspect with you, maybe get some insights into her psyche and possible motivations."

"I have time now. Your place or mine?"

"You still have that fancy coffee machine up there?"

The psychologist had been the talk of the department when she brought in her own espresso machine. She could be heard frothing milk at all times of the day.

She laughed. "I do. Come on up, I'll have a latte waiting."

Patti smelled the coffee the moment she alighted the elevator. If she hadn't known how to find Dr. Lucia's, she could have simply followed her nose.

The psychologist's office bore no resemblance to Patti's: larger and uncluttered, with a comfortable seating area that included a settee, all in a mellow, soothing palette.

Not only did Lucia Gonzales dissect the minds of criminals, she counseled overworked, burned-out, seen-it-all cops—of which the NOPD had an unending supply.

Patti greeted the woman, who motioned toward the sitting area. A frothy latte sat waiting on the table beside a comfortable armchair.

"Thank you," Patti said, sitting. She picked up the cup, sipped, then sighed. "I needed this."

"You look tired."

"I am."

"I hear you arrested a suspect in Sammy's murder."

"Yes."

The woman picked up on the small hesitation. "You have your doubts."

"I do. But perhaps I'm simply not ready for a suspect."

"You want to talk about that?"

"Once his murder is solved, I have to let go."

The psychologist nodded. "To a degree that you haven't yet."

"Yes. I didn't come up with that myself, by the way. Someone I love pointed it out."

"We all say goodbye in our own time and our own way."

Patti cleared her throat. "I have an interesting suspect. Young woman. A stripper. Been on her own a long time. A number of arrests—solicitation, possession, petty theft.

"She may or may not have seen her father kill her mother. At the least, she witnessed her mother's neck-breaking fall. Abuse by the father was suspected but not substantiated."

"Go on."

"She first came to my attention when she claimed the City Park Handyman victim was her former roommate. The roommate disappeared right before Katrina and had been stalked by someone calling himself the Artist."

"And that claim proved false?"

"Yes. She made it up."

"For her own aggrandizement, I'm guessing."

Patti nodded. "Then she came to me claiming that the Artist was actually stalking her, sending her disturbing love letters. Professing his undying and eternal love. She claimed he had broken into her apartment. That he had killed a friend who'd disappeared. She also insisted this 'missing' friend had IDed the City Park victim and told her that this same girl had been receiving attention from the Artist."

"Why did she come to you?"

"For my help."

"Which you gave her."

"I did, even though she couldn't produce any real proof

of her claims. She absolutely believed her own story. Or seemed to."

"So she was convincing."

"Very. And facts began to substantiate her version of the truth." Patti explained about Tonya's body being found, right hand missing, and the Jane Doe ID checking out.

"But?"

"Facts are coming to light that throw suspicion on not just her story, but on her as well. She may be a murderer. Now she's missing."

"What are you asking me, Patti?"

"If she's lying, why? Why come to me with this fantastic story? Did I want to believe her so badly, I looked past the holes in the story? Or was she so convincing because she actually believes her version of events?"

For a long moment the psychologist was silent, lost in thought. "It's interesting to me," she said finally, "that this Artist is sending 'love' notes. Ones that profess his undying and eternal devotion.

"From what you've told me, it sounds as if this young woman had a pretty horrific childhood. One that included trauma, her mother's sudden, violent death, and abuse at the hands of her father. Most probably, she received little love or loving attention."

"Except for her mother, maybe."

"Who died."

Eternal, undying love. Of course.

Dr. Lucia continued. "Could she be creating this fantastical story? Absolutely. Children who suffer extreme trauma or abuse sometimes disassociate from their own memories. It's a kind of breaking free. And it allows them to create another story, to become a part of another life or relationship."

Patti's cell phone vibrated. She glanced at the display, saw it was Spencer, but didn't answer. "You're talking about multiple personality disorder?"

"That disorder has been renamed, more appropriately, disassociative identity disorder. DID for short. Sometimes, in extreme cases, different personalities develop to take over the painful memories. These alter identities can vary in age and gender. Whatever abuse occurred happened to that other person, not them. There are many documented cases of DID."

"I hear a 'but' coming."

Dr. Lucia smiled. "But sometimes the person simply detaches. In doing so, they are free to embroil themselves in another's life—or tragedy. In a fantastical way."

"Can you give me an example?"

She nodded. "There was a highly publicized case a year or two ago. A man confessed to a notorious and unsolved child killing. He claimed to 'have been with her' when she died.

"It was a complete fantasy. The man was actually many states away at the time, but had emotionally invested himself so deeply in the case, he *believed* it to be true."

"So in this woman's case, she could have so invested herself in the Handyman case, she created her own version of it?"

Her cell went off again. Again she ignored it.

"Yes. Absolutely."

"I received this just a little while ago." Patti held out the Artist's note. "What do you make of it?"

The doctor took it, scanned its simple message, then looked back up at her. "You believed her. Supported her. Then you didn't. You betrayed her. 'Interfered' in her fantasy."

"And now she's angry. She wants to punish me."

"Yes, that could be. Remember, however, we're speculating here."

Patti leaned forward. "One last question, Dr. Gonzales. Could she have become so involved in her fantasy that she began…making it real?"

"It's already real to her, Captain."

"Let me rephrase that. Could she begin…playing other roles in the fantasy?"

"Are you asking me if she could take the next step? Take the story from the world of fantasy to the real world? For example, actually kill someone?"

"I am asking that, yes."

"The human mind is capable of creating anything that can be imagined."

"You mean, she could create a role and become it? Like she's playing several parts in a play?"

"Yes." Dr. Lucia smiled. "That said, however, it would be a big step."

Patti's cell vibrated a third time. When she saw that it was again Spencer, she excused herself to answer. "Captain O'Shay."

"Where are you?"

"On four."

"You better get down here. We're going for a ride."

Something in his tone made her blood run cold. "What's going on?"

"Meet me at the elevators on one. I'll tell you then."

64

Friday, May 18, 2007
11:00 a.m.

Spencer was waiting at the first-floor elevators. "Fill me in," she said as they fell into step together.

"Rich Ruston. I called him back. He claims Shauna's missing."

"Missing? What does that mean? Packed up and gone, or—"

"MIA. Said all her stuff was there. Guy was rattled. I told him I'd meet him at her apartment."

Shauna rented half an old Uptown Camelback, a variation on the traditional New Orleans-style shotgun.

They exited the building. Patti squinted against the brilliant May sun; in unison, they reached for their sunglasses.

"He said Shauna didn't return his calls, so he went to check on her and she was gone."

"What about her car?"

"Parked in the drive."

Patti thought of Tonya Messinger. The scenarios were uncomfortably similar. She shook the thought off. "It's probably nothing," she said.

"That's what I told him."

Now you begin to regret your interference.

On the drive, Patti filled him in on her conversation with Dr. Lucia.

When she finished, Spencer whistled. "So, you're saying that Yvette could be punishing you for interfering with her fantasy?"

"According to Dr. Gonzales, it's possible." He turned onto Shauna's street, and Patti experienced an overwhelming feeling of dread. "She also said, 'The human mind is capable of creating anything that can be imagined.'"

"That won't help me sleep at night."

"Tell me about it."

Rich Ruston was waiting on the small front porch. His self-confident air gone, he looked pale and shaken.

"Thanks for calling us, Rich," Patti said when they reached the porch. "Tell me what you told Spencer."

"When Shauna didn't return my calls, I came to check on her."

"You have a key?"

"Yes. But I rang the bell first, then knocked. When she didn't answer, I let myself in."

"How many times did you call?"

"At least a dozen."

"Her cell phone—"

"And home. Left messages on both."

Patti thought of Tonya, of Yvette's many calls to her. She cleared her throat. "When did this begin?"

"Last night. We—" He bit back whatever he had been about to say.

Patti frowned. "You what?"

"We had a fight. I stormed out."

"What was the fight about?" Spencer asked.

The man looked uncomfortable. "Her working so much. She accused me of being jealous of her success."

"Are you?"

"No! Just…it seemed like her painting was getting all her attention and I… We fought about it."

"You 'stormed' out, then had a change of heart and called her?"

"Yes. At first I just figured she was still mad at me. Then I started to worry. Shauna's not the type…you know, to keep a mad on."

She wasn't. She also wasn't the type to try to punish or scare someone who had hurt her.

"Let's take a look around."

He unlocked the apartment; they asked him to wait for them on the porch. "Shauna," Spencer called, stepping inside. "It's me. And Aunt Patti."

Habit from years of on-the-job entering, Patti thought. Announce yourself. Head off ugly surprises.

Shauna didn't respond, which wasn't unexpected. As they made their way deeper into the apartment, Patti noted the "frozen moment" condition of the apartment, especially in the studio. Shauna had left her paintbrushes soaking in turpentine, her palette uncovered. On her worktable lay her iPod, headphones and a half-drunk mochassippi, a local coffeehouse chain's signature drink. She had removed her painting smock and tossed it over the back of a chair.

The hairs at the back of her neck prickling, Patti looked at Spencer. He, too, gazed at the revealing tableau.

"It's like she was working and stopped suddenly."

"To answer the door."

"Or run a quick errand."

Closer inspection revealed Shauna's purse and cell phone were gone. Her clothes and toiletries all appeared accounted for. The message light on the phone was blinking. They returned to the kitchen, to the phone's base station. Patti hit Play. An obviously still angry Rich's voice filled the room. That call had come in at 9:10 p.m. Then another at nine-forty and another pretty much every half hour. As the calls progressed, his tone shifted from angry to concerned. His were the only calls that had come in.

"He called from his cell phone," Spencer murmured, checking the display. "They're 232 numbers. He could have made the calls from anywhere."

Patti brought a hand to her temple. Exactly what she had said about Yvette's calls to Tonya.

"Aunt Patti?" There was no mistaking the concern in his voice. She met his gaze.

"That note you got this morning from the Artist. What did it say again?"

"Now you begin to regret your interference."

"That's what I thought it said. Do you think there's any chance—"

"I don't want to go there, Spencer. Not yet. Let's make certain she's actually missing. Call everyone in the family, find out if they've heard from her and when's the last time they talked to her. Call June and Riley at the gallery, ask the same thing."

"And if none of them have heard from her?"

"Move on to friends and acquaintances. Anyone you can think of. Get a couple of uniforms over to begin a door-to-door, and bring Ruston downtown for further questioning."

"And if none of it pans out?"

"Then we'll talk about the Artist."

65

Friday, May 18, 2007
12:10 p.m.

No one in the family had heard from Shauna. The neighborhood sweep had turned up little except for one neighbor confirming the time of Shauna and Rich's fight and that he had, indeed, stormed out. This information had come from the single mother who lived next door.

Rich had provided a list of friends and acquaintances; the ones they had been able to reach had not seen or heard from her.

Spencer had yet to speak with Stacy, but he didn't hold out much hope that Shauna was with her.

He tapped on Patti's open door.

She waved him in. "How'd it go with Ruston?"

"He stuck to his story like he was glued to it. Never varied."

"You think he's telling the truth?"

"Yeah, I do. He didn't exhibit any of the signs of lying. Kept eye contact, didn't even break a sweat. Seemed genuinely freaked out. Of course, none of that means he was being truthful."

Just that, if he was lying, he was really good at it.

"I want to put someone on Ruston, anyway. I don't want him to make a move we don't know about."

"Agreed." Spencer flexed his fingers, frustrated, itching to act. "This is such bullshit! Why are we sitting here when we should be out there, looking for her!"

"An all-radio bulletin has been sent," she said, countering his emotion with calm. "Every patrol unit has Shauna's description."

"Where the hell's the rest of the family?"

"On their way."

As if on cue, John Jr. burst into the office. Moments behind him was Percy, then Mary. Quentin rolled in last, out of breath.

"Sorry," he said, "I was in court. What's the emergency?"

"Shauna," Percy said. "She's gone missing."

"Gone missing? What the hell?"

"Where's Stacy?" Mary asked.

"Not certain," Spencer replied. "On the job. I'll fill her in."

Patti began, "There's a chance Shauna's been abducted by a killer who calls himself the Artist."

She passed around the note she'd received that morning. While they each read it, she filled them in on the investigation so far—their suspicions about Yvette, the notes, the connection to the Handyman case and the Maytree and Messinger murders.

Spencer stepped in. "This chick's good, no doubt about it. But parts of her story weren't adding up. We called her in for questioning yesterday, then acquired a search warrant. Now she's gone."

"And suddenly the Artist is back in play," Patti added. "In addition, the department psychologist said it's possible that Yvette's acting out a fantasy. When I stopped believing in it, I incurred her ire."

"But why would Shauna go anywhere with Borger?" asked Percy.

"Shauna met Yvette at June's gallery the night of her opening," Patti said. "So she wouldn't have been a stranger. Somehow she convinced her into coming with her."

They all began talking at once.

"I don't like the look of this."

"Welcome to the club."

"Ruston's a creep, he could be lying."

"Could be," Patti agreed, "but we don't think so."

"We have another option," Quentin offered quietly.

Everyone looked at him. "That Yvette was telling the truth about the Artist."

An uncomfortable silence ensued. Mary cleared her throat. "Which could mean the Artist has Yvette *and* Shauna."

Two women's lives in danger.

Spencer's cell phone vibrated; certain it was finally Stacy, he answered without checking the display.

"I was getting worried. Where are you?"

"Malone?"

Not Stacy. "Yeah. Who's this?"

"Rene Baxter. I was wondering if Killian's with you."

For a moment Spencer allowed himself to doubt what he'd heard, then he went cold with dread.

Not Stacy. Please not Stacy, too.

He lifted his gaze—and found Patti looking at him. He shifted his attention back to Rene. "She's not there?"

"Checked in this morning, then disappeared."

"What do you mean 'disappeared'? She's not a goddammed ghost!"

The room around him went silent. He felt as if someone had just set a piano on his chest.

"Chill, man. She was here and went out. I assumed—"

"She say anything to Cooper?"

"No. Like I was saying—"

"Is her SUV there?"

"Didn't check. Just assumed—"

"Check, dammit! Now! I'm on my way."

66

Friday, May 18, 2007
9:00 p.m.

Late that afternoon it had become official—Stacy was missing. No one had seen or spoken with her since that morning. Her Explorer was still parked in the lot that serviced the Eighth District station.

Spencer was out of his mind with worry. The Malone clan had gathered at John Jr.'s and set up a sort of family "command central." The women had strict orders not to go off alone. Same for the children, though Patti didn't believe the Artist would harm them.

The Artist had established his MO: he—or she—went for women, even when the punishment was directed not at them but at her.

Now you begin to regret your interference.

Word had spread throughout the department, and support from the rest of the force had been overwhelming. An incredible amount of manpower had been dedicated to finding the two women—and protecting the others. Off-duty patrols volunteered to cruise neighborhoods or stand watch at John Jr.'s.

This was an act against their own. Against a family who had given their lifeblood to the NOPD. Against a detective who, although new to the force, had stayed during the worst natural disaster in American history and laid her life on the line for their community, their people.

Patti was moved by their support. She prayed it helped keep the people she loved safe. But in her heart she knew the Artist wouldn't rest until she had been punished to his satisfaction.

He had found her most tender spot—her family. He had realized that hurting them would wound her more than any physical act against her person.

Not so long ago, she had thought that she had nothing left to lose. How wrong she had been.

And until the maniac decided on his next move, she, the rest of her family, and the entire NOPD were helpless.

She pulled up to her home. Not a light shone from its windows. The porch was dark. When she'd left this morning, finding Yvette had been her only priority.

What a difference a day made.

Quentin's comment rang in her head. What if the Artist wasn't a creation of Yvette's imagination, but was real? That would mean he had Yvette also. That all three lives hung in the balance.

What did she believe? Was Yvette another of the Handyman's victims, or a damaged young woman for whom the lines between reality and fantasy had become blurred?

Patti parked in the drive and climbed out. She intended to grab a shower and a change of clothes, then head back to John Jr.'s. Spencer was doing the same. They would rendezvous after and design a plan of action.

If nothing else, it would keep them busy, keep them from focusing on "what ifs."

Patti reached her porch steps and stopped. A small cooler sat in front of her door, the kind you could buy at any gas station or convenience store, one big enough for a six-pack. The top had been taped shut with silver duct tape.

Patti stared at the cooler, a tingling sensation stealing over her. Followed by dread. Deep, debilitating dread.

There could be any number of things in that cooler, all innocent. A friend dropping by some fresh shrimp. Or fish. Her neighbor Mrs. Wonch sending leftovers.

Patti's mouth went dry. But that wasn't what was in it. She didn't have to open it to know for certain.

Now you begin to regret your interference.

Patti forced herself to act. Quickly she returned to her car. From the console storage she retrieved a flashlight and scene kit. She fitted the gloves on as she strode determinedly back to the porch, heart hammering, hands beginning to sweat inside the latex.

Patti reached the cooler. She squatted in front of it. Taking a small knife from her kit, she carefully cut the tape. Lifted the lid. Peered inside.

She hadn't been wrong.

A severed hand, nestled in ice packs.

Patti launched to her feet and swung away, fighting for composure. She squeezed her eyes shut. It had been the logical next move—for a psychopath.

Patti took a deep breath. *Get a grip, O'Shay. Divorce yourself. Do the job.*

She returned to the cooler, squatted beside it. She snapped on the flashlight and, forcing thoughts of Stacy and Shauna from her mind, visually inspected the hand.

Female, she saw. A right hand; the real deal. It had been brutally hacked off.

She swallowed hard. Judging by how well-preserved it was, it had been frozen or stored on ice. But whose hand was it?

Please, God, not Shauna's. Not Stacy's. And what of Yvette? Could it be hers?

Patti carefully replaced the lid. She had calls to make. The crime lab. Dr. Elizabeth Walker. Spencer.

Dear God, how was she going to tell Spencer? The rest of the family? What was she going to say?

With a heavy heart, she flipped open her cell phone.

67

Friday, May 18, 2007
10:20 p.m.

Spencer couldn't breathe. His heart beat so heavily against the wall of his chest, he feared it would burst through. He stared at the cooler, afraid to move. Afraid of what could be inside.

His sister could be dead. Or the woman he loved.

He loved Stacy. He had realized it the moment he'd had to admit she was missing. That she was most likely in the grasp of a lunatic.

He had been playing a game of chicken with himself this whole time. He had been so afraid of loving Stacy and losing her, of being vulnerable to that kind of pain, that he'd denied his feelings.

Idiot. Like that had made one iota of difference. He loved her, anyway. And now, along with grief and fear, he felt a great, yawning regret. For what he could have had. What he had stupidly denied himself.

Patti's call had sent them all into a panic. Spencer worked to control his. Quentin and Percy stood on either side of him, also fighting for calm; John Jr. and Mary had stayed behind with spouses and children.

The morgue was eerily quiet. He jumped when Patti asked, "Are you ready?"

He nodded, though every fiber of his being wanted to scream "No!"

Quentin laid a hand on his shoulder. He heard Percy draw a fortifying breath. Patti lifted the lid.

Relief was immediate, dizzying. "It's not Stacy's," he said.

"What about Shauna?"

The brothers leaned forward to get a better look. Percy let out his pent-up breath. "No...no way. Look at the nails."

Shauna was an artist. She worked with oil paints and turpentine every day. Nails would get in the way, so she kept hers very short.

These nails were long. Unpainted. Stained around the edges.

Spencer gazed at the hand, those nails. Long, square-tipped nails. Medium-size hand. Looked to him like it hadn't belonged to a petite woman. Even in its postmortem state, he could see its owner had certainly been out of her twenties. Maybe her thirties as well.

Not Shauna's or Stacy's, and he would bet not Yvette's, either.

Patti looked his way. "Are you thinking what I am?"

"Messinger," he said, then turned to the lab technician. "Are Tonya Messinger's remains still here?"

He checked the computer. "Nope. Autopsy was completed this afternoon, next of kin notified."

"How about photos?"

"Got 'em. You want the real deal or are the digitals okay?"

"Digitals work for me. I'm looking for photographs of her remaining hand."

The technician navigated their system, then opened Messinger's file. Moments later the image filled the screen.

"It's Messinger's," Spencer said. "Her nails were painted. It threw me off."

Patti stepped in. "The bastard knew exactly what he was doing. The bright red nails would have immediately given the identity away, so he removed the polish before making his delivery to me."

"Son of a bitch wanted us to be afraid."

That had come from Quentin; Patti corrected him. "He wanted *me* to be afraid. Wanted to terrorize *me*. This is my fault. My responsibility."

Percy squeezed her arm. "We're in this together, Aunt Patti. We're family."

"And they're still alive," Spencer said. "If they weren't, it wouldn't be Tonya Messinger's hand in that cooler."

"I agree," Patti said.

"We'll need Elizabeth Walker to confirm."

"Already contacted her. She'll be here first thing tomorrow."

"What now?" Percy asked.

Spencer moved his gaze around the circle. "We catch this bastard. And we do it fast."

68

Saturday, May 19, 2007
Midnight

The first thing Yvette became aware of was a stabbing pain in her head. She moaned and opened her eyes—to complete black. No glowing clock face. No ambient light from the street outside her bedroom window or gentle glow of the moon.

She blinked and rolled onto her side. The bedding was rough. It smelled musty. Sour.

Not hers. Not home.

She remembered then. Grabbing her clothes and ducking out of the Hustle. Into the alley.

How long ago had that been?

The bum. The one who had followed her home once.

Yvette struggled to remember. She had pulled her shirt on first, then shimmied into her pants and stepped into the flip-flops.

And looked up to find him there. Staring at her. Her skin crawled, recalling the look in his eyes. Heart pounding, aware of every moment that passed, she'd told him to fuck off and hurried toward the alley entrance.

He had attacked her from behind. Hit her with something, then dragged her into the shadows.

And done what to her? How had she ended up here? Where was "here"?

The Artist. That's how he had known where she lived, how he knew the route she took home. Because he had followed her.

Dear God, that's how he had known about Marcus owing her money. How much he owed her. He had been in the alley the night she and Marcus fought about it. Watching. Listening.

I did it for you.

He had killed Marcus because Marcus had hurt her. The re-alizations rushed over her in a sickening wave. She had to run. Go, now. Before it was too late.

She scrambled to her feet and immediately sank back to the cot, light-headed. Legs rubbery. She breathed deeply, waiting for the dizziness to pass. She was hungry, she realized. Thirsty. What time was it? How long had she been unconscious?

Not out the entire time. In and out. She remembered voices. Whose? A woman's? Urging her to run.

He's going to kill you. Run. Quickly.

Panic rose up in her. She fought it back. She had to keep her wits about her. People would be looking for her. The police Patti would realize the Artist had nabbed her and would—

But would she?

She disappeared after being questioned by the police. They would see her tip money was gone, see the note she left for her landlord.

Guilty. It all made her look guilty.

Riley would have sounded the alarm. But would it do any good? Would they simply think she had planned that, too?

She was in trouble. Deep trouble.

Yvette brought her hands to her head. The woman had urged her to escape.

There must be a way out of this place.

She stood again, this time slowly. Though her legs were still rubbery, she inched cautiously forward, hands out in search of a door or window.

A way out.

She made it to a wall. The surface felt rough, rotten in places, fuzzy in others. She frowned at that. Fuzzy?

She felt her way along it, throat and eyes burning. She came to what she realized was a window. Broken. Boarded over. From the outside.

She felt around it, pressing against the unyielding boards. Her right arm snagged on glass and she jerked back, crying out in pain. She brought a hand to the stinging spot and found it wet and sticky.

Yvette breathed against a wave of dizziness. The blood pounded crazily in her head. She couldn't stop now.

Yvette moved on, straining to see more than a foot in front of her. She stumbled and righted herself, once, then again, the second time landing on her hands and knees. Into something rank.

Something dead.

She sprang to her feet, stomach rising to her throat. She scrubbed her hands against her capris, the sickening smell filling her head.

Get out. She had to get out.

She heard the faint sound of voices. A car door slamming. The Artist? Or a savior?

She moved blindly forward.

Dear God, help me. Deliver me. I'll change, I promise.

It was the same prayer she had whispered during Katrina. He had answered it then, but would He now?

Her hand landed on what felt like a paneled door. Quickly, heart racing, she felt her way to where the knob would be. Finding it, she closed her fingers over it and twisted.

The door opened.

Fresh air rushed over her. The soft glow of the moon. Crying out with relief, the sound of voices growing closer, she darted through the door—and stopped, grasping the metal rail that had kept her from falling.

She stood on a fire escape, several stories up. It swayed dangerously with the breeze and her weight.

Where was she?

She looked out over the moonlit landscape. A wasteland. Piles of rubble. An occasional building, boarded over. Broken. Cars discarded, pushed aside with the rest of the trash.

Like a nightmare world. Post-nuclear.

What had happened between being grabbed in the alley and waking up here?

No. There were trees. Overgrown vegetation.

Not a bomb. The storm. She must be in the lower Ninth ward. Or St. Bernard.

Voices. A voice calling softly to her.

Or was that the wind?

Biting back sobs of fear, Yvette eased forward, finding the first step. She grasped the rusty handrails, found the next and the next. With each step, the metal groaned a protest and she felt certain that any moment it would crumble beneath her feet.

But it didn't. Her feet found solid ground. Heart in her throat, she ran.

69

Saturday, May 19, 2007
7:00 a.m.

Patti stood in the doorway to her office, a cup of coffee in each hand. She gazed at Spencer, sitting at her desk, surrounded by case files. Staring into space. Expression lost.

He was thinking about Stacy, she knew. He loved his sister, but at that moment his heart was aching for Stacy.

"She's going to be okay."

He looked over his shoulder at her. "She's a fighter."

"Yes. A good cop, trained to defend herself." She entered the office, handed him the coffee. "You need to sleep."

"I'm not sleeping until I have Stacy and my sister back."

"Let's get them back then."

They had pulled every file remotely connected to Yvette Borger. The Maytree and Messinger murders. Marcus Gabrielle's. Stacy's notes. The Handyman files as well. Looking for the connection. The thread they had missed.

They were several hours into them with nothing but the same old questions.

"The day before Katrina hits," Patti began, "the Handyman kills Jessica Skye, a dancer at the Hustle. He dumps her body in a shallow grave in City Park."

Spencer took over. "He also kills Sammy. Shoots him with his own weapon. Tosses his badge in the grave with Skye, then discards his gun in the same general area."

"Sammy's body is found uptown. His cruiser located nearby," Patti continues.

"A present-day dancer from the Hustle claims she's being stalked by somebody calling himself the Artist. She comes to us for help. Claims the club's talent manager not only recognized our Jane Doe as Jessica Skye—"

"Which proved true."

"—but insisted the creepy dude sending her notes used to send notes to Skye as well."

"At the same time, she tells us the manager is missing. She fears the Artist may have killed her. She has no proof to support the claims."

"But the manager turns up dead, right hand severed."

"In addition, the dancer's elderly neighbor is murdered. The same night another neighbor's dog is poisoned. Dancer claims the Artist visited her that night."

"You come on board," Spencer went on, "and all communication from the Artist stops. Dancer disappears and he reappears."

"Bent on punishing me."

"To that end, Shauna and Stacy go missing. And Tonya's hand is delivered to your front door. So," he finished, "is it Borger?"

Patti swore softly, frustrated. Stymied. Circumstantial evidence suggested it was. But her gut, the instinct she had built her career on, said Yvette had been telling the truth.

Problem was, she no longer trusted her gut.

"I don't know," she said.

"You think she may be innocent?" He drew his eyebrows together, expression disbelieving. "What is it with you and her?"

"I don't know," she said again.

"We've got plenty of circumstantial evidence against her."

"But no physical."

He thumbed through the Maytree file, then stopped and looked back up at Patti. "What kind of dog?"

"Pardon?"

"The two strands on the victim's robe. The lab was supposed to identify the breed." He flipped through the pages. "I don't see a report. Looks like they never got back to us."

Patti got to her feet, looking excited. "What about the dog groomer's business? Anyone ever run a client list?"

She saw by his expression that he followed her thought—maybe there was a connection there. Match the breed with one of the Perfect Pups' clients and it might lead somewhere.

"Doesn't look like it was done."

"McBreakfast."

Quentin and John Jr. stood in the doorway, one carrying take-out bags from McDonald's, the other a beverage tray.

Spencer's stomach growled loudly. Patti smiled. "Apparently just in time."

The brothers dropped the bags on the desk and pulled up chairs. They all helped themselves to an Egg McMuffin.

While they ate, Spencer explained about the unidentified dog breed and the neighbor's grooming business. "I'm thinking, we finish this and contact the lab. Somehow it fell through the cracks."

"Oh, my God," Patti said, it suddenly hitting her like a ton of bricks.

The Artist was punishing her. By going after the women in her life. The ones she cared about most.

They all looked at her.

"June," she said, standing. "I forgot all about June."

70

June didn't answer her home or cell phone. When Patti rang Pieces, she got the message machine. Patti kept the panic at bay by telling herself it was early, a weekend. Her friend was still sleeping or in the shower. Or taking Max for a walk.

But it felt wrong.

Patti ordered a unit to Pieces, and she, Spencer, Quentin and John Jr. all headed for June's Garden District home.

She and Spencer made the Garden District mansion in ten minutes. Quentin and John Jr. pulled up just behind them. Patti leapt out of the Camaro and ran to the door. She rang the bell,

then pounded. Inside, Max went nuts, yapping and clawing a
the door.

"I'm going in," she called to Spencer.

She fumbled with her keys, found the one June had give
her for emergencies, unlocked the door and pushed it open
As she did, Max darted past her and outside.

"Somebody catch him!"

John Jr. gave chase and Patti stepped into the mansion
"June!" she shouted. "Riley!"

Silence answered. Spencer and Quentin joined her in the
foyer. She looked at them. "Let's split up. I'll start upstairs."

Quentin offered to go outside and Spencer took the main
floor.

Moments later, Patti was on the second floor. She made her
way from room to room, forcing herself to move slowly, to
treat each room like a crime scene. Nothing appeared out o
order. No signs of a struggle. June's bedroom was pin neat
Riley's was a mess. Same with their respective bathrooms.

The spare bedrooms looked as they should—un-lived in
ready and waiting for a guest.

"Anything?" she asked as she rejoined her two nephews
downstairs.

"Grounds, garage and tool shed are clean," Quentin said
"There's one vehicle in the garage. A Mercedes."

Patti's heart sank. "That's June's." She turned to Spencer in
question.

"One broken dish in the sink. Otherwise everything's in
order."

Patti frowned. *A broken dish?* "Could she have cut herself? Maybe Riley drove her to get stitches?"

"It's possible, though there didn't appear to be any blood at the site."

"June's pretty neat. Maybe she cleaned it up."

"*Before* rushing to the emergency room?"

Patti felt ill. Where would June be so early Saturday morning? Without her car. Without Max.

Same MO as Messinger, Shauna and Stacy.

John Jr. returned, out of breath, dog in his arms. "Little shit was almost to St. Charles Avenue before I got him."

Patti stared at the shih tzu. Not the traditional champagne color. A salt and pepper.

Black and white.

She turned to Spencer. "Get the lab on the phone now. I want to know the breed of that dog!"

While Spencer made that call, she made one of her own: Ray's Perfect Pups. Ray himself answered. He sounded frazzled. No doubt Saturday morning was one of his busiest.

"Ray, this is Captain Patti O'Shay. Yvette's friend."

"Captain O'Shay, sure. What can I do for you?"

"I have a question. Is June Benson a client of yours?"

"Benson...shih tzu named Max, right?"

"Right," she answered, then thanked him, hung up and looked at Spencer, who had just finished his call. "Well?"

"A shih tzu."

"And June's a client of Perfect Pups."

They all turned to John Jr., who was still holding the dog.

It all made sense. Riley had been at the scene the night Yvette disappeared. She had confided in him. Perhaps, just as he'd said, Yvette asked him for a ride. Had confided why she needed one.

She had played right into the Artist's hands.

He'd come looking for her at the Hustle all innocent concern. A smokescreen. Covering his ass in case her phone log revealed they'd talked that night.

Patti's mind raced. June confiding in her. That she was concerned about him. What had she said? That Riley gets all head-over-heels stupid about some woman, then when it doesn't work out, he mopes around for weeks, brokenhearted.

After they betray him. And he kills them.

Had June begun to suspect her brother was a murderer? Had she made a connection between Riley and one of the victims? Maybe she had confronted him?

Dear God... If Riley was...that meant he'd——

Riley killed Sammy.

Patti brought a hand to her mouth. This couldn't be happening. The brother of her oldest friend. She loved him like one of her own nephews.

"Aunt Patti? Captain?"

She blinked, focusing on the men. "It's Riley," she said. "Riley's the Handyman."

Her nephews stared at her as if she had lost her mind. Quentin cleared his throat. "Aunt Patti...with all due respect, you're talking about Riley here. He's family."

"You think I don't know that?" She realized her hands were

shaking and fisted them. "You think I don't know what it means? What he's done?"

Her cell phone vibrated and she flipped it open. "O'Shay."

It was the patrol unit she had sent to Pieces. She heard what sounded like a roar in the background. "Captain, we've got a situation here. The art gallery...it's on fire."

71

Saturday, May 19, 2007
Noon

Patti saw the smoke from blocks away. After asking the patrol-man to repeat himself twice, she had grabbed Spencer and together they'd raced to the scene.

June and Riley were both missing. Their business was in flames. This was not an accident. But what would they find inside?

Spencer held the wheel in a death grip. She knew he feared the same as she, and was praying those fears proved unfounded. Praying they wouldn't find someone they loved in that building.

The fire department had barricaded the block. Patti produced her NOPD credentials and was waved through. She rolled in, the smell stronger as she drew closer.

At the first sight of Pieces engulfed in flames, an involuntary cry slipped past her lips. She knew there was nothing she could do, that her work would come later, but hanging back idle was agony.

June could be in there. Stacy or Shauna. Dear God, no.

It looked as if the firefighters were on the winning side of the fire. They had contained it, which was no small feat in the Arts District, where the buildings nestled snugly up to one another.

Patti parked; she and Spencer climbed out. They found the incident commander. "What do you know so far?"

"Damn little. Investigator's been called. He's coming from Baton Rouge."

"Was anybody in the building?"

"Don't know. By the time we got here it was too late to go inside. Whatever was in there went up quick."

All those beautiful paintings. It made Patti sick to think of it.

"When can we go in?"

"As soon as the fire's suppressed. You'll have to suit up."

"Of course. Let me know."

One of the patrolmen she had sent saw her and hurried over. "I found Benson's car."

"Where?"

"In a private lot across the street."

"Great. Spencer?"

They crossed to the lot. The officer explained that he'd gotten the remote from a woman who worked in the building next to Pieces. He activated it and the gate slid open.

Riley's Infiniti sedan was parked in a spot in back. She and Spencer peered in the windows.

"It's empty," the patrolman said, as if to confirm what they were seeing.

"Did you check the license plate number?" she asked.

"Called it in. Vehicle's registered to Benson."

She looked at Spencer. "What're you thinking?"

"He could be in there."

And he might not be alone.

She ran the possibilities through her head. They were all horrific. All involved women she loved.

She glanced at the uniformed officer. "Open it up."

"Captain O'Shay!" The call came from the incident commander. "Fire's suppressed."

She nodded, then turned back to the patrolman. "Search it. Keep me posted."

She and Spencer returned to the now-smoldering gallery. She knew the drill: the fire investigator would look for the source of the fire, follow its trail and determine if it had been accidental or intentional. If the investigator determined a crime had been committed, the PD came on board.

She didn't have a doubt which one this was.

Patti looked at Spencer. "Maybe you should sit this out?"

"Like hell."

"We don't know what we'll—"

"Find?" he finished for her, voice tight. "You think I don't know that?"

She hesitated. As his commanding officer she could order him to stay put, but he was just stubborn enough to defy her.

"Let's do this."

They donned overalls, boots, respirators and hard hats. Though they were cumbersome and uncomfortable, Patti was grateful for the protection as she entered the building and the heat and smell slammed into her.

Patti moved her gaze over the interior. Though the fire hadn't consumed everything, nothing had been left untouched. Shauna's beautiful work was ruined. Some totally destroyed, others only partially burned. None salvageable.

Was this meant to be part of her punishment? Seeing her niece's beautiful artwork reduced to blackened rubble?

It looked as if June had been in the process of installing a new show. A number of paintings were propped against the walls, a number were hanging, and some, judging by blank wall space, appeared to have been removed.

Patti wondered if some buyers had already picked up their purchases. She hoped so.

"Captain O'Shay?" One of the firefighters stood at the burned-out doorway to the gallery's storage area. He motioned her over. "We have a victim."

Her chest tightened. She didn't want to do this. She didn't have to. She could turn and walk away now, leave it for the coroner's office.

She didn't know if she could handle what she might find.

She glanced at Spencer. He stood frozen, his agonized gaze fixed on the blackened doorway.

She would have to handle it.

She forced herself to put one foot in front of the other. She reached the fireman; he ushered her into the storeroom.

The victim lay just inside the door. Body blackened. Mummified. But still recognizable. Odd how fire could consume a body save for a random area. In this case, that area was part of his face. Riley Benson's face.

What did this mean?

She looked at the firefighter. "Just the one?"

"Yes."

"You're certain? You searched the rest of the gallery?"

"Yes. This one's it."

Spencer joined her. "Lord, God Almighty."

She glanced at him; he had tears in his eyes. "I always thought he was a good guy."

"If Riley was our perp—"

"Where are the women?"

Patti turned to the fireman once again. "Could he have killed himself?"

"Possible, but unlikely. Few people choose fire as a means to kill themselves. More often we see the fire used as a way to cover up a homicide."

True. Many a criminal didn't realize that a conventional house fire didn't burn hot enough to incinerate a body, only about one thousand degrees. In contrast, a body was cremated at seventeen hundred degrees.

At one thousand degrees, clothing, hair and flesh burned. The skin melted, although it wasn't uncommon for areas of soft tissue to be left intact. Autopsies could still be performed, determination of cause of death pinpointed.

She squatted near the body, examining it as best she could without touching it. "We need to know if he died in the fire or was already dead when he burned."

The pathologist would make that determination based on whether or not he found smoke and soot in the lungs.

"Coroner's office has been called," Spencer said.

She saw by his expression that he was thinking the same thing as she: how Riley died made a big difference in this investigation. If he had been murdered and the fire started in an attempted cover-up, Riley hadn't been their guy.

Then who was? And where were the women?

Back out on the street, Patti saw she'd had a call. She checked the display and frowned. She knew the number by heart.

It was her home number.

72

Saturday, May 19, 2007
1:20 p.m.

Patti left Spencer to wait at the scene for the coroner's representative and the arson investigator. She had also left him in the dark about her mysterious call.

The Artist. Another move in his game, another punishment. Or should she say *her* game?

Riley was dead. That left one obvious suspect.

Yvette.

It felt wrong. Patti wanted her to be innocent, to be the victim she claimed to be.

Patti had grown to understand her and respect her fighting spirit. She had seen through her sarcasm and anger to a young oman who had been hurt. Who needed love, to be cared for. ot in the physical sense, but in an emotional one.

Patti pulled into her driveway. That may all be true, but she ad a job to do. She killed the engine, then checked her weapon. full magazine, bullet chambered. Locked and loaded.

She opened her console, retrieved the set of handcuffs she ept there. She hooked them to her belt, then climbed out and ade her way to the front door. Was Yvette watching? Would e be surprised when Patti confronted her? Would she try to lay innocent?

Or was this another nasty surprise? Her chest tightened. nother loaded cooler? Worse?

The door was locked. As stealthily as possible, she fitted the ey into the lock and turned. The dead-bolt slid back. She un-olstered her Glock as she eased the door open.

No nasty surprises. Yet.

Patti stepped inside, weapon out. A rustling noise came om the back of the cottage. Her heart rate increased. She rmed her grip on the Glock and made her way soundlessly orward. She knew the house like the back of her hands and voided the creaks and groans effortlessly.

She reached the kitchen doorway and stopped, heart inking. Up until that moment, she had held out hope that she ad been wrong. That Yvette was the innocent victim she had roclaimed herself.

She wasn't.

She stood at the kitchen counter, her back to the door. She vore a T-shirt and pair of sweats that Patti recognized as her own.

"Hello, Yvette."

With a cry, the other woman spun around, soft dri[n]
slipping from her hand. It hit the floor and the cola spewed ou[t]

"Patti! Thank God, you're—" Her gaze went to the gun; h[er]
eyes widened. "What are you doing?"

"That's my question, isn't it? What are you doing here? I[n]
my home?"

"Trying to help. Why are you pointing a gun at me?"

"I think you know."

"No, I don't! Have you lost your mind?"

She backed against the counter. Patti saw that she had bee[n]
making a peanut butter sandwich.

"Where are they?" Patti asked.

"Who? Stacy—"

"And Shauna. My friend June."

"Riley's sister? How would I...I don't know!"

"I believe you."

At the sarcasm, Yvette held a hand out, expression pleadin[g]
"I came back to help you. To help find Stacy and Shauna. [They]
could be in Houston by now."

"A totally selfless act? Sounds like the Yvette Borger I know[.]"

Her eyes filled with tears; unaffected, Patti smiled griml[y]
"I suppose you're going to tell me the Artist got you, but yo[u]
escaped?"

"Yes! I was on my way out of town...I saw a newspaper. [I]
read about Stacy and Shauna, and I—"

"Came back to help?" Patti cocked an eyebrow. "Just like that[?"]

"Yes."

She laughed, the sound tight. "We both know that's bullshit. Here's what really happened. You ducked out of the Hustle Thursday night. You had everything planned and ready. You were angry at me for questioning you, doubting your story. You had decided to punish me by getting to the people I loved. Shauna. Stacy. And now June."

"That's crazy!" Yvette cried. "Why are you saying this?"

"You used Riley to reinforce the illusion you were abducted. Did he figure you out, Yvette? Did he catch you in the act?"

"I don't know what you're talking about."

"Is that why you killed him? He was on to you?"

Yvette went white. "What?"

"You killed Riley and tried to cover it up by burning down the gallery."

Yvette grabbed the counter for support. "Please don't... Riley can't be—"

"Is that why you're wearing my clothes? Are yours bloo—"

"No! My God, I could never—"

"Make this better. Tell me where Stacy, Shauna and June are."

As if her legs gave way, Yvette sank to the floor. "Riley was supposed to meet me," she whispered. "I knew you were trying to pin this on me, so I called him."

"Go on."

"I planned ahead. Left clothes and my wallet hidden by the alley door. I knew no one would expect me to leave right after a performance."

Tears rolled down her cheeks and she wiped them away. "I ducked out into the alley and he was there. The Artist."

Patti made a sound of frustration. She'd thought she w
getting a confession.

"I didn't realize at first. It was this bum who…hung out i
the alley a lot. He'd followed me home once…"

She cleared her throat. "He was staring at me. I yelled at hi
and he…attacked me."

Patti had to admit she sounded convincing. But then, th
was Yvette Borger's trademark.

"What happened then?"

"I don't know. I—"

"You're losing me now. And just when I was starting to bu
your baloney."

"No, it's the truth! I woke up in this place…I didn't kno
where I was. It was dirty and…and I remembered then, wh
had happened."

"When was this?"

"Last night, middle of the night."

"It's the first you remember?"

"Not completely. I realized I had been in and out of cor
sciousness. Maybe he was drugging me, I'm not certain."

She pressed her face against her drawn-up knees, and Pat
wondered if she was composing herself—or hiding a smile.

"Someone spoke to me. A woman, I think. Telling me t
run. To escape."

Patti recalled what the psychologist had said. "Children wh
suffer extreme trauma or abuse sometimes disassociate from their ow
memories. It's a kind of breaking free. And it allows them to crea
another story. Become a part of a fantasy life or relationship."

"How did you escape?"

"I was in a boarded-up room…it was completely dark. I tumbled, hurt my knee and cut myself on the broken window."

"The boarded-up broken window?"

Yvette looked stricken. "Yes! Look—"

She peeled back a handmade bandage, revealing a nasty cut. "And here." She carefully inched up the sweatpants. Sure enough, she had badly scraped her knee. It looked dirty.

"You should clean that," Patti said. "It'll get infected."

Tears filled the young woman's eyes. Patti's resolve wavered. She scolded herself for it, even as she crossed to the cabinet where she kept her first aid kit.

Her aim never wavering from Yvette, she retrieved the kit, then handed it to her.

"Everything you need's in there."

Yvette nodded and opened the kit. Patti watched as she cleaned the wound.

"So how did you escape?"

"I figured, if the woman urged me to escape, she'd left a way for me to do it." Yvette slathered the ointment on the cut, then covered it with a big bandage. "The door was open."

Interesting, Patti thought, that a "woman" told her to escape. Left the door unlocked.

Patti had a pretty good idea who that woman was: Yvette herself.

"If I was guilty, why would I come here? Why would I call you?"

Patti didn't answer.

"I've got my clothes, you'll see—"

"Show me." Patti motioned her up, then followed, gu
trained on her.

Yvette had, indeed, left her clothes in a small pile on he
bedroom floor. She held them up for Patti. They were rumple
and dirty. The knee of the capri pants was torn, bloodstain
marred the pink stretchy T-shirt.

"See? I'm telling the truth." She dropped them. "I can tak
you there. Stacy may be there. Shauna… I just ran. I was s
scared."

What if she was telling the truth?

Her cell phone vibrated. Instead of answering, she retrieve
her cuffs.

"What are you—"

She snapped one around Yvette's right wrist, then the left

"Patti, please! I—"

"Excuse me while I take this call. O'Shay here."

It was Spencer. "Aunt Patti, I'm with Ray Hollister. He
confirmed that Riley was shot. Twice."

"Self-inflicted?"

"He doesn't think so, judging by the entry-point locations
Autopsy will confirm, but his bet is Riley was dead before th
fire reached him."

"Which would most probably mean he wasn't our guy."

"But he may have known who was."

"Bingo. Let's try to find out if he was killed at the gallery o
dumped there."

"You've got it." He paused. "Where are you?"

"At my house."

"Your house? What—"

"I've got to go. Keep me posted."

"You were talking about Riley, weren't you?"

At the choked question, Patti glanced at Yvette. She looked...devastated, as if her world had come to an end.

Patti stared at the young woman. Riley was dead, shot twice. His body had been found in the blackened rubble of the torched gallery. Three women were still unaccounted for—Shauna, Stacy and June.

Riley. The gallery.

Then Patti knew. Beyond all reason. She fought back a sound of disbelief. Of despair.

Riley had, indeed, caught on to the killer. A killer who had connection to the missing women. To Riley and the gallery. The black-and-white shih tzu and Ray's Perfect Pups. A killer no one would have suspected—and everyone would trust. Including her.

That killer wasn't Yvette Borger.

It was June Benson.

73

Saturday, May 19, 2007
2:35 p.m.

Spencer swung the Camaro into Patti's driveway and brake
sharply. Leaving the car running, he leapt out and ran to th
front door. Patti hadn't sounded like herself on the phone
She'd had no reason to be home.

When that had sunk in, he'd rung her back. Several times
She hadn't answered.

Patti had left him at the scene, told him she would get a cruise
to take her back to headquarters. So how had she ended up here

And more important, why?

He struggled to remember what she had been doing righ
before she exited the scene.

Checking her cell phone.

He pounded on the door. "Aunt Patti! It's Spencer. Open up!"

When she didn't answer, he tried the door and found it locked, then went around back. There he found a broken window. Whoever had broken it had used it as a way to enter the house. They had cut themselves going in, he saw. Blood on the glass, the inside sill.

He tried the rear door, found it locked, then reared back and kicked it in. "Sorry, Aunt Patti," he muttered, and slipped inside.

Little out of place. Sandwich fixings on the kitchen counter. PB & Half-drunk Coke. Looked like some had spilled onto the tile floor.

He made his way into the living room, then the bedroom.

There he found a pile of discarded garments. They were dirty. Bloodstained.

He stared at those stains, growing dizzy with fear. Not Aunt Patti. Dear God, not her, too. He closed his eyes and breathed deeply, working to clear his head. Think it through.

Grabbing a tissue, he carefully lifted one of the garments. Capri pants. Ridiculously small. A size 0, or some such number. Aunt Patti was a trim woman, but these were *tiny*.

Yvette's clothes.

They stunk. He wrinkled his nose. But of wha—

He realized then. Of mold and mildew. From water damage. The way the entire freaking city had smelled for a year. The way some parts still smel—

The lower Ninth ward. Pockets of St. Bernard. Son of a bitch.

He unholstered his cell and dialed Tony. "I know where they

are," he said when his partner answered. "Lower Ninth. Assemble a search—"

"What about the captain?"

"MIA. Either with Yvette or the Handyman."

"That makes no damn sense."

"Live with it. Assemble a team. Lower Ninth."

"Wait! That's a big place, Slick. Where do you want this tear to start?"

"Where we found Messinger's body. I'm on my way now."

74

Patti pulled onto a long, gravel drive and followed its graceful curve. The setting was beautiful: gently rolling hills, vibrant green pastures, mature oak, maple and dogwood trees, lush, manicured landscaping.

Folsum. Louisiana horse country. Home to celebrity polo, thoroughbred horse farms and country homes for the wealthy.

"This isn't it," Yvette burst out. "It's so not it."

Patti ignored her, just as she had ignored her the entire hour they had been on the road. Finally the young woman had given up and dozed.

The house came into view then, a sprawling Southern

country house, white with black shutters and a front porch tha
ran the length of the house, lined with white rocking chairs.

Visiting Mimosa, as the Bensons' country place was named
was like taking a step back in time. To a gentle, uncomplicated era

Patti had always found this one of the most beautiful place
on earth. A place where she came to refresh her soul.

Until today.

"I don't understand why we're here."

Patti wasn't sure she did, either. What she was thinking
defied all logic. Defied all she knew to be true—not just with
her head, but her heart as well—about her oldest and deares
friend.

"This is June's country place," she said softly, drawing to
stop in front of the house. "I'm checking out a hunch."

More than a hunch. A horrible, taunting fear.

Yvette held out her arms, rattled the cuffs. "Are you going
to take these things off me?"

"Not until I know I can trust you."

"No! Plea—"

Patti opened her door and slid out. "Wait here." Before
Yvette could respond, she slammed the door and started fo
the house.

The gravel crunched beneath her feet. Her heart beat heavil
against the wall of her chest.

This couldn't be. June was her best friend.

To even consider this, she must be losing her mind. Sammy'
death and the stress of the storm had finally gotten to her.

Patti removed her Glock from her shoulder holster.

All roads led directly back to June. Riley. The gallery. Max. June was the last woman to disappear.

She let herself in. Moved from the foyer into the large living room. The house was perfect, as always. It smelled of flowers and lemon polish; sunlight dappled the interior in a warm, welcoming light.

June stepped through the patio door and stopped dead. She held a big basket of fresh-cut flowers. Her cheeks were pink from the warm day.

"Patti! What in the world are you doing here?"

"Looking for you."

"For me? I don't understand."

"You didn't answer your cell phone."

"I wanted to get away... I've been so stressed. Overwhelmed. Riley's been driving me absolutely bonkers...." She frowned. "Patti, why do you have your gun?"

"We thought you'd been abducted." She took several steps toward her.

"Abducted?" June laughed. "That's just silly."

"You left Max home alone."

"Never. Riley's taking care of him, of course."

But Riley was dead. Murdered.

June shook her head, closed the patio door and headed into the room. "How about I get us an iced tea? You don't have to go back to the city right away, do you?"

Could she really not know?

"Patti? You're acting strangely."

"I need to search the property, June."

"Search the... That's crazy. I don't understand."

"I'm sorry, but there's been an...incident."

"An incident?" June repeated, looking confused. She gripped the basket's handle. "What are you trying to tell me?"

"Riley's dead. The gallery's—"

June shifted her gaze; her eyes widened in surprise. "You!" she cried. "Patti, watch ou—"

Patti swung around. Yvette stood in the doorway, her expression registering surprise, then horror.

Patti realized her mistake, but too late. June charged her, burying her shears in her back. Blinding pain speared through her.

She heard a scream. Yvette, she realized. She fell to her knees, then forward. Her head connected with the corner of the coffee table.

And everything went black.

75

Saturday, May 19, 2007
4:55 p.m.

Spencer fought becoming discouraged. Tony had assembled a large team, many of them off-duty and volunteering their time. They had fanned out, using the spot where Messinger's body had been found as the epicenter.

It was hot, dirty work. The environment inside the buildings was damn near unbearable: stifling hot and airless, putrid. The thought of Stacy or Shauna trapped inside threatened to overwhelm him.

They'd been at it over an hour. Once the sun set they'd be out of luck until morning.

What if his hunch was wrong? Stacy and Shauna could be

anywhere: Chalmette or lower Plaquemines. The Gulf Coast. Hell, they could be Uptown, in a high spot that had never seen one drop of flooding. He could have simply been grasping at straws.

The metro area was too big to search, even if the entire force volunteered.

"Detectives! We have something!"

The call came from a team two buildings over. "John Jr.!" Spencer shouted, already running.

Heart thundering, he reached the three-story building. It looked like the ground floor had been a corner grocery, with a couple of apartments above. Once upon a time, the owners had probably lived above the store. A neighborhood kind of place.

The officer who'd made the find motioned him over, pointed to the wall, near the door, to the Orange *X*.

Spencer went light-headed with fear.

Blood spatter. Definitely caused by a gunshot. He lowered his gaze. A bloody trail to the street. Then it stopped. Made by a victim being dragged to a vehicle.

Spencer was aware of John Jr. coming up behind him, out of breath. Heard his explosive expletive.

A victim. Who?

"Downstairs is clear," the patrolman said. "There's no way to the second level."

Yes, there was. Metal stairs going to the second floor, one on each side of the building.

He darted for the ones on the right, John Jr. the ones on the left.

"Stacy!" he shouted, hitting the stairs. "Shauna!" The metal screamed in protest at his weight but held firm.

He shouted again. He heard his brother doing the same. Their shouts had drawn other teams within earshot.

Spencer reached the door and stopped cold. Padlocked. The lock was shiny, new.

What could be so valuable here, in this post-Katrina hell?

"They're here!" he yelled, drawing his weapon. "Stacy, Shauna, if you can hear me, get back!"

Below him, John Jr. reached the staircase and started up. Spencer fired three shots, blowing the lock apart. He kicked in the door. Light spilled into the darkness, falling over Stacy and Shauna who were bound and gagged—*but alive.*

With a sound of relief, he raced into the room, his brother at his heels. He reached Stacy, removed the gag. She gasped for air, then began coughing.

"Somebody!" he shouted, working at the duct tape securing her wrists. He was aware of his brother beside him doing the same for Shauna. "We need water!"

Within moments, he was handed a bottle of cold water. He held it to her lips.

When she'd had enough of the water, he moved his hands over her face, arms, searching, desperate for reassurance. "Are you hurt? Did he hurt you?"

"N...no—"

"Thank God...thank God... I thought I'd lost you. I—" His voice broke.

"I've got to—" She struggled to speak, her voice a hoarse whisper. "Got to tell you—"

"I love you, too, Stacy. I was such an idiot. I—"

She laid a finger against his lips, stopping him. "I do love you," she croaked. "But that's not... It's June," she managed. "June Benson's the Handyman."

76

Saturday, May 19, 2007
5:10 p.m.

Patti came to. She lay on her side on the floor. She hurt. She tried to move and moaned as pain shot through her.

"Thank God. I was afraid you were dying."

Yvette. Patti cracked open her eyes. It took a moment for her vision to clear. When it did, she moved her gaze over the room.

A bathroom. Luxurious. Garden tub. Marble.

She settled it on Yvette. She still wore the cuffs. June had bound her ankles with duct tape. "Where...is she?"

"I don't know." Yvette drew in a breath; it caught on a sob. "When she stabbed you, I tried to run for help. I didn't get far...I fell and with the cuffs—"

Couldn't get up fast enough.

"She has your gun. She said she'd shoot me."

June. Her best friend. Trusted confidant. How could this be happening?

Patti recalled the sequence of events: turning her back to June; the scissors going into her back; the intense pain, then falling forward; not stopping herself in time and hitting her head on the coffee table; being knocked out.

"How bad am I?" she asked.

Yvette's eyes filled with tears. "Bad, I think. The scissors, they're still in…"

"My back?" Yvette nodded.

"How deep?"

"Pretty deep, I think."

Patti breathed deeply against the dizziness. Obviously June hadn't hit anything vital, but too much could go wrong if she had Yvette try to remove them.

Yvette inched toward her. "What can I do?"

Patti pressed her lips together a moment. "I'm sorry I suspected you."

"The way I acted, like such a brat…I don't blame you."

"We've got to get out of here."

"I tried. There's no way out."

"Window?"

"Glass bricks. One door. Locked from the outside."

"Did you try to kick it in?"

"I was afraid she'd hear me and get angry."

And making June angry would be a bad idea. She had Patti's Glock. And no doubt, the gun she had used to kill Riley and

Messinger—and most probably Marcus Gabrielle. Patti wouldn't doubt she had a couple of bone saws hidden on the property as well.

Yvette started to cry. "I don't want to die."

"You're not going to die, not if I have anything to say about it."

"But you don't, Patti," June said, opening the door.

Patti saw that she did, indeed, have the Glock. *It had a full magazine. Bullet chambered.*

"I'm sorry," June said. "I really am. You're my friend."

"Your friend?" Patti repeated. "You call this friendship?"

"You got involved in my business. My private business."

"You killed Riley!" Yvette cried. "How could you—"

"He got in my way. Starting snooping around. Letting you go was the final straw."

"He let me go? He's the one who—"

"Unlocked the door, yes."

"He warned me," she whispered. "Told me you were going…to…kill—"

Tears choked Yvette, and Patti took over. "Was Riley part of this?"

"Riley? Mr. Incompetent? I don't think so. He began to suspect, somehow. Although frankly, I can't imagine how. And then he involved himself with Yvette. My muse. Mine."

"He was your brother. You killed your own brother."

June looked at her then, her expression terrible. Grotesque. "He wasn't my brother. He was my son."

The words caught her so by surprise, they took her breath. "Your son? How—"

"My parents sent me away to 'boarding school.' That's how they did it back then. An abortion was, of course, out of the question. A good Catholic would never resort to such a thing.

"Besides, Mama wanted another child. So she pretended to be pregnant. They faked the whole thing. No one suspected. No one ever suspects people who live in Garden District mansions to be anything but upright, law-abiding citizens."

A lesson, it appeared, she had made good use of.

"I was fifteen when he was born. I was never allowed to speak of what happened, never allowed to refer to him as anything but my brother."

"Did Riley—"

"Know?" She shook her head. "I gave him everything, devoted my life to him. And he did this to me."

Patti stared at her friend, shocked by the skewed perspective. She'd killed him, but he did *her* wrong?

"And his father," Patti asked. "What of him?"

"You mean *our* father."

Patti stared at her, feeling sick, stunned.

"That's right. Riley and I had the same father. He raped me. More than once, of course."

Her dislike of men. The distrust of them that had emerged every so often.

"Mama figured it out, but looked the other way. After all, she got what she wanted. Relief from her conjugal duties and a *son.*"

If only she had known, maybe she would have been able to help, to get her help. "I'm so…sorry, June. You could have told… Someone would have listened, would have believed you."

She laughed, the sound harsh. "In your world, maybe. Not in mine."

Patti struggled to sit upright, nearly passing out from the pain. "You need help," she managed. "I can make certain you get it."

"No, I needed help at fourteen. Now I'm fine. *I'm* in control. *Me*. I've got all the power now."

"Killing people gives you power?"

"The ones who betray me deserve it. *You* betrayed me, Patti. You sided with her."

"What about Shauna and Stacy?"

Her expression went momentarily blank. Then she shook her head. "It was so easy. I called Shauna, told her a collector wanted to meet us at the gallery. That I was just around the corner and would pick her up. Same with Stacy."

She smiled as if immensely pleased with herself. "You'll like this one. I told her you were having a breakdown. That you'd asked for her, but only her. I knew she wouldn't breathe a word to anyone—to protect you. Brilliant, don't you think?"

"Risky, in my opinion. What if she'd told her captain? Or called Spencer?"

"But she didn't. Here's the secret. I understand people, their behavior. I can anticipate how they'll react."

"You're so smart, are you?"

Her self-satisfaction said it all. "You know what your problem is, Patti?"

"Right now? I'd say it's you."

"You think too small. I can be anyone or anything I want to

be. Old or young. Rich or a bum living in a box. Woman or a man sending love notes to a stripper."

"And how's that? You put on a wig? Some men's clothes?"

"Again, thinking too small. You have to let go and just *become* it."

What Dr. Lucia had said about severe childhood trauma rang in her head. How it could fracture a psyche, cause an individual to create alternate personalities.

But this wasn't DID in the sense of alternate personalities wresting control from the "host," Patti realized. June made the conscious choice to become someone else.

"The human mind is capable of creating anything that can be imagined."

"Why, June? Why the girls? Why take their hands?"

"The girls were weak. They didn't deserve my love. Each time they proved that. But at first…they're so full of life and hope, so filled with tomorrows."

June's father had robbed her of her childhood. Her tomorrows.

Her expression softened. "My muses. They inspire me. Take me to new heights. Make me believe in love and happily-ever-after."

From the corner of her eyes, she saw Yvette ease open one of the cabinets. Searching, she supposed, for something to use against the woman.

Good girl.

Patti worked to keep June talking, fully focused on her. "Then they betray you."

Her expression hardened again. "Yes, they betray me. I see they're weak. And foul."

"The way you were weak?" she said softly. "When your father abused you?"

Her face went momentarily slack with surprise, then a dull flush crept up her cheeks. "No," she snapped. "I loved them. They betrayed me."

"What about Sammy?"

"A horrible mistake. A tragedy. He came to check on the house, to make certain looters hadn't broken in. Caught me driving off with my sweet Jessica. He followed.

"You can't imagine how upset I was. I drove on, hoping he'd give up, realize I was fine. But no, not Sammy. He signaled me to pull over. Get this." She leaned slightly forward, as if still amazed. "To tell me *my trunk wasn't completely latched.*"

"You pulled into Audubon Place. No one was around."

"Yes. It was getting late. Everyone had evacuated. I got out of my car. I hid my Club…that anti-theft thing, behind my back. And I hit him with it."

Patti listened in horror, imagining Sammy, his last thought before he went down.

"I had to do it, had to shoot him. I didn't want to, I really didn't. I loved Sammy."

Patti wanted to scream "Liar!" That she couldn't have loved Sammy. If she had, she wouldn't have killed him.

But confronting a crazy person only made them crazier, and she and Yvette were in enough trouble already.

"What about Tonya?" Yvette asked, voice sounding stronger than before. Patti saw the cabinet was closed and she was holding her hands oddly.

June looked at her. "Tonya wasn't your friend. She tried to blackmail me. She didn't care about you, just wanted money. Stupid whore."

"So you killed her. Hacked off her hand."

"Yes. She approached me at the Hustle. I went there after Shauna's opening. I was angry at you for flirting with Ruston. For going off with Riley."

Patti shifted, wincing at the pain in her back. "You used your left hand to take hers. To confuse us."

She looked surprised. "Not at all. Tonya didn't deserve my kindness, my loving attention and care. That's only for my sweet girls. I took her hand because I could. And I thought maybe I could use it. As usual, I was right."

Patti fought to keep her fear and revulsion from showing. "You were the dark-haired woman the neighbor saw Tonya leave with?"

"Yes. One of many roles."

She smiled and turned back to Yvette. "And I killed Marcus because he hurt you. It was for you, my sweet Yvette. All for you."

"I didn't know," Yvette whispered, voice trembling. Her eyes welled with tears. "I thought you were like the others. All the ones who hurt me."

Patti watched, heart thundering. She didn't have a clue what Yvette had planned, she just prayed it worked because they were running out of time.

"We're alike," Yvette whispered. "You and I. I didn't know. We belong together. We've been hurt by those who were supposed to love and protect us."

"Yes," June said, nodding. "We are. I knew that but you—"

"Didn't," she finished for her. "Will you ever forgive me?"

"You had sex with Riley."

"A mistake. The whole time, I was looking for you, and—" Her voice caught on a small sob. "I didn't see, you were right here."

June's grip on the gun wavered. A tear rolled down Yvette's cheek. "Hold me," Yvette pleaded. "Please…just hold me."

June helped her to her feet, put her arms around her. With a whimper, Yvette brought her cupped hands up, as if to stroke June face.

Instead, with a primal cry, she ground something into June's eyes.

June howled and fell backward against the vanity, clawing at her eyes.

The gun hit the floor. Yvette dove for it, falling hard, elbows cracking loudly against the tile floor.

She got it, anyway, curled her hands around the grip and pointed it at June, her hands shaking so badly the muzzle bobbed up and down.

"Give me the gun!" Patti ordered. "Let me do this."

Yvette shook her head. "I can't. I won't."

"Give me the gun," she said again, more firmly.

"She killed Riley." Her voice trembled. "Sweet Miss Alma. Tonya. They never hurt anybody. They didn't hurt her."

"I did it for you," June said again, dropping her hands. Her eyes were tearing, the skin around them blotchy and bright red. "So they're dead because of you."

"No! That's not true!"

June's stance and expression altered subtly, becoming mor masculine. "If you hadn't come on to Riley, like a little whore—" The pitch of her voice changed, deepened. "If not for you he' be alive."

"Shut up!" The gun bobbed. "It's not tru—"

June lunged. Patti shouted for Yvette to watch out. The soun of the weapon discharging was deafening in the small room.

June stumbled backward, a hand to her chest, a look of utter disbelief on her face. Then she went down.

In the distance came the sound of sirens.

The cavalry. Thank God.

With a sob, Yvette dropped the gun. Drawing her knees to her chest, she began to cry deep, wrenching sobs.

Patti dragged herself to the young woman's side. "You're going to be okay," she said, voice cracking. "We are. Because of you."

She sobbed harder. Patti caught Yvette's hand, curled her fingers around it. "You saved our lives. You saved mi—"

"I...wouldn't...count on that."

Patti's blood ran cold. Feeling as if life had gone into slow motion, she turned her head. June had the gun. She lifted it, aimed at Yvette.

No! The word resounded through her head even as she mustered all her strength and threw herself on top of Yvette.

The gun went off. One shot. Pain. Intense, searing. She heard Yvette's scream, the voices of others, shouts. Spencer.

And then silence.

77

Sunday, May 20, 2007
9:15 a.m.

Patti opened her eyes. Spencer sat beside her hospital bed. He was smiling at her. "Hello, sleepyhead," he said.

She returned his smile, groggy from pain medication. "Hey."

"Doc says you're going to be okay. Bullet went through a fleshy spot, raised a little hell, but didn't do any permanent damage. As for the scissors, you're gonna have one ugly-ass scar."

"Can't kill someone as ornery as me." She found the remote and, with his help, raised the bed until she was in a sitting position. "That's better. How are Stacy and Shauna?"

"Dehydrated. Sick from the mold. Otherwise unharmed."

She curled her fingers around his. "And you and Stacy?"

"We're good, Aunt Patti. Really good." He cleared his throat "You were right about Yvette. And Franklin. And I was so wrong. If you hadn't stuck to your guns, Yvette would mos likely be dead and Franklin standing trial for a murder he didn' commit."

She had found Sammy's killer. Stopped the Handyman from eve. hurting another woman.

Yet she couldn't rejoice. She had been betrayed by someone she had loved.

Seeing Patti's expression, he curved his fingers tighter around hers. "I'm sorry, Patti. I can't believe Aunt June...you know. I just...can't."

Neither could she. She might never be able to truly accept it.

"At least I know the truth about Sammy."

She could let go now. Take the next step in her life.

Yvette tapped on the door. "Can I come in?"

Spencer smiled and stood. "Hey, Yvette. I was just leaving." He kissed Patti's cheek, then straightened. He walked to the door, stopped and looked back at Yvette. "By the way, pepper-mint salt scrub in the eyes? Good thinking."

When the door clicked shut behind him, Yvette turned to Patti. "I've got something for you." She was grinning, obviously pleased with herself.

"What?"

She crossed to the bed and plopped down on the chair. She held out a check.

Patti frowned. "A check? What for?"

"Take it and see."

She did. It was made out to Patti O'Shay in the amount of ten thousand dollars.

The deposit to keep her from running.

Patti looked at Yvette in question.

"When I accepted your offer of fifty grand, I thought it'd be enough for me to start a new life. Give me a fresh start, a shiny clean slate. I'd go to school or start my own business."

"You still could."

"I've already started my new life." She leaned forward. "It was never about having enough money. It was always about what was inside me.

"You took a bullet for me, just because you believed it was the right thing to do. This way—" she reached out and curved Patti's fingers gently around the check. "—I'll have stayed and helped you for all the *right* reasons."

"I don't know what to say."

Yvette smiled. "I could use a friend? A real one this time."

Patti returned her smile. "I like the sound of that. Friends."

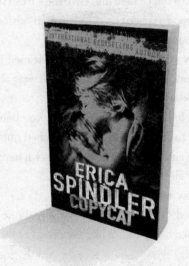